THE GORGON BRIDE

GALEN SURLAK-RAMSEY

A Tiny Fox Press Book

Cover design art by Simon Eckert.

Library of Congress Catalog Card Number: 2018902903

ISBN: 978-1-946501-09-7

Tiny Fox Press and the book fox logo are all registered trademarks of Tiny Fox Press LLC

Tiny Fox Press LLC
North Port, FL

FOR MY WONDERFUL WIFE WHO LOVES ME DESPITE MY SNAKES

CHAPTER ONE

At 9:03 a.m., on a cold Tuesday morning, Alex would get his fifteen minutes of fame. In truth, his share would be closer to one minute; the orca would garner the other fourteen.

Alex's neighborhood of exquisite prairie homes and Jaguar drivers was a whale-free zone. It always had been, and everyone expected it always would be. Thus, when Alex sat down at his Steinway grand piano to practice Chopin's first ballade at 8:30, he considered the day to be routine. But when his doorbell rang a minute before nine, things changed.

Alex muttered a few curses and took to his feet. He opened the front door and felt a twinge to burn the heretic who had interrupted his worship service. Chopin, as far as Alex was concerned, was a god.

At the foot of his doorstep jogged a man of impeccable physique who had his index and middle fingers pressed into his neck. Before Alex could raise a hand to shield his eyes from an unusually bright sun, the man thrust a fancy looking clipboard into his chest. "Delivery for Alexander Weiss," the man said. "Sign here."

Alex hesitated. He took the board and examined the man. He wore a nondescript white uniform, sneakers, and ball cap that screamed athletic commercial. "Who exactly are you with?" Alex asked.

"With?" A puzzled look crossed the deliveryman's face, as if the question had never been posed to him before.

"Yes, with. Who do you work for?" Alex looked at the man's running shoes. The emblem on the sides looked vaguely familiar. "Nike?"

"Gods, no." The man rolled his eyes. "I hate doing jobs for Nike. Always going on about triumphing over adversity. Thankfully, Olympus doesn't have me at Nike's beck and call."

"Olympus, huh? Startup company?"

The man grinned. It was mischievous and the type of grin a child might give after thieving a cookie or two. "No, we've been around for a while."

"Funny, never heard of you."

"We're from overseas. Closed shop for a bit." The deliveryman peered around Alex. "Say, you've got a lot of nice stuff inside."

Alex glanced over his shoulder. "Thanks."

"Really nice."

"Again, thank you."

"Nicest on the block, by far. Care to part with any of it?"

"No, I'm afraid not."

The smile on the man's face grew. "Your neighbor said the same thing about her cookies. But I must say they are delicious. You should help yourself to some."

"Mrs. Nemur gave you a homemade cookie?"

"Well, *gave* is such a strong word," he said with a wink.

"I don't think I want to ask." Alex looked at the form in his hand. There was a single line on it with his name written underneath. No date. No company logo. No tracking number. Only a line and his name. "Sorry. This is too odd for my likes. Let me see this supposed letter."

"It's right here," the man answered, producing a small, bound scroll from behind his back. "But if you want to read it, I must insist that you sign for it first."

"Who's it from?"

"The owner of Athens, Greece."

Alex arched an eyebrow. A personal letter from the mayor of Athens could only mean one thing: a request for an appearance. He quickly signed the form, handed it back to the messenger, and took the scroll. It read:

Athena Parthenos, patron of Athens, to Alexander Weiss, the esteemed protector of the arts and pursuer of scholarly wisdom. I have written to inform you that due to recent events, it would behoove you to have in your possession the standard fare of one obol. An American silver dollar should also suffice.

Sorry about the whale.

Alex looked up, thoroughly perplexed. He tried to place the name, Athena Parthenos, but failed to recall ever meeting such person. He became further confused when he realized that the messenger was gone and his Rolex was missing from his wrist. When Alex stepped onto his lawn for a better view of the street, a full-grown orca landed on his head.

"I'm sorry, but I don't understand what you're saying," Alex said, scratching his neatly trimmed beard. "Run that by me again?"

"Most certainly, kind sir," the man replied. He wore a red tunic and conical hat and stood upon a small skiff. He kept his right hand stretched out and leaned on a pole with his left. "If you wish to cross the Acheron, it will be one obol," he said, slowly enunciating every syllable. "Otherwise, you'll have to join the others alongside the bank."

The man's words seeped into Alex's mind. He looked about and noted that the shore stretched for a hundred yards to each side before being engulfed by a thick fog. Shadowy forms of people dotted the landscape. Some skipped stones. Others meandered. None interacted with one another.

Alex turned back to the man. "And you are?"

"Kharon," the man replied. A smile flashed across his disfigured face. "Ferryman of the unseen."

"Are you telling me I'm dead?"

"No. I'm telling you it'll be one obol if you wish to cross."

Alex shook his head. "I can't be dead. This is nonsense."

"The dead are those who have gone on." Kharon said, motioning with his pole toward the waters. "You're not dead, yet."

"So you're telling me I'm alive?"

Kharon sighed. "Look, this is simple. You can't be squashed by a six-ton aquatic mammal and expect to live."

"So what the hell am I, then?"

"Alexander Weiss, I presume," Kharon said, shrugging. "Though I never asked your name, you do match the description given to me."

"I must be dreaming."

"You're not."

"I'll wake up soon or something." Alex tried pinching himself.

"You won't."

"Yes," Alex told himself. "I'll wait a moment and this will all be over."

Kharon shrugged. "You'll be here awhile."

High above the waters of the Acheron, past the layers of clouds that separated the heavens and the earth, stood Olympus, dwelling place of the gods. Thick clouds and vapors obscured the city's platinum gates from mortal eyes, and the guardians posted outside granted access only to the divine. Zeus had insisted on keeping the community exclusive to keep property values high.

Inside the walls, dwellers and visitors were treated to a menagerie of delights. The finest of architecture, complete with marble colonnades and intricate friezes, shaped each building. Aromas of feasts and sounds of the lyre filled halls inlaid with ivory and gold. Tapestries and sculptures so life-like that no mortal could ever dream of reproducing them adorned rooms that were as countless as the stars.

Yet, despite these ceaseless pleasures, one god felt discontent with the current state of affairs. Ares, God of War, sat naked on a small balcony, scowling. His army was scattered. His enemy approached. All he had at his disposal were a few footmen, one hero, and a king.

"The knight should be strong," Ares said, breaking the long silence and folding his enormous arms over an equally muscular chest. "He is weak, and he should not be. Heroes are worth more than a mere. . .a mere. . .what did you say his worth was?"

"About three pawns," Athena replied before taking a sip of nectar from a silver goblet. She sat opposite him with her legs crossed and was dressed in white robes. In her lap rested an open biography about the United States Marine Corps general and legend, Chesty Puller.

"Three pawns! I would have gladly traded legions of men for the likes of Hector or Achilles! Either of them would cleave your pathetic army with a single hand."

"The knight is as strong as the bishop."

"He's as weak as the priest!"

Athena, enjoying her brother's frustration, drew back the corners of her mouth before returning to her reading. "Did you know Chesty Puller killed a thousand and a half Japanese warriors and only lost seventy of his own?"

For the first time in days, the God of War looked up from the marble chessboard. "Did he? Now that is a man that knows how to win a battle. Not like this pathetic king I must protect—a king that can only move one little square at a time. Would Odysseus have been so frail? My forces are not what they should be."

"We started with the same pieces. It was a fair contest. One that you suggested, I might add."

"I said I longed for combat," he replied. "Not some coward's game that you picked out. Where is the bloodbath you promised? What glory is gained here? I should be out in the fields of battle!"

"Might want to catch up on current events before you do," Athena said. "Humans have been busy the past couple thousand years."

"Let me guess, you want me to read a few things."

Athena nodded. "Yes. They're called books, and they're quite informative."

"Bah," Ares said, shooing at her with a meaty hand. "They still kill each other when they go to war, yes?"

"Very efficiently."

"Good. That's all I need to know." Ares looked at the board and snorted. "What a pitiful field. No ability to flank or use the high ground. What general fights his opponent on equal footing?"

"Are you going to move or not? I'd like to have this done while we're still young." Athena put her book down and straightened. Though she had picked the game and had looked forward to it, her brother's complaints were taking a toll. "And don't think you can get out of our wager. Loser is the winner's servant for a day."

"I haven't forgotten," he snapped. "You'll be sharpening my sword and spear soon enough."

"Athena!" bellowed a deep voice from below. "Where is she hiding?"

Ares looked over his shoulder and grinned. "Sounds like Poseidon found out about the whale."

"Do you think he's mad?" she asked, her question born from idle curiosity, not worry or fear.

"No more so than when you cursed Medusa."

A flying trident impaled the column next to the goddess's head, and Athena gave it a brief glance before returning to her book. She'd seen the weapon coming and knew it would miss her by at least two inches, if not three. "Do you feel better, Uncle?" she said as Poseidon stormed onto the balcony, his white hair and beard blowing as if caught in the fury of a raging sea.

"I shall have you fed to Cerberus, torn limb from limb," he said, stopping but two feet from her.

Athena brushed her now wind-tossed hair back over her shoulder and straightened her robes. "Really, Uncle," she said. "There's no need for all the theatrics."

"Don't you dare brush me off. You will respect your elders," The Lord of the Sea said, knitting his weathered brow. "Do you have any idea what you've done?"

"Are you referring to Stheno? I'll have you know she said I was fat, so I turned her into a whale," she said, not concerned by her uncle's wrath. With Zeus, ruler of Olympus, as her father, she knew most threats against her would never be enforced. Dad would see to that. "Look, I know you're upset, but you have to admit, she looks much better than she did before."

"You said the same thing about her sister," Poseidon replied. He clenched the shaft of his trident and yanked the weapon free.

"Oh, come now," Athena said with a dismissing wave of her hand. "Everyone agreed that Medusa needed her head chopped off. What I did to Stheno isn't nearly the same thing."

"Then you can explain that to her father," Poseidon replied. "He's blaming me for this mess."

"The Old Man overreacts to everything."

"You've humiliated his family yet again, young lady. He has every right to be upset."

Athena smiled as she ran a quick mental calculation of how hard a whale should hit the ground. "I'd think he'd be proud. After all, she made quite the impression when she landed."

Poseidon's face hardened, and his blue eyes shot her a glare that would have dropped a Titan. "Your puns do not amuse me."

Athena sat back and kept her smile. "You'd find this much more entertaining if you saw the look on her face when I launched her into the air. So what happened to her after she hit the ground that got The Old Man so riled up? She's immortal. It's not like I killed her."

"The humans put her into an amusement park where she jumps through hoops for snacks of halibut. People are coming from across the world to see her perform."

"Well, I think that's probably better than letting her turn people into stone, don't you?"

Poseidon stepped forward and towered over her. "Do not test me, young lady," he growled. "Fix this."

Athena looked at the game board and then back to her uncle, who hadn't changed his expression. A chill ran up her spine, one that she hadn't experienced in an eon. Something told her that her uncle wasn't worried about what Zeus would say or do in her defense. "I suppose I could see what can be done to calm The Old Man down," she said, capitulating only as much as she felt was needed to placate Poseidon. "But you ought to tell him to teach his daughters some manners."

"I'll do no such thing," he replied. He leveled his trident at her and said, "Tell him yourself."

"It's your move," Ares interjected. His face beamed, and he leaned back in his chair. "Come. Let us do battle."

"Fine," Athena said, still looking at her uncle. "I'll tell him myself." She then glanced at the game board before picking up her queen and moving it three spaces. "Checkmate."

* * *

Alex, blazing a new path through the ever-thick fog, learned that whichever way he went, he always returned to Kharon and his skiff. Even following the shoreline in either direction yielded the same result. Alex, having reached the ferryman for the seventh time, dubbed himself crazy.

"What the hell kind of sick dream is this?" Alex said, squaring off with Kharon.

"This is no dream. This is the start of the Underworld," Kharon replied. He extended his right hand yet again. "One obol, if you please."

"God," he yelled, throwing up his arms. "Don't you say anything else? Is it that hard to come up with some decent conversation?"

"The weather here never changes, and I'm not paid to chat."

"You get paid to annoy people?"

Kharon pointed to the waters. "No, I get paid to ferry. We've been over this before. If you aren't going to pay, you're going to have to step aside and join the others."

"Maybe I'll stand here," Alex said, refusing to be dismissed. "I'm sick of walking around in circles. Maybe I'll even commandeer your boat. What do you think about that?"

"I think you'd be a fool to try," Kharon said. "You're no hero. You're simply a man on his way to the afterlife."

Alex crossed his arms over his chest. "I'm not dead."

"Yet," tacked on Kharon.

"I'm not even not alive!" Alex made sure his double negative worked as he intended before continuing. "You're simply some made-up piece of my psyche insistent on keeping me stuck in this dream."

"How rude."

"What's rude?"

"Calling me a liar and saying I don't exist," Kharon said with a frown. "I take a lot of pride in my work. I have to deal with enough abuse as it is."

Alex shook his head at the unexpected turn. "No, that's not what I meant."

"You said—and I quote—'you're simply some made-up piece of my psyche.'"

"Look, I'm not here to argue with you, I want—"

"Don't give me any of that." Kharon shoved his pole into Alex's face. "I know what you want. You want to go back to your fabulous life of fresh outdoors and warm sunshine. Never mind the rest of us that are stuck down here in the gloom. Don't you think I'd like to see the sky once in a while or count the stars at night? No, of course you don't think of any of that. All you can think about is how to be rid of me."

"You're damn right I want to be rid of you. I want to be rid of you, this place, this dream, and whatever else is lurking around and get back to my life," Alex said.

"I've had enough of you," Kharon said, taking a seat on the edge of his skiff. He reached into a brown sack and pulled out a large fig. "And I'm not about to put up with your insults any longer. Now if you'll excuse me, I'm going to have a bite to eat."

"No, I don't think so." Alex snatched the fig from Kharon's hands. "Take me across the river this moment, or else."

"Or else what?"

"Or else I'll be forced to take your boat," Alex said, casting the fig to the ground like a gauntlet.

Kharon's eyes followed the fruit as it rolled to his feet. His hands trembled and he shifted his grip on his pole. His mouth opened, and for a moment, no words came out. Finally, the ferryman stood and leveled his pole at Alex. "That was completely uncalled for. Now apologize."

"No," Alex said, standing fast. "In fact, I just realized something."

"What's that?"

"Since this is a dream, I can do whatever I want." With that, Alex lunged at the man and the two became entangled, rolling along the bank of the Acheron.

After a series of hits, kicks, bites and gouges, Kharon got the upper hand and pinned Alex to the ground. "I can't believe you're so childish," he said, keeping his pole pressed against Alex's neck. "Do you yield?"

"Never," Alex said. A few squirms and grunts later, Alex, still pinned by Kharon, ceased his struggles. "This is pointless, isn't it?"

Kharon nodded. "It is."

"You've done this before, haven't you?"

"I have."

"I haven't a chance, have I?"

"Not the slightest."

Alex sighed in resignation and much to his surprise, Kharon released him from the pin and helped him to his feet. "What now?" Alex said, brushing the sand from his body and feeling embarrassed about how easily he'd been beat.

"I'm going back to work," he answered as he returned to his skiff. "We can be friends as long as you learn to control yourself. Until you decide to pay my fare, you can wander the banks, look across the river, or sit down for a spell."

Alex looked over the dark waters and a thought struck him. "I'm a strong swimmer. I bet I could cross it without your silly boat."

"No!" Kharon spun around and placed a hand on Alex's shoulder. "Believe me, you do not want to do that. Even the gods are not so foolish as to touch the waters of the Acheron."

"Why's that?" asked Alex, walking over to the shore and looking at the murky waters. "What's in there that even a god can't kill?"

"Nothing lives there," Kharon replied.

"Is it toxic?"

"To the soul, it most certainly is."

"How do I know you're not saying all this to trick me?" he asked.

Kharon snorted and shook his head. "Touch it and see. It will take only a drop."

Alex knelt by the river and dipped his right index finger into the water. Immediately, it felt as if someone was crushing his finger in a vise. Alex screamed and fell back on the bank, clutching his hand. The pain grew, and unable to do anything else, Alex clenched his jaw and curled into a fetal position. Finally, after what felt like hours, the pain subsided.

"Still think I'm trying to trick you?" asked Kharon.

Alex, teary-eyed, came to his feet. "You could've warned me."

"I did warn you."

Alex, silent, was unsure what to say or do. All he knew was that he wanted to get across the river. Why, he didn't know, other than he felt a draw to the other side. But since swimming wasn't an option, and he didn't have any money to pay Kharon's fare, he was stuck, plain and simple. As he thought about his problem, the gears of his creativity began to spin. From that spinning, an idea was born. It was an idea that lit Alex's face with the brightest of smiles. "Kharon, dear friend," he said. "Has anyone ever beaten you in a sporting contest?"

The ferryman straightened with pride. "Not a one. On my weakest day, I'm stronger than a dozen men."

"What about a race? Are you quick?"

Kharon puffed his chest. "My speed is second only to the gods."

"Then I propose a contest," Alex said. He motioned toward a cluster of rocks off in the distance. "A race, from here to there and back again."

"Stakes?"

"If I win, you take me across the Acheron free of charge."

"And when you lose?"

"I'll be your servant without complaint until you grow weary of my company," Alex replied. "Certainly there is work that could be done. But to be fair, I should disclose that I was quite the track star in my younger days. I even kept up with the famed Chesty Jr."

"Chesty who?"

"A Marine," Alex explained. "You know, the whole 'From the Halls of Montezuma' bit?"

Quietly, Kharon thought about the offer. After a few moments, he tossed his pole into his skiff. "I do not know this Chesty Jr. you speak of, but I accept your challenge nonetheless, Alexander Weiss."

CHAPTER TWO

Inside the rotunda of the U.S. Capitol building, Athena, Goddess of Wisdom, met with Phorcys, Primeval God of the Sea. The location had been picked in advance, being neutral ground since the building's patrons held neither deity's realm in high regard.

Athena leaned against the curved, sandstone wall while lobbyists bustled past. She gave the occasional non-committal gesture, feigning interest and civility in The Old Man's conversation while she critiqued John Trumball's painting, *Surrender of Lord Cornwallis*. She particularly liked the contrast of the blue sky and dark clouds, as she felt it set the serious tone on which observers of the piece should meditate. The mistakes Trumball had made in recounting the exactness of the event—such as who was present and what uniforms were worn—she could overlook, and overall she liked the work. Perhaps when this was over and Ares surrendered to her yet again, she would have Trumball paint that scene as well. If she felt like going down to Hades again, that is.

"Do you not fear the depths?" Phorcys asked, his voice dripping with contempt. The god looked to be a thin man in his late seventies, with sunken cheeks, stringy grey hair, and recessed eyes.

"There is little I fear," Athena said, fully knowing that the god's weak appearance was nothing more than a ruse he enjoyed.

Phorcys straightened, his joints popping loudly as he did. "Mortal and immortal alike are wary of my children. Even your father respects my domain. It is not your role to interfere with my family."

The goddess flicked a piece of lint off her navy-blue short jacket. She loathed the charge that she had nothing better to do than to meddle with The Old Man's children when it was Stheno that had opened her mouth and uttered blaspheme against Athena in the first place. "Your offspring are miserable little monsters and deserve to be treated as such."

Phorcys's hands twitched, and Athena guessed he was doing his best not to revert to his true form and strike her. "And who gave them their snakes for hair?" he asked, popping his knuckles one at a time. "Tell me, oh favored daughter of Zeus, who turned them into the hated creatures they are? Surely such knowledge has not been washed away from your memory."

Athena couldn't help but smile. Of course she knew who it was, and she had always been proud of her creativity when she had meted out the three gorgons' punishment ages ago. Her rational side, however, decided not to gloat, even if she would enjoy toying with The Old Man. Poseidon would make things troublesome, to say the least, should she not at least try to make amends. "What would you ask of me to rectify the situation?"

Phorcys tilted his head and rubbed his hands together as he contemplated his answer. "A peace offering already?" he asked. "Do you expect me to believe the tides have turned so quickly?"

"You are free to believe whatever you like."

A smile spread slowly across Phorcys's face. Athena had not seen that look for three thousand years, but she knew it well nonetheless. The Old Man was about to hit her with something she'd hate.

"Cast your line into the sea of forgiveness and pray it catches something worthwhile," The Old Man said. "Admit you are not my family's captain and are ignorant in our ways, lest you see what a true tempest I can bring."

Athena felt her mouth dry, but she kept her face flat to keep Phorcys's leverage at a minimum. She weighed the choice before her and pondered what the consequences of such an admission would be. She was, after all, the Goddess of Wisdom, not of mistakes. Any blemish on a deity's track record could be seen as a sign of weakness and later exploited. Then again, she thought, there might be a way to quickly and quietly put the matter to rest and save face at the same time. "Fine," she said. "But only if the matter is never spoken of again, between us or anyone else. Furthermore, I only admit that as a courtesy to you, I should have informed you on what had transpired before acting as I did."

Phorcys looked surprised at how easily she agreed to his first demand. "There's more," he continued. "My last daughter, Euryale, is in need. Her crying is what woke me from my slumber in the abyss. Her spirit needs to be lifted."

"What did you have in mind?"

The Old Man waited for a group of tourists to meander by before answering. "Find a suitor worthy of her, one that would resist the call of the sirens to be at her side."

Athena raised her hands and took a step back. "Oh no. That's Aphrodite's specialty. You've got the wrong girl if you think I'm playing matchmaker."

"Athena," he said, the tone in his voice softening. "Navigating the waters of love is treacherous enough where a gorgon is not concerned. Aphrodite lacks both the tact and wisdom to handle the finer details of such a voyage."

Athena mulled the request over. She knew Phorcys was catering to her ego, and it would be nice to show up little miss love goddess, but she felt that the task was still beneath her station, which was probably why he was making her do it in the first place. "Let me make a counter offer," she said. "I'll see to it that she gets a suitor, but I'll only act as an overseer to the endeavor. Someone else will do the leg work."

The Old Man's brow furrowed. "No. This is part of your penance."

"I'm afraid I'm far too busy to be personally involved on this one, Phorcys. So much to do and see since we've been gone so long, but you have my word that the results will be the same. I've got precisely the man in mind."

"Man? You insult me by using a mortal for such a task?"

Athena masked her disdain for The Old Man and gently took his hand with a smile. "I assure you that he will do your daughter the proper service."

Phorcys pulled back. "And what is the name of this hero of yours?"

"Alexander Weiss."

A low growl preceded The Old Man's response. "Your hero's fame escapes me."

"He's perfect," she reassured with a pat on his shoulder. "He's a romantic at heart and the one that Stheno accidently landed on. More importantly, he owes me a favor."

"Details."

"Apollo has prophesied that he's going to insult me."

The stakes had been made, the finish line had been drawn, and the two runners took their places along the desolate bank of the Acheron. Alex, bent over in a perfect, four-point crouch, glanced at his opponent. Kharon, also set and ready, counted.

On one, Alex held his muscles taught. On two, he sucked in a deep breath. And on three, he held fast. Predictably, Kharon bolted forward like a thoroughbred free from the gates. The ferryman's speed was impossible to match, but Alex had no intentions of trying. Instead of taking up the race, Alex leaped onto the skiff, grabbed the pole off the deck, and pushed off.

"My thanks, kind sir," Alex called out once Kharon realized what had happened and skidded to a stop. Alex gave an informal, two finger salute and took pride at how well his ruse had worked. "Fear not. I'll take good care of your ship."

Kharon didn't respond, but stood statuesque on the riverbank, his gaze never leaving Alex as he disappeared into the fog.

The skiff glided silently across the dark waters, and Alex was surprised at how little effort it took to move it forward. As he pressed on, the air grew foul and thick, causing him to cough. The fog closed in, and soon it enshrouded the bow from view. Despite a growing nausea and being all but blind, Alex whistled the first Chopin nocturne he'd ever learned (Op. 9, No.2) and when he was done with that, he was still in the fog, and so moved on to the next. And the next. And the next. Only after he'd finished every nocturne Chopin had ever written and was about to start again, did the fog lift and the air refresh, and the skiff ran aground.

Smiling with relief, Alex hopped off and surveyed his surroundings. The bank gave way to rolling hills of vibrant green. The sky above seemed to be in a perpetual sunset, shimmering with reds and oranges and smeared with a handful of clouds. Regardless of the array of colors, the silent and musty air gave Alex an uneasy feeling.

He wasn't dreaming. This was real. His stomach knotted at the implications, and a pain grew in his chest at all the things left undone. The concerts he'd no longer play. The travels he'd no longer take. His fish he'd no longer feed.

Alex sighed as one final thought came to him: there was a girl he'd no longer be able to call. Perhaps that one was for the best. They'd only been together for some of middle school and high school before she moved, and thus he hadn't seen her for what, eighteen years? It was doubtful she even remembered him all that much. Still, he would've liked to have contacted her at least once before he'd died.

He wondered how soon it would be until he met someone else. He came across a few shadows like those on the banks of the Acheron, but like those other souls, these shades never spoke a word to Alex, no matter how many times he tried to engage them. Worse, the more he went on, the fainter they became, and he soon realized he too would become like them, oblivious to everyone around him.

Tired and stiff from the boat ride, Alex plopped onto the ground and studied the scenery. "If this really is the afterlife, I can't say I'm impressed," he said to himself. "It's like a second-rate Manet painting."

"I think you mean Monet," a voice said from behind.

Alex turned. Behind him stood a woman about his height, dressed in flowing robes and holding a full helm in one hand and a spear in the other. Alex rubbed his eyes, unsure what to make of this new arrival. With high cheekbones and mysterious, grey eyes, the woman had an attraction that far surpassed any woman Alex had ever seen—even more so when he realized her athletic figure was flawless. Two words came to mind, beautiful and enticing, but he spoke neither. Flabbergasted that there was a living, breathing, talking being before him, all Alex could say was, "Pardon?"

"You're referring to Claude Monet," she said. "Crossing the waters of the Acheron will do that to a man, make him lose his memories of life."

"No, I meant Manet. The impressionist. This place lacks detail and feels fuzzy, like his paintings."

"That was Monet," she reiterated, now sounding like a professor clarifying a lesson. "Edouard Manet was a realist and the one that painted the whore."

"Are you sure?"

"Very."

Alex furrowed his brow and pressed his lips, all the while wondering how anyone could mix up something so simple, as if a realist and an impressionist were anything alike. "No, I'm certain it was Manet. I had a few art history courses in college. They teach you things like that, painters' names and whatnot."

"Are you openly challenging me on this?" Her eyes narrowed, and her sex appeal vanished. "By all means, continue to insult me by staying seated."

Without thought, Alex jumped to his feet. She had an air of importance around her, but other than that, he hadn't a clue who she was or why he should care. "I'm sorry, but have we met?"

"Athena Parthenos," she said, offering nothing but an annoyed glare to go with the introduction. "Though some prefer Pallas Athena. You may address me as either."

"Would that be Miss, Mrs., or Ms. Pallas Athena?"

"You can drop the prefix completely."

"And you are?"

"Daughter of Zeus, patron goddess of Athens."

"Oh, that's peachy," Alex said before cursing under his breath. "I really have gone insane."

Athena raised an eyebrow. "Why do you say that?"

"Goddess indeed. You're about as real as the Easter Bunny. I've clearly had some sort of psychotic break and am now probably dribbling in a nut house."

"I assure you, you're not a madman," she said. "If anyone should know about things that afflict the mind, it would be me."

"Pish-posh," Alex said with a wave of his hand. "What do you know?"

A wry grin formed on Athena's face, one that made Alex shift nervously as he questioned the validity of his conclusion. "I was going to give you the honor of running an errand for me, one that I might have even rewarded you for," she said. "But first, I think you need to be taught a lesson."

Athena snapped her fingers, and the two disappeared.

CHAPTER THREE

In the center of an ornate, marble arena, Athena donned her helm and adjusted her grip on her spear. Long ago, she had grown weary of such unimaginative combat, but Ares, who stood a few paces away, insisted on the duel. She had relented not long ago to silence his constant badgering.

"Are you ready?" she asked, hefting a large, bronze shield from the ground and onto her arm. "Double or nothing, yes?"

"Double or nothing!" The God of War thumped his bare chest twice and then twirled his spear before planting its butt in the ground. "Now this is sport. This is a test of prowess and strength."

"I would've thought you'd want a more substantial contest," Athena said, baiting a proverbial hook with which she planned to tease her brother. "Something more war oriented."

"I do not wish to play that game of yours again, where heroes and kings are useless and at the mercy of women."

"Fair enough," Athena replied, adopting a fighting stance with shield and spear. "To be honest, I was relieved that you didn't suggest it."

Ares' grin shone from beneath his helm. "Your tricks of the mind won't work on me, dear sister." He took a half step backward and charged.

Athena deflected the point of his spear on her shield and turned with her brother's momentum. She whipped the butt of her spear around, aiming for his head, but failed to land the blow. The two disengaged, and Athena pressed her lips together. A thousand years ago her counterattack would have connected. Either she was getting slower, or he was getting smarter. She wasn't sure which she'd prefer. "Have we started?" she asked to mask her surprise.

"Warming up," Ares replied. He bounced on the balls of his feet a few times. "Tell me, sister, are you disappointed that you missed?"

"I didn't want to beat you as easily as I did at our last contest," she lied.

Ares grunted. "Had I a real army, you wouldn't have won. Here you shall find defeat."

"One of us will," she said. She hopped forward and lunged. It was a half-hearted attack, and one she knew would miss, but it was meant to underscore her next point. "In all seriousness, I am glad you suggested the duel."

Ares backed several yards, planted his spear into the ground, and raised his helm. "What do you mean?"

"Think about it. If you win here, there is no shame for me," she replied. "But if we'd played chess again and you'd won, I'd lose something I could never get back."

Puzzlement crossed her brother's face, and it was precisely the reaction she was looking for. "How so?"

"Because as of right now, you have never defeated me."

Ares didn't react at first, but once her statement's implications had had time to sink in, he heaved his spear into the air and threw his helm. "You tricked me into this duel!"

"I did no such thing," Athena replied. She was pleased she wouldn't have to spell it out for him. "I only went along with your suggestion for our next contest."

"You wanted to keep the glory to yourself!" he shouted. Cords of muscle bulged in his neck. "You wanted to gloat on your perfect track record for all of eternity!"

"I suppose I could gloat if I wanted, couldn't I?" Athena removed her helm and tucked it under her arm. "Funny how it only takes winning the first game to do that."

"I don't find it funny at all."

Athena spun the helm around with her hand several times. "Shall we continue this duel now or later?"

"We will do neither," he stated. "I demand a rematch. Get the board ready, and this time I play white."

"As you wish," she answered. "But first, I need to go check on Alex."

Alex found that the mountainside he was on gave him an excellent view of the sea. He had always been fond of watching the waves break against a rocky shore, smelling the salty air, and listening to the birds overhead. And he would have been fond of all of that on this lovely day had he not been lying on his back, chained hand and foot to a stone slab. A slab, he noted, that was stained a dark brown.

"This doesn't prove anything other than you're a psychotic bitch!" he yelled. When his cries were answered only by his echo, he thrashed about once more. "Let me out of here right now or so help me god!"

"God? Which god did you have in mind? I don't believe any suffer your plight at the moment."

Alex craned his head over his shoulder to see Athena standing a few paces away. "The real God, if there is one, you sick little monkey. We have names for your kind, you know, and it's not divine. It's psychopath."

Athena walked over, patted Alex on his head, and ruffled his hair. "That's the problem with you mortals, never understanding your place in the world and never grateful for the gifts you receive."

"Don't mortal me. You've still proven nothing," Alex shot back. He was glad that his backbone hadn't disappeared. If something bad was going to happen, at least it would happen while he was still on his feet—or as much as circumstances would allow. "And what gift have I been given?" he added. "My imprisonment?"

Athena tapped him square on his chest. "This."

"My sternum?"

"Your body," she replied. "Or did you fail to notice that as well? I think I did a pretty good job fixing it up after it was flattened and washed off a whale's hide."

Alex paused. As much as he could tell, he looked exactly how he always had. Tall, reasonably fit, and a scar on his left forearm from where he'd broken it falling out of a tree when he was nine. "Oh yeah, my body," he said, returning to the conversation. "I have no idea how I missed it before. It must not be very important if it's been gone all this time."

"It's only important if you want to mostly interact with the world around you," she said with a smile. "Or have the world mostly interact with you."

"Mostly?"

"Yes, mostly," she reiterated. "But don't get too attached to it. It's a loaner and for demonstrational purposes only."

"Right." Alex rolled his eyes. He was tired of the games. "If you're some ancient Greek deity, then where have you been the last two thousand years?"

"On vacation," she answered matter-of-factly. "Something your culture might call paid time off."

"You're the modern goddess now? Stop toying with me and be done with it." He had a brief inclination to spit on her, but his imagination on how she might react to the assault kept him in line. It was easier to be brave when the situation wasn't at its worst.

Athena knelt so she was eye level with him. "Now Alex," she said. "I'm a reasonable goddess, more so than any other you'll meet. I'm not about to butcher you without cause. That would be uncouth. However, I'll not have you uttering blasphemy, nor will I tolerate you insulting my friends."

The tone in her voice made Alex rethink his predicament. He had to admit that there might be a chance she was who she said she was and he hadn't gone crazy. If that were true, that would be—for lack of a better word—bad. A more rational point replaced that thought. "You can't scare me into thinking you're some goddess. Fear does not equate truth."

"Scare? No," she answered. "But we will come to an understanding. As this is your first offense, your sentence will be light. Are you familiar with Prometheus?"

The name sounded familiar, but Alex could not come up with the details. "I'm afraid not."

"No matter," she said. "You will know his fate soon enough."

Alex pulled against the shackles yet again. "What are you going to do to me?"

Athena held up a hand. When he calmed, she whistled sharply. Off in the distance, an eagle cried out in reply. "You see," Athena said, coming to her feet. "Prometheus angered my father, and Zeus, being the disciplinarian he is, had Prometheus bound to this very same spot."

"And?"

The goddess motioned skyward. "During the day, an eagle would come and tear out his liver. But at night, his liver would regrow, thus restarting the cycle."

Alex looked to the clouds and spied a large bird that sported a wicked beak and dagger-like talons. It looked more real to him than anything he'd ever seen in his entire life, and suddenly, he hadn't a doubt that this was not a dream whatsoever. "Okay, okay. Just wait," he pleaded. "You're a goddess. I apologize for saying you weren't. So now we're good."

"I think not," Athena replied. She ran a solitary finger down his chest and poked him in the abdomen. "As you said before, threatening you only makes me a psychotic bitch. Keeping you alive after you've been eviscerated and then regenerating your liver, however, makes me divine. And if you're going to run an errand for me, we've got to have our roles clear from the beginning."

"This is completely unfair! You'd torture me because I didn't know who you were?"

"Torture? Hardly. We can stop by Hades if you want to be tortured," she said. The eagle landed next to her, and she scratched its head. "Think of this as tough love. Children need to be corrected from time to time. Once this is over, I'm certain we can be friends, in a deity-servant sort of way."

The eagle ruffled its dark brown plumage and hopped next to Alex. It lightly pecked once, then twice, at Alex's torso and drew blood.

Alex screamed and tugged at the chains. The sinews in his arms and shoulders painfully strained under the demand he set upon them. That pain paled in comparison to the fire in his midsection when the eagle drove its beak into his abdomen.

Blood poured from the wound and stained both rock and plumage in equal amounts. Alex's body went into spasms, and still the bird tore at him until his liver fell out. The eagle ruffled its feathers, gobbled it up, and flew away.

Alex's body went limp, and his head rolled to the side. To his complete horror, he was still alive and aware of everything.

Athena stood nearby, apathetic to the entire ordeal. She glanced at the ground as she approached, evidently not wanting to step in any blood or gore. "This is how it's going to be, Alex," she said, squatting and resting her chin on folded hands. "Since you still owe me for your petty little insults and outburst from before, you can either repeat today for another thousand years, or you can complete a simple task for me. The choice is yours."

Unable to think or speak, Alex shut his eyes, grit his teeth, and tried his best to push the pain away.

"Think it over," she said. "Be warned. Tomorrow morning your liver will be as good as new, and Aldora likes to eat an early breakfast."

CHAPTER FOUR

Alex woke to the spray of saltwater upon his face. He screamed and tried to jump up, but the shackles held him fast. Immediately, his eyes went to his torso, and he stared in disbelief at the wholeness of his midsection. Slowly, he tore his gaze away and looked about. The eagle, thankfully, was nowhere to be seen. He was, however, still bound to the very same slab of rock, on the very same side of the very same mountain. Only two things had changed in his predicament. First, a night sky loomed above, and second, an aged, hunchback man stood nearby, scowling at him.

"Alexander Weiss?"

"Yes," Alex replied. "And you are?"

"Phorcys, God of the Sea, though many call me The Old Man," he replied.

"Isn't that Poseidon's job?" Alex said, remembering a small amount of his Greek Mythology.

Phorcys's eyes narrowed, and he made tiny, withered fists. "The deep will always be mine."

"Please say I haven't angered you too," Alex said as his gut tightened. "I don't think I can handle two of you after me."

"No. You have not," Phorcys replied. "But I shall no longer weather Athena's games at the expense of my daughter and my sanity."

Alex sighed with relief. "I don't suppose you could get me out of these chains? My appreciation would know no bounds."

Phorcys made a strange gesture in the air. After a brilliant flash of light, he changed into a hideous mix of crab, fish, and man. The Old Man extended a large claw, and with a few quick snaps, he cut Alex free.

Alex scampered away and knocked his head on a nearby rock. "What the holy hell?" he exclaimed. "You could at least warn someone before doing that."

"You startle easily," Phorcys commented. "Odd for a champion of Athena."

"I think any normal person would, hero or not."

"Doubtful," the god replied. The Old Man slithered toward Alex on his elongated fish tail. "For a hero, you are nothing of the likes of Perseus. Strange, isn't it, that she would pick you to steer the fate of a gorgon?"

"I'm not doing anything," Alex said. "I want nothing to do with her."

Phorcys expression soured, and he looked at Alex with skepticism. "Perhaps I should let you run off. I see no heroic qualities in you. Your body is weak. Your spirit lacks salt. And from what I hear, you are filled with hubris that borders on blasphemy. What could you possibly do of worth?"

"If it means getting away from Athena, I can't do a damn thing," he said. He had half a mind to bolt right there, but he hadn't a clue where he was or where he'd go. "All I want to know is how to get out of here so I can put as much distance between me and her as possible."

Phorcys drew back a corner of his mouth. "You think you can run from Athena?"

"I'm sure as hell going to try," said Alex.

"Yes, I'm sure you'll elude her for quite some time." The Old Man said, shooing Alex off with a claw. "Go. Tempt fate and see if outwitting Athena is a course safe and true."

"It has to be safer than staying here," said Alex, glancing to the slab with a grimace and a shudder. He could still feel Aldora's beak tear through him and remember the sickly, sweet smell to his innards. "Besides, I'm sure whatever pointless, meaningless errand she keeps alluding to is going to be a thousand times worse."

"That pointless, meaningless errand is my daughter."

Alex felt the color drain from his face. "Oh. I didn't mean anything by that. I swear."

"For your sake, I should think not."

"Maybe I could help," he said, hoping to smooth things over as quickly as he could since the gods seemed to be touchy on everything. "What seems to be the trouble?"

Phorcys looked warily at Alex. "My daughter needs a suitor, and only a hero would be up to such a task."

"And?"

"And there is nothing more," he said. He looked out over the ocean and made a sweeping gesture across its waters. "I can command it to ebb and flow at my whim. I can draw back its waters to expose the Abyss or summon creatures from those very depths to do my bidding. But I cannot control true love. No one can. Not even the gods."

"Love is not something you control," Alex said, sighing wishfully. His body relaxed, and a smile born from a longing heart spread over his face. "It's a power that draws you in. Shapes you. Controls you. It's the sweet notes of whispers between a couple, the prestissimo charge of lovers reunited, and everything in between. Your daughter only wants what we all dream of, in one form or another."

The Old Man's face softened, ever so slightly. "Maybe you do know the waters she seeks."

"I know them," Alex said, leaning against a rock and letting himself slip back to days long gone, days when Jessica stole his breath and consumed his every thought with her adorable freckle face. But as much as he wanted to indulge himself in thinking about the past, he knew he had to return to the present and deal with the god before him. "For your daughter, would I have to find her someone to marry, or would a date suffice?"

"A courtship would be acceptable," The Old Man answered. "Provided the other was serious about pursuing a relationship with Euryale. Woe to he that hurts my daughter."

"That's it?" Alex asked. "He doesn't need to be anything else? A god? Demigod? Rich? Powerful? Doctor? Warrior? Sea Captain?"

"No," Phorcys said. There was hesitation in his voice. "Euryale will tell you who she wants."

"Might I ask why she's having trouble finding someone to begin with?"

"Mostly it's a matter of her appearance." The Old Man admitted. "Some have had, how I shall say this, bad reactions to her...substantial looks."

"She's a big girl?"

"Man-sized."

"No, I meant is she excessively overweight? Not that it matters, but I know some people are self-conscious about such things."

"Not at all," The Old Man answered. "She's as streamlined as the mako and twice as strong."

"But she looks like a shark," Alex guessed. Maybe it was only her teeth, he hoped. If so, Alex did know a few dentists that could work miracles. But then again, her dad was crab-fish-man. Miracles might not be enough.

Phorcys shook his head. "Not at all."

Alex rubbed his chin as he tried to pick his next words carefully. "But you're saying she's not the most beautiful girl in the world?"

"Before mortals even dreamed of taking to sails, she and her sisters were the envy of many."

"Ah, that's it then," Alex said with a smile. He was glad that the problem was now identified. "Age isn't a problem anymore, not in this day. There are plenty of people out there with a cake full of candles that are looking to meet that special someone, wrinkles and all."

"She's immortal," Phorcys replied. "Her skin has not aged a day since she matured. The problem is with her vipers."

"She has snakes?"

"Yes, they are—"

Alex waved his hand and cut in. "Snakes shouldn't be a problem. Are they dangerous?"

"Yes, but—"

Alex waved his hand again, proud that he finally understood it all. "No, I get it. She has a bunch of poisonous snakes for pets, and they scare off her prospects."

Phorcys nodded slowly. "In a manner of speaking, but—"

"No need to explain," Alex said. Confidence soared within and exuded in his voice and posture. "I can do this. A nice eligible herpetologist and we're all set. The last thing I want is you feeling like you need to make excuses for your daughter."

"There are no excuses. Only facts."

"If I can find the perfect girl for John Puller, a marine more obsessed with finding the best way to kill a thousand men than remembering to open the door for a girl, I can find a date for your daughter," Alex said. "What do I get in return when I succeed?"

"Are you agreeing to my request?"

"I'm leaning that way. What do I get in return?"

"You'll have enough of my gratitude that I'll see to it you have a companion when you return to the fields of asphodel in the Underworld. A dog, perhaps, to keep you company. A much more agreeable existence you'll find than being a shade without companionship or purpose for all of eternity."

Alex cringed at the thought, and he hoped he could sweeten the deal. "Any chance at getting a little extra?"

Phorcys motioned to the slab with a pincer. "Your extra will be Athena will keep you free from those chains and Aldora's beak, provided your tongue is kept in check."

Alex looked at The Old Man, back to the rock and chains, and then to The Old Man once more. "Sounds fair."

"A wise choice." Phorcys smiled, moving closer. "Now, there is one more matter to address."

"What's that?" Alex asked. Not liking the sound in The Old Man's voice, Alex retreated a few steps. Unfortunately, those were all that were to be had, and Alex found himself pressed against a rock wall.

Phorcys closed the distance. "Athena wants your body back. Hades would be irate if he knew you were inhabiting it again."

Before Alex could even think about protesting the remark, Phorcys struck him on the side of the head.

Upon Ares' request, the chess rematch was moved to one of the open courtyards in Olympus. There, both he and Athena sat next to a large fountain and basked in the warm sunlight. Ares insisted on it because he claimed the light would, "stimulate his tactical thought." Unlike the first game, Ares played white, and Athena played black. In seven moves, Ares had lost a rook. Four more after that, he lost both of his knights while taking only one of hers. Six moves later, Ares' position wasn't any better. Some might say it was worse.

"These surroundings are not conducive to combat," Ares said with a weary voice. "Our battle should've been moved to the armory where I can get in the mood for conquest. Not out here where puffy clouds and the smell of spring seek to weaken my resolve."

Athena looked up from her book on 20th century existentialism and caught her brother adjusting the position of one of his pieces. "I loathe bringing this up, dear brother," she said, "but if you touch a piece, you have to move it."

"I am aware of the rules," he snapped, pulling his hand back. "You knocked it aside on your last turn."

"Then I apologize," she said and returned to her reading. She knew her hand hadn't graced that side of the board in over an hour, but she found her brother's frustrations amusing, and his excuses more so. "It was only meant as a harmless comment."

"Keep your comments to yourself. They're distracting."

Athena marked her place in the book with a finger and closed it. "You've been distracted this entire game. I had nothing to do with it."

"I have to be somewhere soon," he explained. "Somewhere more important than here with this silly game."

"Oh? Did you finally find a war to join?"

Ares picked up his king and castled, queen side. "No, I have to see someone."

"Who? Dad?"

"No," he replied. "Someone else. It's your turn."

"Ah," Athena said. A large smile grew on her face. No one, save Aphrodite, Goddess of Love, was ever referred to in such an aloof manner by her brother. "Back to having an affair I see."

"It's not like that."

"What else would you call it? Better yet, what would Hephaestus call it?"

"Quiet, woman. Lest my wrath spill on to you."

Athena laughed and slid her queen across the board, creating an absolute pin on Ares' sole bishop. "At the very least, I hope you two are more discreet than last time."

Ares stared at the chess board. Minutes passed, and he neither replied nor moved an inch. Ares reached out, hesitated, and shot out of his chair. "Who let your human in here?"

Athena spun and scanned the courtyard. "Alex? Here?"

"Oh, never mind," the God of War said. He sat back down and made his move. "It's Hermes."

Athena turned back and studied the board. Aside from the rook Ares had moved, another piece, a pawn, was out of place. Her brother was also trying—unsuccessfully—to maintain a poker face. "I should probably be going," she said. "I need to check on Alex to make sure he's dealing with Euryale as per our agreement. Phorcys said he could motivate him, but I have my doubts. Perhaps we should end things here?"

"Resigning?"

"Offering a draw. I'd like to grab something to eat before I get moving."

Ares leaned back with his fingers interlocked behind his neck and grinned. "A true warrior does not settle for mediocrity."

Athena set her book aside. "Is that a no?"

"That's a no."

Athena looked down at the board and smacked her lips. Three quick moves later, the game was over, the table was broken in two, and Ares had stormed off to find consolation in Aphrodite's arms.

CHAPTER FIVE

Alex shut his eyes and screamed. Something loud popped in his head, and the dull thump of a heavy object hitting the ground followed. Slowly, he opened one eye and then the next. Phorcys stood nearby and brushed bits of goop off one of his claws.

"You winced like a coward," The Old Man said, "especially for someone who has already tasted death."

"What did you do?" Alex asked, perplexed.

Phorcys motioned at the ground. "See for yourself."

Alex jumped. At The Old Man's feet was a body, twisted and covered in blood. When the initial shock wore off, Alex remained confused. He hadn't seen anyone else in ages and certainly not someone sporting the same polo shirt as he wore. "Who did you kill?"

"Look closer."

Alex did. "He looks sort of like me. Though not as good looking."

"It is you."

Alex laughed. "No."

"Yes."

Alex's inspection took on a surreal quality. Finally, Alex's spirit decided that Alex's body was indeed lying on the ground. "You killed me?"

"You seem upset."

"Of course I'm upset! Why shouldn't I be?"

Phorcys pressed his lips together and grunted. "Man your helm and get your bearings. Would you cower in the hull of your ship as the storm approaches? Would you let it be tossed by the sea without trying to steer your own course? For my daughter's sake, I hope you would not."

Alex stared at his body and slapped himself in the face several times. "Okay, okay, okay, okay," he said. "This isn't too bad. I can work with this. Not quite what I expected being dead would be like. Maybe I just need a drink."

"You drink?"

"Never have," Alex admitted. "But if there's ever a time to start, I think this would be it."

"Many a captain has taken a fancy to rum," The Old Man said as he put his arm around Alex's shoulder and led him away. "Euryale, however, has only wine. But she is a gracious hostess. I'm certain she'll offer you some."

"At this point, any alcohol I think would be fine."

Phorcys nodded. "One last thing, you're not quite dead, yet."

"Right, so I've been told."

Home. That's what Euryale called it. But to Athena it was a tiny island stuck on the western edge of the world and was nothing more than a large, useless rock jutting out over the sea. It was not only useless, but also barren and worthless. In short, it was the perfect place for Athena to have banished a blasphemous trio of sisters.

Athena picked her way along a rocky foot path and headed for the island's sole cave where Euryale dwelled. She paused at the top of the cliff and admired the ocean view. The evening sun dipped into the horizon, silhouetting a half dozen mismatched sailing ships that had anchored in the bay. Beneath their tattered sails and barnacled keels, Athena could make out the shadows of a larger fleet, a fleet that had made its final home on the sea floor. How and why the mortals kept coming was beyond her.

Athena took a deep breath and sighed. The sooner she finished her visit, the sooner she could get back to her pursuits, and with some luck, Alex would have a good start on his task. As she started to walk again, Athena made a note that Phorcys didn't appreciate whales in the family.

"Athena!" Alex shouted as she entered the cave. He jumped to his feet, scampered past a dozen stone statues and threw his arms around the goddess. "I'm so glad you could make it!"

With a puzzled look, Athena gently removed his arms. "Alex?"

"Sorry," Alex said, blushing. "Really, sorry." He stepped backward and ended up stumbling as he fought for balance. "It's only that I thought you might not come, being mad at me and all."

Athena ignored Alex for the moment and turned to Euryale. "What did you do to him?"

The gorgon, wearing a bright green peplos with bronze clasps, sat next to the fire pit. A smile graced her gentle feminine face while a delicate hand twirled one of the many serpents that adorned her head. "He's had some drinks," Euryale explained. "Care to join us? Or are you looking to donate more to an aquarium?"

The goddess's eyes narrowed. "Bite your tongue or you shall see how creative I can be."

"Let bygones be bygones, I say." Alex said. He grabbed a chalice from the ground and hoisted it into the air. "Let's toast to my friend, Athena, Goddess of Wisdom and stuff!"

"You're drunk." Athena seized the chalice and cast it aside, spilling what little wine was left onto the rocky ground.

"What's wrong with a couple drinks?"

"Seven drinks, Alex," Euryale corrected.

"Two, seven. Same thing." Alex flopped down and started eating a fig from a nearby basket. "And I'm not drunk. But I could use a stick of beef jerky, if you had one."

Athena's lips flattened. "Are you looking to argue with me again?"

"You're really being a stick in the mud," Alex said. "Hey Athena, you know what's really weird though?"

"At this point, I can't imagine what's going through your mind."

"I'm not dead, yet. But I'm drunk."

Euryale reclined on one elbow. "He's been trying to figure that one out for an hour."

"Seriously, drunk," he said. "How weird is that? No body, but I'm drunk. I'm only ghost. That's all that's left of me. Maybe that's why they call it spirits?"

"Mortals," Athena said, shaking her head. She leaned against the cavern wall and massaged her scalp. "You're giving me a headache."

"So what if I'm drunk?" Alex asked, his voice sharpening. "What's the big deal? No responsibility. No having to listen to inner critics. No worrying about this and that or what could have been. It's pretty nice actually."

"I can't abide drunks," she answered. She began to enumerate on her fingers as she continued. "They're boorish, mindless, and do nothing to further society. They say things that get them in trouble and don't do what they should. Case and point, you."

Alex took to his feet in the most ungainly of ways and brushed off the dirt that clung to him. "Nothing for society? I'll have you know, I'm quite the pianist. I slew the Totentaz! With less than a year's practice I might add!"

"Which matters little to me," Athena shot back. "What does matter to me is you finding Euryale a suitor, which you obviously haven't even begun to start working on."

"Psh!" Alex, smiling bright and eyes half closed, walked behind the gorgon. "We've been chatting, getting to know one another—you know, the stuff you have to do to make a relationship. Can't really find her someone if I don't know her myself, can I?"

Athena gave the tiniest of approving nods. "What do you know about her?"

"I know enough that I'll have this angel a date in no time."

"Angel?" Athena echoed.

"Have you ever seen anyone near as beautiful?" he slurred, kissing Euryale on the cheek. Alex pulled back, face red with embarrassment. "Sorry about that."

"Don't apologize," Euryale said softly.

A tingle ran through Alex's body and he felt his pulse quicken. "Okay, well, I'll admit that the snakes freaked me out at first," he said, running his hand through Euryale's reptilian hair before jerking it away when a red viper took a nip at it. "And yes, it's annoying when they bite. But once you get past that, she's perfect."

Euryale blushed.

Athena's mouth hung open.

"She's not just a pretty face either," Alex went on, finding himself swept up in the moment. "She's got great taste in wine. She's got her own place. Her dad is affluent and part of the who's who of the universe. And...and..." His monologue trailed off while he attempted to recall the list he'd made previously. "Oh, yes! She's the most fantastic of artists."

"Oh, she is, is she?" Athena asked with a bemused smile.

"Yes, she is," Alex replied. He stumbled over to a pair of life-sized statues and hung his arms around the neck of the one on the right. "Look at this guy," he said. "I've never seen such fine detail in a carving, have you? I'd swear this guy was alive. His face is so full of emotion that it's downright scary."

"You think she carved those?"

"I never said I was a sculptor," Euryale cut in. "I merely said they were my creation."

Alex looked at the two of them with ambivalence. He couldn't care less the exact method of working with the medium. "Does it matter? She's obviously a master at her craft—the markings of a true genius. The point, however, remains. I'll have no trouble finding her someone. Might not be one that is classy, as I can't see any of my friends wanting to live in a dumpy cave, but it will be someone nonetheless. A nice someone. A someone that she can bring home to her dad. I bet I can do it in half a week."

"I happen to like my cave, thank you," Euryale said, scowling.

"I'm sorry," Alex said. "It's a nice cave, as far as holes in the ground go. But if I were you, I'd think about hiring someone to spruce the place up. Maybe we should put that on our to-do list. Something that says you're a successful artist, not a starving one. You know, one you'd bring home to mother."

"Would you bring her home to mother?" Athena asked.

"Well, no," Alex stammered, unprepared for the question. "But only because that would be a little hard at the moment, don't you think?"

"Point taken," Athena said. "I'll tell you what, if you find her someone in three and a half days, I'll forget your behavior tonight. I'll even get you something special if you do."

Euryale stood and came to Alex's side. She ran one hand along the small of his back and rested her head on his shoulder. "Don't worry, Athena. I think he'll do. I think he'll do nicely. I'll let you know soon if it works out."

Alex smiled. "See? She's got faith in me."

"Oh, that she does, Alex," Athena said with a laugh. "She has more faith in you than you realize."

Alex shrugged, not quite understanding what she meant, or why he felt a tiny pinch on his right butt cheek. But whatever. He was happy that the matter would soon be settled, and he hoped that if things went well, he might be rewarded with more than a canine companion to join him in the afterlife.

CHAPTER SIX

Alex slept for nearly a day. He woke in the evening to the smell of Euryale making dinner. After a meal of poached fish and a few ponderings as to why he had to eat at all, Alex discovered that being a daughter of a god was not without its perks. He watched Euryale open a massive oak chest tucked away in the back of her cave. Inside, she dug through numerous piles of clothes, weapons, pots, and spices before finally pulling forth a pair of fine sandals.

The footwear was leather and superbly made. The sandals sported snug straps, a comfortable sole, and a set of small wings on the heels for quick travel. The latter trait Alex had trouble getting used to, as Euryale made moving at the speed of thought look much easier than it was.

But the gorgon had the patience of a saint, and by midnight Alex was zipping about her island without difficulty. By the time the morning sun's glow warmed the horizon, the two were in the driveway of his former home, staring at the whale-sized imprint on his front lawn.

"I'm sorry about your sister," Alex said. He couldn't think of anything meaningful for the moment, but it felt awkward, and in the back of his mind he felt like he should at least say something.

"Thank you," she said, turning her gaze from the small crater. "But you're the one she landed on."

"Flattened, from what I understand," said Alex. With nothing else to further the conversation, he started for the door.

Euryale grabbed him by the arm. "A moment, Alex, if you would. We must be sure no one is at home."

Alex stopped, puzzled. "Why would there be?"

"I should have asked before," she said, "but I was caught up in the moment and in my haste, I did not."

"Ask what?"

Euryale chewed her lip momentarily before clarifying. "Have you a wife?"

"I never married."

"What about your family?"

"I have none that are still alive," he replied, his eyes never leaving the door. "Thanks for reminding me."

The gorgon slumped. "I apologize if my questions were painful. Do you want to talk about it?"

"Not particularly."

Euryale pulled her serpentine hair back and attempted a fast knot tie, but without something to clamp the reptiles down, they easily slithered free from the bun she created. "As you wish," she said. "But let me warn you, if anyone saw me, it would not end well."

"Because of the snakes?"

"In part, yes," she answered as she pulled up the hood of her cloak. "I don't think you understand for whom you are trying to find a suitor."

"Look, the snakes are weird and will freak most people out," Alex replied, hoping that it didn't sound as bad as he thought. "But can you imagine what would happen if the neighbors saw me walking around? I think a walking corpse tops snake-girl any day of the week."

Euryale patted him on the shoulder. "You don't have to worry about that. No one can see you—no mortal at least."

"No one?"

"Not a soul, Alex. You've been killed, remember?"

"Figures. Maybe I'll start tossing some lamps around to get their attention. That could be fun."

"I'm afraid that won't work," she said as she smacked a stray viper back into place.

Alex smirked. "They can't see lamps now either?"

"No, it's not like that," Euryale replied. She hesitated and then motioned toward the house. "Try the doorknob and you'll see."

"Right, the doorknob," Alex repeated with a wary voice. He reached out to give it a turn, then a second, and finally a third time before he realized that his hand was passing through with each attempt. "Now that's bizarre."

"You'll need a body if you want to use anything around here. That includes being seen, heard, or otherwise noticed by people. And since you've been killed...well, you understand now, I'm sure."

"But you can see, hear, and interact with me."

"I'm also the daughter of a god," she said with a wink.

"So, you're telling me what, exactly?"

"I'm telling you that you won't be doing anything on your own."

Alex took a deep breath and exhaled sharply. "Well, hell."

Ares paced the bedroom, occasionally kicking various garments that had been tossed on the oak floor. His mind was elsewhere, while Aphrodite, Goddess of Love, sat in bed with pink silk sheets drawn up to her neck and a crass look on her face.

"Well that was unfulfilling," she said with a huff. She fluffed the large feather pillow behind her and sank into it. "A mortal would have lasted ten times longer."

Ares grunted while he continued to walk about. What mortal could gaze upon her immaculate, milky skin and not turn into a stuttering idiot? Or kiss her lips, full and red, and not do the same? And could a man ever touch her legs, long and sculpted, let alone see her perfect breasts or curvy hips and not drop dead?

Aphrodite threw a pillow at him, interrupting his train of thought. "Are you going to leave me in want all night?"

The God of War stopped, clenched a fist, and then forced himself to relax. He enjoyed his time with her immensely, and he knew that she expected more of him. Perhaps he could still salvage the evening. "I'm sorry, my love," he said, taking a seat at the foot of the bed. "Stress. Pressure. Frustration. It's all taking its toll. I'm not the warrior I once was."

Aphrodite scooted toward her lover and massaged his shoulders. "Talk to me."

"It's Athena," he said, leaning back into her. Even in his aggravated state, her soft touch brought welcomed relief. "She's cheating somehow. I should be driving her into the ground and crushing her skull beneath my heel. But these war games all end in her victory, and I know not why."

Aphrodite kissed the side of his neck and face. "You shouldn't let little sis bother you so."

"She has no love of war, true war that is," Ares went on. "How can one like she win our contests? Not once has she drank the blood of the fallen or sent corpses sailing over walls to frighten her foes."

"Ignore her." Aphrodite slid her hands under his arms and around his chest. "She's not worth your time."

Ares twisted to face her and savored her warm embrace. "But you are."

The goddess smiled seductively. "We both know who the strongest is. Let her play her games, and let us play ours."

Ares silently agreed, kissed her, and let the thought of his little sister fade from his mind. He nibbled her ear and relished the sweet smell that floated from her skin.

"It's not like she does anything important," Aphrodite added with a laugh.

"You're probably right."

"Of course I am," she replied. "What's the little priss doing now?"

"Mixed up in some business with The Old Man," Ares said. He grabbed her about the waist and slid her up to the head of the bed. "She has to find Euryale a date."

"A date?" Aphrodite's hands stopped caressing his back. "What sort of date?"

"More like a suitor," he said. "The gorgon wants to be loved."

"What?" The goddess pushed him off, and she sat up. "Athena is arranging a marriage?"

"Phorcys forced her, but yes."

"*She* is encroaching in my domain?" Aphrodite stammered as she tried to spit out the rest of her thoughts. "How could anyone think she's qualified? She's never even kissed another!"

Ares put his arms around her and kissed her on the cheek. "Let it go. Like you said, it's only Athena playing games."

Aphrodite shoved his arms away from her and jumped out of bed. "No, I won't let it go," she said. Her cheeks flushed. "And neither should you. This is an insult to my reputation and my honor. You of all gods should be defending me and putting a stop to this nonsense."

"What does it matter?" Ares said. "She doesn't know what she's doing."

"Doesn't know? Doesn't know!" she shrieked. "Of course she knows! She calculates every little thing she does!"

Ares took her hands in his and tried to soothe his lover. "Light of my life, even if Athena succeeds in the task, no one cares if Euryale marries. You will always be the Goddess of Love."

"She'll have a perfect track record!" Aphrodite said, heaving a pillow at him. "She'll be able to gloat for eternity that she's never failed!"

"And?"

"And excuse me for not wanting to tend to every mortal's persnickety desires, but after a few billion couples, you tend to mess up every now and then."

Ares, still not following, dared to ask his follow up question, even though he felt like it was a bad idea. "What does that matter?"

"What do you mean what does it matter? Who do you think she'll say is the true Goddess of Love?"

Ares, feeling stupid, didn't respond.

Aphrodite groaned and threw up her hands. In a whirlwind of activity, she grabbed her floor-tossed robes, threw them on, and fixed her golden hair. "Keep this in mind, *dear*," she said as she headed for the door. "If Euryale gets married while Athena is involved, don't bother coming to see me ever again."

A heartbeat later, she was gone, leaving Ares alone and wondering what his lover was about to do. Maybe start a war. That was never a bad idea, and one he liked for himself as well. The only question was, with whom?

Alex and Euryale stood outside the office of Dr. Martin, matchmaker extraordinaire. The building—single-story, brick and boring—was the sole occupant of this block and had a well-manicured lawn encircled by a low-lying stone wall. Though the building had been built on a small side street with little traffic, Euryale was ill at ease. With each passing car, she ducked her head and adjusted her wide-brimmed, white hat.

"You'll be fine," Alex reassured. He tried to sound confident. "Trust me."

"That's easy for you to say," she replied, checking for stray serpents. "No one can see you. I wish you'd listen to me about what I want."

"No," Alex said. "It's my ass on the line, so we're doing it my way."

"That's rather controlling, don't you think?"

Alex nodded. "It is."

"Are you always this way?" she said, crossing her arms and smiling. "Or just with girls you are trying to find someone for?"

Alex paused, his eyes drifting upward and his mouth twisting to one side as he thought about his answer. "I can be," he said. "At least, when it's something important. Look, I know this isn't the most romantic solution. Hell, it's as far from romance as you can get, but right now we need to play the numbers, so humor me. If this doesn't work, I'm all ears to do it your way. I promise. Besides, we both want the same thing." When Euryale gave a reluctant nod, Alex tacked on. "You do realize that eventually you'll have to take that off, right?"

"The hat?"

"And sunglasses."

Euryale balked. "I think I need to explain a few things to you, Alex. As much as I love entertaining your ideas, this plan isn't going to work."

"You're beautiful, snakes and all. But don't mention the being immortal and daughter of a god right away. People will think you're crazy." He checked the spot on his wrist where his watch used to be and cursed to himself. "I've got to stop doing that," he said. "Regardless, it's probably time for your appointment. You brought the monies?"

The gorgon held up a small pouch. "I did."

"Are you sure you don't want me to come with?" he asked.

"I'm sure."

Alex stared at the gorgon, uncertain what to make of her defiant tone. In the end, however, he decided she would need the help, whether she agreed or not. "I could always haunt the corner of his office while you find a date, just to make sure nothing gets screwed up. You won't even know I'm there."

"No," she replied, forcefully. "And if you keep insisting, I won't go in at all. Do try and show some patience, Alex."

With that, Euryale headed for the door before Alex could say another word.

CHAPTER SEVEN

Euryale had spent thousands of years wandering, both on her island and in the wilds across the globe, but the trek up the cobble path that led from sidewalk to office door was the longest yet. As she made the journey, she could feel panic rising within her chest. She had tried on several occasions to warn Alex that his idea would end horribly, that she would inadvertently kill anyone who saw her, but he would hear none of it. Or rather, he heard none of it. Perhaps it was his unbridled optimism that this Dr. Martin could help, or the fact that for the first time in eons someone other than her father was genuinely enjoying her company, but whatever it was, she couldn't bring herself to enlighten him about the curse she bore. Nor could she enlighten him on her growing fondness of him. Not yet at least. Not while the risk of rejection still loomed.

Patience, she reminded herself, was a virtue. She would play his game, and hopefully Alex would come around. If not, then perhaps Alex wasn't the one and someone who'd decide to love her would cross her path.

Euryale turned one last time as she reached the doorstep, hoping that Alex would understand, or see her angst and call her over so they could leave and stop this nonsense. Instead, he offered her an encouraging wave to go inside, which she begrudgingly did.

The front office was not what she had been expecting. While the building's exterior was dull, flat, and unassuming, the interior's design held to an organic style of architecture that she enjoyed. It was a mixture of stone and wood, with colorful lights shining down on countless pictures of happy couples that lined the curved walls. Soft music played from mounted speakers, making her feel warm and fuzzy. The air even had a peculiar scent to it, as if romance waited in the next room.

Front and center was a lavish, semi-circular desk, currently occupied by a tanned, rosy-cheeked secretary. "Miss Euryale, I presume," she said, putting down her celery stick.

"I am," Euryale replied while trying her best not to make eye contact.

"Dr. Martin is eager to see you. I just need you to fill out some paper work, first." The girl handed her a clipboard with several forms attached. "And how will you be paying?"

"Coinage." Euryale raised her leather pouch. "Cash, I mean."

Euryale took the forms and filled them out as best she could. She hadn't a clue as to why this businessman wanted to see her name written on so many sheets of paper, nor what the difference was between a printed name and a signature, since they both referred to the same person. As she read through the paperwork, most of her questions revolved around a section entitled *Limitations of Liability*. Ultimately, she decided it must be the standard way of doing business now and said nothing. The less attention she could attract at this point, the better.

Once the completed paperwork was back in the hands of the secretary, Euryale followed her down a short hall and into a room filled with metal contraptions the likes of which she had never seen. Lining the walls on all sides were things that blinked, beeped, flashed, wobbled, and chirped. At the far end of the room was a small, round desk. Behind the desk was a man who stood barely four feet tall and wore grey pants with a bright blue blazer.

"Miss Euryale!" the man said with enthusiasm. He ran over to her and warmly extended his hand. "How lovely to finally meet you. I'm Dr. Martin."

"Finally? I first called you this morning," she said, perplexed.

Dr. Martin kept his cheerful disposition and ushered her further into the room. "True enough, but it isn't every day a client is willing to pay extra to see me before regular business hours. Nor have I ever talked to anyone else in such a hurry to find love."

"Money is of no object to me or my family," Euryale said. "As for my hurry...let's say my situation is unique and the details aren't important."

"Well I'm certain this will be a wonderful relationship for the two of us," he answered. He motioned toward one of the couches that occupied the room. "Please, have a seat."

Euryale sat down. She tried to relax as she ran her fingers over the satin cushions. So far, she felt things had gone well, but she wondered if she was being too formal, too strong. Probably. Most definitely. Men didn't want to be intimidated by a female, maybe even more than they didn't want to be turned into stone. They were stupid like that.

"If I remember our conversation correctly, you said your father will be pleased when things go well?" Dr. Martin asked. He took a spot across from her, clipboard in hand. "Tell me more."

Euryale tossed him her leather pouch. "There's plenty more if you get me who I want."

Dr. Martin peered inside and pulled out a gold coin. It was no bigger than the tip of his finger. It had the head of a female on one side and a winged person on the other. "I think there's been a misunderstanding," he said, putting the coin away and handing her the bag. "By cash, I mean U.S. currency. I'm not even sure where this is from."

"Greece," she answered. "The one you had is a gold stater."

"Ah, yes," he said. He ran his hand over his balding head. "Well this isn't an exchange house, and I fear that you'll need more than a purse full of change to pay for this appointment. Perhaps we should use plastic?"

"I'm not familiar with plastic." Euryale tossed the sack back to him. She tried to keep herself calm, but she could feel the impatience rising in her voice. Her nails sharpened, ever so slightly, as did the tips of her canines. "I assure you that those coins are more than enough compensation."

Dr. Martin reached into the bag and pulled out a coin similar to the first. "Let me be frank with you, Miss Euryale," he said. "I don't know what Greek coins look like, but these look like crude forgeries. They aren't even round."

"That's because the one you are holding is about two and a half thousand years old. I've been told that it will easily fetch several thousand of your U.S. dollars."

Dr. Martin's eyes widened. "This is ancient?"

"According to your people, yes."

"This is gold?"

"Yes." Her body relaxed as they were finally getting somewhere.

"A moment," he said. He scuttled over to his desk and pushed a button. "Ms. Carrington? I need a curator or a coin expert of antiquity to come over right away, one who would recognize something from Ancient Greece. Thanks, you're a doll."

"I assume you'll help me now?" Euryale asked. "Because I have a man in mind, but I'm not sure he knows it."

"I'll gladly help, provided these are authentic," he replied. "Why don't you take off your hat and sunglasses so we can get started?"

Alex meandered about the front of the building as he waited for Euryale. His mind drifted back to the short time they had spent together, back to her sweet demeanor and melodic laugh. He replayed kissing her on the cheek a thousand times over, remembering every detail about it, from the sensation of her skin against his lips to the brief glint in her eye as he pulled away.

The more he thought about it, the more he realized he longed for more such moments. And for the first time since Jessica had stolen his heart in middle school, he felt a warmth in his soul grow—a warmth he thought he'd never find again.

Alex blew out a long puff of air and caught himself longing for a gorgon-filled future, one where this warmth would grow, consume him, let him swim in a sea of bliss till the stars faded and time grew weary of existing.

This wishful high was short lived. Reality smashed his dreams and his heart sank. The daughter of a god would never settle for him. Even if she did, Alex knew she wanted more than a date. She wanted marriage, and even with the ethical questions of dating a client or using her to escape a lonely, shadowy fate aside, could he envision himself with a demigod for a wife? Surely that would be a lot more complicated than any human relationship he'd had, and save for the one with Jessica, none of those had turned out too well.

Alex huffed with frustration and distracted himself with the people that came and went. Some passed by in fancy cars, others in designer shoes. None paid him any heed, and he felt that being stared through, or in some cases being passed through, was an experience in and of itself. Only once did he feel that a living creature might have noticed him, and that was when a German shepherd was taking his master out for a walk. He moved about in circles, taking several sniffs in Alex's direction. In the end, it turned out the dog had been looking for a place to pee.

An hour passed, and then two. Cars filled the small parking lot and their drivers went inside. No one came out. When the noonday sun broke free of the clouds, Alex was staring at the building, hoping, praying that she didn't come out happy.

Alex took a deep breath and steadied himself. "This is stupid," he said to himself. "You like her. Go get her already. It's not like she's going to make you get married in Vegas tomorrow."

His words became action. Alex zipped through the front door of the office, intent on dragging Euryale out one way or another. Even if he folded at the moment of truth and failed to tell her how he felt, at the very least they could spend one more afternoon together. Tomorrow he could find her someone. He worked better under pressure anyway.

The office was quiet inside, and not a soul could be seen. Alex paused near the secretary's desk and admired a pair of life-like statues that hadn't been shown on Dr. Martin's webpage.

"Hello?" Alex called out, wandering through the office. "Anybody home?"

From down the hall, he heard the muffled sounds of someone crying.

Alex came to a stop at Dr. Martin's door. "Hello? Can I come in?"

The crying turned into sniffing, and then stopped altogether.

Alex sucked in a breath and stepped through the door. Inside the office were more statues, most having similar looks of shock upon their faces, and one looked like a garden gnome in a business suit. On the couch to his left sat Euryale, her head buried in her hands, hat and sunglasses lying at her feet.

"I told you this would happen," she said, rubbing her eyes. "I told you, and you didn't listen."

"You told me what would happen?" he replied, confused. Alex replayed every conversation he could remember that they had had and came up empty.

"This!" She made a sweeping gesture at the room. "I did this to them, and they were only trying to help."

"You brought them statues?"

"I turned them into statues, you dolt!" she cried. "Haven't you heard of Medusa?"

Alex took a seat next to her, and his mind wondered about the absurdity of the question. "Of course I have. Who hasn't? Mean girl. Snakes for hair. Turns people to stone when looked at, and—" He stopped mid-sentence. The confusion on his face was replaced by dread. "Oh. Oh, god. It all makes sense now."

Euryale laughed and wiped away a tear. "It's about damn time, Alex."

But the moment was fleeting, and she soon buried her head in his shoulder and sobbed. Alex sat silent and uncomfortable as her tears ran down her face.

An urge came along and grabbed him. Before he could think, Alex lifted her chin and planted a kiss square on her lips. He brushed her cheek, while a delicate hand, hers, pressed into his chest with a slight tremble. No doubt she too could feel his heart pounding away.

As quickly as it had happened, Alex pulled back and felt his face flush. He was being too forceful, too overbearing, and completely taking advantage of the situation. Not to mention he'd already shown himself to be a failure. A failure who didn't listen, at that. "Sorry," he said. "Really, sorry."

Euryale's mouth hung slightly open. Her tears had stopped, much to his relief. But her eyes glazed over and her fingers gently traced her lower lip. "No...no...it's fine. Unexpected, but fine."

"It was uncalled for," Alex said, trying to recompose himself and put a rational explanation to it all. "For a second there I was twelve again, and it sort of hit me."

Euryale didn't say anything, and Alex desperately sought to fill the awkward void. "And I was getting flustered, and I wanted you to feel better, and it seemed like a good idea."

"Oh, I see," she replied, though Alex was certain she didn't.

His mind looked for an easy out and momentarily turned from the situation at hand and thought about the particulars of what she could do. "Why can't you hurt me? Or Athena?"

"She's a goddess, and you've already been killed, stupid." Euryale snapped out of her shock, laughed, and blew her nose into a pillow. "My curse won't affect either of you in the least."

"Ah, yes. Hadn't really thought of that."

"You want to quit and run away."

"No, quite the opposite," he said. His eyes met with hers and held their gaze. They were beautiful, sparkling, hopeful, and scared, all at the same time. Most of all, Alex found himself unable to turn away.

"Why are you looking at me like that?"

Alex took her hands in his and decided to go for broke. Words bubbled out, but they were nowhere near as smooth as he'd envisioned. "You know, when I was outside, I got to thinking that maybe you'd like to spend some time with me instead of trying your luck with some random guy. I mean, I know that part was my idea, but it was a stupid idea, I think."

Euryale giggled before having to blow her nose into another pillow. "Are you sure you know what you're getting into?"

"I hope so," Alex said, trying to contain the nervous energy brewing inside. "But it's not like I'm proposing or anything."

"No, you're not. I'll let you save that for tomorrow."

CHAPTER EIGHT

Alex and Euryale managed to return to his home without petrifying anyone else. Once there, time passed for Alex far too quickly. Before he knew it, the night had long settled and four movies had played on his TV that neither of them had watched thanks to the endless conversation they were stuck in.

"And that is how you tickle the Charybdis," she said, leaning back on the couch as she played with a viper.

"Nuts," said Alex. "I can't imagine trying that on a ship-eating monster."

"Best you don't," she replied. "Excessive laughter makes him hungry."

"More so than usual?"

"He's a big guy. Burns a lot of calories for someone that big to roll with laughter." The gorgon stretched and glanced toward the kitchen. "I'm a little parched. Can I get something to drink?"

"Of course," Alex replied. "What's mine is yours."

Euryale went hunting for refreshment, and Alex wandered over to his piano and plopped down on the bench. Instinctively, he reached out to play a few runs, but his hands passed through the keys and not a note was played.

"This is so unfair," Alex muttered. He looked at the bench where he sat at and then back to the piano. Once again, Alex raised his hands above the keys and dropped them down, only to have them pass through once again. "Now *that* is bizarre."

"What is?" Euryale said, coming back with a glass of orange juice.

"I can sit on this bench, but I can't play a single note."

"It's no mystery," she commented. "It's always easier to sit on your ass than to do something."

Alex cracked a half smile, but his heart was too heavy to keep it from fading. "This is worse than being on that slab. At least that's over and done with. I'll never play again."

When Alex tried to play a third time, Euryale sat down beside him and held his hands. "Some things don't change, Alex," she said. "No matter how much you want them to."

Alex slumped and resigned himself to her point, but it didn't make him feel any better. "The subject can always be changed."

Euryale placed his hands back in his lap and smiled. "For you, certainly," she said. Her eyes scanned the room. She took to her feet and went over to an enormous mahogany hutch. She picked up an award plaque, studied it for a moment, and turned to Alex. "What's a Marine jay-row-toc?"

"That's JROTC," he said. "It's something I did in high school. Kids who want to join the military do it sometimes."

"You were in the military?"

Alex shook his head. "No. Although JROTC was enjoyable at times, you can't be a career officer and concert pianist at the same time. I had to pick one or the other."

"I see," she replied. "What did you get the plaque for?"

"Best platoon leader in a war game," he explained. He laughed. "Spanked the tango with minimal losses."

"I'm glad you enjoyed it," she said. Euryale put back the award, and her eyes drifted downward to a small, plastic pony that stood on a shelf. Before Alex could protest, she scooped it up and turned it about in her hand. "Oh, now this is far too serious for you, Alex," she said. "Was it a toy of yours when you were little?"

"No," Alex replied, his nerves mounting and his voice starting to waver as she gave it a few playful tosses in the air. "Mind putting that back?"

Euryale grinned and began galloping it across the hutch. "Not until you tell me whose it is," she teased.

"I mean it," Alex said with more force than he'd intended. "It's old. The hinges are wearing out."

Euryale stopped her playing but kept the toy in hand. "Calm down, Alex. I'm not going to hurt it, but I do want to know its history."

"Would you please put it back?" he said as he rubbed his temples.

Euryale remained motionless, staring and not saying a word, and when Alex could take it no longer, he asked a question he already knew the answer to. "You're not going to let this drop, are you?"

"No, I'm not," she said with a smile. Euryale returned the toy to its home as if it were crafted by Apollo himself. "But take this as a token gesture of my goodwill."

Alex relaxed as best he could. "It belonged to a girl I knew, okay?"

"And?"

"And her name was Jessica."

"I'd like more than a name, Alex," Euryale said.

A moment passed and neither moved.

"Gah." Alex rolled his eyes and crossed his arms over his chest. "She was my first and only love through school until she moved away. She gave it to me our last day together."

"She sounds like she was special."

Alex nodded. "She was."

"What did your mother think of her?"

Alex shrugged. "Mom died before all of this."

"Can I ask what happened to her?"

A hint of amusement touched Alex's face. "You can ask."

"But you won't tell," she finished.

"No. Not tonight, at least."

"Shall we call it a night, then?" she offered with a stretch and a yawn. "That is, if you would be so kind as to provide me with a place to stay."

Alex tossed her suggestion over a few times. Perhaps a rest would do him some good and a part of him—a large part—wanted to know what it would be like to wake next to her.

"There's one thing you should know," he said as he took to his feet. "And I hope you don't mind, but there's only one bed."

"Only if you don't mind sleeping with snakes."

CHAPTER NINE

Alex woke. Euryale, still asleep, had her head resting on his chest and one arm thrown across his torso. Though the warmth of her body against his satiated a longstanding hunger of his lonely soul, the fact that her hair quietly slithered about his neck and shoulders gave him the willies.

"Euryale?" he said, gently reaching for her head as he argued with himself on how best to wake her. He closed his eyes, took in a deep breath, and let himself savor the moment. "Are you awake?" he eventually asked, opening his eyes.

"Awake?" she replied. Euryale lifted her head off his chest and gazed deep into his eyes. It was not fierce, but intense. And patient. Then she returned to her official snuggled position, running one of her hands up the side of his face and through his hair. "I am awake, Alex. The important question is whether or not *you* are awake."

"Erm, yes," Alex stammered. He wasn't sure what to make of the gorgon who'd attached herself to him, or if he really wanted her to move. A glance down to the lower portion of his spiritual body showed that part of him *really* didn't want her to move. The libido, it seemed, truly knew no bounds, but somehow ravishing her didn't seem appropriate. Or wise. With a little luck, Euryale wouldn't notice or take offense. "What do you want to do today?"

Euryale patted his head and sighed. "I'm content to stay here a while. Are you?"

Alex adjusted his position. Apparently, not having a body didn't mean the soul was free from all forms of stiffness—memories from life, perhaps. "Does this mean we're becoming a couple?"

"I hope we're more than that," she said. "At the very least, for the sake of your liver." Euryale paused as one of her two red vipers tasted his nose. "But I tease. Will you give me your heart? You certainly can have mine."

Alex balked at giving a reply. This was going far beyond anything he was familiar with, and Euryale was quick to pick up on it. "You can't love me?" she asked.

"Sure, one day, right?" Alex said. He grimaced and quickly added to his reply. "Sorry, that sounded a lot worse than I intended. What I meant was, I've only known you a short while. I like you a lot, but love seems like a strong word, no?"

"Love is a strong word," Euryale replied. "But we choose to love whomever we want, do we not?"

"I don't know. Love always seemed like a feeling that you just knew was there when it was—like being hot or cold or happy or sad. Can you really choose it?" Alex's admission surprised him as much as it appeared to surprise Euryale.

The gorgon slipped out of bed. There was a hint of fire in her eyes. "Would you rather have Jessica?"

Alex shook his head as he took to his feet, but even before his reply passed his lips, he wasn't sure of his sincerity. "No. That was a long time ago. Anyway, I'm sure she's moved on."

"If you'd rather be with her, I understand. I'll find someone else, but tell me now."

"No. She's not here. You are, and that's what matters."

Euryale narrowed her eyes. Her features seemed harsher, nails longer, and teeth sharper—a trick of the lights, Alex told himself. "Promise me that's true, and I'll believe you. Know this, however, nothing makes me angrier than being lied to."

Alex, mind still reeling at how fast this morning was moving, sucked in a breath. "If part of me is stuck on her, I'd rather it not be," he said softly. "I liked you from the moment I met you, and I'll give you my best, whatever that's worth. That's all I can do. The rest will come with time."

Euryale pulled him close and kissed him, softly at first, but the pressure increased with the intensity of a volcano about to pop its top. Eventually she let him go and said, "That's all I'll ever ask, and that's what you'll always get from me. Everything will be wonderful. You'll see."

"Good." Alex laughed. "Aren't you worried I'm only courting you out of necessity?"

"If you are, you should be more worried than I," she replied with a grin. "I know Father hinted at what he'd do to anyone who broke his little girl's heart."

"That's the last thing I want to do," he said.

Before Euryale could say anything else, the doorbell rang and Alex jumped. "Someone's at the door," she said, looking over his shoulder.

"Who on earth would that be?"

"Perhaps it's Athena."

Alex's brow furrowed. "Why would she ring the bell?"

"Why not?" Euryale countered with liveliness in her voice. "It's the polite thing to do in your culture, is it not? Shall we see who is calling?"

The doorbell rang again.

"Let's not. Maybe they'll go away."

"Alex, that's not very nice of you," Euryale said, releasing her grip about his neck. She straightened her robes and grabbed her sunglasses and floppy hat. "I'll answer it myself if I must."

"You didn't even want to be seen the other day, and now you're going to entertain guests? In a house that shouldn't even be occupied, I might add."

"My heart soars. What can I say?" she replied as she headed downstairs.

Alex, unable to think, say, or offer any sort of protest, followed. By the time he reached the bottom of the staircase, the doorbell had sounded a third time.

"Well, speak of the Fates," Euryale said, opening the door. "We were just talking about you."

On the other side stood Athena, dressed in a leather cuirass and holding both spear and helm in hand. She wiped the sweat away from her forehead and gave an indifferent wave to Euryale. "Good morning, Alex," she said as she stepped through the doorway. "I trust things with you are well?"

"For the most part," he replied. "And you?"

"I'm a little tired. Having to fight Ares first thing in the morning will do that to you."

"Coffee?" Alex offered, thinking it was the only polite response to her comment. "I have some, though I can't make it. But you're welcome to anything in the cupboard."

"No thank you. Honestly, I can't stand the stuff. It tastes too much like watered down beans." Athena made her way to the living room, tossed her helm and spear to the side, and took a seat in a leather recliner. "So, Alex, should I be pleased with the progress you've made?"

"Well, I'm not really sure if I can attest to such a thing," he said, and that was the truth. Though he was happy, and more importantly, Euryale was happy, he couldn't help but wonder if Athena would see his new-found relationship with the gorgon as a way to cheat at the task she had set before him.

Euryale crept up behind Alex and slid her arm inside of his. "Your champion is mine and I am his."

Athena took to her feet with vigor. "Lovely. Now we can all move on to bigger and better things."

Alex, shocked that Athena had taken the news so well, managed to restart his brain enough to reengage the conversation. "You're okay with this?"

"Why wouldn't I be?" Athena replied. "If she's happy, Phorcys is happy. And that means I'm happy."

"You can stop worrying, Alex," the gorgon said, leaning in and giving him a kiss on the cheek. "I told you things would be fine. We'll be married before you know it, and all of this will be behind us."

"Married?" Alex echoed. "When, exactly?"

Euryale went from excited to ecstatic with her face bright and her vipers energetic. "Soon as we can plan the wedding. I've wanted this for so long. I don't think I could bear putting it off any longer."

"Shouldn't we wait and spend some quality time together?"

"What for?" Euryale asked, snuggling in to him. "We've already spent time together, and I've chosen to love you, and you've chosen to love me. What more is there?"

Athena threw Alex a wry grin. "Yes, Alex. Why wait?"

Alex resigned the argument before it had a chance to take off. He slumped into a nearby couch and stared at his feet. "This is just going much faster than I'm used to. I think I would've liked to at least ease into a marriage. You know, be engaged for a while to make sure it's what we want."

"But you said you'd give me your best after you slept with me," Euryale said, confusion surfacing in her face.

"I didn't sleep with you," Alex replied.

"Yes, you did. What do you call last night?"

"We slept in the same bed," he said, trying to explain what he meant. "But that's not sleeping together."

"What would you call it?" Athena interjected.

"No, I mean, that we didn't..." Alex said, tripping over his words. "I just don't understand what the big deal is over sharing a bed."

"You can't expect to sleep with a girl and not have her think it's important," Athena scolded.

"It's just...look, where I come from, there's a lot that happens, relationship wise, before you actually get married is all."

"Where we come from, marriages are set up faster than Hera cursing a harlot," Athena countered. "Consider this as us meeting you halfway. Besides, what's the divorce rate in your culture again? Not sure I'd be bragging about the way you do things if I were you."

Alex looked at Euryale, whose earlier bliss was starting to dim. In that moment, he decided that continuing the argument wasn't what he wanted. It wasn't as if he hadn't known she was looking for a husband from the start. And he had doubts that he even wanted to find her someone else, anyway. Sure, they were moving faster in their relationship than a whale falling at terminal velocity, but his heart said that they could manage, somehow. Maybe he was being stupid, rash, and desperate to avoid a thousand years of torture, but being with her felt right, even if he didn't agree with her idea of choosing to love. Love chose you, not vice versa as far as he—and every other romantic that had ever lived—was concerned.

Alex reached back and took her hand. "It doesn't matter. We can get married whenever you like."

Euryale leaned over and kissed him. "Thank you."

"Wonderful," Athena said, again taking her seat. "Your father ought to be happy now, and even more important, he ought to stop hounding me."

"He's going to be thrilled," Euryale corrected as she massaged Alex's shoulders. "Stheno might be a little jealous about not being married first, but we'll manage."

"Well now that that's out of the way, it sounds like you two have quite a lot to do," Athena said. "There's just one last thing to take care of, and then I'll leave you two lovebirds alone. And that would be the matter of your reward."

Alex perked. "You're giving me a reward?"

"I said I would, and I am a goddess of my word," she replied. "Think of it as a wedding gift. What would you like?"

"Is this a free wish kind of thing?" Alex asked.

"Close to it, so make it a good one," she answered. "Since you're marrying into her family, you'll get to live with her on her island and avoid being turned into a shade—so you have that going for you already. For your gift, all you need to say is, 'I wish' and fill in the blank. But nothing cute like asking for more wishes. Try that one and I'll give you a fruit cake instead."

Alex drummed his fingers on his leg while he thought about how best to use his one wish. He thought about asking for his body back, but wondered if he would be selling his wish short on such a request, and being able to float through walls never seemed to get old. He considered power or riches, but given that his fiancée was the daughter of a god, he decided he would get that anyway when he became the new son-in-law. With only one wish at his disposal, getting it perfect was paramount. Thus, without having an immediate answer, he decided to ask Euryale for her input. "What would you wish for?"

"I already got my wish," she said, snaking her arms around him and giving him a squeeze. "Get whatever you want."

Euryale had barely finished her sentence when the front door disintegrated into a hail of splinters. Alex leapt off the couch as an enormous, muscular man clothed only in a loin cloth strode into the foyer.

"Gods, Ares," Athena said with embarrassment. "Couldn't you have rung the doorbell like everyone else?"

CHAPTER TEN

Alex bolted outside. He had seen a lot of things in life, but never had he seen gods battle. In truth, no one that resided on his block had either. All of that changed, however, when Athena insisted that she and Ares take their argument elsewhere—to be polite to Alex, of course—and Ares heaved a 2010 Mercedes-Benz SLR at his sister. Its sleek, W196-F1-inspired design, rear spoiler and fine Anglo-German engineering made it an exceptional missile for any enraged deity. A fact that Alex became aware of as the vehicle missed Athena by a hair and tumbled down the street.

"Hold still, you little cheat!" the god bellowed over the now blaring car alarm. His eyes scanned the road for something else heavy to chuck.

Alex felt that he should object to the destruction of his neighbor's properties, but given that the Mercedes belonged to Mrs. Nemur and she had never given him any cookies, he decided not to risk afterlife and limb.

"Honestly, Ares," Athena said with a grin. "If you aren't going to learn to lose graciously, I'm not going to play with you anymore."

She paused to brush back her hair as her brother, flustered, continued his search for the perfect missile.

"Game?" he roared. "You think this is a game? You antagonizing Aphrodite is no game."

"Ah. So, this isn't about you. It's about her."

Another auto-turned-missile flew down the road, and Athena dodged once again.

Alex, now fearing for the safety of all in the area, finally decided to get involved. "Could you take this elsewhere? The police will be here soon."

"What are they going to do, arrest me?" Athena said with amusement.

"I don't know, but this is a pleasant neighborhood, and it doesn't deserve to be obliterated."

"Stay out of this, mortal." Ares gave him a very convincing death-to-you-by-divine-fury look. "This matter will be settled right here, right now, in its entirety."

Athena ducked under the fist of her brother's clumsy attack and kicked him playfully. "It's not good for you to be upset about something so silly. You know I'll exploit it and make you look like the fool."

"I'm not the one that's upset," Ares said as he managed to get a hold of Athena's wrist. He yanked her off balance and gave her a hip toss. "Aphrodite is." Ares paused and enjoyed his small victory while letting his sister take to her feet. "She was so distraught that her fires of passion were snuffed, and she could not be intimate."

"Feel better now, or do you need to prove you can win?" Athena replied, brushing herself off. "And I doubt that the little tramp was the one having issues on performance."

"I'll feel better when you beg for mercy." Ares balled his fists and charged, but Athena sidestepped the attack. "You shouldn't be meddling in affairs of the heart."

Athena clutched her chest. "Me meddle with love? Surely you jest." The shock on her face might have passed for authentic if a wry smile hadn't formed a second later.

Ares ripped a street lamp from the ground and held it above his shoulder. "Don't feign ignorance with me, little sis. We all know you are trying to find Euryale a husband."

"Correction, I have found Euryale a husband."

Ares kept the streetlamp high, but did not swing. Clearly, this statement was not one he had expected to hear, and he was probably trying to figure out which to do first: either drive the lamppost into his sister's stomach or pump her for info. "You seek to enrage me further," he finally said, taking a deep breath. "No one would marry a gorgon."

"Alex is about to," Athena replied, motioning toward him. "They agreed to the union this morning, in fact."

"They did, did they?" The God of War dropped the light pole, and it hit the ground hard enough that Alex could feel the thump in his feet. "Congratulations, little mortal," Ares said, turning to Alex. "I'm certain you will find many a heroic battle defending her honor."

"Thank you," Alex replied as he inched back. It was not the reaction he had expected from such a raging hulk of muscle. But with the look Ares now had in his eye, Alex wondered if it might be a good idea to run back inside.

"Don't take this personally, Alex," Ares said as he walked toward him. "But I can't allow this wedding to happen. Not while Athena is involved and my lover is not."

"What?" Alex said, back peddling on his front lawn, arms outstretched defensively. "Keep me out of this."

Athena intercepted her brother and put a staying hand on his shoulder. "Oh stop, Ares," she said. "We both know you'll not touch Alex or Euryale under my watchful eye. Now run back to Aphrodite and tell her what you will."

Ares grabbed her wrist and growled, "Do not tell me what to do."

"It's over," she said, freeing herself as easily as she had countless times before. "Now if you'll excuse me while I gather my belongings, I'd appreciate it." Athena turned away and walked back in the house.

Alex watched Ares' skin color go from a light shade of pink to a bright crimson. Judging by the curses the god swore under his breath as he chased after Athena, Alex guessed that what was about to happen would be nothing short of cataclysmic.

Thus, Alex remained outside, thinking it would be wise to stay away from the argument. He wondered if it might not be a bad idea to leave the city or even the state. A moment later, Euryale bolted from the front door and grabbed him by the arm, dragging him into the street. All that came out of her mouth was the single word, "Run."

A heartbeat later the house exploded, sending bits of plaster, wood, furniture, pillows, plates, electronics, and piano in every direction. From the midst of the smoking crater, Athena, Goddess of Wisdom, and Ares, God of War, rolled forth, arms firmly locked about one another.

"We should go while we still can," Euryale said, tugging on Alex's arm.

Alex didn't respond. He looked down at a single piece of debris that had come to rest at his feet. It was a fragment of one of his piano keys, middle C, and he would've recognized it anywhere. He reached down, gently picked it up, cradled it in his hands, and growled.

Euryale put a hand on his shoulder. "Alex? Dear?"

"Hold this," he replied, placing the key fragment in his fiancée's hands. He brushed off his chest, which was more for show than for purpose, but it made him feel good, and marched forward.

Athena and Ares continued to wrestle, each trading blows, locks, and kicks. Obscenities flowed as freely as their punches, and neither took note that Alex was now looming above them.

"I have had enough of you two!" he shouted as his hands trembled. "You've ruined my life. You've demolished my house and my piano, killed my fish, destroyed my souvenir horse, and for what? To argue about who gets to set up Euryale?"

Ares, whose arms were still locked about his sister, looked up, perplexed. "You have fish?"

"Yes, I have fish!" Alex said, balling his hands into fists. "I love my fish. They aren't constantly demanding things of me, or taxing my patience, or wanting me to perform this that and the other, unlike a few certain deities I know. I wish the both of you would leave me alone!"

Athena smiled, and in the blink of an eye, she deftly slipped from her brother's hold and took to her feet. "I like you Alex," she said, keeping her smile. "You've got some spunk. And if I didn't owe you a wish, I'd peel your skin for a thousand years over that little outburst. But since I do, I will uphold my word and be gone from your sight."

Ares' face brightened. "You'll have nothing to do with their wedding?"

Athena nodded. "If Alex so desires for his present."

"Why do I even have to spell this out?" Alex said. He looked up to see the sidewalks filled with onlookers and their cameras, while Euryale moved away from them all, hiding beneath her floppy hat. Alex breathed deep before continuing. "Please go before you kill someone else. You're already going to be on the news for mass destruction. We don't need to add mass casualties to those reports."

Ares looked to Athena, and Athena in turn shrugged. "I'm ready to go home," she said. "Tell Aphrodite she can see them wed and offer her blessings as she likes."

"Victory at last!" he shouted. Ares crushed Alex in a massive bear hug and hoisted him into the air. "Come, little warrior, and bring your bride! We shall have you wed in Olympus and celebrate the day that Athena surrendered!"

As Alex was dragged away, he couldn't help but notice Athena happily humming to herself. Moreover, he couldn't help but worry what it meant.

Ares, with lightness in his step and a face full of joy, ran into the bathhouse and skidded to a halt on the mosaic floor. Aphrodite, lying in an immense basin filled with water and lilies, opened an eye at his intrusion. Her lips parted, but before she could speak, the God of War reached down and plucked her from her bath.

"My love," he said, spinning her about. "I have come with the most glorious of news."

"Put me down at once," she insisted. The goddess pushed against his chest but could not free herself from his embrace. "Hephaestus will see us."

Ares squeezed her even more. "I care not," he said while he kissed her several times over. "There is nothing that can be said or done to besmirch the news that this day has brought."

Aphrodite turned her head to the side as his lips brushed her neck. For the moment, she held her objections. Her hand drifted across his chest and down his side. "Tell me then, what news has given you such energy?"

"Your honor has been restored. Athena has abandoned the gorgon."

Aphrodite grinned and ran fingertips down his back. "You've done well, my love."

Ares hoisted her further, and she wrapped her legs about his waist. "Shall we pick up where we left off?" he asked. "Hephaestus, indeed no one, will be around for hours."

"Oh?" she replied as she nibbled at his ear. "What makes you so sure?"

"They are all preparing for the wedding."

Aphrodite's hands and lips stopped their caresses. "Wedding?"

"Euryale has been betrothed to the mortal. The wedding is today, in less than an hour, and all are attending."

The goddess shoved him off and looked him square in the eye. "Are you trying to be funny?"

"No," Ares stammered. He took two steps back as his mind reeled. "I thought you would be glad that Athena has bowed out of the picture, wedding or not. She even deferred to you to bless Euryale's marriage."

"How obtuse can you be?" she yelled, pushing him in the chest one more time. "There's a wedding! A wedding! She brings two lovers together and somehow me getting to play second fiddle by granting them a token blessing is supposed to make me happy? It's no wonder she beats you in everything. You really are as dumb as a boar."

The sense of humiliation came first, but as quickly as it rose, Ares pushed it down. His skin burned red, and he drove his fist into one of the room's columns. Chunks of stone flew in all directions, and his face was covered with a fine powder. "You're infuriating."

"And you're useless," Aphrodite said. She stomped off to the other side of the bathhouse and grabbed her clothes. "Where is this mortal now?"

"I'm not sure," he answered. "He was wandering around near the garden last I saw. Why?"

"Because I'm tired of your ineptitude. I'm going to fix everything once and for all."

"You could challenge him to combat," Ares replied thoughtfully. "Perhaps tearing his arms out of his sockets would make you feel better."

"So playwrights and poets can write stories of their tragic love for centuries? Are you crazy?" she replied as she slipped on her sandals and headed for the door. "No, I'm going to ensure one breaks the other's heart."

"Try a spear," said Ares. "Its ability to pierce the flesh is unequaled."

Aphrodite stopped in her tracks, spun about on her heels, and squared off with her lover once more. "Don't be stupid. I mean I'm going to ensure Euryale's new love abandons her."

"How?"

"The details aren't your concern," she said. "I don't need you trying to help. All I want you to do is to lock Euryale up somewhere and not let her go until I say."

"I'm not kidnapping The Old Man's last daughter," Ares said, hands raised. "He is a mighty foe and no doubt would carry the favor of many other gods."

"You deny my heart's desire?"

"I will not start an unjust war with The Old Man, nor his daughter," Ares replied with defiance. "They have done nothing. My list of enemies to defeat is long enough already."

"Fine. I'll tend to my own needs. Again." Aphrodite then stormed out of the bathhouse with disgust.

CHAPTER ELEVEN

"Why are you doing this to me? To us?" Jessica sobbed. Her body collapsed on her desk, her sandy-brown hair covering her face and her arm scattering a plethora of travel brochures onto the ground. "I've been good to you. I've taken care of you. I've loved you with all I am and more, and this is how you repay me?"

Silence reigned in her one-bedroom apartment, and Jessica pushed herself up. She brushed the hair out of her tear-stained face, grabbed a recently opened Diet Coke, and was about to curse her betrayer, her Nikon D5 DSLR camera, to the fiery pits of hell when her cell phone rang. Had the caller ID not shown it was her editor, and had she not already known he'd call her nonstop until she picked up, she'd have let voicemail answer.

"Hi, Chris," she said, picking up the line. "How are you?"

"Wonderful. Couldn't be better," he said. His words were fast and a half octave higher than normal, which meant the truth was opposite to what he was saying. "I wanted to see how your trip went now that you're back and settled in."

"I've been home not even a half hour," Jessica replied. "Hardly settled."

"Long enough for you to update your Facebook and Twitter," he said. "Good enough for me."

Jessica stifled a sigh and smacked her head. Of course he saw that, but at the time, she was on cloud nine and eager to download a slew of pictures from her camera. Now she was in a pit of despair with a corrupt memory card and one, maybe two salvageable shots at best. "I know, but I'd love to get a shower before I sit down and talk shop for an hour, if that's okay with you."

"You don't need my permission," Chris said with a nervous chuckle. "I'll get right to it then. How did the shoot go?"

"Good."

"Good? That's it? Not amazing? Fantastic? The best thing since sliced bread?"

Jessica's gut tightened. Did she dare tell him the truth? No. Not yet. Not while there was some slim chance someone could rescue the pictures off her SD card. Who did she know that could work miracles? Someone on her friend's list, for certain. She decided to run with that. "Shoot was all that and more. You're going to flip out, I promise."

"You hesitated."

"You're reading too much into this," she said, trying to sound upbeat. "You'll have a gorgeous spread for the next journal."

Chris let out a soft whistle. "Wonderful. Sorry if I was a little uptight. Some of the execs got on me for okaying the trip, said it wasn't a good use of company resources to fund a month-long excursion to Indonesia."

"That figures," she muttered.

"No worries though," he said. "Send me what you've got. I'm sure they'll be happy."

"No. You know I don't give anything out before the post-processing is done."

"Tomorrow is fine."

"Do you know how long it takes to get one shot done?"

"Do you know what they're going to do to us both if I tell them to wait?"

Jessica groaned. "I'll work tonight and give you one shot tomorrow," she said, doublechecking that yes indeed, one file on her card was still readable. "It'll be a week before I can get all the rest done. That's the way it's always been."

"Okay, I'll see what I can do. But I need those shots a week from today."

"You'll get them," she said before ending the call.

Jessica leaned back in her chair and cleared her eyes. Tension mounted in her shoulders and neck, and her head lolled to the side. Out of the corner of her eye, she caught the sight of a hairy eight-legged creature climbing the glass side of its tank.

"What?" she said to her pet tarantula. "I'll think of something. I've got a few days. Worst case is what? I fly back out to Indonesia on my own dime, live off credit cards, and declare bankruptcy in time for Christmas, right?"

Mr. Peepers stayed silent, which was fine with her. As much as she loved her pet—the easiest thing she'd ever cared for when it came to a critter—given the day she'd had thus far, she might have thrown herself out the window had it talked.

The doorbell rang. And again. And again, and again. Figuring things couldn't get worse and it might be cathartic to behead whoever was soliciting whatever at her door, Jessica answered it.

There, standing at the foot of her door, was a man dressed as if he were about to run the Boston Marathon, jogging lightly in place with two fingers pressed into the inside of his wrist.

"Jessica Turner?" he asked.

"Yes," she warily replied.

"The same Jessica Turner who once courted a Mr. Alexander Weiss?"

Her jaw dropped. That was a name she hadn't heard in a long, long time. Thought of? Yes. But heard? No. Well, not counting the news report she'd seen this morning at the airport about his untimely demise that was tied to a mysterious, skydiving whale.

"Is that a yes?" the man asked.

Jessica nodded, her mind still trying to get a handle on the ton of weird that had been dumped on her today.

"Message for you," he said as he shoved a clipboard into her chest. "Sign here."

Jessica signed on a line that was below a slew of other signatures, handed it back to the man, and then took the scroll he gave her. It read:

Aphrodite, patron of Cyprus and Goddess of Love, to the lovely Jessica Turner, photographer of all things beautiful and dear friend to Alexander Weiss. I have written to request your presence at a wedding in Olympus. Compensation for your time in monies, adventure, and whatever else your heart desires will gladly be provided.

P.S. Don't forget your camera.

Jessica folded the parchment in half and looked at the man with the same look she gave one of her coworkers when he claimed he used to hunt grizzlies in Africa with a bowie knife. "I don't know what game you're playing or who you're with, but I don't appreciate you using my dead friend like that."

"No game here."

"Mhmm," she said, crossing her arms. "I suppose that makes you Hermes, right?"

Hermes bowed. "The one and only. Now can we get moving? I still have twelve hundred deliveries to make before sunset." When she balked, he outstretched his hand and added, "Take it if you don't believe me."

Jessica eyed him. He did have an air of...regality surrounding him, even if he looked like a fitness freak. And the wings on his shoes were a nice touch to his story. And they did look feathery, and incredibly authentic for ancient Greek footwear. But this was nonsense. There was no way this guy was a god. There was no way Aphrodite was real, or even if she was, that she'd extend her an invitation to a wedding in Olympus (though she did admit to herself that such an opportunity would be nothing short of amazing should it come her way).

Hermes dangled her Nikon D5 in front of her face. "Come on," he said. "I've got you packed."

Alex sat on a cold stone bench at the center of Olympus's largest garden. He was flanked on either side by the bright flowers of countless pomegranates, laurels and jacarandas. Although their fragrances were pleasing, and the breeze that blew through them was refreshing, they did little to restore his peace of mind. He longed an intact piano that he could play to reduce his stress, but instead of playing Schubert or Beethoven, he was now entangled in the affairs of the gods, his wedding was imminent, and Phorcys had just joined him.

"For the first time in eons, I am at a loss of words," The Old Man said while his claws clacked loudly at his side. "My daughter is to be wed within the hour, and while my heart should be overflowing, it is not."

"Not due to anything I've done, I hope," Alex said.

Phorcys slithered behind Alex and draped a heavy claw over his shoulder. "Not in what you've done, but who you are."

"Who I am?"

"Yes, who you are." The Old Man put his other claw on Alex's other shoulder. "You are not what I had envisioned for Euryale, but I cannot deny that she's determined to love you more than any other."

Alex swallowed and shifted under Phorcys' pinchers, hoping he wouldn't be sheared in two. "I thought you wanted her to find someone."

"Ultimately, yes," he answered. "And that is why I remind myself that her desires trump mine in this matter. But that doesn't mean I must like it."

Alex didn't know what to say, and he'd learned not long ago that the wrong words to an Olympian could be far worse than no words at all. Thus he stayed silent as The Old Man came around and halted directly in front of Alex's feet.

"I have only one question, Alex," he said. "Will you love my daughter more than I love the sea?"

"Euryale has me smitten," Alex replied. That much was true, regardless of how short an amount of time they'd spent together. She was easy to be around, intelligent, quick witted, appreciative of art, and in great shape. And though the snakes had freaked him out at first, they didn't bother him at all now. "I can only pray that the love I have for her now will pale compared to the love I'll have for her tomorrow."

"Flowery words mean little to me." Phorcys said. "Love does not pull a man like the currents pull a ship, rather it is an action—a dedication—like a captain intent on reaching port through any storm."

"Of course," Alex said. "When the heart beats for another, what can get in its way?"

"Do not confuse reaction with action," Phorcys said, much to Alex's surprise. "I do not take kindly to those who hurt my daughters. Do you have any idea what I would do to you if you broke her heart?"

"I think I can imagine."

"No, mortal, you cannot," The Old Man replied, shaking his head. "I have fed blasphemers to the leviathan, piece by piece, who would now sing my praises for eternity had I placed them on Prometheus' slab. Unless you wish to join them, do not cross me."

"I have no intentions of doing that," Alex replied. "Aside from keeping Euryale happy, what do you expect of me?"

Phorcys slapped him playfully on the side. "Rise to the challenge and tame the sea-born storm, Alex," he said with a hearty laugh. "Or will you let your frail father-in-law intimidate you forever? Think where we'd be if Zeus had not stood up to his father, Cronos."

Alex straightened and his brow furrowed. "You'd like me more if we argued?"

"I'd like you more if you would stop acting like a cowardly potter from Athens," he replied, smacking Alex again. "You're a son now, or will be shortly. Our family reigns with strength and power. We stretch lines across the shore and tell the waters how far they can go. The Scylla heels at our command, and fissures open at our whim. I'll not have you be our weak link in Olympus."

"Easy to say when you're a god," Alex pointed out. "Seems whenever I stand up for myself with any of you I'm either chained to a rock or threatened with some other everlasting torture."

"Respect, Alex," The Old Man explained. "A difference of opinion is one thing, but even the saltiest captain respects the power of the sea and dares not risk incurring her wrath."

"So, you're saying..." Alex said, his voice trailing off and his mind not sure where this was headed.

"Be mindful what steers your tongue," Phorcys said. "Contempt will not be suffered by any of us, but neither will cowardice find our favor. Polite disagreement is what you must strive for."

Alex grinned as his newest thought lightened his mood. "You're telling me that if you ask something of me and I tell you to stuff it up your ass, respectfully, you wouldn't care?"

"Stuff it up my ass?" The Old Man repeated the line once more before moving on, puzzlement never leaving his face. "Your kind has some interesting retorts. The imagery is unique to say the least."

"So, you wouldn't care?"

"Words do not bother us, Alex," Phorcys stated. "Actions and attitudes do. The sooner you learn that, the easier of a time you will have. Surely the senators of your land would model such behavior. Perhaps you should learn from their wisdom."

"I can't stand politicians," Alex commented. "All they care about is appearances. They're completely incompetent at what they do. If they spent their time actually practicing their craft instead of writing stump speeches, the world would be a much better place."

"Yet they know that even their enemies must be addressed properly," Phorcys said as he brought Alex to his feet. "You've got a long way to go to be the son-in-law I desire, but worry not. As my gift to you both, I'll craft you into a true champion, one who carries the favor of all the gods, as well as the finest of fishermen. The Charybdis will swallow your foes, and the tides will lap at your feet."

"I'd rather have my Steinway."

Phorcys grunted. Whether it was a grunt of indifference or disgust, Alex couldn't tell. Instead of continuing the discussion, The Old Man led Alex down the garden path and back toward the festivities. As the two walked, Alex tried to imagine what eternity with Euryale would be like. He wondered what their home would be like, and if they would have children. More importantly, he wondered if they would have snakes for hair and whether or not they would turn their playmates to stone.

Phorcys halted outside the colonnade of the Banquet Hall. His jaw tightened and his claws snapped.

"What?" asked Alex.

"I smell the perfume of the goddess." The Old Man took another whiff of the air. "She draws near."

"Who? Athena?" asked Alex. Before Phorcys could respond, Alex had his answer. It was not Athena. A different goddess approached, clad in a thin, red, silk garment that did little to conceal a figure that could only have been forged in the heavens.

As the goddess walked toward the two, her golden hair bounced playfully, and her eyes drew Alex into a world of blissful captivity and lust.

"Fortune is mine today," she said, coming to a stop before the pair. The tip of her tongue grazed her lips. "How often does a girl find exactly who she is looking for?"

"Aphrodite?" asked Alex, unable to imagine any other name that would fit.

"He's as smart as he is handsome," the goddess said to The Old Man while tousling Alex's hair. "I see why your daughter likes him."

Phorcys took a half step forward. "Have you come to celebrate or have you a storm brewing behind that smile?"

"I've come to see who would be married without my say," Aphrodite answered. "Rumors abound that Athena had her hand in this. I'm here to learn the truth of such whispers."

Phorcys put himself between Alex and the goddess, and for the first time since Alex had met the god, he was grateful for The Old Man's bulk. "I forced her hand," Phorcys said. "I found it a fitting punishment for what she did to Stheno."

"No need to be defensive, love," Aphrodite answered, running a hand up The Old Man's chest. "My quarrel is not with you, and may the hearts of Euryale and Alex forever yearn for one another. But I do have a score to settle with my troublesome sister."

Phorcys remained steadfast in the face of the eternal flirt. "You shall bring no ill wind to either my daughter or son-in-law. Bring your grievances to Athena directly and leave us be."

"You have nothing to fear, Old Man," she purred, making Alex's hairs stand on end. "When has my tongue spoken deceit?"

The Old Man laughed. "Your tongue has been entwined with many others, despite your vows to your husband."

"My personal business is my own," she shot back. The anger faded from both her face and her tone, and Aphrodite continued. "Despite your opinions on my affairs, I have never broken an oath or given curses in lieu of blessings. I only wish to bestow the greatest of pleasures upon our dear Alex."

Alex stepped forth from behind Phorcys. "What do you want of me?"

"Only to listen to a gentle reminder," she replied. "Though it's one I hesitate to say, for I fear it might hurt you."

Alex cocked his head to the side. Though he knew he was completely enamored with her already, he couldn't imagine what words she might speak that he wouldn't savor. She could ask him to gnaw off his arm and he was certain his only reply would be if she wanted that done above or below the elbow.

"I'll take your silence to mean you're eager to hear," she said, toying with her hair. "Know this, Alex. The love you have for Euryale is like the rose that has been planted haphazardly, whose roots are not strong."

Alex felt his mouth run dry, and a bead of sweat trickled down the back of his neck. "I don't follow."

Aphrodite took his hand and pulled him close. She brought her forehead to rest against his and ignored The Old Man's roll of the eyes. "I wish you the best in your marriage, Alex. But Athena may have erred in bringing you and your wife together as quickly as she did, despite her best intentions. Marriages have trouble, and the love required for them takes time to grow. Thus, I fear, when trouble comes, the rose that is your love will die with the storm, for your love for one another never truly took hold."

"No," Alex said, shaking his head.

Aphrodite placed a finger on his lips and drew him in with her eyes once more. "Fret not, sweet Alex," she purred. "Come to me, if the need arises, and I shall see that the both of you are eternally happy. Understood?"

"Understood," he repeated.

Aphrodite closed her eyes and pressed her lips against his cheek. Alex's mind went to mush, and a few moments later she pulled back, running her fingers through his hair. "Promise you won't forget?"

"I promise," Alex mindlessly repeated.

"Good." she replied. She then threw The Old Man a wink. "I'll see you boys inside."

As she left, Phorcys smacked Alex in the back of the head.

"What the hell was that for?" asked Alex after he stumbled.

"For looking at her as you should Euryale," The Old Man explained. "Even if Aphrodite is irresistible, don't ever do it again."

"Oh Alex," Aphrodite said, stopping a half step before disappearing inside. "There's something I forgot to tell you."

"What's that?"

"I brought you a guest," she said.

Alex turned, and his heart skipped at least two beats. Coming down the garden path was Jessica with her hair in a bun and life radiating from her eyes. Her hands clung to her camera while a Tiffany Blue cocktail dress clung to her body. Alex wanted to say something, anything, but she tied his tongue the very same she had on the first day of the school year, when he'd gotten assigned to sit next to the new girl.

CHAPTER TWELVE

"Alex?" Jessica said as she hurried to him, her high heels clacking on the stone path. "Is that really you?"

All Alex managed was a feeble nod since he was still brained by the imp called Stupidity. Thankfully, it only took a moment for him to find his voice. "What are you doing here?"

Jessica wrapped her arms around his neck and squeezed him tight. "It's so good to see you again! I got back from this disaster of a trip and—" Jessica leaned back. The joy in her face disappeared, and her shoulders slouched. "I'm dreaming, right? I mean I must be. You're dead, and I didn't meet Aphrodite."

"I'm not quite dead, yet," Alex said with a half grin.

"No, you are," she said. "Your death was all over the news—mystery of the century people are calling it. I passed out at my computer, and this is my subconscious working out things I always felt were left unfinished with you. I'll wake up in a second."

"I tried that. You won't."

Jessica pinched her arm. "Huh. That didn't work either."

"Tried that, too."

Slowly, Jessica looked over his shoulder and her face lit up. "I'm not dreaming. I'm actually in Olympus."

"Yep."

"The Old Man!" she exclaimed, dashing by Alex. She circled the monstrous god with wonder, her hands moving back and forth like a little girl who's dying to touch something she's not sure if she's allowed to. "I can't believe it. The gods. The myths. They're all real!"

The Old Man extended a claw and nodded approvingly. "Go on. Behold the Primeval God of the Sea."

Jessica grasped the massive pincer with her left hand, and when that wasn't enough, she laid her head against its hard shell. "This is so cool. He exudes power across every inch. I can feel it tingle in my skull."

The Old Man laughed. "See, Alex? I told you not all mortals scamper away in fear."

"Her liver is still intact, too," Alex said. "All things considered, I'd say I handled that little incident as well as any other."

Jessica disengaged and ran back to Alex. She snatched his hands and bounced on the balls of her feet. "This is incredible! Do you know how much of the cosmos you can see with Hermes? Or how fast you can go from bleh to gorgeous with Aphrodite doing the styling?"

Alex could guess at the foremost, but didn't need a single hint for the latter. Jessica looked nothing short of divine herself. "You look lovely as always."

"You should've seen how much of a mess I was earlier," she said, fumbling with her camera. After a few twists of a dial and a couple pushes of buttons, she herded Alex next to Phorcys. "Stay right there."

"What are you doing?"

"Taking your picture," she said, scooting back a few paces and bringing her Nikon up.

"Because?"

"Because I'm Aphrodite's personal photographer for the festivities!" she said with the most excited eep Alex had ever heard. "She said I have to follow you around for everything and I'd get whatever I wanted—not that I'd actually have to be paid for this. God, I can't wait to get back and publish all these photos! I'm going to be the girl who documented the return of the Olympians!"

Alex's list of questions shot up a hundred fold, but instead of having the opportunity to get answers to any of them, he was manhandled for the next fifteen minutes by Jessica as she took shot after shot of him and Phorcys in the garden, in deep thought, and even in mock combat. Alex had thought The Old Man wouldn't have liked such a thing, but to Alex's surprise, the god enjoyed the photoshoot, and per Jessica, was remarkably photogenic as well.

"How much more time do we have?" she asked after snapping yet another burst.

Phorcys glanced at the sun and sighed. "None. Come, we must hurry, lest we suffer Zeus's wrath for being late."

The Old Man escorted them both to the banquet hall. Inside was a massive table, easily a hundred yards long, and at it sat countless deities and demigods. Most were shouting at one another, some being playful and others antagonistic. Dozens of women, scantily clad in fawn skins and topped with crowns of vine, danced about. In one hand they carried staves tipped with pinecones, and in the other, pitchers filled with wine that constantly poured out for the wedding guests.

Of all the attendees, Alex only recognized Aphrodite and Athena, each sitting far from one another and occasionally exchanging glares as they chatted with fellow gods. To Alex's dismay, Euryale was nowhere to be seen, and a longing for her settled in his heart. At least he had Jessica to keep him company.

Upon being prompted by Phorcys, Alex and Jessica took their seats, at which point The Old Man settled into his spot on Alex's left. On the other side of The Old Man was the head of the table, and there sat that largest god of them all upon a chair of ivory and gold. His bright skin shone like bronze, and his white hair flowed like a tempest behind him. Thunderous laughter bellowed from his mouth, and miniature bolts of lightning shot from his hands as he clapped them together. There could be no doubt that this was Zeus, ruler of the Olympians.

"The mighty Alex," Zeus said, hoisting a goblet in his direction. "I can't recall the last time mortals were in our hall, let alone being wed into the family."

"Thank you. It's all very exciting, your majesty," Alex said, unsure how he should address or respond to the ruler of Olympus.

"Majesty? Ha! Such funny words," Zeus said before downing his wine with one large gulp. The god leaned over the table, resting his bulk on his enormous forearms, and spoke softly. "Let me ask you something. As you are about to be a married man, who do you say should run the house?"

"I suppose it would be whoever is most capable."

Much to Alex's relief, Zeus didn't argue the reply. "Would you agree then, Alex, that whoever is in charge doesn't need to justify every action taken? Need a parent explain all things to a child, for example?"

"I suppose a parent would not," Alex replied after some thought. "It would be annoying and unproductive to literally justify everything."

Zeus leaned back with a smile before turning to the goddess on his left. "Hera, my incessant harrier, even this mortal knows where your place is."

The goddess, with fair skin and sharp features, turned from the conversation she was having with one of her servants. Large, cow-like eyes narrowed at Zeus's words and then cast their gaze upon Alex. "You dare suggest that a husband be unfaithful?" she said. "Perhaps you should make such beliefs known to your bride. Or her father."

Phorcys leaned over to Alex and whispered in his ear. "Furl your sails, mortal, and proceed at your own peril. Hera has rightfully suspected Zeus of sleeping with young maidens again."

"Thanks for the warning," Alex replied. He turned his attention toward Hera and Zeus and chose his words carefully. "I think such matters are best handled by the parties involved. Seeing how I'm not privy to all the details and my wisdom is nowhere near divine, I couldn't make a fair judgment."

Jessica prodded Alex with a gentle elbow to the ribs. "Nice save."

Both Zeus and Hera relaxed in their chairs, and an air of smugness settled about the pair. Phorcys laughed and took a swig of wine. "For one as headstrong as you, Alex, you're a fast learner. It seems like only days ago you were insulting Athena, and now you're playing politics with none other than Zeus and Hera."

"It *was* only a few days ago," Alex pointed out. "That aside, where's Euryale?"

"You won't see her till after the feast when you wed," Phorcys explained. "She's having her bath and sacrificing her childhood toys to both Athena and Aphrodite as we speak."

Alex felt his shoulders drop, and he wondered if Aphrodite's words were a curse or a blessing. Euryale continued to weigh on his heart, and he wondered how unbearable her absence would ultimately become. Before he could give it further thought, large, meaty hands gripped his shoulders from behind and gave a friendly, though crushing, squeeze.

"Mortal!" Ares said, standing behind Alex, grinning from ear to ear. "Who's this maiden you've brought us?"

"Jessica," Alex replied. "Old friend from school."

Jessica clutched her chest and an exaggerated hurt splashed across her face. "Friend? Is that what I've become?"

"You know what I mean," Alex said. "We dated when we were kids."

"A fine companion then to see you wed," Ares said. He paused as his eyes darted to Zeus, whose attention was elsewhere, and then spoke in hushed tones. "Though keep her from Father, yes? Your friend's beauty will not last if Zeus takes a liking to her and Hera has her revenge."

"Yes, Alex," Jessica said, laughing. "You best protect me from the gods."

"Perhaps some of the gifts you receive will help you in that endeavor," said Ares.

Alex raised an eyebrow. "Gifts? From who?"

"From everyone, of course," Ares replied. He gave him another crushing squeeze on the shoulders before finally letting go. "Though mine must wait till tomorrow." Ares leaned close and whispered in Alex's ear. "Tomorrow you shall be my partner for the games. I have never lost, and as such, you will be assured a place in the victor's circle. Glory shall be ours!"

"We're having Olympic games?"

"Would there be any other?"

"I suppose not," said Alex, feeling dumb.

"Just don't fail me, little Alex," Ares said, his voice touched by both threat and promise. "I would hate to be in your sandals should your performance be an embarrassment to me."

"What does that mean, exactly?"

"You must take second place, Alex," he replied. "I'll tolerate nothing less. We are to be the champions on the field of battle, not pathetic footmen struggling to keep up."

Before Alex could reply, Zeus stood, raised his hands above his head and unleashed a bolt of lightning from one hand to the other. The minor display of power was both bright and loud enough to quiet the banquet hall and have everyone present give him his or her undivided attention. Most continued to wear smiles upon their faces, but more than one had traded the look of merriment for concern.

"Before we start the feast and in accordance with the traditions of man, I wish to propose a toast," Zeus said as he hoisted his goblet. "Let us drink merrily to the health and lasting relationship that Euryale, the daughter of Phorcys, and Alex, the recently deceased, have found with one another. Although I know not why a man would wish to be wed for all eternity, having to see the same woman day in and day out, night after night, being nagged and pestered about every little detail that goes on under the sun until his will is broken and his mind charred black, we wish him all the best just the same."

Phorcys thumped his claws on the table, and Hera let loose a sigh of discontent that did not escape the ears of those around her. Alex buried his face in his hands, hoping that others did not attribute the toast to his own feelings, while Jessica had her camera up and was snapping off a plethora of pics.

Zeus looked at Alex, keeping his goblet high in the air, and grinned. "But I jest, of course," he went on. "With the blessing of Aphrodite and Athena, and such a fine bride in Euryale, whose beauty has never been anything short of legendary, happiness shall surely flow throughout the days for you both. With that, let us drink—and drink well—lest we have to sit through another lecture from Dionysus."

"That's not quite how we do toasts," Alex said, leaning over to Phorcys and lowering his voice. "Maybe I should give one that's more uplifting?"

"Zeus does not take kindly to correction," The Old Man replied in a low tone. "Unless you have an affinity for bolts of lightning, I would steer to calmer waters."

Alex grimaced. "Got it."

Zeus clapped his hands together, and the feast commenced. Satyrs bounded from every entrance, their hooves clacking loudly on the marble floor. Some skipped about with flutes and pipes in hand, while others cradled large plates of food in their arms. Flat breads, served with olive oil and vinegar, along with dried figs, chestnuts and chickpeas came first. As those were eaten, racks of lamb, filets of fish, and cooked game birds of all kinds soon followed. Though the meat offered was plentiful, its numbers paled to the amounts of fruits, vegetables, and cheeses that accompanied it.

Alex ate it all, and more than once he noted that there was always room for more. Though he talked with The Old Man, Hera, and even Zeus throughout the meal, most of his conversations were with Jessica. Sometime after talks of childhood adventures and in the middle of confessions as to how neither could still fully believe they were dining with the gods, Alex noticed that the wine in his goblet was a different color than what the others drank.

"It's grape juice," the satyr explained, evidently noting Alex's confusion.

"Because?"

"Because I thought it best, given what happened last time," Phorcys interjected. "Euryale found it amusing, but others that sit at this table might not find your drunken blasphemy as funny, especially when you are about to take your vows. First impressions, if you haven't noticed, are very important around here."

"Ah," Alex replied taking another sip. "Point taken."

As the meal ended, gods and goddesses went their separate ways. Some were laughing. Most, however, were squabbling about this, that, and the other. The satyrs came and cleared the plates from the tables and refilled goblets one last time before disappearing altogether. Alex, with his elbows on the table and his chin resting on his hands, had only Jessica, Zeus, and Phorcys to keep him company.

"These deities are a hoot," Jessica said as she started scrolling through the pictures on her DSLR. "I never would have guessed that Ares would have been so into having his picture taken. Aphrodite? Of course. Mister God of Wine and Parties, Dionysus?

Certainly. We redid him posing with his maenad groupies at least a dozen times before they stopped slobbering all over each other for half a second to get a decent shot. But Ares? Why him?"

"Probably sees it as something fun he can do to show off his glorious skills in combat," Alex said after a moment's thought.

"Good point," Jessica replied. "You know, I always loved reading about these guys. The books and stories were so rich. But here we are walking among them. What more could you ever want?"

"My liver to remain hands off," Alex said.

"Come again?"

Alex shook his head and laughed. "Never mind. I don't want to spoil the mood if you're having a good time. Nothing you need to worry about anyway. You always were the social butterfly, not me."

"When do I get to meet this bride of yours?" she asked. "I'd love to get a shot of her in her gown before you see her and the service begins."

Alex felt the color drain from his face as up until now, he hadn't even thought about what would happen should the two meet. He lunged at her without thought, practically mauling her as he covered her eyes. "You can't. Oh, god, you've got to get out of here right now."

Jessica laughed and fought him off. "You think I'm leaving and not being a part of all this? You're crazy. What's this bride of yours going to do, eat me?"

"No, she'll turn you to stone."

"She will?" Jessica cocked her head before shooting out of her chair. But instead of terror gripping her body, it looked like mania had instead. "Of course, Euryale! Sister of Medusa and Stheno! She's the one who has a couple red snakes in her hair, too, right? I can't believe I didn't realize who she was."

"Exactly. You've got to go before you become a permanent fixture."

"A tiny chance at petrification isn't going to scare me off." Jessica dug in her purse and whipped out a crème-colored compact mirror. "See? I'll be fine. She can't turn me to stone if I look around using a mirror."

"I don't think it works that way."

"It most certainly does," she countered as she practiced surveying the room via reflective surface. "You'd know that if you'd ever bothered reading your mythology in Miss Dolen's class. How do you think Perseus slew Medusa?"

Alex shook his head. "Doesn't matter. You can't walk around with that thing in front of your face all day. Too much can go wrong, and it looks stupid."

"Well what's so special about you then? How come you won't turn to stone?"

"Already been killed. Perks of getting squashed."

"Enough. I'll take care of it," Phorcys said after a heavy sigh laced with annoyance. "Aphrodite should've already done all this if she was going to bring you here."

"Do what?" asked Alex.

"Protect her from my daughter," he replied.

Phorcys shut his eyes and a deep crevasse formed in his brow. His body shrank, and in the span of two breaths, he once again looked like a hundred-year-old human, small and frail. He grabbed an empty goblet from across the table, filled it with a small amount of wine, and then swirled it with an index finger, all the while chanting something Alex couldn't follow. The water glowed yellow and wisps of acrid smoke rose from the surface. He passed the concoction to Jessica and said, "Drink."

Jessica brought the goblet to her lips, wrinkled her nose at the smell, and then quickly shut her eyes and tossed the drink back like she was doing a shot. A coughing fit took hold of her—one that prompted Alex to whack her on the back—but when it was done, the goblet was empty and not a drop had been wasted. "There. That wasn't so bad," she said. "She won't hurt me now?"

"For a week's time, yes," The Old Man replied. "That will be more than enough for you to participate in the festivities. Once they're done, I suggest you return to your own land."

"Awesome sauce," she said. "Speaking of, when is the wedding?"

Alex shrugged. "I don't know. Soon?"

"Whenever Zeus is ready," The Old Man replied.

"I'm ready. I'm ready," said Zeus as he finished his own wine and set his goblet aside. "I suppose we should let you take your vows now and put on your yoke of eternal servitude."

Alex glanced around the hall, and when he noted his bride was still nowhere to be seen, he asked, "Shouldn't Euryale be here?"

"Not for the ekdosis. You'll see her once you're wed."

"This doesn't sound like any wedding I've been to. What do I do?"

"Say 'I do' when you're supposed to and we'll be done. Is that simple enough?"

Alex nodded.

The Old Man, after Zeus gave him a short wave, took to his feet and cleared his throat. "Alex, I give you my daughter, Euryale, into the bonds of marriage, so that she may bring you offspring as numerous as the creatures in the sea. Do you accept?"

"I do," said Alex.

Phorcys nodded and continued. "I also give you a dowry in the form a pledge. I pledge before the Fates and Zeus that I shall not tear your body to pieces, nor allow Athena to chain you to the slab of Prometheus, for as long as you remain in wedlock to my daughter and love her as you should. Do you accept?"

"I do," Alex said, quicker and more forceful than before.

"Congratulations," Zeus said, ending the exchange. "You're married for all of eternity now, waking to the same girl day in and day out. Try not to let the nagging and questions get to you—and if you need to slip away for a few days, provided you offer me a proper sacrifice, we can find a few maidens to ease our minds."

Alex, uncomfortable and unsure of how to respond, gave a sheepish grin.

Phorcys, on the other hand, scowled.

Zeus, noting the reaction by The Old Man, leaned back in his chair and laughed. "Fret not, Phorcys," he said taking to his feet. "I'll merely use Alex to look out for my cow of a wife. I wouldn't dream of enticing Alex to stray from your daughter, let alone share any of my mistresses with him. They are far too lovely for the likes of him."

Phorcys held his glare as Zeus left. Once he was gone, The Old Man stood and motioned for Alex and Jessica to follow. "Come. It's time you received the rest of your gifts before going to meet your wife."

They left the banquet hall, and now that it was all finished, Alex realized he felt cheated from the whole ordeal. For such a momentous, life-changing event, he would have liked to actually have a ceremony he'd remember, one where he'd see his bride come down the aisle wearing a gown tailored by the gods and looking more radiant than the sun. He wanted a ceremony where even the groomsmen would cry, and at the end, he'd plant such a kiss on her lips that all in attendance would have their collective breath sucked away. But no. What he'd received was little more than the pushing of a legal contract.

Maybe the gifts would be better. If not, he decided, he'd have to spend some extra alone time with Euryale to make the day a memorable one.

Chapter Thirteen

Alex found himself alongside Jessica at the base of Apollo's temple, watching a pair of large palomino horses stand idly by. They looked happy enough, even if they were yoked to a heavy chariot made of bronze and purfled with gold. The nearest one gave a brief glance as Alex extended his hand. It nickered, snorted, and then turned away.

"Stupid horse," Alex said as he dropped his hand to his side. "It's a wonder cars weren't invented sooner. I bet all you do is eat and poop."

"It's a horse," Jessica said. "What did you expect?"

"Around here? Anything. Everything."

"Get closer to it and pretend you like it anyway," she said, raising her camera. "The lighting here is outstanding."

"Alex, my good man," called out a young, beardless and muscular man as he bounded down the temple stairs. Though Alex had never seen him before, a quick whisper from Phorcys told him that this was none other than Apollo, God of the Sun and Giver of Prophecy. The god stopped and put a hand over his chest as he sucked in a sharp breath of air. "And you, Jessica, so nice to finally cast eyes upon your lovely self, at least, literally. Seeing your future is not the same as seeing your present, yes?"

"If only I could!" she said.

"But then where would the fun be in all of life's surprises?" he replied. "You wouldn't want to ruin that, I assure you. Stay in the moment and enjoy your life here and now. Relish the sun's rays against your skin and enjoy the fresh air that abounds. What more could one want?"

"Being by my wife's side might be nice," Alex replied with a smile.

"Ah, love. The ultimate want!" Apollo added, patting Alex on the shoulders with both hands. "My heart soars knowing you've found it." The god stopped when his eyes met with Alex's. "It seems I may have misspoken," Apollo said once his scrutiny was over. "Not love, no. Not yet at least."

Phorcys let a low growl slip, but said nothing.

"Fear not, either of you," the sun god went on. "Love can still easily grow from this infantile infatuation you and Euryale have now. I tell you the truth, Alex, there's no stopping what has begun and what the Fates have in store. Your wife will be the center of your heart before you know it."

"What's in store for me?" Jessica said, face full of excitement. "Love, too? A new house? A lifetime supply of pumpkin spice lattes?"

Apollo stepped in front of her and lifted her chin with a single finger. His eyes seemed to study every facet of her face. When he started, his mouth held a half grin, but by the time he finished, it was twisted and his eyes looked strained. "Strange," he said looking between her and Alex a few times. "You two are entwined yet again, but for how long, I can't say. Nor can I in regards to how it relates to Euryale, only that the three of you will be in conflict."

"With someone else or each other?" Alex asked.

"Both, I think," Apollo replied. "The Fates have hidden much from my eyes."

"Maybe it's something silly," Alex offered, knowing full well he was tricking himself into believing such a thing. But one good feeling did come of Apollo's talk. A pit grew in his stomach, one that had him long to be at Euryale's side, and thoughts of her put a smile on his face. "Is there at least a happily ever after for everyone?"

"That will depend on you," Apollo said, taking him by the arm and walking him slowly around his chariot. "I know you're eager to rejoin your wife, so I shall move things along, but remember, you've all of eternity to spend with her. Life is not meant to be so narrowly focused. Even with her absence, there is much to see, do, and enjoy."

"Like enjoying horses that eat and poop?"

"Yes, my dear man!" Apollo's face beamed, and Alex found himself shielding his eyes for the moment. "They're Akhal-Tekes, by the way, and a source of joy for all those that get to know them. They love sharing music and poetry, if you happen to have some good bits of either, and they'll never tell a lie. I think I like that the best about them."

"They can talk?"

"Well of course they can talk," Apollo replied, giving the nearest horse a good scratching behind the ear. "How depressing would it be if they couldn't? They would have all sorts of fine things to say to the world but be completely unable to get it out for us to enjoy."

"Well the last thing we would want is a bunch of depressed, non-speaking horses," Alex said with a grin. "I mean, what would the world do with those kinds of beasts?"

"See? You still jest," Apollo said with a playful punch to Alex's shoulder. He then reached into a small pouch at his side and pulled forth a pair of sugar cubes. "Here," he said, placing one of the cubes in Alex's hands. "If I am to teach you to drive a chariot, it is important that you first give our good friends here a little snack. These Akhal-Tekes are a good breed, but their loyalties are tied to their stomachs, I'm afraid. It's something I've complained about to Poseidon, but he cares not to remedy the problem. Do you know how long it takes to pull the Sun across the sky when all they want to do is graze nonstop?"

Alex shrugged his shoulders. "Ten, twelve hours maybe?"

"Ten or twelve hours?" Apollo repeated with a laugh. "My boy, not only are you handsome, but you are as clever as the sphinx. But back to these obstinate equines, it really depends on the time of year. In the winter, when the cold nips at their backs and the foliage is scarce, the day's work goes by much faster."

"Ah, and here I thought it was due to the tilt of the Earth," Alex said. The two's eyes met and held each other's gaze but for a moment before Alex looked down and shifted about. Though he was growing accustomed to hobnobbing with the Greek gods, he was now particularly uncomfortable. In the short time he had spent in the god's presence, this was now the second time he felt as if he had been mentally undressed by the deity. "You were saying about me learning to drive a chariot?"

"There are many things I could teach you, should I suit your fancy," Apollo said, adopting a more serious tone. "But I suspect your wife would be jealous and frown upon such things."

"That's, um, very nice of you," Alex said, feeling his skin, or whatever the spiritual version was called, crawl. "But I think it's best we stick to the horses for now."

"Relax, my good man," Apollo said as he stepped into the chariot and then helped Alex in. "You've nothing to fear with me. Besides, do you know how many Greeks and Romans would kill to be in your sandals right now? To be taught the finer points of chariot racing by Apollo himself?"

Alex gave a knowing smile. "None, if they knew they'd be seeing a gorgon shortly after."

"I would wager you're right," Apollo said with a nod. "Perhaps you can teach Hades a thing or two about humor. I loathe seeing such a depressing individual, always going on about death and dying, but we must, I'm afraid, to pick up the last of your gifts. And to do all of that, we'll want my chariot. Afterwards I was thinking we could take in a play, or an opera. Jessica could join us when we get back, too, if she likes. It would be a fine place to introduce her to your wife."

Jessica, who had wandered off a few paces and was talking to The Old Man, perked at the mention of her name and turned around. "What's that?"

"Apollo wants to know if you'd like to join us after we make a run to Hades."

"After?" she said. "I don't get to go?"

Apollo shook his head. "The Underworld is not a place for the living. I have no domain there, and I'd fear for your safety."

"Right," Jessica said. "Then I guess I'll catch up to you when you get back. Maybe Phorcys would be kind enough to show me some of the secrets of the deep sea?"

"I'd be happy to take you to places that will leave you in awe for the rest of your life," The Old Man replied.

"Then I am but your humble follower," she said with a curtsey.

"I guess that's that," Alex said. "What are we getting in Hades, anyway?"

Apollo smiled. "Your new body, of course. Hades said he would fashion you one, and it will help you greatly in the upcoming games, you know. Not to mention your wife ought to appreciate it as well."

"Oh, of course," Alex said. Before he could add another word, Apollo took the reins, gave a sharp tug, and the chariot bolted into the sky.

For two hours, Apollo drove the chariot above the clouds. Occasionally he gave Alex the reins along with instruction, but more than once he snatched them back when Alex would inadvertently plummet them toward the ground. Eventually, Apollo dove to the waters that covered the Earth. There they skimmed along the sea for another half hour before Alex spied a tiny peninsula on the horizon.

"Is that where we're stopping?" Alex asked.

"No, my good man," said Apollo, spurring the horses on. "But it is our last waypoint before we go under."

Alex gripped the body of the chariot as the God of Prophecy and Sun snapped the reins once more, driving the horses ever faster. It wasn't so much the extra speed that made Alex nervous, for watching the dark waters below speed past was exciting, but rather the fact that the chariot streaked toward one of the many pitch black water caves along the peninsula's coastline with no indications of slowing or changing course.

"Fear not," Apollo said, glancing toward Alex. "I could fly this route with my eyes closed."

"Oh good," Alex replied with a nervous laugh. "Because you might as well."

And with that, the chariot drove into the cave's inky black.

"If you think I'm getting near *that*, you're sorely mistaken," Alex said as he pointed a shaky finger at the most monstrous of dogs.

"What? Why?" replied Apollo, jumping off the chariot and striding across the cavern floor. "Cerberus only keeps the dead inside. He won't bother you in the least."

"Somehow, I doubt that," said Alex.

"Alex, trust me. He only hunts down the dead, not those married to the divine. And if you ever wanted something of him, I'm sure a little bribe would go a long way. You know, scratch behind the ears or a nice severed limb to chew on."

Regardless of Apollo's reassurances, given that the dog's three heads had yet to take their combined six eyes off of Alex, he had no intentions of leaving the relative safety of the chariot, let alone giving the dog a friendly pat. And his feelings about those three heads didn't even include the creature's mane full of snakes, nor the serpentine tail.

"How about I wait here, and you open them instead," Alex said, referring to the wrought iron gates on the other side the dog.

"I could do that, but if you're going to come and go from this land, you must get over this irrational fear of yours."

"I'm not being irrational," Alex replied. Then a curious thought dawned on him. "How often do you think I'm going to be making this trip?"

Apollo gave a wry smile. "More than once, I'm sure. Cheer up. It could be worse."

"How's that?"

"You could be here without any light at all," said Apollo. The god winked, snapped his fingers, and the ball of light that had been with them both since they'd first entered the cave disappeared.

Alex tightened his grip on the chariot and held his breath. He couldn't see anything other than darkness, even when he waved his hand in front of his face. While Alex's vision had gone, however, his hearing had not. He could hear Cerberus panting a few yards away. The sounds of the dog taking to its feet followed, and Alex heard the repeated clack of approaching claws on the limestone floor. Within moments, hot breath assaulted the back of his neck.

"Get away!" he yelled.

The light reappeared, hovering a few feet from Apollo. To Alex's embarrassment, Cerberus hadn't moved from his spot at the gates, though now the canine (if it could be called such a thing) was sprawled out on its side, its tongues hanging out of its mouths, and tail smacking the ground in slow, rhythmic thumps.

"Go on," Apollo said, pointing to the gates. "Open them and conquer your fear."

"You said he hunts the dead," said Alex.

"Quite well," Apollo replied. "You might say he has a nose for it, or three."

"And he won't think I'm dead because...?"

"Because at best you're not quite dead, yet," answered Apollo with a wink.

Against every fiber of his being, Alex eased off the chariot, half expecting Cerberus to rip out his throat. But when he didn't, Alex sucked in a breath, tip-toed past the dog, and pulled the gates open.

Apollo gave an approving nod and carefully drove the chariot through, being mindful not to run over Cerberus' tail. "Worry not, good Alex," he said, smiling. "I know much of your story, despite what the Fates have hidden. I promise it does not end here."

Alex exhaled with relief. He stepped back in the chariot as the iron gates swung closed. A snap of the reins by Apollo sent them moving once more. Faster and faster they raced through the tunnel before they burst out into an open land of gently rolling fields and asphodel flowers.

"Oh no," said Alex, letting his enthusiasm for the land show. "Not this place again."

Apollo pulled the reins, and the horses drove the chariot up into the air. "Don't be so glum. There are only two things to remember while you travel the Underworld."

"What would those be?"

"First, don't insult any deity you find roaming around," he said. "And second, don't eat anything, even from Hades."

"What if he offers?" asked Alex.

"Especially if he offers."

"Why is that?" he asked, brow wrinkling. It seemed to Alex that not taking offered food would be insulting and therefore bad.

"Any mortal that swallows even the tiniest of crumbs is bound by the Fates to stay here forever. And Hades, despite ruling the dead, is ever lonely, always wanting more company."

"Note to self then: no food, and no pissing him off. How hard can that be?"

* * *

Aphrodite strode into the abode of Pallas Athena unannounced and uncaring that she was. After marching through the front doors, she crossed the inner courtyard without as much as a glance here or there and headed straight for Athena's great room, for she knew the Goddess of Wisdom would be there, reading, studying, or doing something "smart" like she always did.

"Sister," Aphrodite said, halting a pace inside the study. She paused to take in the décor. She had hoped Athena would have changed how she lived by now. After all, it had been what, two or three eons since the two talked about such things? But to Aphrodite's dismay, Athena had not hung up one tapestry on any of the bare walls, nor replaced any of the bookshelves with things of beauty, like sculptures, full-body mirrors, or display cases (to show off the better gifts from adoring, would-be suitors, of course). All she saw were books, books, and more books, along with the occasional oil lamp.

"Yes?" Athena replied, snapping Aphrodite's attention back to their encounter. Surprisingly, however, Athena was not reading a book. She stood over a table filled with parchments and a small model of a temple, complete with miniature walls and statues. "Is there something you wanted?"

"Only to offer you my congratulations," Aphrodite replied. "You must be proud that your one and only attempt at love turned out so well."

Athena smiled warily and never let her grey eyes leave her sister. "I am."

"I admit I'm jealous at such a record," Aphrodite said, but her face did not reflect those words for an impish grin followed.

"Let's drop the charade, shall we?" Athena said. "Tell me what you're up to."

"I suppose I should know better than to try and push something past you," she said. She stopped when she noticed what Athena was working on. It was not some random temple project. It was a temple to Aphrodite herself.

"You were saying?" Athena prompted.

Aphrodite growled. "I was saying, that despite you trying to usurp my domain and evict me from my own temples, I'm not mad. I had a thought that put everything in perspective..."

Athena rolled her eyes at her sister's intentional trailing off and continued to scribble notes. Such dramatics were unnecessary and wasted as far as she was concerned, but still, she knew she'd have to play along if she were to be rid of her sister. "And that thought was?"

"You haven't succeeded," she said smugly. "You see, my dear, the love I've created for countless men and women has been tested and strained. My love weathers time, whereas yours is a shadow at best. A simple illusion."

Athena dropped the pen she held and straightened. "You think Alex hasn't been through enough?"

Aphrodite shrugged. "Have the gods not placed a hedge about his marriage? Does he not mingle with Olympians and travel the Underworld freely?" she asked. "His father-in-law alone will see to it that neither he nor Euryale will face a single danger, yet mortals on Earth face them daily."

"What, then, do you propose?"

Aphrodite seemed to grow, both in presence and height, as she continued. "I propose a true test of their marriage. Stand back whilst I strike him," she said. "He will either persevere and prove his love for Euryale, or he will abandon his vows, and leave her to ruin. But you cannot claim victory in my realm until you've tried him and tried him well."

"Do you plan on trying to break him today?"

Aphrodite shook her head, and she appeared as sweet, innocent, and sensual as ever before. "I thought we could at least give him and his bride one night of bliss together."

"Then you plan to do this at the games," Athena finished.

Aphrodite nodded. "I do, and I want this contest bound by oaths. It's only fair."

Athena remained silent, and to Aphrodite's delight, she grew neither angry nor combative at her request. "Very well," Athena replied. "Let's see who can make the better match. I swear by the River Styx, everything he has is yours, and I will not interfere as long as you swear by the same not to lay a finger against his life or liberty."

"With a body made by Hades, his life is hardly in jeopardy," Aphrodite replied. She then placed a hand against her chest. "But to your demand, with you and the Fates as my witnesses, I so swear by the River Styx, I shall neither destroy his body nor his freedom while he's put to the test."

Alex drummed his fingers on a massive table of gold inlaid with diamonds, rubies, and sapphires, and tried to appreciate his surroundings. It wasn't easy. The few lit braziers barely illuminated their bases, let alone the dining hall. Thick, ankle-high fog carpeted a mosaic floor, and shadows smothered the cracked and worn frescos on the wall. But at least his company was nice. The queen of the Underworld, Persephone, sat a few chairs down and had thus far been a gracious and warm hostess.

"Hades will be here shortly," she said. A royal gown, white and flawless, clung to her slim figure and seemed utterly impervious to any stain or smudge it might encounter in such a dark world. As she waited, she occasionally brushed aside a curly lock or two that escaped her ponytail or toyed with the silver tray in front of her. "Though," she added, taking a pomegranate seed from the tray and popping it into her mouth, "he may be here already."

Alex twisted in his high-back chair, but saw only Apollo who sat nearby. "Am I missing something?"

"Nobody misses me," said a voice. "That's for certain."

Alex turned back around and found a man, nay, a god, he corrected, sitting at the head of the table and placing a helm and bird-tipped scepter at his side. "Hades?" Alex asked.

"That's me," he said. The God of the Underworld leaned forward with his elbows on the table and rested his cheek on folded hands. His gaze was not at Alex, but Persephone, and the look in his eyes was not a joyous one. Grief, was it? Alex wasn't sure. Perhaps it was the anticipation of something painful.

"Well, good morning," Alex offered in an uncomfortable moment of silence.

"Good morning, Alex," Hades replied. "If it is a good morning, which I doubt it is."

"Is something the matter?" Alex asked more out of politeness than anything else. He wanted to get home as quickly as he could, as this place continually raised his anxiety.

"Winter has come, and spring will soon arrive," Hades said. "We can't all be excited for that."

"How so?"

"You don't need to feign interest in me," said Hades. His voice drifted off, and the god took the tray from Persephone and helped himself to some of the pomegranate. "But if you want to carry on with your pretense, have a bite to eat."

With a flick of the wrist, Hades sent the tray sliding over to Alex, who in turn was very impressed with the fact that both the tray reached him from so far away, and all the seeds remained on it.

"Thank you, but I've already eaten," Alex declined as politely as he could. Out of the corner of his eye, he caught Apollo shifting in his seat, perhaps to object on Alex's behalf, but the God of Sun and Prophecy did not.

Hades nodded slowly, and what little life was in his face fell to gloom. "I don't blame you," he said. "I suppose you'll be wanting your new body now. Though I can't say I'll make a good one. Or even if I want to. It's hard to make something nice when your efforts go unappreciated."

Sorrow filled Alex's heart. Sorrow and pity. Hades' lament struck a chord in him, unnatural and divinely inspired, perhaps, but all Alex could think of was how an eternity spent under rock and clad in shadow would drain the merriness out of anyone, gods included. "It's not that, really," Alex said, hoping he might smooth over the rejection of hospitality. "It's not you. It's me. I just—"

"That's what they all say," Hades said, cutting him off and waving his hand. "People don't want to spend time with me, I know. You want to get back to your wife. I envy you for that, Alex, to know she'll be at your side day in and day out."

"I do want to see her soon," Alex admitted. "But it's not like that."

Hades expression didn't change in the least, and Alex, feeling horrible about being the source of Hades current depression, decided to make an offer. "If I try one seed, would that be enough to show I mean no offense?"

Hades sat up in his chair, a hint of life now showing in his face. "It would be a start," he said as he took up his scepter and helm. "And I might even put an extra effort into your wedding present if you did."

"Then so be it," said Alex, grabbing a seed and popping it in his mouth. He chewed slowly, deliberately, and a few seconds later, Alex swallowed, smiled, and wiped his mouth. "Not bad," he said. "For a seed."

Hades stood, pushed his chair under the table and motioned for Alex to follow him. "Come, Alex," he said. "Let us build you a body even Heracles would envy."

Apollo groaned, and Persephone covered her mouth with her hands. Alex was certain she was about to say something, as he could have sworn he caught the tiniest of noises escaping from her lips. A caution, he'd guess, if he had to wager, but it didn't matter. Not anymore at least.

"Prometheus shaped your kind from mud," Hades bellowed as he stood upon a rocky precipice. Lava flowed underneath, bathing both the god and the cavern in a deep red and giving the scene an ominous tone. "But you, Alex, you who marry into the gods, will be shaped in a proper fashion. A fashion, I might add, that won't leave you petrified by your wife's infamous gaze."

"Thank you," Alex said, taking a few steps back. Heat rolled toward him in waves, and he wondered how much more of it he could stand before he roasted. More concerning to him, however, was the sudden change in Hades' attitude. The god's depressive state was no more, and instead of the slow movements and apathetic conversations of the past, Hades worked and spoke swiftly with purpose and power. "I take it you enjoy this part?" asked Alex, hoping something sinister wasn't in store for him.

"It keeps me from having to think about my wife's soon departure from my realm. How I long to be with her for all of eternity, but we can't all have what we want," Hades replied. As he spoke, the cave dimmed and the air cooled. His shoulders fell, and his scepter, now outstretched over the lava flows, dipped. But all of this was only temporary. A second later, his head snapped back, and he raised his scepter high. "With this scepter I can raise the dead, shape the earth, and snatch immortality away from anyone short of a god," Hades said proudly. "With it, I shall form your bones from iron, and bronze shall cover your skin. Any injury you suffer shall be healed by dawn of the next day and death shall never come for you."

Out of the lava floated an amorphous, glowing mass. Up it went until it hovered an arm's length from Hades. It stretched and bent in five different directions, and all the while Hades waved his scepter to and fro. Alex watched in amazement as the form took a human shape. Its features turned masculine, a strong jaw set into a chiseled face, one that looked much like his own when he was alive, save without any imperfection or hint of weakness. Its shoulders were wide, something one might set the world upon. Its back rippled with muscles, its chest the same. Its arms bulged, and its hands looked as if they could turn coal into diamonds without trouble. A washboard stomach and powerful legs complemented the upper torso, each something Olympic athletes could only dream of attaining.

Hades lowered his hands, and the body gently floated to the ground on its back between him and Alex. The white-hot skin cooled, and Hades blew sharply upon it. Instantly, the metallic look disappeared. Flesh, dark and toned, took the place where bronze once was, hair sprouted, and the chest slowly began to rise and fall.

"Lie inside and take your gift," Hades said. With his work now done, the enthusiasm in both his face and voice fell away. "And do try and remember all I've done for you," he added as he walked away. "Not that you really care."

Once Hades was gone, Alex looked at Apollo for direction. "So how do I use this?"

"You only need to lie down inside," Apollo said. "The rest will happen on its own."

Alex straddled his new body and sat in its abdomen. A tingle ran up his spine, one that intensified as he stretched out his legs, shut his eyes, and eased back.

He felt as if he were sinking into a bed filled with blankets fresh from the dryer. Alex enjoyed the sensation for as long as he could, but it soon faded away, and all he could feel was the hard rock beneath his skin and hot air hanging over his face.

"Is there anything you want me to tell your wife when I see her?" Apollo asked.

Alex opened his eyes and noted that the god stood over him with an offered hand. "No," Alex said, gladly taking the help to his feet and admiring his new body. "I think I can tell her everything myself."

"You want me to bring her here then," Apollo replied. "I suppose you should be the one to tell her how and why you confined yourself to an eternity in Hades despite my warnings."

"I don't really think that'll be an issue," Alex said with a grin.

Apollo, apparently, didn't share Alex's optimism, for his face looked grim, an unsettling characteristic for such a light-hearted being. "You think you're special?" he asked. "Even Persephone, daughter of Zeus and Demeter is confined to this place during the winter, and her place in the Universe is far greater than yours will ever be. No Olympian will argue your case on your behalf, and even if they did, you would fare no better than she."

Alex, still beaming, held out an open hand. In the center, covered in saliva but not chewed in the least, was a single pomegranate seed. "I suppose it's a good thing no one will have to."

Apollo laughed heartily, rays of golden light bursting from his face. "Alex, good man," he said, wiping away a tear. "I should never have doubted you or my own foresight for that matter. Come, let us see to your bride and leave before Hades learns of your deception. I fear he would not take it kindly."

CHAPTER FOURTEEN

Alex, standing in the middle of Euryale's island cave, held his bride in his arms, completely enamored. With the stars covered by clouds and the fire pit burning low, there was little else to see in the cave other than Euryale, but he didn't care. He loved watching the firelight dance on her red chiton and trace every curve the silk made as it clung to her body. Shadows played on the hood she wore, and the sparkle from her eyes pierced the veil that covered her face.

"You're beautiful," he said, pushing the veil aside and letting the hood slip back.

Euryale blushed and rested her head on his shoulder. Her serpents wrapped around his neck while the pair of red ones tasted his cheeks. "I'm glad you think so," she said. She looked up slowly. "Alex," she said. "Will you always love me?"

The question caught him off guard, and he reflexively pulled back an inch or two. "Why would you ask that?"

"Will you?" she repeated.

"Always," he said. "I promise."

Euryale smiled and snuggled back into his shoulder. "I only ask, Alex, because I fear I may have bullied you into this. I was impatient that day, and I knew what Athena had threatened you with. It would be tempting to marry me simply to avoid Aldora's beak."

"I know, but that's not why I did," Alex said. A sliver of doubt ran through his heart, but he pushed such thoughts away before they could gain strength. There was no need to trouble her with such things, anyway. "I admit this went faster than I'd anticipated, but waking up at your side was a thousand times better than waking alone."

Euryale's hands drifted down and she gripped his forearms as she stepped back. "Who was the girl with you at the feast?"

"You know about her?"

Euryale's eyes darkened. Her nails felt unnaturally sharp against his skin. "Who was she?"

"Jessica."

The gorgon's grip tightened, her teeth lengthened, and a faint hissing came from her head. "Your Jessica. Your love."

"Former," Alex corrected. "Nothing happened. I swear."

Euryale laughed. "Do you always toss around oaths so lightly?"

"No, that's not what I meant."

"Am I frightening you?" There was an ancient power to her voice, one that could cause dragons to heel or hurricanes to silence.

"Concerned," Alex said. He tried to pull away, but her grip intensified and her eyes mirrored the burning coals in the fire pit.

"Tell me why you've brought this woman back into your life."

"I didn't!"

"Tell me!" She bellowed.

Alex staggered. The flutter in his heart worried him, but that was nothing compared to the fear he felt when he saw the foliage nearby wither. "Stop it," he said. "Why are you being like this?"

"Because you need to see who I am," Euryale said. She shut her eyes and breathed deep. The strength in her grip faded, and her claw-like nails all but disappeared. Once again, she was the soft beauty Alex had always seen before.

"What's going on?" he asked.

"I apologize for working myself up so, but we all have our ugly sides. I wanted you to taste mine."

"Taste?" he said with a nervous laugh. "Is your actual ugly side that much worse?"

Her head dropped. "It can be, and I hate myself when it gets the better of me. I want you to know all that because if I ever do...change, please love me, stay with me. I'll come back to you...eventually."

"What's eventually?"

"A week? A month? It's not that long, considering we're immortal."

"Maybe we could find a way so you don't have to change," Alex said.

"It's tied to my anger and something only the Fates can remove," she said. Euryale shrugged as she went on. "Part of my curse."

"So essentially you're the Greek Hulk on steroids."

"The what?"

"Never mind. Look, I promise I didn't have anything to do with bringing Jessica to the banquet. Yes, I was happy to see her, but my life with her is over. My life with you is what's important now."

"Do you swear that is true?"

"On everything I hold dear."

Euryale grabbed the back of his head and kissed him. "Then let's leave discussions of the past alone and look to our future."

"As long as we're confessing," Alex said once they parted. "I hope I can perform as well as you expect."

"Are all famed artists this troublesome?" she teased. "If anyone can perform, it should be you."

"It's not the same. My days were filled with getting a piece to perfection," he said. "It drove me crazy to make mistakes, even if no one noticed them but me."

"I have no illusions of perfection, Alex," she said. "But if it troubles you so, perhaps you should spend those countless hours practicing a new craft."

"Such as?"

"Learning how to be with me," she replied. "With such dedication to everything else, how can you not rise to greatness in my eyes?"

With his worries melting, Alex opted to change the subject. "How do you like the new body?"

"I like it very much," Euryale said. She ran her hand up his muscular chest and gave his biceps a squeeze. "Hades spent some time remaking you. Have you found it suitable?"

"Aside from being a little horny, it's fantastic," Alex admitted. His fingers were making their third round trip across her body as they spoke. "Apollo says it will also help in the games, so I'm trying not to be nervous about it."

"Trying, but not succeeding," she said with a smile.

Alex nodded. "Any advice?"

"Do your best and the rest will work out in time," she said. "Anything else I should know?"

Alex thought for a moment, but came up empty. "Not that I can think of."

Euryale rose on her tiptoes and peeked over his shoulder at the clump of packages that had been brought to their home. "Shall we open our presents?"

"And take my eyes off you?"

"I appreciate the flattery, but I think we should see to our gifts."

Alex squeezed her and kissed her forehead. "I think we should retire for the night," he said, looking to the bed in the corner. With the coals all but out in the fire pit, the mood lighting was perfect. "We can keep each other warm."

"No, Alex." she said, laughing and pushing him away. "The bed will always be there. Surely you can wait five minutes?"

"Around you, how could I?"

"There may be days when you will have to endure much more than that. Think of this as good practice," Euryale grabbed a log from the wall nearby and tossed it into the fire. Within a few passing breaths, the fire came to life, and their cavernous abode was lit once more. Euryale made her way to the pile of gifts that sat atop a large, oak table. "Now are you going to join me or not?"

"Fine, fine. I'm coming," he said, all the while deciding whether or not he really wanted to suppress his libido. A hop, skip, and a smooch on Euryale's cheek later, he was at her side. "I'll be good," he said as the gorgon rolled her eyes at him. "I promise."

"I've heard that before," she remarked.

"Yeah, well, have you seen this before?" Alex reached down and plucked a small, golden-wrapped gift box and placed it in his wife's hands. He tried to appear calm, but his nerves weren't making such a look easy.

"From you?" she asked, reading the note attached. She gave the box a shake and brief inspection. "A ring?"

"Maybe." Alex said, trying to keep his face straight. "It's a little something I made on the way over here. It's nothing fancy."

"I'm sure I'll love it." And by the look on her face, when she pulled out a sharply folded origami ring—one that perfectly fit her finger no less—she did. "It's perfect," she said, admiring its new home on her hand and giving him a kiss. "I'll treasure it always."

Alex's eyes shifted to the pile of gifts. "What did we get?"

Euryale reached down and grabbed a long javelin, complete with a pink ribbon and small card attached. She gave it a twirl before handing it to Alex. "Envelope is addressed to you. See what the card says."

Alex reluctantly took the weapon from her, unsure why someone thought he needed an impaling device, or why it was an appropriate wedding present to begin with. Must be a cultural thing, he decided as he took the card and read its contents. "To Mr. and Mrs. Alexander Weiss, blah, blah, blah," he said. "I, Artemis,

Goddess of the Hunt, do hereby bless the consummation of your marriage, blah, blah, blah, and I pray that this javelin will serve you well."

Euryale raised an eyebrow. "Blah, blah, blah?"

"Well, that was the gist of it."

"Perhaps I should read them from now on," she replied. "Does it say anything else?"

"There's a P.S. at the bottom."

"Stop ogling my body and tell me what she said."

"Right, sorry." Alex tried to sound sincere in his apology, but he was certain he failed. Not that it mattered, anyway. As if he needed to excuse such things. "P.S. I was going to get you a bow, but Aphrodite insisted that you would rather have one of my javelins, so I obliged. Let me know if you'd like the bow instead."

"That was thoughtful of her," Euryale commented. "Sounds like she spent some time on it."

"I don't want either, to be honest," he replied, dropping the card on the ground. "I mean, what am I going to do with a spear?"

"It's a javelin, Alex, and not the same thing," she said, scooping up the card. "And whatever you do with it, where on earth are your manners? Don't throw cards away. It's rude."

"Sorry, bad habit. What else is there?"

Euryale went through the pile and found a pair of swords. "How sweet of Hephaestus. Do you know what these are, Alex?"

"Swords?"

"Of course they're swords, Alex. What kind?"

"Short ones that don't have a card attached?"

Euryale sighed. It was the type of sigh any male might receive after not properly identifying the latest Prada, lace-up, round toe booties with covered heels and leather soles—or whatever their mythological, Greek counterpart was. But instead of answering directly, Euryale flipped the scabbards around and pointed to the name engravings made on each.

"He made us His and Her swords?"

"Close enough." Euryale laughed and placed the weapons to the side.

"What kind of god gives His and Her swords?"

"The kind who's the God of Smiths," Euryale replied. "He's made countless weapons and armor for the Olympians. Why wouldn't he make us some as well?"

Alex shrugged. "Don't know. But it's not what I was expecting."

"Don't be like that, Alex," she playfully scolded. "Appreciate the gift. It was sweet of him to give us something so personalized."

"Eh, I suppose," Alex replied. He looked over his shoulder to where his new chariot was parked. "I guess it's a little manlier than the wagon and ponies."

"It's a chariot and I happen to like the ponies."

"Well I'm glad one of us does." Perhaps it was fate, or merely a long-lost friend calling out to him, but whatever the reason, Alex shifted his eyes from his wife's ass long enough to spy a small package tucked away and neatly wrapped. The paper used was smudged with something dark, chocolate or fudge perhaps, but was otherwise folded neatly. Alex held it up to his ear and gave a rattle, but was unable to determine what was inside the box. Shrugging his shoulders and at the prompting of Euryale, he read the card:

To Alex.
From Hermes.

Thought you might like one of these. Give a whistle if you need anything else!

Alex carefully unwrapped the gift as if a wrong tear or overeager rip would detonate a miniature bomb inside. When all the paper had been removed, and the lid to a small box opened, Alex found himself looking at a Rolex—*his* Rolex, to be precise.

Euryale yawned and stretched. "Come, Alex," she said, taking him by the hand and pulling him toward the bed. "You'll need your rest before the games tomorrow."

Alex followed without question. Given the way she looked at him over her shoulder, he was quite certain several cups of coffee would be needed in the morning.

CHAPTER FIFTEEN

If it hadn't been for her father, Zeus, Athena would have never bothered attending the games, celebration of a wedding or not. Everything about them rubbed her the wrong way, from the misogynist views about who could compete, to the smugness of each god that won his respective event. The latter of the two further highlighted what a bore the games had become. Hermes, as always, won every foot race without any difficulty. Likewise, none could catch Apollo's chariot as he blazed around the track, though she did admit that Alex's ponies were the most adorable pair of creatures she'd seen in a long time. And Hephaestus, even with his limp, had won the boxing event, staying true to his nickname of *The Hammer Fist*.

Athena yawned, stretched, and shifted in her marble seat. For the amount of time and resources Zeus had put into creating such a lavish stadium, she wished he had put more thought into the comfort aspect. Having access to three dozen separate food vendors and instant replays splashed across the clouds above meant little to her if her legs constantly went to sleep.

For the majority of the day, Athena had been reading her latest book, *Howitzers: Artillery Explained*. While she loved the writing and the detail the author put into it, sadness struck her heart for Ares. In the two thousand years since the Olympians had been away, there were plenty of momentous battles that he would have been overjoyed to take part in.

The past, however, was the past and nothing could be done about that. As such, Athena kept reading and when she finished chapter nine, *Forward Observation for the Coordinately Challenged*, she realized something was amiss. Like most somethings that were out there, whatever it was, it wasn't clear, only a nagging feeling.

Athena marked her place, put the book down, and looked about. Zeus was demanding more wine and threatening a satyr with a two-billion-volt enema if it didn't return posthaste with a new pitcher. Hera sat next to him, crass faced as always and probably still demanding to know where his daily activities had taken him. Two rows below, Artemis was arguing with Poseidon, the topics being that she should be able to compete if she so wished and that archery should be included in the Olympic Games. It was a tired argument, one that was brought up every time Zeus organized a sporting event.

Near the sidelines, Ares was warming up, javelin in hand, while Alex stood a few paces away, nervously fumbling with his own. Neither held any lasting interest for the goddess, and it was clear neither was the source of her unease. Then Athena spied Aphrodite, who wore a tasteful yellow sundress and was seated a dozen rows beneath her, pleasantly chatting with Euryale and Jessica.

Athena raised an eyebrow. Upon further inspection, she noted her sister glowed with genuine excitement and wasn't faking it to be polite to the gorgon and Alex's old love as Athena had originally assumed. Something was about to happen, and it bothered Athena that she didn't know what that something was.

A cry, guttural and warlike, drew Athena's attention away from her visual sleuthing. On the game field, Ares had just made his first of three throws. The God of War bounced lightly on the balls of his feet, watching his javelin arc high in the air. It was a fine throw, one that would best most of his previous attempts over the years, and when it landed, everyone knew he'd walk away the victor. His second and third throws only solidified the prediction, and he returned to his place, boasting so all could hear.

Athena turned her attention back to Aphrodite. The Goddess of Love gave quiet applause, seemingly unimpressed by her lover's success. However, her disinterest in the games faded when Alex took to his feet and she happily directed Euryale's and Jessica's eyes toward him.

"What are you up to?" Athena whispered under her breath.

It was at that moment she noticed the javelin Alex carried and put the pieces together.

As Alex prepped for his throw at the start of the runway, Aphrodite looked over her shoulder, locked eyes with Athena, and mouthed two little words. "Game on."

Alex grunted. It was a manly, *watch me skewer this crash of rhinos and live to tell about it,* sort of grunt. Though his rational side would later come up with a rational explanation—precisely the sort of thing it was good at—at that moment he was certain the almighty grunt of manliness had been the cause of his success. Any other explanation was poppycock.

The javelin Alex hurled sailed through the air as if it had been launched by Ares himself. It sailed past the fifty-meter mark, passed the one hundred, the two, and then the three, before landing at the far end of the field.

Alex squinted. Exactly where his javelin had landed was hard to see, but he was sure it was at least a competitive attempt.

Thankfully that meant he wouldn't have to slink away as he had when he was lapped three times in the chariot race.

Heavy steps approached, shaking the ground. Ares planted himself in front of Alex. His face twisted and muscles bulged, and the god showed as much restraint as a rhino that had recently been skewered.

Alex, feeling like a feeder rat tossed in front of a python, spoke first. "Was that a good throw?"

Ares narrowed his eyes and spoke slowly, enunciating every syllable. "What sort of subterfuge is this?"

Alex's mouth hung open, unsure of what words it could form that would spare him a grisly end. He averted his gaze, adjusted his loincloth, and looked to those in the stadium, hoping, praying, that their reaction would offer some insight on what he should say or do, or at least what the hell was going on. Sadly, all the Olympians, the minor gods and goddesses, and creatures of myth and legend, stood from their seats, unmoving and without word, their eyes fixated on the far end of the field.

"Answer me!" Ares demanded, drawing a yelp from Alex. Ares lifted him by the shoulders and carried him across the field.

Alex struggled, kicking and pushing against him. Though he failed to free himself from Ares' grasp, he found his backbone in the process. "Let me go!"

"Explain how a mortal throws as you," Ares said, tossing Alex to the ground.

Alex picked himself up and dusted off. From the other end of the field, it had been hard to see how far his throw had been. But now that he was closer, the source of Ares' rage was apparent. Sticking in the ground at a perfect forty-five degree angle was Alex's javelin, the head being five or six paces farther than Ares' best mark. "Beginner's luck?" offered Alex.

"You say this was luck?"

"Well, no. Maybe something like luck," Alex said. For the second time in the past few days he wished he had brushed up on his stalling skills. "I mean, I was a decent athlete back in my day. Good at baseball, too. Had a killer swing. Maybe this new body, courtesy of Hades by the way, tapped into that. Maybe you should blame him?"

"Blame him? Blame him!" Ares yanked the javelin free and shoved it in front of Alex's face. "You've brought dishonor to yourself and tried to cheat me of my rightful victory. If it is battle you seek, it is a battle you shall find."

"I've done no such thing," Alex said. "I don't know what happened, but I didn't cheat. Maybe you should've practiced more."

The moment the words passed his mouth, Alex's brain scolded him for relinquishing control of his tongue. Ares seemed to have a similar thought but decided to issue his reprimand physically. By the time Alex had thought about ducking, he was flat on his back, vision blurred and spinning.

"That's enough," someone yelled. Someone nearby. Someone who, much to Alex's later thanks, stopped Ares from stomping Alex's brains out. "These games are in celebration of his wedding, and you have no cause to accuse him of cheating."

Alex redoubled his effort to focus, and when his vision cleared, the large, meaty hand of Zeus pulled him to his feet.

"Everyone saw," Ares said, arms crossed and foot recently stomped. His voice had lost the harsh, unyielding tone but still held its spite. "No one can out throw me. No one."

"Unless he is judged a cheater, he is under my protection, and you will not touch him," Zeus said, squaring off with Ares as thunderheads filled the sky. "I have run these games flawlessly since they began, and I'll not have you throwing accusations around of being unfaithful."

Ares spat. "I demand a war to settle this matter and to reclaim my honor."

"I'm not going to war over something this stupid," Alex said, not wanting his fate to be decided by another. "I'm no cheater, and I shouldn't have to prove I'm not."

Zeus slapped him playfully on the back. "That you don't. No man need prove his faithfulness. If Alex does not wish to fight you, Ares, he does not have to."

"Gather your men, mortal," Ares said. The God of War leveled his finger to emphasize the rest of his statement. "You will fight, of that you can be certain. Mark my words, by the week's end we shall be pitted against one another in glorious combat."

Zeus rolled his eyes as Ares stomped off. "Don't worry about him. He says that all the time."

"All the time?"

"All the time. Two nights ago, he declared war on his soufflé when it failed to rise. If I were you, I'd forget him and take your wife home and make love to her while you can still stand the sight of her."

CHAPTER SIXTEEN

Alex, inside the cave of their island home, stood behind his bride, stupefied. "What do you mean, no?"

"I thought that answer was clear enough, Alex," Euryale answered as she braided her serpents. Sunlight poured in from the mouth of the cave, giving her ample light in which to work as she stood in front of a full-length mirror. She turned this way and that, inspecting the little, black, scoop-necked dress with matching gloves and heels, and making whatever proper adjustments the moment called for. "When I get back, I'll relish your touch, but I've got to get going or I'll be late."

"Pfft," he scoffed. "You can afford it."

Euryale ignored his remark and smoothed out her dress for the fifth time. "I'm not sure I like this design your culture has developed. Jessica said I should give it a try. Do you think this looks good on me?"

"I think it would look better off you." Alex's fingers went for the laces on her dress, but when they were batted away, he decided to take a different approach to his seduction. "Did I tell you I won the javelin event? It was a thousand times more awesome than any fencing tourney I've been in."

"Yes, my dear." She turned around and kissed him on the cheek. "Only a dozen times. I also heard it from everyone else twice as much in the stands, and that was only moments after I saw it myself."

Alex put his arms around her waist and leaned in close. "You know you want to."

"Yes, I do. But the answer is still no." Euryale squirmed free of his grasp. "I mean it, Alex, I do not want to be late. Aphrodite is hosting the party, and it's not wise to cross her. She can be as vindictive as Athena, if not more so."

Alex sulked. "What if I wither and die from lack of affection?"

"That's a risk I'm willing to take." Euryale grinned and pressed a small, leather pouch into his hands before kissing him once more. "Here, take this. It will alleviate this longing you have for me."

Alex looked down. "What is it?"

"My first wedding present to you."

Alex opened the pouch and peered inside. With hands that moved more slowly and more carefully than a surgeon's, Alex pulled forth his small, plastic pony. "Where did you get this?"

"I found it in the wreckage after you left with Ares," she explained. "I knew it meant a lot to you, so I thought you might want it back."

Alex turned the toy over a few more times. "This was given to me by another."

"I know," she said. "It's okay."

"No," he replied. Alex took a deep breath and gave it a squeeze, breaking the toy in half. He then threw the two pieces into a nearby brazier and never looked back. "I'm not married to her," he explained. "Happiness should come from you, not the past."

"I want you to be happy, but I'd be lying if I said your gesture wasn't appreciated," she said while pressing a second pouch into his hands. "But maybe you'll find this to be more to your liking."

Alex opened the next pouch and gave a look. "Money?"

"Yes, but I'm ordering you to buy something with it," she explained. "A piano. Whatever the best money can buy. You were upset at what happened to your last one, so I thought the least I could do was get you a new one."

"I'm buying my own present?" Alex looked at the gold coins once more. "I thought that was a faux pas."

"It is. In your case, however, it'll be therapeutic."

"I'm not sure this is the best of ideas."

"Why is that?" she asked, her excitement fading. "I was under the impression that you'd love a new one."

"I would," Alex explained. He leaned a shoulder on the wall and debated how much he should share before continuing. "I don't think you appreciate the monster you're about to create."

Euryale laughed, her snakes seemingly joining in at the same time. "I think I know a thing or two about monsters. You are no monster, Alex."

"I will be if you sit a piano in our home," he said. "I'll play it constantly and neglect you at best."

"And at worst?"

"Berate you for saying something sounds good when it sounds terrible." Alex tried to stay detached and as matter of fact as possible and kept his eyes away from hers. "It never fails. It's driven away what few girls I've dated over the years."

Euryale, to Alex's surprise, giggled. "That's it? I turn people to stone, and you yell at them and play music?"

"Well...yeah..." Alex replied, now feeling as if he'd made a mountain out of a molehill. "But it's a mean bit of yelling. You'll probably cry."

"No, I'll get even. I've spent thousands of years perfecting the art," she teased. She pushed the monies pouch into his chest, leaned in, and kissed him softly. "I know what I'm getting with you, and I can handle it. Besides, I don't need you at my side every waking moment."

"You don't?"

Euryale shook her head. "No. I don't need you to complete my life, Alex. I only want you to share it."

"What does that mean?"

"It means I want you to live your life as well and let me be a part of it," she said. "Enthusiasm for music will not drive me away. If anything, I shall love to sit and listen to you play."

"Don't say I didn't warn you."

"That's a good boy," she said, patting him on the head. "I'll be home in a few hours. Now go and enjoy yourself."

Alex pulled her close and placed her arms around his neck. "I love you."

"You still aren't getting me in bed, Alex," she replied.

"I know. I just wanted to tell you that before I left." Alex kissed her, letting her lips hang on his for a moment before parting. And then off he went, wondering if he had indeed found the best wife to have ever lived, reptiles included.

CHAPTER SEVENTEEN

Euryale had never been to Termessos before, and she wondered why Aphrodite would pick such a place for a party. Once she reached the city's theater high atop the Taurus Mountains in Turkey, however, she knew the reason. Even with the city in ruins, scrub taking hold in both the streets and in the pockets of crumbling walls, the theater held a mystical air to it, a place where only the clouds kept one company, fresh, cool air kissed the skin, and the world bustled below, oblivious to anything that happened above.

"Right on time," Aphrodite said the moment Euryale arrived. She stood in the center of the stage with a plucked rose in hand. She turned the flower over several times before offering it. "For you, my dear," she said. "Though I suspect it will wilt without its roots in a day or two in such a dry climate. I hope that doesn't bother you."

Euryale took the flower. She was perplexed by the gift at first, but when she looked around the theater and saw that there were no others about, nor food nor decorations in place, she realized the gift did not represent a token of good will. "There is no party, is there?"

"No, there isn't."

"And there is no one nearby," she said,

The goddess's lips drew back into a thin smile. "There is no one nearby," Aphrodite repeated. "Not for miles."

A vindictive look shone in Aphrodite's eyes, and Euryale knew she was about to bear the brunt of the goddess's anger. "Why are you doing this?" the gorgon asked.

"Does it matter?" Aphrodite replied, trailing a finger on the gorgon's shoulders as she walked around her. "The only thing that really matters at this point is that there is no one around to hear you scream."

A massive hand with an iron grip clapped down on Euryale's wrist. She jerked her head around just in time to see that Ares was attached to said hand before a sack went over her head and her wrists were bound behind her back.

Images of her being separated from Alex for untold swaths of time flashed through her mind. She strained against her bindings, and they cut into her hardened skin. Feeling her blood run down her wrists only fueled her anger, heightened her strength. Her lungs filled with air, and she bellowed while jerking against the ropes. The bindings snapped, and every creature for hundreds of yards in every direction fell over dead.

"A warrior's spirit!" Ares said, laughing as he clamped down on her upper arms. "I admire the fire in you!"

"You've no idea what you've started," she said.

"I know exactly what I've started."

Euryale replied by trying to drive her forehead into Ares, but with the sackcloth over her head, her aim was terrible and she headbutted his shoulder. The God of War's laughs only infuriated her more, and since she couldn't see nor move her arms, she sent her serpents to do her bidding.

Seven vipers burst free from the sack, and all seven buried their fangs into Ares' skin. The venom they dumped into the god's body was enough to fell a thousand legions, but it was not near enough to cause Ares to drop her, only enough to cause him to howl.

"Good night," he growled, thumping her once on the head.

Euryale's world went black.

Pritch's Pianos. That was the name of it. Its elegant, black and gold logo of a double P had cost a hefty sum and provided endless delight for kindergarteners in need of a laugh. The store's showroom of exorbitantly priced pianos catered to a select group of people—people who filled Kleenex boxes with hundred dollar bills and could buy Ferraris with their lunch money.

Alex stood outside the store, staring through the full-length glass windows, and salivated over the selection inside. Would he buy only one? Or maybe a dozen to ensure that wherever he went on the island, a set of ivory keys would always call to him. He could have one on each beach, too, for when the sun rose or set, so that he'd have the perfect scenery for an uplifting ballade or a somber nocturne.

With a smile larger than a titan, Alex strode into the store. He walked past the Kohlers, the Kawais, the Yamahas, and headed straight for the Steinways. Most of the store patrons went about their business, looking at or playing with various models of uprights and baby grands. Only a couple took note of Alex's entrance, and when they did, they offered themselves a handful of whispers and snickers. Precisely what those whispers said eluded Alex's ear, but judging by their expressions and gestures, he suspected their comments were directed at the white chiton he wore.

Alex waved to each one and wondered if they'd truly appreciate the free concert they were about to witness. He soon reached the back of the store where the Steinways were, the least expensive one only a dollar below six figures. Nine feet long and almost a half a ton, they were beasts yearning to be tamed. No, they were not beasts, but rather perfection incarnate, having Sitka spruce headboards, sugar pine ribs, heavy brass pedals and a variety of high-gloss finishes.

Alex chose the nearest of three grand pianos and sat down, completely ignoring the *Please ask for assistance* card that had been left on its top. After flexing his fingers and cracking his knuckles, a practice his first teacher always hated but had never managed to stamp out, Alex let his right index finger drop on middle C. The tone resonated in his soul and seemed to hang in the air long after the strings stopped vibrating.

"Excuse me, sir," the salesman said, dressed in a charcoal coat and tie and coming to a stop a few paces away. "Might we have a word before you try out that particular model?"

"Don't talk," Alex said, both his hands hovering over the keyboard. He needed to warm up. Some Czerny? No, no. Something more complete, more emotional. The perfect piece sprang to mind.

Alex dropped his fingers to the keys, ever so soft. As his left played descending octaves with a somber tone, his right started the perpetual triplets to Beethoven's first movement of the Moonlight Sonata. Alex shut his eyes when his little finger delicately picked up the main theme, a single, grave voice that sang above a rhythmic undercurrent. Alex continued to play with a gentle touch born from decades devoted to constant practice. Only when his hands lifted from the keys and the performance truly sank into the hearts of all those around, did Alex direct his attention to the man at his side.

"Masterfully done," the salesman said. "Now if we might—"

Alex held up a finger with such command that the man instantly hushed. Alex's fingers took to the keys once more, skipping the second movement to the Moonlight Sonata and heading right into the third. The second was quaint, as Alex would put it if he were being polite (for he found it annoying and unworthy of his time), but the third movement was as much of a sight to behold as to hear.

Alex's fingers blurred as they raced up and down the keys, giving *Presto* all new meaning. His notes came off as fierce and fiery. The chords he struck were nothing short of bolts of lightning. And when it was over, some five or so minutes later, everyone from the store crowded around and whispered in awe.

"Meh," someone dared to say from the back, breaking the silence. "Your phrasing could have been better."

"What the hell do you—" Alex said, twisting around and ready to disembowel whoever the blasphemer was. But when he saw Athena push her way through the crowd, he held back the rest of his comment.

"Quick study, Alex," she said, smiling and coming to rest at his side. She leaned against the piano with one elbow. "Glad to see my lessons were not lost on you."

Alex grimaced at the memory. "Yes, well, with all due respect, might I ask why you're here now? I thought you were done with me."

"Oh, I am, Alex. I am," she said. Before she went on, she directed her attention to the salesman still standing near and shooed at him with her hands. "Be gone," she said. "You have things to do."

The man blinked and straightened, as if some long-forgotten thought suddenly came to mind. "I have things to do," he stated. "Please excuse me."

The small crowd dispersed, and once Alex was certain they were having a private conversation, he asked the only question on his mind. "You were saying?"

"Fear not, Alex," she said. "I've not come to torment you."

"Oh, thank god."

"There is something you ought to know, however."

Alex froze, both in breath and in thought. "Do I want to know?"

"Up to you," said Athena with a shrug. "Though you'll find out sooner or later, certainly by the time you get home."

"Speaking of getting home, I need to get back before Euryale gets worried." The corners of his mouth drew back into a smile as he reminisced. "She has the cutest expression when she gets anxious—even when she says she's not. She flips her hair around and the snakes keep tasting the air." Alex sighed a happy sigh. "Maybe I should get her something nice on the way back."

"That would be thoughtful of you," Athena said. "But if you do, don't get her anything perishable."

"Why not?"

"She's been kidnapped, so your gift might spoil before she has a chance to get it."

The smile faded from Alex's face and his mind tried to wrap itself around what Athena had said. "Come again?"

"My brother, Ares, took her," she said. "It seems he's still upset about you beating him in the Olympics. You really shouldn't have used that javelin from Artemis. Of course it's going to sail far, and of course that's going to piss him off."

Alex stared blankly. "This is a joke, right?"

Athena shook her head. "No joke, Alex. Your wife's gone."

Alex's muscles tightened. His jaw set. He could smell the anger wafting from his skin and feel the temperature in his body rise tenfold. "This is insane!" he said, jumping to his feet and knocking the piano bench over in the process. "Why won't everyone leave me alone?"

"Ares will, once he's satisfied he's pummeled you enough."

"And how long will that be?"

"If you admit to cheating and beg for mercy, I'd wager a couple hundred years ought to do it.

"A couple hundred years?"

"Three tops," Athena said. Though that response was cheerful, she grimaced a half second later. "Unless..."

"Unless what?"

"Well, if Ares is still sore about an incident involving a hydra, you might be looking at spending three centuries at war instead of two," she said. "Four tops. Definitely no more than four."

"Now it's up to four?"

"If you count by millennia, it'll be over before you know it."

"I'm not doing that," Alex said. "I'm going to Zeus. He said he wouldn't let Ares do this."

"Dad really isn't one to get involved in things like this," Athena said. "Besides, he's disappeared again. Young maidens and all."

"Fine, you know what? I'll get her myself then. Where is she?"

"Termessos. It's a quaint mountain area, complete with an ancient fortress and a large tower that's perfect to hold someone prisoner."

"Then that's where I'll go to get her back," he said, stepping over the fallen seat and heading for the door.

"Oh Alex," she called out, stopping him dead in his tracks. "How do you plan on doing that? Ares isn't going to hand her to you."

"I'll reason with him." Alex said. "If that doesn't work, I guess I'll have to beat him in a duel somehow."

Athena laughed and doubled over as she did. "That's rich, Alex," she said, trying to recompose herself. "You are in no way, shape, or form ready to do that. If you're going to challenge him in combat, you'll need lots of practice. Or an army. Or both."

"I was a good fencer in college. I even competed in the nationals," Alex said. "I'm not that helpless. I could win."

Athena raised an eyebrow. "Oh, is that so? Perhaps a little demonstration of your abilities is in order. Maybe I've underestimated you."

Athena snapped her fingers and in an instant, two spears, six feet in length with iron heads, ash wood shafts and bronzed ends, materialized in her hands. With a flick of her wrist, she tossed one to Alex. "If you can run me through, I'll concede your point and send you on your way with blessings. If you fail, however, you'll shut up and listen to me."

"I said I was a fencer, not a Spartan. Give me a saber."

"You'll still lose," Athena said with a shrug. "But suit yourself, if that's what you want."

A second snap of the fingers later and Alex's six-foot spear was replaced by an M1860 cavalry saber. The sword itself was a little heavier than the sabers for sport he had once used, but the weapon was still light and easy to handle. "Ready when you are," Alex said, giving the saber a few turns in his hands and then taking a half step back with his left leg.

Alex's saber thumped to the floor before he realized what had happened. He was fuzzy on the details, but he felt as if Athena had knocked it there since the inside of his forearm was bruised and she had the point of her spear resting against his neck.

"You were saying?" she said, smiling.

Alex gently pushed the spear tip away and grabbed his weapon from the floor. He flinched as he picked it up, noting a terrible gash in a piano leg it must have caused on its way down. "I could always sneak up on him."

Athena rolled her eyes and partially suppressed a laugh. "Well make this one count," she said, turning around and leaning on her spear.

Alex lunged, intent on driving the tip of his saber clear through her spine, but Athena stepped backward and turned so his blade slipped harmlessly by. As momentum kept him moving forward, Athena wrapped her left arm around Alex's right and pinned his weapon hand against her side. She then drove the butt of her spear into his solar plexus. Alex doubled over. She swept his left leg, twisted his saber from his grasp, and threw him into the side of an upright Everett.

"Do you yield?" she asked.

Alex stumbled over his reply, and Athena drove the head of her spear deep into the Everett's side, less than an inch from Alex's head. "Do you yield?" she said again, more forcefully than the last.

"I yield! I yield!" Alex spit out. "Christ, you didn't have to destroy the place."

"The place is hardly destroyed," she said, looking around. "You've got some inborn talent, I'll grant you that, but you're far from the perfect swordsman and not at all ready to face my brother."

"Well I don't exactly have the time or desire to perfect the craft, especially while my wife wastes away in some dungeon."

"Tower," Athena corrected.

"Close enough," said Alex as he went for the door again. "I still have to get her back."

Athena grabbed him by the shoulder. "Listen to me, Alex. I only get to say this once. If you want to be reunited with your wife and avoid being Ares' punching bag, you'll need to get help. Who, what, when, or where you find said help is up to you."

Alex turned her words over in his head. He did need help. He knew that, and he hated how rash he'd been only moments ago. Who was he to think he could defeat The God of War? His fencing skills—as demonstrated by Athena—wouldn't be near enough. "If you're offering to help, I wouldn't turn it down."

Athena shook her head. "I can't."

"Why not?"

Her eyes darted to the sides before she answered. "There are...events...that go beyond you and Ares, events that prohibit certain deities from doing certain things."

"And you're one of them."

She didn't reply.

"Is anyone else not allowed to do anything?"

She didn't reply again, and Alex was certain at this point that any other questions would be met with the same answer.

"That figures," he said with a huff. "Well, at least I know someone who will be eager to help free Euryale."

Alex broke from the conversation when he realized that people were fleeing out of the store. The only person not fleeing was the salesman that had attended to Alex when he had first arrived. That man was currently clutching a phone and peering around the doorway to a corner office.

"Don't worry, we're leaving," Alex called out. As he made for the exit, Alex tossed the pouch of coins Euryale had given him to the salesman inside. "Sorry about the mess."

Chapter Eighteen

On the southern edge of Greece, Alex stood along a powdery white shore, ankle deep in the rising tide. There he watched Phorcys, novice of architects, help Jessica build a sand castle.

"I can see why the humans enjoy this," The Old Man said as he filled a plastic bucket. "Though it doesn't hold together as well as coral, it's fun nonetheless. I have yet to discover, however, the secret to the larger structures. I either add too much water or too little, and my work collapses. You mortals have the advantage on me in that regard."

"Takes practice," Jessica said, straightening the top to her green bikini. "Do you want to stay for a bit and build the barbican, Alex?"

"No, I don't have time," Alex said, realizing he was looking at Jessica a little longer than he should. "I came here because I need help with Euryale."

Jessica snickered. "Lover's quarrel already?"

"No, she's been kidnapped."

Jessica dropped her jaw an inch. "What? Who on earth kidnaps a gorgon?"

"Ares, which is why I came here for help."

The Old Man pushed himself up off his knees and stood tall. "I'm aware, and though I'm not fond of her imprisonment, you will not have my aide."

"But you're her father!" Alex protested. He ran his fingers through his hair and dug them into his scalp out of frustration. "Don't you always have to rescue her? Isn't that part of the job?"

"I have spoken with...others about this matter already," he replied. "If you love my daughter and desire her at your side, then you will win this fight without me."

"Who have you been talking to?" Alex demanded. "Athena?"

The Old Man's face gave no indication either way. "Does it matter? A captain is responsible for his own vessel regardless of the route he must take, regardless of who sails with him and who does not. I have made up my mind. This voyage you will do without my help. But remember what I said before, I do not take kindly to those who hurt my daughters."

"Then help me! Ares is the one hurting her, not me!"

"Not until you prove your dedication to Euryale first and your saltiness with Ares second. When you've shown yourself to be a true member of this family, I will lend you strength and power beyond reckoning, but until then, you're on your own."

"Gah!" Alex shook his head and blew out a stress-filled puff of air. "Can you at least give me some resources? Or suggestions on what I might do? Athena said I'd need an army."

The Old Man said nothing, which only further frustrated Alex. How he hated feeling like their plaything, and how he hated the fact that he didn't know where else to go even more. If Euryale's own father wouldn't help him, who would?

"We could try Hades," Jessica said. "Lots of dead people there that have fought in wars, right?"

Alex's face lit up. "That's not a bad idea at all," he said. "That's actually a pretty damn good idea. I'll go to Hades and raise an army of the dead."

"*We* will go to Hades and raise an army of the dead," Jessica said. "No buts. I'm coming with."

"It's dangerous. You heard Apollo. The living aren't allowed."

"I don't care what he said," she replied, squaring off with him. "You think I'm passing up the chance of a lifetime and *not* seeing what the afterlife looks like? *Not* photographing the God of the Underworld? *Not* helping the person I care about and *letting* him face danger alone?"

Though Alex's heart warmed at her determination and friendship to be at his side, he couldn't risk her wellbeing on such a treacherous journey. As such, he looked to The Old Man. "Little help here? Tell her what's what."

"I've said already, you are on your own," he replied. He looked to Jessica as he went on. "And you, Apollo was right in that the living are not allowed to walk freely to and from the Underworld, but that doesn't mean it hasn't been done before."

Jessica's eyes lit up. "Orpheus!"

The Old Man nodded and left without further word.

"Who?" asked Alex.

"Orpheus went to Hades to go after his wife and got by with his buttery voice and musical talents."

"I'm hardly epic-voice man," Alex said. "And I can't tote a piano around."

Jessica shrugged and hopped into his chariot. "We'll think of something. Important thing to take away from all of this is that Hades can be bargained with."

"And if he can't, what happens to you then?"

"Guess I'll become the second person you have to save," she said with a playful wink.

Having slipped by a sleeping Cerberus an hour prior, Alex pulled the reins, and his fiery mane ponies came to a halt outside Hades' abode. He hopped off the chariot and helped Jessica down. Ahead of them stood the massive double doors that led to Hade's abode.

"How does this work? Do we knock?" Jessica asked.

"Probably best," he said. "I don't want to be rude, since I think I might have already upset him."

"How's that?"

"I tricked him by not eating a pomegranate that he offered. I'm sure by now he's figured that out."

"Ah," she said, stepping back. "Well, you do it then."

"What happened to helping me through thick and thin?"

Jessica laughed and stepped back again. "I never said through thick and thin. Anyhow, you're the immortal one now, remember? You can take whatever's coming. I'd rather not die and be stuck here forever."

"Glad to be your meat shield," he said as he grabbed one of the large, iron knockers and used it to announce their presence.

Alex folded his arms and drummed his fingers on his bicep as they waited. He prayed he hadn't made a mistake in coming here or in capitulating to Jessica's demand to help. To top things off, he still didn't know what he was going to say to Hades to smooth things over or how he could go about getting an army of the dead from him.

The doors swung open, and Alex blew out a puff of air when he saw that it wasn't Hades who answered, but Persephone. She still wore her royal dress and her golden crown. Her hair was still fixed the same since they had last parted, but her eyes were different. Gone were the hints of fear and uncertainty Alex had seen before. Instead, they had a touch of life to them, almost desire.

"I need to speak to Hades," Alex said, thinking that he might as well state his intentions upfront.

"Of course," she said. "Who have you brought with you?"

"Jessica Turner," she replied, practically leaping over Alex to get in front of the queen. "You have no idea how excited I am to meet you. I must have read your story a hundred times when I was a child."

Persephone tilted her head. "You're not dead, are you?"

Alex butted in before she could reply. "She's here on Aphrodite's orders, more or less."

"More or less?" Persephone chuckled. "I wonder if that will be enough. For your friend's sake, I hope you have something to offer my husband that will appeal to him—he's already cross with you. But if I were you, Jessica, I'd take those ponies and wait for Alex back in land of the living."

"I'm staying," Jessica said. "We can work something out."

"If it were up to me, we could," she said, bidding them to follow her inside with a wave of her hand. "I imagine you're here about Euryale, then? I can't think of any other reason why you'd risk coming back."

Alex raised his eyebrows. "You know?"

"Everyone knows," she said, leading him down the hall with her hands folded behind her back. "Before Ares had even finished turning the key that locks your wife away, Hermes had told everyone."

"That fast?" Alex said, impressed.

"That fast," she repeated. "She is the daughter of a god, after all."

"I'm hoping Hades might help me," Alex said.

"As do I," she said.

"Why?" asked Alex.

"Oh, that someone would fight over me," she replied. A smile, small but true, appeared on her face and she wiped away a tear. "Mother did, of course, when she made demands to Zeus to have me freed, but no one else."

"I don't follow," said Alex.

"My mother is Demeter, Goddess of the Harvest," she explained. "Long ago, when I was free and able to roam the Earth above, Hades swept me away to be his bride. I was innocent, a little naïve perhaps, and before my mother could find me, I ate some pomegranate seeds Hades had offered."

"Binding you here in the Underworld," Jessica finished.

Persephone nodded and continued. "Mother didn't give up, to her credit. She hounded Zeus for my release, threatened the Earth with famine, and so he gave in, partially at least. To satisfy the Fates, Hades, and my mother, Zeus allowed me to roam the Earth for three seasons each year, but during the fourth, I'm to live in the Underworld. So you see, though mother fought for me, it's not the same, is it? It's not like a lover risking it all to be at my side."

"I suppose not," Alex admitted.

The conversation paused, and the three of them navigated the twists and turns of the dark halls in silence. Only a single, long red carpet and periodic braziers offered any sort of decoration. The foremost muted their footsteps as they traveled, while the latter held waning fires that could barely melt an ice cube. As the minutes ticked by, Alex wondered if Hade's abode had always been so barren, or if it had started out as an extravagant home that had slowly eroded under an eternal depression. Either way, he could scarcely believe the contrast between this place and Mount Olympus.

Finally, they reached the throne room. Hades sat on an ebony throne, hunched forward with his elbows on his knees and his hands clasped together. His face looked drawn, and his shoulders sagged, as if the weight of the world above pressed down upon them.

"We have company, dear," Persephone said, walking up a few steps to be at her husband's side. She did not sit on her throne beside him, but simply placed a hand on the god's shoulder. "Alex, husband of Euryale, son-in-law of Phorcys, humbly requests an audience, and he has a guest with him, a woman named Jessica, who comes at the direction of Aphrodite."

Hades shifted in his seat, and rested his chin on one hand. "I'm surprised you came back, Alex," he said. "Everyone else just wants to run away. Not that I blame them."

"Well, I'm not everyone else," said Alex when he couldn't think of anything else to say.

"No, no you aren't," Hades replied. "But I'm still certain you want something from me."

"I've come for your help," said Alex.

"And why should I help you?" Hades quickly retorted as he straightened in his seat.

Whereas moments ago, Hades had regarded Alex with indifference, the curt reply and change in posture told Alex that at least one flame of anger burned inside the god. So instead of challenging the god on the question of why, Alex opted to take a different approach. "You have no reason to," he said. "I tricked you into thinking I had taken some of your food for my own reasons when I should have been upfront and honest that I did not care for any."

"Go on," said Hades with a weary voice.

"For that offense, I can only offer my apologies," Alex said. "But my wife has been taken from me, and I need an army to get her back. Surely you can empathize with my plight. You know what it's like to be separated from the one you love."

"Yes, I do," said Hades, holding his wife's hand. "But you're still like the others. Always wanting. Never giving."

"I don't know what I have that you want," said Alex.

"You have nothing I want." Hades replied.

"Surely there is something I can do."

Hades' brow furrowed. "I said, you have nothing."

"Yes, you did," Alex said, feeling like what little wind was in his sails had been taken away and now he risked Hades' wrath if he stayed. "I'm sorry for taking up your time. I'll see my own way out."

Alex turned and began to walk away, intent on finding a new way to raise an army, but Jessica grabbed him by the arm and was quick to speak. "If I may, your most powerfulness," she said. "I know you're saddened for your wife to leave the home you two have made for the next few seasons, but perhaps I can do something to help alleviate that pain of separation."

"What can you do, a mortal?" he scoffed.

Jessica raised her camera. "I can take pictures of her and you two together, so you'll have fond memories to look at until she returns."

"Paintings."

"No, not paintings. Similar in a sense, but not the same. If I may." Jessica slowly approached the throne and showed the preview screen on her DSLR to the god where she flipped through all the pictures she had taken thus far. "These would be made as big as one can print, if you so desire."

"Show me."

To that request, she did. Jessica had Persephone drape her arms around Hades' neck and lean into him, her forehead resting against his, and with a little extra direction, she struck the perfect balance between longing and loving in her eyes. Then, Jessica only had to spend a few extra moments setting her ISO and shutter speed to account for the gloom before snapping off a dozen shots from three different angles.

"I'm not that impressed," Hades said. "They are decent depictions of us, but nothing special. Certainly not worthy of having an army raised over."

"I'll need to do the processing at home. When I'm done, the colors will be more vibrant, the mood and framing perfect," she said. "I could easily take a hundred more of your lovely wife throughout your kingdom while you help Alex. I swear to you, what you see now are only shadows of what could be."

"You expect me to believe you'll work elsewhere and come back on your own, especially when your friend gets what he wants up front?"

Jessica shook her head and looked as helpless as Alex felt. "I have to have my computer. These pictures are raw. They aren't near finished."

"Tempting, but no," Hades said.

"Please, though I'll do whatever it takes to see Euryale back to me, I'd prefer having your assistance," Alex said. "All I can offer in addition to Jessica's service is my gratitude and service at some other time. Being the son-in-law of Phorcys must count for something."

"It along with Aphrodite's involvement with your friend is barely enough for me not to keep her here forever. I do not like the living coming and going from my realm as they see fit. Now go."

"Wait," Persephone said, grabbing her husband by the shoulder. "For my sake, help him."

Hades looked up to her and shrugged. "I see no reason," he said. "I'm tired enough as it is."

But Persephone did not relent in her request. She bent down and kissed him on his forehead. "Take Jessica's offering and help Alex. Should he succeed, I'll stay with you another fourteen days on my own accord."

Hades remained silent for a few moments, and Alex waited anxiously, fidgeting as he did. Finally, the god nodded. "Only if you swear by the River Styx," he said.

At which point, Persephone quickly interjected, "I so swear!"

"And, you, Alex," Hades continued. "You must win. For if I help you, and you fail and my wife does not stay, you'll bear a fury like no other. Before I'm finished peeling away your sanity, you'll beg to be made mortal again and let your body give up the ghost."

Despite the grim warning, Alex smiled broadly. "Thank you," he said. "Thank you. I won't rest until she's in my arms again."

"Then take my scepter and go," Hades said, offering it to Alex with one hand. "Raise your army and rescue your bride, but be sure your heart is in the work, lest the quality of men you raise suffers."

* * *

In a large clearing, some five or ten miles south of Termessos, Alex, covered in grime, blood, and gore, looked at the countless sets of bones and half-formed corpses and wondered what he was doing wrong. Everything, probably. Hades had given no real instruction on the use of his scepter, and thus far, Alex had tried a variety of grips on its shaft, all the while trying to "will" an army to raise from the ground. Whatever the hell that meant. But since his previous attempts had ended in the most magnificent of corpse explosions, Alex decided he needed to reevaluate his plan. Perhaps his heart really wasn't in it after all, or simply not enough.

Alex's brow furrowed as he tried to recall every little detail he could when he had watched Hades work. The god had made it look so easy, Alex thought, but then quickly reminded himself that that was the mark of a true master, to make the complicated, the impossible, look simple. But even a master was a novice at one point. Even a master had to start with his first creation or performance, no matter how long ago that was. Everyone started at the beginning. Everyone. Still, he was up for suggestions.

"Any ideas?" he said to Jessica.

"Yeah, conjure up a hazmat suit for each of us," she said, shaking a bit of gore off her boot. "And then some new clothes to change into as well."

"I meant in making an army."

"Maybe you're trying to take on too much," she said. "Start simple."

Alex eyed the scepter as he thought about her remark. Maybe she was right. With that thought, he outstretched his arms, held the scepter horizontal, and began to envision a single, solitary soldier—not the vast army he originally had been trying for. The man he envisioned would be from World War II, only because Alex had read and seen enough documentaries about the period that he felt confident in knowing every detail in how he'd look. Besides, Alex couldn't very well raise a Spartan and thrust a gun into his hand, now could he?

The image in his mind took shape: the man would be six feet even, short hair, brown, cleanly shaven. A muscular build, but not brutish. A grin that said the man kept his humor, but a thousand-yard stare that said he'd seen combat, and plenty of it. His uniform would be a form-fitting M-42 jumpsuit over a wool shirt, green of course. He'd need rank, as well. Sergeant stripes would do. In his hands would be an M-1 Garand, and atop his head would be the iconic helmet that all the US soldiers wore. As Alex thought about all of this—the more he pictured the way the man moved, spoke, even smelled—a tingly sensation ran through his arm.

Soon Alex realized his hands were moving rhythmically through the air. He continued to concentrate on what he wanted, and at the same time, he tried to relax and let the energy flow through him unimpeded. The ground several yards away rumbled and slowly peeled back. A second later, a bare hand shot forth, perfectly formed.

"Keep it up!" Jessica said energetically. "You've got it!"

Alex watched, amazed, as the hand groped both air and dirt as it sought some unknown thing. But as quick as it came, it stiffened and sank back into the ground. The energy that had flowed freely through his body only moments ago dwindled to almost nothing.

"No! Get back to whatever you were doing!" Jessica said.

Alex shut his eyes, knowing his spell was on the verge of collapse, but frustration kept him from progressing further. He sighed heavily. "I'm too tense."

Jessica slipped behind him and massaged his neck and shoulders. "You can do this. I've never seen you not be able to do anything you've wanted to do."

Alex nodded as he let his body enjoy a bit of pampering. As she continued to work on his muscles, the tension melted away, and his mind relaxed. He soon found himself replaying one of his favorite orchestra pieces in his head, *In the Halls of the Mountain King.*

The simple theme started low and quiet with cellos and bassoons. While they tip-toed through the notes, Alex tip-toed through the picture of what he wanted to the tune of the melody.

I need one who's tall and lean,
Just as mean,
Dressed in green,
If I'm to save Euryale from Ares' evil things

He must have a rifle too,
Aim it true,
Hair cut crew,
He must have an attitude that always says can-do

In his boot's a fighting knife,
To take life,
For my wife,
He will charge right into strife, day or night too.

Shovel will be on his back,
With a pack,
Ammo sack,
On his feet are boots of black, good, not cracked too.

He'll be fearless at my side,
As we hide,
And decide,
The very best way that we can go and save my bride.

At that point in the song, when the tempo of his mental recital picked up, Alex became acutely aware of two things. First, the energy he'd so earnestly sought now coursed through his body. And second, someone had just given a throat-clearing cough. Someone who was neither Jessica nor feminine.

Alex opened his eyes. There, standing a few feet away, bewildered but otherwise looking fine, was the soldier Alex had envisioned, right down to the frayed nametag and weathered combat boots.

"Sorry to interrupt, but where the hell am I?" the man asked.

"Termessos," Alex replied with a growing smile.

"We still at war?"

Alex nodded. "We're at war, but not the one you're thinking of."

The man looked about and adjusted the sights on his M1 Garand. "Is it just us?"

"No," Alex said, shaking his head. He sucked in a deep breath, stretched out his arms, and shut his eyes once more. "More are coming. Many, many more."

CHAPTER NINETEEN

Alex, standing in his chariot and dressed in an M-42 jumpsuit, raised his hand to shield his eyes from the midmorning sun. A hundred yards ahead of him stood a gargantuan fortress, the likes of which Alex had never dreamt about.

Two sets of walls, thirty and sixty feet high respectively, formed the bulk of the defenses, and those were protected by a ditch that looked at least ten feet deep. At regular intervals along the walls were at least a dozen watch towers, each with a catapult on its top. If Alex squinted, he could make out the movements of troops inside. How many there were, he didn't know, nor did he care. The only thing Alex wondered at the time was what Ares was about to do, for the God of War was waiting for him at the iron gates.

"Mortal!" the god cried out as he trotted over to Alex. Sunlight sparkled off the Ares' sweat-drenched skin, at least, what portions weren't coated in mud and dirt. "Do you like my fortress?" he asked eagerly. "I built it last night for this very day!"

Alex's ponies snorted and shook their heads with flattened ears. Alex pulled their reins in a preemptive move to keep them from bolting. "I've come for my wife," he said once the ornery creatures settled down. "I hoped we might settle this without bloodshed."

"You make demands of me without a fight?" Ares erupted in laughter so deep that the ground shook. The god turned scarlet, and he gripped his side, the humor he found apparently getting the best of him. Finally, Ares regained his composure. "What, little mortal, makes you think you have any such standing?"

"I'm serious," Alex said. He held out Hades' scepter for Ares to see and tried to sound as strong and confident as he could. "I wield power over the dead and this scepter obeys my commands."

"That scepter can only strip the immortality of one who is not a god."

Alex steeled himself, feeling his courage falter at the lack of Ares' fear. "I also have an army the likes of which you've never seen."

To Alex's dismay, Ares stepped forward with a glint of bloodlust in his eye. "Yes, Alex. I know you have an army," he said, grinning from ear to ear. He pulled an ivory horn from behind his back and raised it up. "I have an army as well. When the day is done, we shall see who is able to make demands from whom."

Ares put the horn to his lips, and from it came a low, mournful blast. The gates behind him swung open, and from inside, double file, came countless men on horseback. In their arms they carried shield and spear, and on their backs flowed bright red capes. On their heads sat helms of brass, and to the sun they showed their bared chests.

Despite Ares' unexpected cavalry, and despite their still unending numbers, Alex vowed to win the day. "So be it," Alex said, turning the chariot around. A snap of the reins set his ponies into a trot, back to the tree line some six hundred yards away, back to where his troops lay hidden.

"Go Alex," Ares called. "Go to your men and lead the charge. I shall welcome you on the field of battle."

Alex waited until he was half way across the field before taking out the hand-held radio he had tucked away. "Yeah, I'll welcome you too," he muttered, punching the radio's buttons, "right into modern combat."

The call he placed was quickly answered. "Alpha company here," a radioman said in Alex's handset. "Bravo and Delta are in position."

Alex shut his eyes and sucked in a deep breath to prepare himself. Sadly, it didn't work. His hands picked up a tremor as he thought about what was soon to take place. Not because he was leading five hundred gun-toting soldiers against god-knows how many on horseback. That battle would be a slaughter, especially with the few tanks he had managed to bring up, courtesy of Hades' scepter once more. No, Alex was worried because amongst that cavalry was a god, and truth be told, even with artillery and tanks, Alex had no idea whether his men could actually take Ares down. And that scared the crap out of him.

The radio sprung to life and snapped Alex out of his thoughts. "Orders, sir?"

Alex thought about his wife and pushed aside his fear. "Fire at will," he said. "Arty first. Everyone else open up once those shells hit. Don't stop until they're all dead."

Thunder sounded in the distance, and Ares, mid speech, paused in his troop address and turned his head. Not a cloud could be seen in the sky, nor could he see his father, Zeus, lurking about. Before Ares could discern its origins, a new sound filled the air. A whistling sound. One that drew nearer with each passing moment.

And then the world exploded.

Rock and debris flew in every direction. Large, dust-filled craters appeared where rows of men had been an instant ago. The tree line erupted in white flashes and loud cracks. Bullets tore into Ares and his warriors. The bullets were not nearly as large as the ones used in slings, but they proved deadly nonetheless. Some left colorful trails in the air, while others zipped by almost unseen. All, however, felled horse and soldier alike. Despite the carnage and Alex's clever ambush, neither Ares nor his men faltered.

Ares raised his spear high overhead and charged. "Come men!" he cried. "Come and claim your glory!"

The sound of a thousand charging horses filled the air. Ares glanced over his shoulder and savored the image of his men surging forward in a mass of horse and spear. As he turned his attention back to the tree line, he spied Alex on his chariot, still out in the open.

"Now, Alex, you'll see a true warrior in battle," Ares said, slowing his stride and shifting the grip on his spear. A second later, he gave it a heave.

A hundred yards to the tree line, Alex's shoulder exploded in pain and he toppled over the side of his chariot. Down he went, tumbling to the ground and striking his head at least three times over. When he finally rolled to a stop, he lay flat on his back, out of breath and disoriented. In the back of his mind, the sounds of gunfire and hoof beats registered.

Before he could stand, let alone think of something to do, a large hand grabbed him by the jacket and hoisted him into the air. He then found himself staring face to face with Ares.

"Brave, Alex," the god said. "A reckless, stupid ambush, but brave."

"Let me go," Alex said, trying to bat Ares away. The attempt was feeble, however, for the strength in his left arm had all but gone and his right hung limply at his side, nearly severed at the shoulder.

Ares ignored the request and instead turned Alex around so he could see the field of battle. Bodies littered the field, and the ground was stained in untold amounts of blood. All the dead that Alex could see were Ares' men, and as far as Alex could tell, not a single one had reached the tree line. "Your soldiers are deadly, Alex," Ares said sounding impressed. "I will enjoy killing each one of them."

Alex smirked. "Yeah, that's what you think." With that, Alex reached down with his left hand and pulled his 1911 pistol from his belt. It was an awkward grab, and the weapon felt clumsy in his hands, but at point blank range, he couldn't miss.

Ares looked down right as Alex pressed the .45 caliber pistol against the god's muscular chest and pulled the trigger.

The gun kicked in Alex's hand, and again and again as he continued to fire. Though Alex emptied the magazine in under three seconds, all eight rounds hitting home, Ares stood tall and proud as ever. Maybe slightly annoyed. But certainly not dead. Or even mortally wounded. It was definitely not what Alex had been hoping for.

"Not today, Alex," Ares said, dropping him to the ground. "Not today."

Alex shut his eyes and clenched his fists as another wave of pain washed over him. He tried not to whimper as he waited for it to subside. He wouldn't give Ares that satisfaction. When the fiery throbs went from excruciating to merely god-awful, Alex opened his eyes and found himself alone.

Euryale found it hard to see the battle from the tiny window afforded to her in her tower prison. She had managed to see Alex summon powerful explosions that tossed Ares' men like chaff, and she was both impressed and pleased that her husband had such abilities. Sadly, her shoulders and smile had long since fallen, as Ares had not been stopped, and now she had no idea what was taking place. Worse, her imagination was doing a fine job filling in the gaps.

"This won't last, you know."

Euryale set her jaw and refused to face her tormentor. "Alex will fight more than you know."

Aphrodite laughed with notes of condescension and pity. "I was talking about your relationship and his supposed love for you."

"What do you know of love? You can't even stay true to your own husband."

Aphrodite let loose a tiny growl, and Euryale tensed. The goddess, to her credit, recomposed herself as quickly as the reaction had come. Her words stayed sickeningly sweet.

"Oh, Euryale," she said. "For a girl who is eons old, you'd think you'd be more realistic about all of this. I mean, really, what's keeping the two of you together? You, I understand. Ugly. Lonely. Both sisters are gone, and your father sleeps most of the time. Of course you'd latch on to the first guy that pays you any attention. But what of Alex? Why would he actually want to be with you? Is it your stunning beauty? Your social grace? Your standing with the Olympians?"

"Quiet!"

Aphrodite giggled. "Is it your temper? He never struck me as the type who likes girls with no self-control. Now that I think about it, I don't think he's the type who would be happy in a forced marriage, either."

"It wasn't forced," Euryale said as her hands tightened around the bars to her window.

"What would you call being under threat of Aldora's beak?" Aphrodite countered. "We both know he didn't find it kinky."

Doubt stabbed through Euryale's gut and into her heart. Her eyes watered, as there was at least a small amount of undeniable truth to the goddess's words. "He said he'd love me," she finally replied, clinging to his words to keep her grounded. "That's enough."

"Men say all sorts of things when they lust after a girl or when they flee from danger," Aphrodite replied. "And I'll grant you that perhaps he has a snake fetish, but those feelings won't last. Those feelings aren't love."

"Love isn't a feeling," Euryale said. "It's something you do. Something you promise."

"And when he chooses to abandon you, what will you call that? Is that love, too?"

"Quiet!" Euryale said as she strained against the bars. Her breathing deepened, and her heart pounded. Her tongue pricked against sharpened fangs, and she could feel her nails grow an extra inch.

"Ah, there it is," Aphrodite said. "My words are getting through, aren't they?"

"Leave," Euryale growled.

"I'm going. I'm going," Aphrodite replied with amusement. "When you've settled a bit and decide you want me to end all this, let me know. Happiness is but one sweet divorce away."

Ares sprinted through the woodland terrain and darted behind a boulder. Dirt, rock, and bits of plant debris kicked up on all sides as bullets whizzed by and tore into the landscape. Individually, Ares regarded them as mere nuisance. But the heavy incoming fire that nipped his skin threatened to sap his strength should it go on for another hour or two. And the last thing Ares wanted to do was take a small break to catch his wind. Not when there were still a good three or four dozen men to kill.

"You fight like babies," he called out, wiping his bloody spear on the ground. "What will you do now, cowards, since your rifles cannot save you?"

The distinct sound of a turbine engine drew Ares' attention. He turned around as one of Alex's steel beasts came crashing through the foliage. Ares thought he overheard someone call it a tank, or a Patton. Regardless of what its name was, Ares had now faced a half dozen such monsters, and he was not impressed with them in the least.

"Bring it on, little mortal," Ares whispered, crouching as the tank leveled its 105mm cannon at his position.

As if responding to the god's taunt, the tank fired, flame and smoke spewing from its barrel. Ares leapt high into the air, grinning to himself, as the shell slammed into the ground where he had been. His leap carried him the full distance to the tank, and before it could run or fire a second shot, Ares tore into its armored hide. He wrenched the tracks from the tank's wheels and bent the cannon into a perfect L-pipe. Then, like all the others he had destroyed, he picked it up and sent it flying.

The tank hit the ground and rolled. Flame poured from the openings, and sparks and bullets flew in all directions. A moment later, the tank exploded.

Ares crouched and looked for his next victim, but none could be seen. The battlefield was silent, strangely so. He could no longer hear the fearful beats of hearts, nor whispers of panic between frightened soldiers. He could not even smell their sweat-soaked bodies. Had they admitted defeat? Fled the field in cowardice? Taken their own lives to avoid capture?

Ares stood tall and proud. "Who else shall test his might against me?"

No one answered the challenge. Thus Ares headed back to where he had left Alex, hoping the mortal would still provide him with some sport.

"Oh, god, Alex, please be alive."

Alex, flat on his back and wracked with pain, craned his head up and to the right to see who was calling to him. It turned out to be a pale, wide-eyed, Jessica standing over him with a trembling body.

"I'm alive," he said as she dropped to her knees at his side. "Can't move very well, though."

"Save your strength," she said. Tears stained her cheeks, and she eased his head down and stroked his hair. She snorted and looked at the sky before laughing out of grief. "I never thought I'd have this conversation, not with you, at least."

"About what?"

"All the things I should say," she whispered. "Want to say."

"As much as I'd love to milk a deathbed confessional out of you, don't worry. I'll live."

"Did you miss the fact that half your blood is on the rocks?"

"Hades said all this will heal by morning, somehow," he replied. "Can you get me to my feet?"

Jessica pulled an olive satchel with a red cross off her back. She emptied its contents on the ground and sifted through the bandages, needles, thread, rubber tubing, and tape before finding a small pack of morphine syrettes. "Found this off a dead corpsman," she said as she stuck him with the needle. "Thought it might come in handy."

"I thought you were going to stay back where it was safe."

"I thought you were going to win," she said. "I wanted pictures."

"Stupidly dangerous," Alex said as his arm warmed and started to numb.

"Hush. I wasn't in any more danger than any other wartime photographer," she said. When Alex raised an eyebrow, she capitulated his point. "Okay, it was dangerous. But god, look at you. You can't tell me you'd rather be alone right now."

"Not particularly," he said.

"Exactly. Anyway, I have no idea how your arm is supposed to heal," she said. "And I can see your shin bone in your left leg, too. Can't imagine what all that feels like, and honestly, I don't want to know."

"Give me some more morphine and I'd call it a hair less painful than what I imagine childbirth is like."

Jessica stuck him with another syrette before taking a tourniquet and cinching it down around what was left of his shoulder. "I said I didn't want to know."

Alex sucked in a breath and grit his teeth as another wave of agony washed over him. When it was over, he managed a weak smile as he looked at her. "You've got quite the stomach for this. Surprised you're not puking everywhere."

"I'm not the one that puked in anatomy class. You were," she said, patting his head.

"I think that was understandable given we were watching a video where they peeled off some guy's face."

"That was so cool."

"That was so not. Look, I'm glad you came and glad you helped, but you should go now. It's not safe here."

"The hell I will," she said. "No one is going to pry me away from you and make you spend the night alone—not in the shape you're in."

Alex, without the strength to argue, closed his eyes and distracted himself from the pain by focusing on Jessica's angelic touch as she stroked his head. The bliss he found, however, did not last long.

"Up, little Alex," came the command, but not from Jessica. No, Alex knew that rough voice all too well know. It belonged to Ares.

Alex opened his eyes, and with Jessica's help, he managed to sit upright. "I want my wife back."

"You and your army are in tatters," Ares said. He ran a finger across his grime-covered forehead and showed it to Alex. "I bathe in the blood of your men. The day is hardly yours."

"The day isn't over yet," said Alex. Had he been of right mind, he might have thought better of such a challenge. There was no telling what Ares might do if he thought the battle was still on. But since the morphine was clouding his brain, the reply rolled right off his tongue without a second thought.

Ares smiled and shook his head. "It is for you, Alex." The god planted his spear in the ground, stuck his fingers in his mouth, and whistled sharply. Alex's ponies, still drawing their chariot, appeared in the distance. "Tomorrow we shall battle again," Ares said, watching the ponies approach. "For your sake, I hope you offer more of a challenge."

"He'll be lucky if he can walk with crutches in a month, let alone pick up a gun," Jessica said, putting a protective hand on Alex's shoulder.

"A body of Hades needing a month to heal?" the god said, chuckling. "You'll be good as new by nightfall, mark my words."

The ponies arrived, and Alex put his arm across the back of Jessica's shoulders. "Help me up," he said, his eyes locked on the chariot. "We've work to do."

"Yes, Alex," said Ares with a dark tone. "You've much work to do. But there's something you should know before tomorrow comes."

Alex, now on his feet, sighed and shook his head. "Always something," he muttered. "What is it?"

"To the victor go the spoils," Ares said, holding up Hades' scepter. "Since I won this day, this shall be my prize."

"No!" Alex cried out, lunging, tumbling forward as he did. Thankfully, Jessica caught him before fell completely. "That's not yours."

"Take it from me," said Ares, folding his arms across his chest. When Alex couldn't meet challenge, the god nodded curtly and began to walk away. "Rest well, Alex," he said over his shoulder. "Tomorrow we'll see if you can gain back your wife and your precious scepter."

CHAPTER TWENTY

Alex sat in a folding chair under a cloudless sky, deep within his remaining army's camp and sighed. He already longed for days that weren't filled with the crack of rifles, explosions from mortars, and severing of arms by god-thrown spears. He longed for days that filled him with joy, not those that sapped his strength and taxed his body. In short, he longed for the war to be over and for Euryale to be at his side once more. At least the words Ares had spoken were true. Alex's arm and leg had all but fully healed. There was some stiffness in both, but they worked. At least that was something.

"Shouldn't you be preparing for tomorrow?" Athena asked, glancing over the book she was reading. She sat near a campfire, and thus far, hadn't said much except to wish Jessica well when she trotted off to photograph the night sky.

"This helps me think," he replied as he licked and sealed an envelope and then used a small ribbon to tie it to a balloon. With his left hand he held the ribbon tight, letting the envelope dangle below as the balloon tugged toward the stars. When the wind was right, he gave the letter a quick kiss and let it go.

Athena raised an eyebrow at the sight. "How many is that?"

"Forty-eight." Alex checked the near-empty bag at his side. Only one balloon remained inside. "No, forty-nine."

"Hallmark card?"

"Yeah," he said as he grabbed the last balloon. "Took the chariot out a couple of hours ago and picked up some things. Hallmark cards, balloons, Jessica's laptop, some more beef jerky."

"You bought beef jerky?" she asked with surprise.

"Want a piece?" he said, reaching into a plastic bag and pulling out a stick of *Hot-N-Tuff*. "This is the granddaddy of jerk right here."

"No, thank you," Athena replied. "But getting back to the balloons, of all your ideas, I think this is the worst. Worse than the pigeons, even."

Alex paused his balloon making. "How else am I supposed to talk to Euryale? It's not like Ares will let me waltz in and see her. There's no phone or internet. I would've tried pigeons, but I'm not sure how they work, let alone where to buy some. Thus, I'm using something that's cheaper and easier to manage—i.e. balloons."

"Delivery method aside," Athena said, "flooding your wife with impersonal cards isn't the way to do it."

Alex huffed and stuck a piece of beef jerky in his mouth like a cigar and slowly chewed on the end. His taste buds exploded in a deluge of spicy goodness. Sure, it brought a few tears to his eyes, but they were good tears. Tears that celebrated the perfect jerk. However, his state of masticating bliss didn't last. His thoughts soon returned to the war, Euryale, and her continued absence. Frustrated, Alex grabbed a nearby stone and threw it into the campfire. "I'm sick of this."

"Please don't do that," Athena said, lowering her book. "You're disturbing the light and there's no moon out. Selene took the night off and Artemis isn't covering for her."

Alex grunted. "This isn't fun, not that it ever was."

"It's day one and you're already turning in the towel?" she said, rolling her eyes. "Absence makes the heart grow fonder. You should be taking this opportunity to develop your romantic side."

"No, absence drives you crazy is what it does." Alex did have another, a more vulgar and insulting response, one that would challenge her knowledge of anything romantic, but he chose to keep it to himself, for his liver's sake. Despite his verbal self-constraint, his knew his face soured, mirroring his thoughts. Fortunately, Athena had returned to her own reading and took no note.

The conversation ground to a halt, and for several more minutes, Alex stewed about the current state of affairs in silence. Finally, he groaned out of frustration. "That's it," he said as he took to his feet and brushed himself off. "I'm done. I'm done. I can't take this anymore. Everyone knows I can't beat him. I'll surrender and be done with it. I'll admit I cheated, even if I didn't, and give into whatever demands he wants."

"What if he wants you to leave Euryale?" Athena said, looking at him disapprovingly. "You going to give her up too to avoid a little pain?"

"A little? I got pulverized out there today!"

"And lived to tell the tale. You'll do better next time."

"He has my scepter," Alex replied. "That means no more army, and no immortality for me anytime he chooses. He can literally break me anytime he wants."

"That does complicate things on your end. But if I were you, I'd consider what 'whatever he wants' might entail."

"Euryale will understand," he said. "She wouldn't want me to be pounded into jelly on her account. Besides, it's not like we can't get back together after this is all through."

"Unless those are the terms of your surrender."

"Ugh!" Alex threw up his hands. "Why are you pushing this doom and gloom scenario so much?"

Athena closed her book, keeping a finger to mark her place. "Because if you're going to ruin an experiment this quickly, I don't want you to have any excuse afterward as to what the consequences might or might not be."

"Experiment?" Alex said, unsure if he heard her right. "What are you on about?"

"What does it matter?" Athena said, returning to her book. "You obviously don't love your wife if you're giving up after the first day."

"You stole my wife to see if I'd try and get her back?"

"Ares stole your wife, Alex. I'm merely observing," Athena said.

"This is why you won't help?"

"I can't falsify the data. I need to see if the match I made is the real deal," she said. "By the way, you're really starting to give the name Alex a bad reputation."

Alex set his jaw and clenched both of his fists at his side. "Oh I am, am I?"

"Yes, you are," she said. "You'd be much more likeable if you followed in the footsteps of Alexander of Macedon. Do you have any idea how much of the world he conquered by the time he was thirty-two?"

"I bet he wasn't fighting a war against Ares so some stupid goddess could feel good about herself."

Athena placed her book down and took to her feet. Her march around the campfire was stopped when Alex took to his and the two squared off. "Do we need another lesson, Alex?" she said, jabbing him in the chest with two fingers and narrowing her eyes. "I thought you knew better than to make such careless remarks."

"Threaten me all you like," Alex replied, keeping his defiant tone. "But it won't change the truth. Dismissing my suffering—my wife's suffering—as some grand test isn't a scholarly pursuit of wisdom. It's for your own selfish ego, and it's positively evil."

Athena stepped forward and pushed him into his chair. "Let's get something very clear, Alex. You are in no position to make any judgments about anything I do."

Alex opened his mouth to speak, but with Athena towering over him, he opted to shut it and remain silent.

"Perhaps some clarification is in order," she went on with a smirk. "Were you around when man was fashioned or Elysium was made?"

"Of course not."

"Then certainly you can pull the sun across the sky," she added as she circled him. "Or did you bind the Titans with the greatness of your strength?"

Alex shook his head. He didn't need a map to see where this was headed.

"Did you slay Argus? Tame Cerberus? Undoubtedly you've done something to warrant this attitude of yours," she said, drumming her fingers on folded arms. "By all means, boast of your accomplishments and take your rightful place amongst the Olympians if your deeds are as great."

"I spoke out of frustration," he said, choosing his words carefully. He despised her chiding nature, and though the temptation to argue was still there, he decided that at best all he could win was a Pyrrhic victory. It was time to get back on track. It was time to save his wife. "I've done none of those things, but you ask the impossible of me. You can't expect me to hear any of this and not be angry."

"The only thing I expect you to do, Alex, is to beat my brother and rescue your wife," Athena said. The unyielding tone eased in her voice, and the goddess took a step back. "Whether or not you have the desire to do so, is up to you."

"Beat him without your help," added Alex.

"Yes, without my help," she said.

"I have an idea," Jessica said as she stepped into the circle of firelight. When Alex and Athena turned toward her, both surprised at her arrival, she smiled and went on. "Sorry, I kept quiet when you two were arguing since I didn't want to catch a stray curse."

"See, Alex? Here's a mortal I like. She knows who's in charge," Athena said.

Alex forced the tension out of his back and neck as he let the goddess's statement go. "What's your idea, Jessica?"

"Well, since you're fighting Ares, I thought Hephaestus might be willing to help."

Alex dropped his eyebrows, not following her logic. "Why would he?"

"You never did read your mythology," Jessica said with a huff. "Ares and Aphrodite had an affair. Hephaestus was none too pleased when he found out."

For the first time since his last encounter with the God of War, Alex's face lit up with hope. "You think he'd want revenge?"

Jessica shrugged. "Worth a shot."

"Think he could actually make me something to take Ares down?"

"He could make you a banana that would take him down," Jessica said before snatching a piece of jerky from Alex's pouch. "He's the God of Smiths, after all. I'm sure in that magical forge he can make anything into a weapon of legends."

Alex chuckled as a thought came to him. "A banana?"

"I think you'd want something other than a banana," Jessica said.

"I'm not planning to attack him with fruit," he said, "but that did give me an idea."

"Care to elaborate?"

"Yeah, give me a sec." Alex ducked inside his nearby tent, rummaged through the contents of a small chest, and returned to the campfire with parchment and quill in hand.

Though Athena's anger seemed to have subsided upon his return, her sarcasm had not. "Going to pen an epic poem?" she asked.

"No," he stated. "I'm going to challenge Ares to a duel."

Athena and Jessica watched as Alex penned the letter. On the scroll he wrote:

To Ares, son of Zeus, God of War and lord of battle, from Alexander Weiss, husband of Euryale.

In the light of this drawn-out campaign, I offer that all matters between the two of us be settled by manner of individual combat, to take place tomorrow morning at 9:00 a.m. in the arena.

Athena took it from him and read it over. When she finished, she handed it back and regarded him with an arched eyebrow. "Since we all know you will never defeat Ares in one-on-one combat, why don't you indulge our curiosity as to what you are planning."

"Let me see if he agrees first. Otherwise it's pointless," Alex said. He then gave a sharp, three-note whistle, and before he could draw another breath, Hermes stood before him, jogging in place. "I have a message for Ares," Alex said. "If you would be so kind as to deliver it for me, I would be eternally grateful."

Hermes took the letter and glanced over Alex's shoulder. "That's a nice tent you have. Real nice."

"Don't even think about it."

Athena chuckled.

Alex didn't.

Hermes tucked the letter away and smiled. "Only a comment." The messenger god took a deep bow and left. Less than two minutes later, he returned with letter in hand. "Reply for a one Alexander Weiss, sign here."

Alex took the parchment and looked at the reply:

Weapons?

"He'll never agree to anything modern, if that's what you're planning," Athena said after she read over his shoulder. "And even if he did, I'm certain he'd still beat you."

"Maybe you should insist on Ares having a handicap and forcing him to use a banana," Jessica suggested.

"I'm going to use a pineapple," Alex replied as he wrote his reply. "Ares can use whatever he wants."

Jessica tilted her head. "A pineapple?"

"Yes. A pineapple."

To Alex's surprise, Athena patted his shoulder. "Clever, Alex," she said. "Very clever indeed. Skirting on deceitful, but within the rules, I think. I suppose it can't be held against you that my brother refuses to read a little history and know what's what."

"Thanks." Alex handed his letter over to Hermes once more, and Hermes, in turn, left and came again before anyone could say *Parthenopeus*. Alex read through the final exchange and then set his mind to the task at hand. "Well, I guess I need a pineapple now."

"He agreed to the terms?"

Alex looked at the letter again to make sure he hadn't misinterpreted it. "I'm assuming. There's a smiley face at the bottom. So I should go."

"We should go," Jessica said.

"He lives in a volcano, right?" Alex said. "I think you should sit this one out since you don't have an immortal body, and I'd rather not see your face melt."

"Point taken," Jessica said, plopping down in her folding chair. "Have fun, and try not to fall in any lava."

Alex kicked the ash off his winged sandals. Looming in front of him was the volcano of Hephaestus, stretching high into the night sky. It was the sole occupant of some nameless island in the middle of the sea. From its top, great columns of smoke made their way into the heavens, and deep within its belly came the rhythmic sounds of a hammer striking an anvil. In the back reaches of his mind, Alex wondered if this was such a good idea after all.

Alex picked his way up the side of the volcano, pausing every so often as it rumbled. He ignored the strong smell of sulfur, and while a large part of his brain prayed that there would be no sudden eruption, a small part—the useful part that insisted on his survival by considering all points—reminded him that spewing lava wasn't the only method a volcano had that could do a person in. Case and point, poisonous fumes were just as lethal, and a gasmask wasn't part of his usual personal belongings.

Thankfully, no eruption took place, and no noxious clouds poured forth. Alex eventually found himself at the mouth of a dark cave. He entered, and after fumbling in the dark and procuring several new bruises on his shins and head, he emerged from the tunnel and found the forge he sought.

On the other side of the chamber stood Hephaestus with a hunched back and a withered, twisted leg. Powerful arms slaved away at the hammer and anvil. Upon Alex's entry, Hephaestus snorted and stopped his work. "Alex, Alex, Alex," he said. "You dare rob me in my very presence?"

Alex swallowed hard and wished he had brought a drink. Nothing too strong, mind you, but enough to calm his nerves. Maybe a keg or two of mead, as he could then share it and break the tension. Blacksmiths were keen on mead. That much Alex knew. At least, he corrected, according to a number of books and movies that depicted their alcoholic preferences, they were keen on the stuff. But without any drink to offer either himself or Hephaestus, Alex was forced to get straight to the point. "Rob? No," he said. "I was hoping you would fashion a weapon for me. A unique one at that."

Hephaestus flipped the hammer in his hand, end over end. "Yes, yes. That's what they all say. Make us a weapon and never mind what we're doing while your back is turned. Never mind at all."

"No, no, that's not it at all." Alex threw up his hands defensively. "I need your help—"

"Silence!" Hephaestus yelled. He picked up a glowing steel bar in his bare hands, turned it over, and held it out for Alex to see. It was about three inches wide, tapered and curved at one end. "They lust for my wife. Their desire burns hotter than any bar in my forge. We know this well. All of us down here."

"I would do no—"

But as quickly as the words came out, Hephaestus stepped forward, and Alex shut his mouth. Despite the god's limp, Alex did not doubt the divine strength that rippled throughout the god's arms and chest. "I can smell her on you," he said, leaning close. "Even the forge cannot cover such a thing. They think the outcast knows nothing. That they can do whatever they please and I'll be none the wiser. You, Alex, are not near as clever as they. I know you want her. I know you've been with her. Insult me no more."

"I'm only here to save Euryale," Alex blurted out, terrified what the god might do next. "Please believe me, I would never pursue another man's wife."

"Believe you?" Hephaestus said, pointing and laughing at Alex. "With one breath we lie to my face, and the other we whisper sweetness into her ears."

"I am not stupid enough to try and deceive you," Alex said. He hoped a new line in the conversation would pan out better. And if it didn't, he hoped he might be able to at least talk his way out in one piece. "Your perception is as strong as the anvil you use."

"Yes, yes it is. Deceit is not something you can craft, is it?" Hephaestus backed off and eyed Alex with newfound respect. "Do you know what this will become?" he asked, nodding to the brightly glowing piece of metal.

"No," Alex replied. He glanced to the walls where countless numbers of arms and armor hung, hoping to find the answer, but none seemed to match. "Cow tools?"

Puzzlement crossed Hephaestus's face. "Cow tools?"

"I don't know," Alex said, wondering what he was thinking as well. "It was the first thing that came to me."

Hephaestus murmured his disappointment and put the bar down. "Go. Leave me be. I have work to do."

"I can't leave empty handed," Alex said, bordering on begging. "I need your help to save my bride and my sanity."

"Your bride? Your bride!" Hephaestus spun around and threw his hammer. End over end it flew until it struck the far wall, carving out a portion of rock. "You would have me save your marriage as if I have no problems with my own? Tell me, Alex, why are your problems my concern? Tell me, or I shall not intend to miss with my second throw."

Alex picked himself off the ground, glad the god had not separated his head from his shoulders. "They are not your problems," Alex admitted. "But you know what it's like not to have your wife at your side. I'm asking that you might have some compassion for my predicament, especially since I face Ares in the morning. I need you to craft a pineapple for me. You're my only hope."

Hephaestus's anger faded and the corner of his mouth drew back. "Ares, you say? You seek to defeat him?"

Going by the expression on the god's face, Alex dared to hope Jessica's prediction would prove true. "I do."

"Humiliation..." the god's voice trailed. His face grew brighter until it outshone the fires at his back. "Are you ready for his anger, mortal?"

"Probably not," Alex replied. "But I haven't a choice at this point. I've already issued my challenge."

"He thinks he is clever, lusting my wife while believing I'm not paying attention." The god limped across the forge till he stood next to Alex. "We trapped them once," he said taking a golden, chain-linked net that hung on the wall. He held it up for Alex to see before giving it a tug. The net disappeared in the blink of an eye. "Stronger than any god, and unable to be seen," he said. "Yes, yes. This worked well, but not well enough. Maybe it is time to show them all what we are capable of."

"Does this mean you'll help me?" asked Alex.

Hephaestus hung the invisible net back on the wall at which point it reappeared, its golden links catching the forge's light. "Indeed we will, Alex. Indeed we will. After this is done, we will be great friends. Trusted friends, that is, but you must promise to come see us again."

"Help me win back my bride, and we'll visit often."

"Do you promise?"

"I do," said Alex.

"Swear by the River Styx, will you?"

"Whatever oaths are needed," Alex said. "But I don't even know what that means."

"Gods that swear by the River Styx and break their oaths lose their immortality," said Hephaestus. "Those who are not divine fare far, far worse."

"Sounds serious."

The corners of Hephaestus's lips drew back. "Which is why we insist you swear such things."

"If you help me, I swear by the River Styx I will not forget what you've done for me and will visit often, fate willing."

"Good, good. We are lonely here and will enjoy your company." The God of Smiths limped his way back to the anvil before continuing. "Promises, Alex, are not to be given lightly. I will hold you to them, but now that we are friends, tell me about this pineapple of yours so that I might fashion one without rival."

CHAPTER TWENTY-ONE

Two minutes before nine in the morning, Alex waited in a small alcove inside the stadium for his duel with Ares to begin. He could hear the roar of the mythological crowd above him, eager to see what this contest would bring. Tension mounted in his shoulders and neck, and he tried—unsuccessfully—not to think about how half-baked and desperate his plan really was.

"I think you've got a good shot at this," Jessica said, massaging his shoulders. "But you've got to loosen up. You freeze out there, and you're dead."

"Right now, I'm giving my odds of success at about seven hundred and twenty-five to one," he admitted.

Jessica slipped around to his front, keeping her hands on him as she did. "Everything like we practiced, yes? Think of it like any other performance you've done. You'll be fine."

"I hope you're right."

"I am and you'll see." She hugged him tight. "When this is done and you're even more famous than before, don't forget me, okay?"

"I've never forgotten you."

"Me either," she said, tightening her embrace. She held it for a couple heartbeats longer than he'd have guessed. When she finally pulled away, her eyes had a sheen to them. "I mean it, though. I'd like to see you again before another decade or two passes. Since I can't exactly come visit you at your new house with your new wife, you're going to have to come see me, you know?"

"I'll be looking forward to it. I promise."

A loud voice, muffled but strong, carried over the crowd's noise, and their energy grew tenfold. Jessica sighed longingly. "Your wife's a lucky girl," she said before kissing him lightly on the cheek. "Not many would willingly face a god for someone they've known only a short while. Now go, before I keep you for myself."

Alex laughed and slipped free of her grasp. Though her tone was playful, he wondered if he detected a hint of seriousness to what she said, and then wondered if it wasn't her, but him, that wanted what she said to be true. Before he could will himself to pursue the topic, trumpets blasted. "I guess we're starting," he said. "Any last-second words of advice?"

"Yeah, look good for the camera," she said, holding up her Nikon. "Might as well finish this adventure of yours with drama and style."

"Will do."

With that, Alex dashed out of the alcove and into the center of the Olympians' arena, his helm in one hand and a small sack in the other. The sun was bright, the weather perfect, and the stadium was filled. Most of the spectators kept their conversations to themselves, but a few offered the occasional jeer or bit of encouragement to Alex for undertaking such a risky endeavor.

"So, this is it then," Alex said loudly enough for both the crowd and his opponent to hear. "If I win, I get my bride and scepter back, and you leave us alone. If you win, then I surrender to whatever terms you offer and admit to wrongdoing at the Olympic games."

Ares, who stood a dozen paces away, thumped his bare chest. "I agree to your terms, Alex," he said. "You are brave, more so than my sister, who hides behind her legions and plays games on boards. It will be a shame to destroy you."

"I'll hate to be destroyed," said Alex.

"How do you want to mark the victor?" Ares asked. "First blood?"

Alex shook his head. "How about first killing blow? For a mortal that is. We both seem to be able to take a little more punishment than normal."

"It's not my fault I am the strongest and toughest," said Ares. "Why should I handicap myself?"

Alex shrugged nonchalantly. "I figured you were skilled enough to not need the extra help."

Ares' eyes narrowed. "Fine," he said. "Whoever scores the first blow that would kill a mortal shall win."

"Are you ready?" asked Alex. He loosened the string that kept his sack tied, pulled out his pineapple, and gave it a small toss in his hand for good measure. It was a little heavier than he had expected, weighing perhaps a pound, give or take.

Ares pointed at him with his spear. "What is that in your hand? What manner of trickery have you brought?"

Alex tried to look as innocent as possible. "No trickery. It's a pineapple, as I said."

"I know what a pineapple is, and that is not one."

"What else would it be?" Alex said. Though he felt like his nerves were under control, he hoped his voice did not betray him. Using an old pianist trick, he tried to picture his opponent naked. Sadly, Ares seemed as scary naked as he did dressed in a loincloth.

Ares extended an open hand. "It looks more like a rock than a fruit. Let me see it."

"It *is* more like a rock than a fruit; a painted rock at that." Alex hid the pineapple behind his back and took a deep breath. Confidence. "I'm not about to let you play with it. You'll probably break it and then where will I be?"

"Dead."

"Yes, dead," Alex said. "And despite what you say it is, where I come from, we call these rocks, pineapples. So let's begin, or are you scared of rocks now?"

Ares glared. "Your people are strange, indeed."

Alex shrugged.

Ares charged, the point of his spear leading the way.

It was a half-hearted attempt, even Alex could see that, but it was more than enough to send Alex scrambling. Whether Ares' motive was to probe his reactions or to simply toy with him, Alex wasn't sure. What he was sure of was that he would not survive a real attack. He needed to stall. He needed distance. "That was fun."

Ares bounced on his feet and twirled the spear over his head. "Your reflexes are sharp," he said. "With some training, you would make a fine warrior."

"Seems like I already have to be." Alex took a few steps back. Hephaestus had mentioned that he should be at least ten paces away, preferably fifteen or twenty. That, above everything else, was paramount. Alex wasn't about to test otherwise.

Again, Ares charged, and again, his actions seemingly had no other purpose than to send Alex running. The God of War took a break from his assault and rested his spear on his shoulder. "You run like a frightened rabbit. Are you going to cower all day? For my sake, at least, put some sport into this."

Alex hopped backward and wriggled his nose. He wasn't sure how convincing of a part he played, but with some luck, the theatrics would mask his intentional retreat. "You wouldn't happen to know where I could find a carrot or two?" he asked as he put two more steps between himself and the god. "I'm a touch hungry."

"You should eat before battle," Ares replied, stepping forward. Ares shifted his grip on his spear. It didn't mean much to Alex on its own, but when the god lowered his stance, he suspected that playtime was about to end.

"There's one thing you should know before you come at me," Alex said.

"What would that be?"

"This!" he shouted as he sprang into action. With one swift motion, he pulled a small, metal ring from the top of his pineapple and gave the weapon a heave. It sailed through the air, landing with a dull thud and making a quaint impact crater in the sand.

Ares picked up the missile and snorted. "Your aim is abysmal."

Alex, who had been counting in his head, dropped to the ground and covered his head. A split second later, the mark two fragmentation grenade, affectionately known as a pineapple by those who once threw them, exploded in Ares' face.

Ares decided that having a 20th century hand grenade detonate in his face was a disagreeable experience. Moreover, Ares felt torn from it all. On the one hand, he thought that Alex had been deceitful and should be ripped limb from limb several times over. But on the other, Ares had to admit that there was an underlying bit of fun in seeing something so small explode with such force. And if tossing these sorts of pineapples back and forth was how man now waged war, he could see the appeal.

Ares also decided that he would have to wait for another time to give the notion some more thought. At this moment, there were more pressing matters. Ares was lying on Aphrodite's bed, arms crossed over his chest while the goddess leaned over him, picking pieces of shrapnel out of his face. It was a painful, bloody affair that would have ruined any normal pair of sheets, but Aphrodite's stainless bed set had been tailor-made to accommodate her eclectic sex life.

"Fruit, a mighty foe." Ares balled his fists as Aphrodite dug into his right cheek. "How is such power trapped in such a tiny thing?"

Aphrodite stroked his cheek. "That wasn't a real pineapple, my love. Not in the fruit sense, at least."

"Yes, I know." He winced as another metal fragment came free. "When we get done here, I will shatter the mortal's body time and again. I will make him tell me all he knows about these pineapples and from whence they grow. And when I tire of hearing his cries, I'll have him push a boulder for eternity. No, I'll strap him to a wheel of fire. Or better yet, torture him with insatiable thirst and hunger."

Aphrodite kissed his forehead and dabbed his wounds with a wet cloth. "All of those have been done before. Do try and be original."

"Fine. I'll do all three."

"You'll do no such thing," she snapped. Her voice was as sharp as the shrapnel in his face. "We're in enough trouble with you losing that duel. How could you do something so stupid?"

"Do not lecture me." Ares pushed her hands away from his face and sat up. "And what nonsense is this 'we' you speak of?"

"*We* yearn for the same pleasure. Or have you forgotten?"

"The punishment of Alex?"

Aphrodite scowled, pushed Ares back down on the bed and began cleaning his wounds once more. "No, my dear." Her voice dripped with impatience. "Alex is a play toy, nothing more. We both yearn for Athena's humiliation and the restoration of my honor. Have you forgotten these things already?"

"Alex is more than a play thing," Ares said. "Twice now he has cheated me out of my rightful victory. I may have to return his wife, but that doesn't mean I can't torment him until time's end."

Aphrodite, to his surprise, leaned over and kissed him softly on the lips. "You needn't return his bride. We're far from beaten."

Ares' brow furrowed. As much as he tried to understand why she said what she did, he could not follow. "The contest was binding. I must."

Aphrodite pulled the last fragment out of his face and placed it in a clay bowl with the others. "I think I have a way around that, love," she said, running her fingers along the sides of his face. "That is, of course, if you are willing to do me a tiny favor."

Ares rolled over, locked his eyes with hers and flashed a wry grin. "If I am blessed with your company tonight, I am yours to command."

Aphrodite placed her fingers on his lips. "Quiet," she said. "Work first and then play. You only have to return Alex's bride if the contest stands. But, if someone were to have it annulled..."

Ares shook his head. "Father is the only one who can make that judgment, and he's not likely to grant me such a kindness while Alex has so many other gods favor him."

"Ye of little faith," Aphrodite said. "Go to Father and tell him how Alex is both a liar and deceiver, and that the weapons you agreed to for the duel are not the weapons he brought to battle. Throw a tantrum if you must—you're good at that—but don't let up until Father agrees the contest was unfair. Mother caught him with a maiden again and she's been relentless. I promise he's in no mood to argue over a human."

Ares raised a clenched fist in the air. "Then I can tear him limb from limb."

"Yes, my love," Aphrodite said as she stroked his hair. "But do not wipe him out. I only want you to send him running, licking painful wounds."

"To what end?"

"To the end that Alex must leave his wife when he feels he will never beat you," she instructed. "He must not fall while he fights for Euryale, lest he be an icon of tragic romance."

"I care not for such silly things."

"I do!" she snapped. "I swore by the River Styx his life and freedom would not be harmed while he was tested. Even if I hadn't, Athena would gloat to the Fates and back if her one and only pet project ended in such fashion."

"Fine, I shall do as you wish," Ares said, capitulating to his lover's desire. He did so, partly because he understood what she was driving at, but mostly because he wanted to spend the night with her and figured it was a good way to get in her dress.

CHAPTER TWENTY-TWO

Free from Zeus's congratulations and Athena's never-ending, post-battle conversation, Alex flew home as fast as his little winged sandals would carry him, his heart overjoyed and his mind hoping he'd beat the thunderstorm that was now brooding. He replayed the battle in his mind dozens of times and relished every second of it, from the way he had nimbly darted about the arena floor, to the expression on Ares' face an instant before the grenade had exploded. Most of all, however, he relished the fact that this would mark the end of the two-day war and the return of his bride. All that he needed to do was get home, clean up, and make the place presentable before Euryale arrived.

When he got home, however, all was not as he expected. The cave was swept, the vegetation cut, and the oil lamps were lit. Near the fire pit was a small, oak table that had a trio of identical places set, each with a succulent lobster on a bed of pasta, surrounded by scallops, and paired with a glass of chardonnay.

"Hi, Alex," Jessica said, stepping out of the shadows. A navy dress with a straight neckline and off-the-shoulder cap sleeves graced her body while a simple pearl necklace hung around her neck. "I'm glad you're finally here."

Hints of perfume floated through the air, one with vanilla notes that stirred long dormant memories of his first date with her. As he tried to think of something to say, he could only wonder if she was as love-struck by him as he was of her.

An arm, slender and graceful, slid across Alex's back as Aphrodite came to his side. "Sit, Alex," she whispered into his ear. "We have much to celebrate."

At the sound of the door opening, Euryale jumped off the wooden bench in her cell and grabbed the bars. Having heard of Alex's triumph in the arena not even five minutes ago, she knew her wonderful husband was coming with key in hand, and they would finally be able to enjoy their honeymoon and the rest of eternity together. Somewhere along the way, perhaps they could even rub their victory in Aphrodite's face. The bitch deserved it.

To her confusion, Hermes zipped through the door, his face red with embarrassment. "Addendum on that last message," he said. "Afraid I got ahead of things. Slight change of plans."

"What do you mean? Alex is still coming, right?"

"Hard to say, or rather, I can't say."

"Why not?"

"Strict instructions from others regarding speculation," he replied.

Euryale shook her head. Of course things weren't finished. She'd been a fool to believe otherwise. She didn't know how, but she knew Ares had succeeded in cheating Alex out of his victory. The thought of having to spend more time in isolation and away from the man she loved only further brewed the anger growing in her soul. She felt like a caged animal under constant torment who needed to break free. No, who had to break free.

Euryale set her jaw as plans for the future unfolded. She'd escape this prison, raise an army composed of the foulest monsters from the Abyss, creatures that the gods themselves didn't know. She'd take that army, smash through the gates of Olympus, and rip Ares and Aphrodite apart for all to see.

Wanting blood, Euryale rammed the bars with her shoulder three times over. They didn't give at all, and smashing into them hurt, a lot, but she'd be damned to another thousand years of solitude if giving in to that impulse didn't feel good. She repeated the action a few more times, and then when she'd calmed enough for further conversation, she looked at Hermes with narrowed eyes. "What can you tell me?"

"Only that Alex has decided that before coming to see you, he wanted to meet up with some old friends...or rather, an old friend."

Euryale's nostrils flared. "Which friend?"

Hermes shrugged. "Never got the name. Nice looking girl, from what I remember. Kind of a blur though. You know, since I have to keep moving and Aphrodite had other messages that needed to go out. If I'm told more, I'll let you know. Have a good one!"

Before Euryale could question him, the messenger god was gone. Part of her refused to believe his words. Another part tried to reassure her that Alex wouldn't give up after coming so far. A small part, however, a growing part, started plotting her revenge if this friend happened to be who she thought it was.

Ares trotted through the courtyard and into the Great Hall of Olympus. Tapestries hung from towering walls, and the vaulted ceilings were high enough for a crop duster to work with ample room to spare. Five empty thrones lined either side, each shaped out of varying stones and precious metals, each adorned with emblems of the gods and goddesses they were meant for. At the far end, up a rise of seven colorful steps, were two more thrones, far larger and more imposing than the others.

On the left was the seat of Zeus, intricately carved from black marble, decorated with gold, ram's fleece, and a ruby-eyed eagle perched above. To the right sat an ivory throne with a cow-skin cushion and a full moon hanging above. Only one was occupied, the left, and as Zeus there sat, he rested his forehead in his palm while Hera stood in front, apparently taking a momentary pause in her berating.

Ares paused halfway down the hall and waited to be acknowledged.

"This is a private matter," Hera said, not once looking back. "Leave us."

Zeus let out a groan. His fingers clenched one of the armrests and tiny sparks shot forth. "Listen to your mother, Ares," he said with a weary voice. "Two of us need not suffer her rants."

"You'll suffer more than my rants if you don't come clean about this harlot of yours," the goddess hissed. "You've tested my patience enough."

"Mother," Ares dared to speak, his muscles taught and ready to dodge whatever curse she might throw at him. "I have something to say."

Hera spun sharply on her heels. "If this is about your war or the silly games you are playing with Euryale's husband, leave now while you still have a chance. That matter was settled today."

"No, mother," Ares said. "This does not concern Alex. It concerns you both."

Zeus's eyes lifted and his posture straightened. "Speak, my boy. Let us hear about matters of true consequence. I tire of hearsay and speculation."

"Father is innocent of your charges, mother," Ares said, bowing his head. "It was me. I took the girl."

Hera's eyes narrowed, and her gaze remained as spiteful as ever. "You dare suggest my trusted circle would lie to me about what they saw themselves?"

Ares shook his head and hoped her wrath would be contained long enough for the ploy to work. "No, mother," he said. "What they saw was true, but it was not him. The girl would not have me, but found Father pleasing. So, I took his form and tricked her to be with me for the night and the nights after."

"Neither of you are as clever as you would like to believe," Hera said as she crossed her arms and slowly circled her warrior son. Her eyes remained fixed upon him, studying every facet of his expression and every move he made. "When did your father put you up to this?"

"May I be cursed to a thousand years of pacifism if Father knew any of what I'm telling you now. By the River Styx, Father did not put me up to this."

Hera spent a few moments in quiet contemplation, and when such thoughts were finished, she turned and began to walk away. "I'll leave your fate to your father then," she said, never looking back. Three dozen footsteps later, she was gone.

Ares stood, patiently waiting for his father's response, which to his surprise took some time in coming.

"I will not be coerced," said Zeus. "Your actions here give you no power over me."

Ares put up his hands defensively and raised ever so slightly on the balls of his feet. Dodging lightning wasn't as easy as it looked. "I ask only a favor. A small one at that."

Zeus eyed his son. "We should discuss this matter elsewhere, then."

"For privacy?"

Zeus put a sole finger on his lips and began walking.

Ares grinned, knowing his task was complete, and followed him out the door.

"What are you doing here?" Alex said. His heart pounded in his chest, both eager and afraid. His mind, however, was having difficulty coming up with anything of meaning, as his memories felt washed away.

Jessica stood and hurried over before taking his hands in hers. "Long ago we had something," she said. "And before I'm forced to leave you again forever, I need to tell you a few things."

"I don't know what to say," said Alex.

"I don't think she wants you to say anything, Alex," Aphrodite said as she pressed a glass of wine in his hand. "All you need to do is listen."

"I can do that," he said. At this point, however, he was only half listening. His eyes were tracing the contours of Jessica's sides, neck, and shoulders, and his heart loved every second of it. He'd always found her attractive, but never had he been so convinced that the artist who had sculpted her body was nothing short of divine.

"I've got a problem, Alex," she said. Her eyes glanced at the ground before she took and deep breath and continued. "That problem is you."

"What did I do?"

"Everything," she answered, looking up to him with hints of pain. "You amaze me to no end. You're talented, determined. Beat a god not once, but twice, and since my parents moved me away from you, I've always wondered—longed—for what could've been. These last few days only solidified things."

"Those days feel like a lifetime ago and only yesterday at the same time."

"Did you ever think about me?"

"Yes, but—" Alex felt his head spin. Everything about this conversation was everything he had wanted for so long, yet at the same time felt as if it were the worst path he could be treading down. The more he tried to figure out why, the more his head clouded. "This isn't right...I don't think."

Aphrodite put a gentle hand on his forearm. A prickly sensation ran up through his shoulder at which point his chest warmed. "Don't think, Alex. Feel. Feel and open your heart to her."

"My world ended the day you left," he confessed to Jessica. "I poured all that energy and grief into my piano for god knows how many hours and years—probably the only reason I'm as good as I am."

Jessica pulled him close, put her arms around his neck, and whispered, "Then let's stop dancing around these feelings that have lasted a lifetime. Aphrodite can make things right."

"I'd like that," he said before his brow furrowed. There was *something*—a splinter in his mind—that would not stop digging at his conscience. "But there's something not right with this."

Aphrodite rubbed his shoulders from behind and spoke softly in his ear. "I know thoughts of Euryale are still on your mind," she said. "But even now, even with me bringing her up, she's fading."

"My wife..." he said, voice barely audible. He stiffened as he looked straight at Jessica. "I'd run off with you in an instant if I weren't married."

"Married, yes, but not to who you should be," Jessica said. "Come on, Alex, be honest. If half of what I heard about the arrangement is true, you were coerced, even if you did like her."

Alex shook his head, hating how true her words sounded in his ears. "I still agreed. A husband should not back out so quickly. But even if I did divorce her, her father would destroy us both."

"He wants his daughter to be happy," Aphrodite said, leaning in. "As do you. Do you think Athena forcing you together is what's best for you both?"

"Yes." Alex nodded, but knew his sincerity was in want.

"How can you say that when I'm the one who's in front of you?" Jessica said. Her eyes teared, and her voice quivered. "I'm the one who's known you since childhood, who stole your first kiss, your first heart, who's risked life and limb to travel with you through the Underworld. What has she done?"

"Nothing," Alex said. "Because she's been locked away. But she'll be back soon."

Aphrodite guided Alex to the table and gently pressed him into one of the seats. "I don't think you'll want to be standing for this," she said. "Euryale's not coming back. Ares has pled to Zeus, saying you were deceitful in your victory, and Father agreed. Right now, it is as if the contest never was. Euryale is still his captive."

"What? He can't do that!" Alex tried to jump to his feet, but Aphrodite easily kept him down with her hands.

"He can, and he did," the goddess said. When Alex tried to rise a second time, she dropped her face in front of his and spoke sternly. "Look at me, Alex. Is Euryale worth an eternity of war? Because that's how long it will last if you continue down the path you are on. Ares will never stop coming for you. Ever."

Alex sighed and slumped in the chair. That was one thing he felt would always be true. The God of War would always come for him, and he would always suffer by Ares hand, and so would Euryale. Then again, Alex didn't see how being with Jessica would change that, which is what Aphrodite seemed to be insinuating. "If that's true, that's all the more reason I can't be with you," he said to Jessica. "You're mortal. At least Euryale can't be killed while I'm fighting with Ares."

"No, Alex, me being mortal is why you should be with me," she replied, kneeling next to him. "Who will understand you more, Alex, the monstrous daughter of a long-forgotten god, or a human, flesh and blood like you?"

Alex downed his wine before refilling his glass and repeating the process. He wanted to be deaf to her words, but his ears took all of them in. Though he couldn't refute her point, his tongue found a way to argue. "Euryale is counting on me."

"She is," Aphrodite said. "Alex, listen to me. You won't be letting her down. You'll be saving her as you promised."

"How?"

"Dedicate yourself, your love, to Jessica, as it was supposed to be from the start," the goddess replied. "Do that, and I'll intervene on your behalf and make sure Ares, Athena, and even Phorcys leave you alone."

"And Euryale?" he found himself asking. "What of her?"

"I'll mend the wounds to her heart that Athena is responsible for, and then I'll make sure she's with someone perfect for her. Happily ever after doesn't have to be a bedtime story, Alex. I can make it happen for everyone here."

"You can?"

Again, Aphrodite placed a hand on his forearm. Again, tingles raced through his body and his chest warmed. "Look at Jessica and tell her how much you love her."

Truth bubbled from Alex's lips, uncontrolled and in the moment, unwanted. "I don't even know what love means, anymore."

Jessica pressed her lips into his, long and hard. "Then let's figure out what that means, together."

CHAPTER TWENTY-THREE

Athena crested the rise to find Alex, Jessica, and Aphrodite seated around a near-finished meal, drinking wine and laughing. As she approached, Alex began singing André Rieu's lyrics to Ode to Joy. With every note he hit, Athena winced. His German was terrible, and his pitch made her want to drive hydra fangs into her eardrums. When she came up behind him, she knocked him on the back of the head.

"Cease that awful singing at once," she ordered.

Alex turned around, tipping to the side as he did. "Oh, Athena. It's you. Figures you wouldn't like a good rendition of a classic."

"Beethoven would tear his skin apart if he heard the way you hacked that," she replied while hoisting him up. "And that's just your German. I shudder to think what he'd say about the actual quality of your voice."

Alex, now upright, fumbled to keep his balance. "There, I'm up. Happy now?"

"Not particularly. You know how I feel about drunks."

Before she could go on, Alex interrupted her with the most marvelous of ideas. "Hey Athena, you know what would be fun?"

"You sobering?"

"No, Athena. That would not be fun whatsoever. I think that might be one of the least fun ideas you've come up with in a while," he said, shaking his head and then wishing he hadn't. The world spun three times over before it finally stopped. "What would be fun, however, is if you got us another bottle of wine, shared a glass, and then joined in a few Irish drinking tunes. What do you say?"

"Ares lost," Athena said, glaring at her sister. "Whatever you're doing here changes nothing."

"I haven't done anything, dear," she said, leaning back and sipping her wine. "These two have done all the talking. I merely gave the two lovebirds a place to enjoy their company."

"Not if I have anything to say about it," Athena said, fist tightening.

"But you can't. Remember? Part of the rules."

Alex, who'd gone on to staring into Jessica's eyes and holding her hand, perked. "Rules? What rules?"

"Nothing," Athena replied. Her lips pressed together in a fine line as she studied the two mortals in front of her. There were flecks of lipstick on Alex's upper lip, and Jessica's fair skin was slightly flush. It was clear where things had gone, and worse, where they were headed. Still, Athena refused to give up without exploring every facet of this situation. "Tell me, Alex, what do you think Euryale will say when she finds out about this?"

"I don't know," he lamented. "I can only hope she understands and wishes us well."

"Are you telling me you've decided not to love her?" Athena said. When Alex balked, her voice turned venomous. "Go on. Say it. Say you will not love your wife, and that you want to be like Father who runs around on the woman who chooses to love him, despite all his faults and ability to be an ass."

"I..."

When Alex's face twisted in confusion, Athena tilted her head. She drummed her fingers on her side as she wracked her brain to find what was off about the encounter. Then a faint scent teased her senses, and she slowly made her way around the table, concentrating on every aroma and fragrance that came to her.

"What?" Jessica said, looking up at the goddess with equal parts fear and surprise.

"Stand up." Once Jessica had, Athena leaned in so her face was only an inch from where the woman's neck met her shoulder, and she inhaled long and deep. Then she snapped her fingers in Jessica's face. "Snap out of it."

Jessica blinked and rubbed her eyes as if she'd been asleep for half the day and was trying to reconcile the fact she was no longer dreaming. "What's going on?"

Aphrodite shot out of her chair. "No helping!"

"And no working against his liberty," Athena countered. "That includes charms, and you know it."

"I didn't charm him, I merely suggested a perfume she might like to wear."

Athena growled. "This ends now."

"Only if you want to break your oath."

Athena ignored her sister's threats. Not that there wasn't a validity to them, but you don't get to be the Goddess of Wisdom and not know how to skillfully navigate situations that could end in disaster. She marched over to Alex and grabbed him by the shoulders. "Listen up, Alex. I'm going to ask you a few questions, and you're going to answer me, quickly and truthfully. Understand?"

Alex nodded.

"Did you kiss her?"

"Yes."

"Why?"

"I don't know," he said. "The last few hours have been a blur."

Athena cursed under her breath. "Did you have sex with her?"

"No."

"Are you sure?"

Alex nodded again. "I'm sure."

"Have you decided to leave your wife?"

"You know what?" Alex said, a sudden fire springing to life in his body and voice. "I'm really getting sick and tired of everyone being so interested in what I'm doing with Euryale. That should be between me and her, don't you think? Why the hell are you two hammering this so much?"

The muscles in Athena's arms tightened. Though she had the urge to chain him to the slab once more and let Aldora feast on his innards for the next week to bring him back in line, she was both relieved and pleased he still had strong feelings for Euryale. The relationship could be salvaged. Perhaps.

"Well?" Alex asked. "No one's going to tell me?"

Athena and Aphrodite exchanged looks, and Athena was the one to reply. "No. No one is going to tell you. But you know what? That doesn't matter. What I want for you to do is stop whining about it and get your shit together."

"My shit together?"

"Yes, your shit together," she repeated. "Granted things for you are fubar—"

"Wait, what?" Alex interrupted. "Fubar? Where the hell are you coming up with this stuff?"

"Fucked Up Beyond All Recognition," Athena explained. "I picked up some of it from my reading. Even if it is crass, it has certain color to it, don't you think?"

"I suppose that's one way to put it."

"Now then, as I was saying, I want you to stop flirting with another woman and act like the husband you ought to be."

"This sounds an awful lot like helping," Aphrodite said.

"I'm not," Athena replied. Try as she might, however, she couldn't hide the nervous edge to her voice. Maybe she had crossed the line. "I'm definitely not helping—certainly no more than you did not affect Alex's liberty. All I'm doing is telling him what I'd like to see."

"You know what I want," Alex said, the fire inside of him raging once more. "I want my love at my side. I want her in my arms. I want to see us together till the stars die off, and I want the world to leave us alone. That's all I've ever wanted."

"The golden question still lingers, Alex," Aphrodite said, sickeningly sweet. "Will you love a gorgon, a monster, who you've barely come to know? Or will you love the girl you grew up with and the one who first stole your heart? Who will you choose?"

"I don't know," he admitted, self-loathing clearly in his voice. "All the warm fuzzies, the happy dreams, and blissful wishes—everything that love is, has, and will always be—vanished since the start of this stupid war. Would I like to love my wife? Damn skippy, but right now, I'm just so damn tired and can't see an end in sight. I'm starting to wonder if Euryale was a happy fling at best, because I'm not feeling the love I thought I had for her."

"It's not a feeling, Alex," Athena replied. "And you can't look to us for the answer since no one can tell you who you love. Not Aphrodite. Not Jessica. Not me. If you don't know what your heart is willing to do, I'm afraid only the Moirae could, and they answer to no one. Not even the gods."

"The who?"

"The Fates," Jessica said. "They're the ones who control everything."

Alex straightened. "The Fates? They're real?"

"Of course they're real," Athena replied. Genuine shock splashed across her face. "You didn't really think you were doing any of this on your own, did you?"

"Well, yes, I did, actually," Alex answered as his face went downcast. "It sort of takes the fun out of, well, everything, doesn't it?"

"We can get into a philosophical discussion later," Athena said. "You need to decide whether you're going to love your wife or not."

"No," he said, shaking his head. "If the Fates are who I need, then it is the Fates who I will see. I have to know where my heart is before I make any decisions. I can only pray they will tell me."

CHAPTER TWENTY-FOUR

Nestled in a gully in the Pindus Mountains, flanked on either side by large pine trees, was the house of the Moirae. To those who were in desperate need of shelter, it would suffice. To those looking to sell a home, it was small, quaint, and had ample opportunity to allow buyers to test their fixer-upper skills. But to Alex, it was just a piece of crap. It stood, barely, at a modest height of ten feet and appeared to be about that in both length and width. The walls were made of sun-dried bricks and the roof of clay tiles, both of which looked like they could scarcely weather a perfect day, let alone any of the elements. But in the end, Alex decided if the three most powerful beings who had ever existed wanted to live in a dump, who was he to say otherwise?

"I need to tell you something," Jessica said as the two disembarked the chariot.

"Something about the Fates?" Alex asked. They'd barely spoken since leaving Euryale's island, and it had been an awkward trip. Alex feared this conversation might prove more so.

"I'm not a homewrecker," she blurted out.

"I know."

"I mean it," she said, this time looking him in the eyes. "After your duel with Ares, Aphrodite came with some perfume, said it was a bonus for taking all those wonderful pictures—which remind me later, I still have to actually print and send—and next thing I know, I'm in dreamland confessing a steady stream of Hallmark cards to you."

"It's fine," Alex said. A twinge of pain ran through him, one that he hid well, one that reminded him that he had loved hearing those sweet words she'd spoken to him. As quickly as that thought came, feelings of guilt smashed into him as well. "Neither of us were ourselves," he added, trying to move on. "Thanks for still wanting to help, though. It would be easy to call it quits after something like that."

"I feel like I need to redeem myself," she said. "And you're still my friend, I hope, and friends don't abandon each other."

They reached the front door without further conversation, and tacked on its warped wood was a small note. Alex plucked it from the iron nail that held it fast and gave it a read:

Dear Alex,

We had to satisfy a chocolate craving, and we'll be back in five. Feel free to come in but kindly have Jessica wait for you outside. It'll be easier for everyone that way. Try not to touch anything.

Yours,
Clotho, Lachesis & Atropos

Alex, perplexed, looked the note over once more, front, back and front again, and then decided to jam a stick of beef jerky from a fresh bag of *Hot-N-Tuff* into his mouth as he pondered what to do. "Well? What do you think?"

Jessica shrugged. "They're the Fates, and I think I should wait here. I honestly can't imagine anyone else worse to cross."

"Point taken," Alex said. He knocked on the door, and when no one answered, he gave it a push and it swung open with little effort. "Hello?" he called out. "You guys home?"

No one replied, and Alex looked down at the note one last time.

P.S. Why are you knocking? We said we were out.

"Now that's creepy," Jessica said, reading over his shoulder.

"Let's hope the creepiness stops there."

Alex stepped through the doorway and once inside, made his way down a long, wide hall, whose sides were crammed with spindles of yarn of every size, make and color. At the other end was a door, much like the first, as it too was misshapen and easily opened, but instead of leading to the outside, this tattered door opened to a large, circular room.

Inside was a tapestry that looked like it could have been the napkin of the Titans' big brother. It was easily thirty feet across and twice as tall. It hung from a domed, mosaic ceiling, open at the top, and the tapestry's frayed, unfinished end was about four feet from the floor. The pattern itself, full of color and repetition on countless levels and scales, looked like a fractal from the Mandelbrot set. The more Alex looked at it, the more he was drawn in, and the more he was drawn in, the greater the urge to reach out and touch it grew. It grew, that is, until a hand grabbed his own.

Alex jumped. At his side was a young girl, fifteen or sixteen, with red hair pulled back into a long pony tail and a half-eaten chocolate bar in hand. She wore a thin, open front dress and carried a distaff in her other hand. "Clotho," she said. "I'm sorry I scared you, but anything else wouldn't have looked as good in the tapestry."

Alex laughed and tried his best to be calm and collected. "I was more startled than scared."

"Lies are not you, Alex. You are scared now," said the woman behind Clotho. She was in her thirties and looked like a mature version of her little sister, though her clothes were far less revealing. She took Alex's hand in hers and gave it a shake. "I am Lachesis, by the way. My sister is rude and fails to give proper introductions. The eldest here is Atropos."

"But you already figured that out," Clotho tacked.

"The note you left helped," Alex admitted. "Having the names on it and all."

Atropos, who was shrouded in a cloak, hunched and supported by a cane, hobbled over to Alex. "Will I like what you're going to say?"

"I'm not sure," Alex said, unnerved. Her face was leathery and wrinkled, and her eyes looked as if they'd lost her soul. "I hope so, but you three already know why I'm here, don't you?"

"We've always known," Clotho said. "We knew before the world was made all that you would do, say, and want. I spun the thread of your life and gave it to Lachesis who measured it out. When the proper length was found, Atropos cut it, signifying the end of your life, and together we wove it into the tapestry."

Before Alex could respond, Lachesis added, "But you don't believe such things. You want proof of our power."

"Will we ever give in to such demands?" Atropos finished.

"Not a demand," Alex said. He wondered what they could do to him if he brought out their anger, and if the gods were wary of the three, he decided he never wanted to find out.

"That was the right decision, Alex," Clotho said with a wink. "But we've had demonstrations in the past, even if they were only for fun. Haven't we?"

"That's all you want, we know," said Lachesis. "You want to see that fate is our creation and the gods bend to our will. You hope that if this is true, we can help you to reunite with your lost love, or rather, find who you can love so you can go to her."

"Yeah, more or less." Alex replied. He felt like he belonged in preschool, having his own thoughts and feelings laid out for him and not being able to articulate them for himself.

Lachesis pulled Alex by the hand to the far side of the tapestry and pointed to a small section. "Look at this thread," she said. "This is your existence. All the other threads it touches are events and moments in your life that have shaped both you and the world. I can make it so you never even were by pulling it loose. Or by shifting it a hair to the side, I can make you have the head of a chicken."

"Will you ever stop your exaggerations?" Atropos said. She shuffled to the two of them and using her cane, gave her sister a whack on the knuckles. "You'll give the poor boy a heart attack and then where will we be?"

"Hush. I'm having some fun at his expense," Lachesis said with a roll of her eyes. She patted Alex on the back and gave him a squeeze. "He's handling it fine."

Alex, however, did not feel fine, and if the rising bile in his throat was handling the situation, he didn't want to see what losing it would be like. "Since we're all on the same page, sort of, are you willing to help me? My request is simple enough."

"You know, Alex," Clotho said as she spun some thread from her distaff to the spindle. "All who came before you sought answers, and all before you left with none. What made you think you'd be any different, especially when it's something so minor?"

"My wife isn't minor to me," he said. "I have to ensure our future together, or at least, a good one for both of us."

"You know nothing of fate," Lachesis rightly pointed out. She took out a small rod and began making measurements against the thread Clotho spun. "Yet you are here, presenting yourself as if you know how it works."

"Please tell me whether I love her or only married out of pressure. That's all I ask."

"Fate has always worked out in the funniest of ways," Clotho said with a smile. "I've told perfectly healthy men that they would die soon, and guess what? They did. It was only the power of persuasion, many a time. They heard something and assumed it to be the end."

Atropos grabbed Alex by the ear and pulled him close. "What will you do when you learn that you will never reunite with Euryale, and that Ares will be the least of your troubles?"

"I don't know," Alex stammered. He let loose a sorrow-filled sigh as the last remnants of hope were extinguished. "I guess that means Aphrodite was right. My heart isn't in it."

"See?" Clotho laughed. "Nothing's happened, yet you think you know our will and have resigned yourself accordingly."

"Are you telling me I'll save her?"

"We answer to no one," Lachesis said. "You know Athena has spoken those very words to you."

"You three aren't being very helpful."

"We aren't here to help," said Lachesis. "We're here to work."

"Which is something you will be doing," Atropos finished. "Once you think things through."

Clotho offered Alex a chair. He wasn't sure what he was supposed to do with it, as sitting seemed off, given the environment. But after he stood a while and none of the Fates said anything more, he sat.

The three Moirae went to work, singing as they did. Clotho sang of things long passed, of empires and nations that had come and gone, and the men and women who led each to their respective fates. Lachesis sang of what was happening now, which made for a rather dull song at times because there were only so many ways one could sing lyrics about a tapestry before it became repetitive. Atropos's song was the most interesting. However, it was also the most cryptic. She sang of things to come, but never of events that involved Alex, as best he could make out. They were always about the manipulations, conflicts and deaths of others.

Eventually, Alex, tired of listening to their songs, decided he needed a Plan B. Or maybe it was Plan C or D. Whatever plan it was, the point remained that in light of the Moirae's unhelpfulness, he needed to adapt. He still felt that he needed to know where his heart was before continuing one way or another.

Alex stood up. "Do you—"

"Know someone that could help you?" Lachesis finished. "Yes, we do."

For a moment, Alex dared to hope. "Will you tell me where this person is?"

"In Hades," she replied. "Past the fields of asphodel is a place known as Elysium. He wanders that land, happy and blissful, and goes by the name Odysseus."

"Odysseus?" echoed Alex. "How will I know him? Or find him?"

"That is something you will figure out on your own," said Atropos. "Be warned: you will pay a heavy price for an answer from him."

"There's always a price," Alex said with a sigh. He popped his knuckles and took in a deep breath, trying to mentally prepare himself for whatever this unknown leg of his journey might entail. Given his adventure thus far, it couldn't be anything good. "Is there anything else I should know?"

"There is much you should know," Lachesis said with a wink.

"But no more will we tell," Atropos tacked on.

"Thank you, then," said Alex. He gave a friendly wave to all three and headed for the door.

"One last thing," Lachesis said, stopping him in his place. She motioned to a box that held all sorts of balls and scraps of yarn. "Take the brown one," she said.

Alex looked at the ball she mentioned, but did not immediately take it. "Thanks, but I don't crochet."

"Think of it as a souvenir," she said.

"Who knows what you will weave," Atropos interjected.

"Better to have and not need than need and not have, yes?" Lachesis then said.

"I suppose," Alex said, taking the ball from the box. Though he still had no idea what he would want it for, or why they pushed it so, he figured being impolite to the Fates was probably not a very good idea. He then said his goodbyes again and quickly left the room. As he made his way down the hall and back outside, he heard Atropos call out to him one last time. "If you see Euryale," she said, "tell her we said hello."

Chapter Twenty-Five

"He doesn't look happy to see you," Jessica said as she slipped behind Alex in the chariot. "You go unlock the gates."

Alex nodded, his eyes never leaving Cerberus. The three-headed dog was not only fixated on Alex, but was salivating like a pack of rabid bulldogs who had no intention of letting Alex pass.

"Shouldn't you be watching out for dead escapees?" asked Alex, wishing the dog had been snoring like the last time he was here. When Cerberus didn't budge, Alex steeled himself before slowly making his way to the gates. Hopefully, Apollo's words were still true and the hideous pooch would let him pass.

Cerberus barked and lunged. With his heads low, ears back, and mane slithering, he growled.

"Whoa! Whoa!" Alex said, freezing in place and putting his hands up. "I'm not dead. Not dead!"

Cerberus's heads continued barking and two even nipped at each other. But at least he didn't attack, and for that Alex was grateful. A few terror-laden moments later, Cerberus sat on his haunches and whined.

"Think he wants something?" Jessica asked.

"I'm hoping it's not a pair of human chew toys," he replied. He kept his hands up and inched forward, his muscles taught and ready to propel him away from a trio of mandible death.

Two steps into his advance, Cerberus came at him with a flurry of barks.

"Christ!" yelled Alex, scrambling back into his chariot. "Don't you have dead people to chase?"

Cerberus tilted his left head while the other two panted, salivated, and then yawned.

Jessica nudged Alex with her elbow. "Bribe him."

"Say again?" he asked, but when he followed her gaze to his bag he had on the chariot's floor, he understood. "That is some good jerky. Think it'll be enough?"

"Only one way to find out."

Alex grabbed the bag and before he was upright, Cerberus shot across the cavern floor. The canine raised on his hind legs and dropped his fore legs over the side of the chariot. Jessica leaped back with a yell as one head slobbered everywhere and the other two sniffed the bag.

"You can have some if you're nice," Alex said, trying to sound in control while reaching in the bag and taking out some jerky. "Now sit."

Cerberus did, and Alex rewarded him by tossing three pieces at him, one for each head. Those three pieces vanished in a snap of teeth and a spray of drool. An instant later, the hellhound was back on the chariot's side, barking for more.

"Fine, fine," said Alex, giving in and reminding himself he had another pouch tucked away. "Take it."

Jerky flew, and Cerberus snapped this way and that. Soon the bag was empty, but Cerberus and his demanding ways remained.

"That's all I have," said Alex, throwing up his hands. "Now let us through so we can find Odysseus."

Cerberus sniffed the air. One head glanced over his shoulder, but the other two looked more interested in the chariot than anything else. Before Alex could react, a trio of black, wet noses pressed into Alex's side and between his legs.

"Oh no," he said, hiding the remnants of his jerky supply behind his back. "Not on your life. Help me get to Odysseus first."

Cerberus lunged forward, and Alex tried to get away. But instead of getting anywhere, the hellhound jumped onto his back and sent him sprawling to the floor.

"Get off me, damn it!" Alex cried, trying to hold on to his bag and protect the spicy strips of jerky inside. "These are mine!"

A massive paw landed on the back of his neck and pressed his head into the ground. Alex wiggled out from under the pin, but he still couldn't get free of the nitrate-crazed dog. Cerberus dropped his full weight on Alex's shoulders, biting and clawing for the bag he clutched in his hands. Alex curled into a fetal position with the bag pressed against his chest. Cerberus jabbed two of his noses into Alex's armpits and barked repeatedly.

At first, the sensation of stinking, furry heads poking his ribs was more annoying than funny, but eventually those heads hit a few nerves the right way and Alex burst into laughter.

In that moment of hysterical release, Alex shot his hands out and the bag went flying. Cerberus jumped and snatched his prize mid-air. Once he landed, the dog tore the bag apart with all three heads in a wanton display of jerky violence. When it was over, Cerberus yawned, stretched, and sat, wagging his serpentine tail and licking all his chops.

"I can't believe you let me get mauled like that," Alex said, picking himself up off the ground.

With her camera in hand and face beaming, Jessica shrugged unapologetically. "This might be my best set of shots yet. Your face was priceless."

"I'm glad my suffering gave you such pleasure."

Jessica stuck her tongue out. "You've had worse."

"Maybe, but now he probably won't help us since he's had his fill."

To Alex's surprise, Cerberus ran to the gates and pawed at them with a trio of whines. Alex opened them up and drove his chariot through, and Cerberus bolted ahead.

"Do you think he should leave the gates like that?" Jessica asked.

"No idea, but you can try and wrestle him back here if you want," Alex replied. "I'm going with the idea that the slayer of jerky knows what he's doing."

They followed Cerberus out into the asphodel fields and along the banks of a river Alex wasn't familiar with. Shades mingled with one another, and they reminded Alex of the shades he had seen when he met Kharon. These spirits were different, though. They didn't look miserable, but at the same time they weren't overflowing with eternal, heavenly bliss. They simply were.

Cerberus raced upstream, and Alex and Jessica soon left the shades far behind. On they went until Cerberus broke from the river and shot off on a tangent. The musty air and fuzzy look that accompanied the asphodel fields gave way to the smell of salt and soon a rocky beach. Cerberus ran only a short while more before halting at the tip of a small peninsula. He looked toward an island on the horizon and barked.

Alex stopped the chariot next to Cerberus and squinted. Try as he might, he couldn't make out any details across the water. "Odysseus is there?" asked Alex. "That's Elysium?"

Cerberus spun around, wagging his tail.

Alex scratched the hellhound behind all three sets of ears. "Thank you," he said, still looking at the isle. "Once this is done, I'll bring you some more jerky. I promise."

Cerberus barked one last time before licking Alex's hand and running off. Alex wiped the slobber off on his chiton and snapped the reins.

As his ponies flew across the waters, Alex said, "What do you know about this Odysseus fellow? Do you think he can help?"

"He's clever, strong, and the very epitome of a hero," Jessica replied. "If he can't help you, I'm not sure who else could."

"Wonderful, but do you think he could ever relate to being away from his wife?"

Euryale sat on her bed and watched the sunrise through the gaps in the iron bars that made her window. It wasn't the most beautiful sight she'd seen—her small island home always gave such wonderful views at both dawn and dusk— but given she was being held captive atop a mountain and inside a tower, she could not deny the grand view she had.

"Here she is," said a voice, rough and harsh.

Euryale turned as Aphrodite strode through the door with Ares following a step behind. As always, the goddess looked gorgeous, as if she had a personal entourage tending to her hair, keeping it ever shining, bouncy, and mat-free. As much as Euryale longed for her freedom and to be at Alex's side, seeing the goddess also made her acutely aware of how much she longed for curling locks once more instead of the venomous snakes she bore.

"Good morning, sweet Euryale," said Aphrodite while she toyed with the scepter from Hades. "I hope all is well."

"You can stop the act," she said, crossing her arms and leaning against the wall. "You know things are not well."

"I could make things better," Aphrodite said. She beckoned Euryale over with a wave. "Take my hand. Let me make things right."

"I already said I will never give up Alex. Let me go or let me be."

Pity filled Aphrodite's eyes. "For your own sake, I wish you'd reconsider."

"My Alex will come for me," Euryale replied, her voice as strong as the stone around her.

Aphrodite withdrew her hand and paced like a tiger inside a cage. "Are you so sure?" she asked. "Twice now he's been beaten by Ares and sent home licking his wounds and his pride. Even now he questions his love for you."

"You lie," Euryale replied while her serpents hissed in agreement. "He loves me. This I know more than anything."

Aphrodite stopped and faced the gorgon. "Euryale, my fight is not with you," she said. "I apologize for the distress I've caused you, but I can't have Athena meddling in my affairs or giving false hopes to lonely souls. You deserve a lover that won't turn tail when danger rears. All I'm doing is demonstrating this for all to see and to put Athena in her place."

Euryale looked away and bit down on her lip. She tried to ignore the goddess's words, but Aphrodite's voice could never fully be tuned out, not by anyone. Knowing this, the gorgon kindled her inner fire, one that burned with anger and hate, and used it to drive away her fears of being abandoned. "Alex is not wrong for me," she said as her brow dropped and her muscles tensed. "He will come for me."

"I hate to tell you this, Euryale, but he's gone," Aphrodite said, as if she were breaking dreadful news to a recent widow. "Right now, he's scouring Hades, desperate to convince himself he loves you. And what will become of that? We both know it will be nothing."

"Leave me be—"

"I cannot," said Aphrodite. Her head dropped forward. Her shoulders slouched and her bottom lip quivered. "It pains me to think you'd refuse my help when bliss is but a single statement away. A mere utterance that you long for another, a true love."

"Never."

A large, clay basin with water appeared in Aphrodite's hand and she placed it on the floor near Euryale's cell. She chanted softly while keeping a hand over the water's surface. Ripples formed in the center while colors swirled throughout. An image of Euryale's island home formed in the reflection, and the goddess stood. "Do you know who he's with?"

"It doesn't matter," the gorgon replied, though in her heart, she didn't believe a word she said.

"You don't care who he shared an intimate meal with and who he confessed his love for?"

Euryale tried not to look, but her self-control failed her. She glanced at the basin out of the corner of her eyes, and when she saw Alex with Jessica, she couldn't stop herself from staring as the woman hung from Alex's neck and wine flowed between them. "No," the gorgon said, her heart pounding in her chest. "You're trying to trick me."

"Even you don't believe that," Aphrodite answered.

"No. No. No." With each word the gorgon spoke, her eyes darkened. Razor claws grew from her hands, and her skin hardened. She grabbed the sides of her head and growled. "Stop this."

Aphrodite raised an eyebrow, impressed at the gorgon's continued resilience to her suggestions. Anyone lesser would have been a raging storm of jealousy by now. Still, Aphrodite knew even a daughter of The Old Man could not resist her forever. She only needed a little extra push to break. "I can find you someone else," Aphrodite offered. "Or I can leave you be with a man who is in love with another."

"I said stop!"

"Shouldn't Alex be the one who should stop?"

"I mean it!"

"As do I," Aphrodite said, her words horribly sweet. "His heart is with the girl who got away. He's thought of her all his life. Honestly, Euryale, what chance do you have?"

"HE'S NOT LEAVING ME!" Euryale bellowed, and Aphrodite staggered from the blast. The gorgon, fully transformed into a monstrous hulk of muscle, claw, and scale, threw herself at the bars and tried pushing them apart.

Had her jail not been divinely created, Aphrodite was certain Euryale's rage would have been enough to rip the bars from their foundation. As the gorgon continued her attempts to break out, Aphrodite went to a window and leaned out to inspect Euryale's damage. When she saw the now-withered foliage that stretched for miles, she couldn't help but whistle long and slow. "As hideous as you are, you've got some lungs."

Euryale paced her cell, fiery eyes never leaving the goddess, and her only reply was a snarl that promised vengeance the moment she was loose.

"Can you hear me in there? The real you, the you who's being cast aside for a pretty little mortal?"

Euryale slammed into the bars. Her arms shot through the spaces, but they were nowhere near long enough. All she could do was claw the air in a vain attempt to get to Aphrodite.

"How predictable," Aphrodite said, laughing. "But it's not me you're mad at. Or even Alex, is it? Be honest. It's her. It's Jessica."

The gorgon finally spoke, her voice commanding such power that any demon would have cowered before her. "I'll destroy you both."

"Don't kill the messenger." The goddess nudged the basin closer so the gorgon could see her husband and his lost love enjoy each other's company. With a wave of her hand, she made sure the scene looped continuously, starting when Alex had first arrived on the island and ending a few moments before Athena spoiled the party. "Oh, one last thing before I go. I know it's hard for you to control yourself when you get worked up like this, but for your own sake, try not to imagine what happened after."

Aphrodite left, smiling as the gorgon howled again. She'd come back in a few days, once Euryale was so distraught that no words would reach her—not even her husband's. And when she was in that uncontrollable state, Aphrodite knew she could checkmate Athena in one, swift move, for who could ever love such a vile, rage-filled monster bent on murdering a loved one?

CHAPTER TWENTY-SIX

The isle was not what Alex had expected. Larks and warblers hopped about. Swans and geese sailed the air while herons and egrets walked the shore. Flowers dazzled the landscape with their large petals, yellow and white, blooming full and welcoming all those who might take in their fragrant aroma. Trees of every kind dotted the land, some bearing flowers of their own, others dangling a wide variety of the most delicious looking fruits Alex had ever seen a mere five feet off the ground.

"Oh, god, I'm going to be sick," Jessica said, suddenly leaning over the chariot's side.

"What—" was all Alex got out before his nostrils were assaulted by the potent smell of rot and decay. He forced rising bile back down his throat and looked for the source of the horrific odor. "Where is that coming from?"

Jessica covered her mouth and nose as her eyes watered. "I don't know, but I vote we go in the opposite direction."

Alex squinted. Far down the shore he found where it was coming from; a bloated monster of immense proportions lay rotting on its side. Had there not been a couple of people nearby, he'd have gone the other direction, but since he needed to find Odysseus, he approached them and prayed his stomach would hold long enough to get some directions.

As Alex drew near with Jessica, details of the creature could be seen. It had the head of a shark, the body of a whale, and a dozen tentacles sprouting from both, though half looked recently severed. Blood flowed and pooled from countless wounds, only to be washed away with each surge of the tide. A spear stuck out from the creature's side, and another protruded from the top of its head. At its side argued two men, each dressed in sea-soaked loincloths.

"The kill is mine!" yelled the first.

"Only because I stole its breath away!" yelled the second.

"A move you could only make after I held its attention!"

Not wanting to be subjected to the stench any more than he had to be, Alex interjected himself into their conversation. "Excuse me," he called out, "but would either of you mind helping me a moment?"

The nearest of the two spun around with a welcoming smile. "Hail there, hero!" he said, waving enthusiastically. "It feels like a thousand years since someone new has come to our isle."

"Thank you for the welcome," Alex said. "Is this Elysium?"

The second man trotted over to Alex and slapped a powerful hand on his shoulder. "Yes, hero, it is!" With his free hand, he grabbed Alex's and shook it with a vise grip. "I am Heracles, son of Zeus and Alcemene, husband to Hebe, and father of Alexiares and Anicetus."

The first man was only a step behind Heracles, and like his friend, he too shook Alex's hand with a crushing grip. "And I am Odysseus, son of Laertes and Anticlea, husband to Penelope, and father of Telemachus."

"Holy snort!" Jessica said. "Heracles? The hero's hero?"

"The one and only," he said with a bow.

"It should be illegal how ripped you are," she said, gawking like a schoolgirl.

When Heracles tilted his head, Alex offered an explanation. "She's saying you have lots of muscles."

Heracles flexed a bicep that looked like it could curl a cyclops all day and never tire. "It's important to stay in shape, especially out here. Who might you two be?"

"My name is Alexander Weiss," he replied before motioning to Jessica. "And this is my best friend since I was a kid, Jessica Turner."

"Alexander Weiss?" Heracles repeated. His brow furrowed and suddenly he began snapping his fingers. "I know this name," he said, still thinking. A moment later, recognition flashed across his face. "Odysseus!" he cried out. "This is the man I was telling you about! He who married a gorgon and beat Ares in the Olympics!"

Odysseus laughed. "You did such a foolish thing?" he said to Alex. "Ares' anger knows no bounds."

"Unintentionally, but yes, I beat him," Alex said, thoroughly confused at this point. "How do you know me?"

"His father is Zeus!" Jessica said, laughing and punching him in the shoulder. "You think he wouldn't know?"

"Precisely," Heracles said. "News like yours does not escape my ears."

Alex felt is mouth hang open as he tried to wrap his mind around the man's family. "Zeus is your father?"

"Of course he is!" Heracles said, taken aback. "Did you not hear me the first time? And if you didn't, could anyone as incredible as me come from any other line?"

"I hadn't really thought about it," said Alex.

"My feats are legendary!" Heracles went on. "Why today alone I've slain three monsters in Elysium!"

"You have monsters in Elysium?" said Alex, unsure if he'd heard correctly. If he had, he found it perplexing as to why that would ever be a good thing.

"What do you call that?" Heracles said, jutting a thumb back to the carcass on the shore.

"A monster," Alex conceded. "But if this is paradise, what the hell is that thing doing here?'

"Can a potter truly be called a potter without clay to work?" asked Odysseus.

"Or a king be called a king without a land to rule?" Heracles added.

"Or a hero be called a hero without adversity," finished Alex.

Heracles slapped him hard on the back. "Exactly! So relax and enjoy an afterlife well earned, Alexander of Weiss." Heracles' face suddenly reflected an inner puzzlement. "Hold on a moment. If you've married into a divine family, why are you here?"

"That," Alex said with a deep breath and subsequent sigh, "is exactly why I'm here. Ares took my bride after the games. I was told Odysseus could help."

"I'm afraid you were told wrong," Odysseus gravely replied.

"How can you say that?" Jessica said. "Your forces drove Ares off at the Battle of Troy."

Odysseus chuckled. "Diomedes had that honor, not me, and when he did that, he had divine help. Sorry, Alex, I've led many a battle, but Ares is a foe I cannot beat. Perhaps it is Heracles' aid you should seek."

"It's not Ares I need help with," said Alex. His voice suddenly became weak. He looked away, off to the lush green fields beyond, ashamed of what he was about to say.

"Tell us what's on your mind, hero," Odysseus prompted.

"I'm not sure if my heart is in this fight," Alex finally confessed. "I'm not sure if I married my wife out of love or out of necessity. The Moirae said you would help in that regard."

Odysseus thought for a moment, arms crossed. "To be clear, you want to know if you love your wife?"

Alex nodded.

"And if you love your wife, the Fates said you can beat a god?"

Alex shook his head. "No. But I need to know before I commit to any sort of action. I have...a means to end the war, but to use it,

I must leave Euryale. So if our marriage is doomed, I might as well end things quickly. On the other hand, if I love my wife, I can worry about how to beat Ares later."

"I see," Odysseus replied. "You need to know what love is."

"No. I know what love is," Alex said. "It's a wonderful song with notes of passion, refrains of joy, and undercurrents of inspiration and intimacy."

"You misunderstood," said Odysseus. "I wasn't asking a question."

"Hero," Heracles cut in. "No one can tell another whether or not to love another."

"I am 'no one,'" Odysseus said with a wink. "But he's right, Alex. I can't tell you to love your wife or not. That is your decision, and yours alone."

"If knowing my heart was in it was that simple, I'd have done it by now," said Alex. "The fire I had for her is being snuffed out by this infernal war, and I'm afraid what's left of my feelings for her won't last. Can't you consult an oracle or cast some bones to help? Why else would the Fates send me to you?"

Odysseus drummed his fingers on his arm. "There is something we could try."

"What?" Alex asked, jumping at the idea. "Tell me, please!"

"The potion of agape," Odysseus said. "Its brewing is known to me, but it needs a few ingredients that aren't easy to get."

"I don't want to love Euryale because I'm under a spell," said Alex, now thinking he'd reached a dead end. "I want it to be real."

"No, no, my good man," he replied, shaking his head. "It won't force anything on you, but it will allow you unequalled introspection. Soul searching, if you will. I'm confident it will give you the answer you seek."

"If that's true, thank the gods," Alex said with a heavy sigh.

"Thank the Fates," Odysseus corrected. He knelt and drew in the sand a map of an island. When it was finished, Odysseus stood. "On this island lives someone called Polyphemus," he said. "He keeps a special type of mandrake in his home, and that will be the first thing you'll need. He stores the mandrake in a silver jar, trimmed with gold. The jar, kept by the spices, has an engraving of Poseidon's trident on its bottom. You can't miss it. Bring me three mandrake leaves and we'll go from there."

"Am I to steal this?" asked Alex, wondering why a price or bartering instructions hadn't been included.

Odysseus nodded. "He won't part with it willingly, and don't bother reasoning with the poor fellow. He's not the most gracious of hosts. So, yes, if I were you, I'd steal it. Try and strike a deal at your own risk."

"But—" Alex protested.

"I've told you what I would do," said Odysseus. "The choice is yours whether you want to follow my advice or not."

Alex looked down at the map and threw up his hands. What was one more stop, even if it ended in a little robbery?

The sun had crept high into the sky and was beating down on Alex's neck by the time Polyphemus's island came into view. It turned out that it was only a couple hours' ride as the ponies fly, and for that Alex was thankful. As he and Jessica flew over a tiny cove, flanked on three sides by sheer cliffs, Alex silently prayed that finding this friend of Odysseus's wouldn't prove to be too much of a bother. But given how everything else in his afterlife had gone, it probably would.

Over the shoreline cliffs they flew, all the while scouring the grassy fields below for the signs of the first landmark they were to take. For all the gifts the gods had bestowed upon him, Alex wished a GPS system would've been part of them.

"How about that one over there?" Jessica said, pointing to a twenty-foot, rocky outcropping in the distance. "Looks like a rock as tall as three men, yes?"

"So does the one over there," Alex said, spying a similar rock, maybe a half mile away from the first. "And that one, and that one, too."

"For a hero, Odysseus gives pretty crappy directions," Jessica said as she adjusted her pony tail.

"Damnit to hell," Alex said, pulling the reins so they came to a stop. "This is stupid."

"Maybe we could see his house if we flew higher," Jessica suggested. "Or maybe we should start looking for a lightning-scared tree. How many of those can be around?"

"Who says it even still is?" Alex tugged the reins a few times, directing the ponies wherever his indecisiveness pointed him to. After the fifth time, one of them looked back at him and flipped its head, no doubt growing impatient at his indecision.

"Don't look at me like that," Alex scolded. "We've got two more landmarks to find after the first. I can't pretend to know where to go."

The pony flicked an ear and turned back around.

"Oh sure, you'd like wandering around this place, eating all the grass," said Alex with a huff.

"Can't blame him," Jessica said, laughing. "I'm sure he would rather be eating grass than pulling you all over nowhere."

"I suppose. What do you know about this Polyphemus guy? Anything that could help find him?"

Jessica tapped the sides of the chariot and a wrinkle appeared above the bridge of her nose as her brow dropped. "I feel like I should," she said. "His name sounds familiar, but that's about it."

"I thought you were the guru of Greek Mythology."

Jessica stuck out her tongue. "Even the master has her weak spots. Besides, do you know how much there is to all these myths? Anyway, at least I knew who the father of your bride was."

"I still say that was luck. But you really can't remember anything?"

"I want to say he was with Odysseus on his way back from Troy," Jessica said with a shrug. "Or he met him somewhere along the way? I'll be honest, I never really got into the Odyssey."

"But he's not like a high priest or anything for one of the Olympians, right?" Alex said as he thought about whether or not he wanted to commit a robbery. "I mean, seems lately everything I've done has had some sort of divine consequence, and I'd rather not be cursed with a dozen plagues and festering boils when someone realizes I helped myself to some mandrake."

"Afraid I don't know," Jessica replied. "Sorry."

Alex's heart grew heavy at their lack of progress, but when he spied someone walking a herd of sheep far to the northeast, hope grew in his soul. "Let's ask him," he said, pointing.

"Oh, hang on a minute," Jessica said. "I think there was something about Polyphemus and sheep. That can't be too bad, right? I mean, how many shepherds sling curses?"

"None as far as I'm concerned," he replied.

Alex skimmed the chariot toward the shepherd, all the while praying that if this man wasn't Polyphemus, he'd at least be able to point them in the right direction.

About a hundred yards from the shepherd, the ponies ground to a halt, nearly throwing both Alex and Jessica over.

"Oh, come on!" groaned Alex.

Alex's words got caught in his mouth as for the first time he got a good view of the shepherd. Even with a hunched back, the man towered over his sheep by seven feet at least. He had legs like the trunk of an old oak, gnarled, rough, and wide. His skin wrinkled and sagged, but it still hinted at powerful muscles beneath. In the man's bony fingers he clutched a walking stick that had more in common with a small tree than a full-length quarterstaff. Most surprising of all was the single eyepatch upon the man's face—a single eyepatch that covered the only eye socket the man had.

"A goddamn, blind, one-eyed giant," Alex muttered. "Figures."

"Cyclops," Jessica corrected.

"Yeah, that. Think he's friendly?"

The giant turned in place, hobbling on his staff as he did, and sniffed the air. A few seconds passed, and the creature kept his nose aloft as best as his broken frame could. Finally, he lowered his head and rested on his walking staff. "Who goes there?" he asked in a rough, scratchy voice.

Alex froze. Jessica dug her nails into his arm. Even the ponies held still, aside from a few nervous twitches of their tails that made Alex wonder how close they were to bolting on their own.

"Don't torment me so," the giant said, sniffing the air once again. "You know I can't see you. Or hear very well."

Alex didn't answer and the creature continued its lament. "What threat is an old cyclops like me? Have you come to steal my sheep? Rob me blind? Woe is me, I say. Woe!"

Alex, taking pity on the creature, whispered to Jessica. "Stay here."

"You don't have to tell me twice," she whispered back.

Alex stepped off the chariot, cleared his throat, and raised his voice as he approached. "My name is Alex," he said. "I'm looking for someone named Polyphemus."

"Polyphemus?" the cyclops replied, bobbing his head. "What for?"

"You know the man?"

"I know Polyphemus," he replied. "But answer me first. What do you want with him?"

"I come bearing a message from Odysseus," he lied.

The cyclops straightened a couple of inches at the hero's name. "Odysseus? You come on his behalf?"

"I do," said Alex.

"You are his friend? His comrade?"

"In a sense, yes," said Alex, growing impatient. He didn't want to sit all day with an over-the-hill monster and chat about who knew whom. "Will you tell me where I can find Polyphemus?"

"I'll take you to him myself," the cyclops replied. He then stuck two fingers into his toothy mouth and whistled sharply. His herd of sheep, some thirty in all, jumped at the command, and in a loose blob, began heading north toward the island's sole mountain. "Come, come. I need this done before dinner."

Alex followed the cyclops and his sheep along a well-worn path, one that darted through sparse woods and up a gentle incline to the base of the island's mountain. The hike lasted about thirty minutes, and the pace the cyclops kept surprised Alex.

A large fire pit was the first thing Alex saw when they reached the creature's home. Coals smoldered in its bed, and two spits were in place, each as thick as Alex's wrist and each skewered with large chunks of raw meat. A thick cloud of flies buzzed about, while an equal number sat on the uncooked food.

On the other side of the pit were animal pens, which the cyclops herded his sheep into. The animals readily complied, giving the occasional bleat as they did.

Alex wrinkled his nose and grimaced. A whiff of the air suggested that the muck-filled pens hadn't been cleaned in a long, long time. "And here I thought the sea monster reeked," he said to himself.

"What was that?" said the cyclops.

"Nothing," Alex quickly said, hoping not to offend his guide. "I was just wondering if Polyphemus was far."

"No, he's not far," the cyclops answered, locking the pen and shaking it once for good measure. "But we will need the key to his home if we are to see him."

Alex crossed his arms and tapped his foot as he watched the cyclops enter a nearby cave and get swallowed by the darkness.

"At least he doesn't need to worry about light," he said to keep his mood upbeat. Just once he'd like something simple. No more, "See the Moirae, Alex." Or, "Grab this mandrake, Alex." Or, "We need a key to keep going, Alex." Just in, out, and done.

A loud crash sounded from deep in the cave, causing both Alex and the sheep to jump. Before his nerves settled, the cyclops called out with a strained voice, "Are you there, friend?"

Alex took a tentative step toward the mouth of the cave. "I am," he said. "What happened?"

"My foot got caught and down I went," the cyclops replied. "I fear my shelves have crashed upon me."

Though Alex had pity for the creature, he did not like the scene before him. The hairs on the back of his neck stood, and goose bumps raised on his arms. "I'm not sure how I can help," he finally said. "Or if I can. I can't even see you back there."

A whimper, low and mournful, echoed from the darkness. "Please, stranger," the cyclops said. "At least come and see what might be done. There should be an unlit torch nearby. You can light it with the coals from the pit."

Alex saw the torch near the mouth of the cave, propped up against the wall. "One second," he said, sighing and capitulating to such a simple demand.

With the lit torch in hand, Alex cautiously moved though the cave. The floor glistened beneath his feet, and twice he nearly slipped. Alex hoped whatever coated the cavern floor was just water, but shuddered at the thought of what else it might be.

"Hurry, kind sir," the cyclops groaned. "Pain fills my back."

"I'm coming. Keep your big giant pants on," said Alex. About fifteen yards in, he stopped. To his right stood a large set of poorly made shelves. How it remained together, Alex had no idea, for the wood splintered and cracked in a half dozen places, and the entire thing leaned to the side so much that he was certain one sneeze would send it all toppling over.

On the top shelves sat a variety of cheeses, most being haphazardly placed. Beneath those were pails and bowls of milk, and judging by the smell, all had passed their due date. At the bottom sat several jars, some clay, others metallic. Plants grew out of most, save one. That one sat tucked in the back, capped.

Alex leaned in with the torch for a closer look. The jar that caught his eye was made of silver and along the top and bottom edges ran rings of gold. "Oh, no way," whispered Alex, taking the jar in hand. He turned it over and sure enough, a tiny trident was engraved on the bottom.

Alex looked up. "Polyphemus?"

A large set of hands grabbed Alex from behind, hoisting him into the air. "Does Odysseus think I'm that stupid?" Polyphemus yelled. "Does he think he can rob from me, take my eye, and I would forget?"

Alex struggled in the cyclops's crushing grip. "Get the hell off me!"

Alex was thrown through the air. Though he lost his grip on the silver jar, he managed to keep hold of the torch as he flew. Unfortunately, it didn't help much when he struck his head against the rocky wall. Dazed, Alex slowly pushed himself off the ground. The torch had gone out, and all he could see was the mouth of the cave, some forty yards away.

"Tell me, stranger, where can I find Odysseus?" the cyclops called out in the darkness. "Oh, how I've longed to chew on his bones! Tell me stranger, and I shall make your death a swift one!"

Alex kept quiet, thinking any sort of reply would invite a colossus-sized beat down. Carefully, he inched toward the exit of the cave, holding his breath the entire time.

The back of a fist met Alex's chest, and again Alex slammed into the wall. The wind flew out of him, and pain laced his ribs. Gasping for breath, Alex looked up to see Polyphemus standing nearby, perfectly silhouetted against the mouth of the cave.

"I don't need an eye to hit you, stranger," the cyclops laughed. "You smell of weakness and fear. I can hear the tremble in your breath."

Alex pushed away the pain, and still refusing to answer, opted for a more direct and speedy approach. Now able to see his adversary, he made a beeline for the exit, hoping to skirt the cyclops's long reach. But like his last attempt, Polyphemus hit him with a crushing blow, one that again sent Alex flying back.

"Tell me where Odysseus is or I'll snap every bone in your body!" the giant demanded.

"Okay, okay," Alex said, coughing and sputtering. He panted heavily, partly because he was short of breath, but mostly because he wanted to buy himself a little time. As he did, he shifted his grip on the torch.

"I won't ask nicely again," the Polyphemus growled, taking a step toward him.

Alex threw the torch in a high arc. "He's right behind you!"

The torch thumped on the ground, and Alex nearly yelled in triumph as the cyclops took the bait. The giant spun around, swinging wildly, as Alex bolted for the exit. When he neared the giant, Alex slid feet first between the giant's legs, and not a moment too soon. Polyphemus came back around with an open hand, grazing the hairs on Alex's head.

Alex shot to his feet before the off-balanced giant could recover. A few strides into his run, Alex kicked something hard.

The silver jar suddenly appeared in the outside light, sailing high and far out the cave. The sight of the prize redoubled Alex's determination and he dug deep, demanding more speed, more power out of his legs.

Polyphemus gave chase, his heavy footsteps thundering behind Alex as he broke free of the cave.

"Hit him, now, Odysseus!" Alex yelled when the giant came into the light.

Polyphemus stopped at the mouth of the cave and tore a chunk of rock out of the mountain the size of a baby grand. He shifted his grip on it once before throwing the boulder at Alex with uncanny accuracy.

Alex leapt to the side, and an impact crater, complete with massive boulder, appeared where he was only moments ago. "You'll have to do better than that, old man," Alex taunted. A second boulder, one that was even closer to finding its mark than the first when it landed, made Alex reconsider aggravating Polyphemus any further. Instead, Alex bolted for the jar.

"How many more can you outrun?" Polyphemus said, tearing off a third rock and sending it Alex's way.

Alex stopped dead in his tracks, the boulder taking some skin off his chin as it flew by. He froze and held his breath. The jar he desperately sought lay about twenty yards away, and he could probably get to it, but he wasn't sure how much longer his luck would hold out. The next rock the cyclops threw could very well be the last the monster would need.

As Alex stood still, planning his next move, Polyphemus held a fourth rock overhead. For the longest time, neither of them moved, but eventually, the cyclops lowered the boulder and raised his nose and sniffed the air. A toothy smile spread across the giant's face, and Polyphemus began a slow approach, nose leading the way.

Alex cursed silently, knowing he couldn't stand where he was much longer. But to run would cause noise and that would invite more boulders to fly his way. Even if his spirit would never shed his immortal body, the last thing he wanted was to be the Polyphemus's eternal plaything.

An idea popped into mind, and a smile grew on Alex's face. Quietly and with as much haste as he dared, Alex shed the chiton he wore. Carefully, he tiptoed toward the boulder, all the while wiping as much of his sweat and stink onto the cloth as he possibly could. Once he arrived at the rock's final resting place, he jammed the chiton underneath and slinked off not a moment too soon.

Polyphemus reached the boulder not even a half minute later. He felt the ground and discovered a piece of the chiton protruding from underneath the former missile. "Come out, come out, wherever you are, stranger," the cyclops teased. "Or have you lost the will to run?"

Alex, a good way off, kept silent, bent down, and gingerly took the silver jar.

Polyphemus grunted and gave the boulder a hard shove. It rolled over several times before coming to a stop. The cyclops searched the ground, smiling as if his latest kill was but one pat away. That smile faded once he grabbed Alex's clothes. The giant tore at them, hit the ground fast and furious, and howled with rage.

Alex backed away cautiously, being sure no leaf or noisy stick would be trodden underfoot, all the while congratulating himself on the fine job he'd done. Then the wind changed.

Polyphemus jerked upright and sniffed the air twice. He charged Alex with a speed that belied his decrepit frame. "You'll never leave this island alive," he yelled.

Alex took off running, lungs gulping massive quantities of air as his legs burned, trying to keep up with the demand he set. He occasionally glanced over his shoulder as he sprinted through the forest, and more often than not he had to dive away from a granite missile. Thankfully, each time Polyphemus stopped to throw, Alex managed to get a few more strides in before having to dodge, and thus Alex soon had a sizeable lead on the cyclops.

On this went, the running, the dodging, the running again, until Alex burst from the tree line. The joy of being almost free vaporized in an instant. He'd come out of the forest too far south. Jessica and the ponies were a good half-mile away, likely closer to Polyphemus than to him.

"Get over here!" he yelled, waving his arms and running for his chariot. At first, neither Jessica nor the ponies seemed to hear him, so he kept yelling over and over, until finally they started for him.

Polyphemus bolted out of the forest in front of him, boulder in hand. He skidded to a stop and readied for a throw. He balked momentarily, turned his head, and then launched the missile at Jessica.

"Look out!" Alex yelled.

To Alex's never-ending thanks to the Fates, the ponies didn't want to die as much as Alex didn't want to see them all crushed, and they shot high into the air, narrowly avoiding the cyclops's attack.

The ponies swooped down, and a second boulder clipped the back end. The chariot twisted to the side, and Jessica screamed as she held on for dear life.

Alex crouched as Polyphemus tore yet another rock from the ground and readied for a throw. This time, however, it was clear the cyclops knew where the chariot was headed, as he was waiting a moment to flatten Alex, the ponies, and Jessica all in one shot.

Fearing that Polyphemus' aim might be that good, Alex summoned every ounce of strength he had and crouched so he could launch himself as high as he could. He shook a single finger over his head, not daring to call out his idea and praying Jessica— or at least the ponies—would understand.

The cyclops hurled the boulder with deadly accuracy. It came faster than all the others, and Alex was so in awe at it's speed, he almost forgot to jump.

"Cripes!" he yelled as his legs shot him up. Ten, twenty feet he sailed while his former girlfriend—smart, in tune, and there to save him—drove the chariot so it was at his side at the peak of his jump.

"Gotcha," Jessica said grabbing his forearm and helping him swing inside the chariot.

"Holy crap that was close," Alex said, laughing. As he watched Polyphemus's island disappear, he glanced at the jar and smiled. "I hope this does the trick. I don't want to have to do that again."

"Me either," Jessica said. "Could've been worse, though."

"How's that?"

"Instead of rocks, you could've been dodging whales."

Chapter Twenty-Seven

Alex jumped off his chariot and stormed across the sandy shore to where Odysseus stood ankle deep in the surf with a net in hand. "Got a question for you," Alex said. "Did something slip your mind about your friend? Did you forget he was a one-eyed giant that wants to eat you?"

"I did tell you to steal the jar and not engage him," Odysseus said, lowering his net. "I'm sure you've figured out by now that he's not the nicest of fellows. It's not as if you would've been stealing from a widow."

"You could have at least warned me!"

"Or mentioned he was the guy whose eye you poked out," Jessica added. "I nearly took a rock to the face over all this."

Odysseus shrugged. "Life and love are unpredictable, get used to it."

"I don't ever plan on getting used to fighting a cyclops."

"We rarely get all that we plan for," said Odysseus, casting his net into the sea. "But that is another matter. Tell me, Alex, what happened once you found Polyphemus?"

"I asked him for directions, since neither of us knew who he was," Alex answered. "He led me back to his cave. We got into a fight. I almost had my brains splattered against the wall, but I still managed to get away with the jar."

"Knowing him, that must have been a giant fight, no pun intended," Odysseus remarked, pulling up an empty net. "He's always been an unrelenting one."

"It was a big fight," said Alex. "A bloody one at that."

Odysseus tossed his net to the side. "I'm impressed you made it out in one piece. Many men fell to Polyphemus, many good men. What was your secret?"

"Quick wits and quicker reflexes," Alex said, reliving the fight in his mind. "For a moment I thought that would be the end of me."

"And?"

Alex shrugged. "And nothing. I got away."

"Don't mind me," Jessica said. "I only caught you midair as you ran for your life."

Alex smiled. "Sorry, yes. She one hundred percent had a hand in whisking me to safety."

Odysseus looked out to the horizon and pressed his lips together. He stood in silence for a moment before grunting. "After such a struggle, one filled with uncertainty and no promise of success, did you at least find what you need?"

"I said I got the jar," Alex said, handing it to him. "The mandrake is inside."

"These are leaves, but not what you need," Odysseus said as he opened the jar and inspected the contents.

"I need the potion, which you said you could make with the leaves."

"I said you need to know what love is."

"And I said I need to know who I love," Alex corrected. "Or at least, should. Ergo, I need that potion."

"Still bent on making it?"

"You make it sound like there's an alternative."

"There are alternatives in everything. Love. War. Life. They all have choices we make and none of them come with guarantees," Odysseus said. "Who you love is no different than doing what you love—be it for duty or pleasure. However, since I can see you're going to still argue with me on that, we should move on and focus on what's next."

"Wonderful," Alex replied, rolling his shoulders and working out some of the stiffness that had settled in. Regardless of his Heraclean body, he hurt after repeatedly being slammed into a cavern wall. "What do I need to get now?"

"Let me say first, I'm glad you're dedicated to see this through, because Polyphemus was the easy part," Odysseus said as he tossed his net to the side and started drawing a map in the sand. "In the northeast part of Peloponnese lives the direct descendant of the famed Nemean lion."

"It's not an ordinary lion, is it?" Alex asked, fearing it was some sort of multi-headed, fire-breathing, petrifying monster that snacked on armies. Not that he had met one yet, but it had to be coming sooner or later.

"Heracles had to kill the Nemean lion as part of his twelve labors," Jessica filled in. "Trick was, however, its golden hide could not be pierced by any weapon. As you can imagine, it wasn't a walk in the park."

"Lovely," Alex said. "Let me guess, I've got to do the same."

Odysseus nodded. "Yes. A life of love takes courage, Alex, and at times that life includes terrible fights that we'd rather not undertake. Thus, we'll need that lion's teeth and mane."

Alex ran both hands through his hair and locked his fingers behind his head as he thought the scenario through. "How did Heracles beat this creature?"

"With a club and his bare hands," Odysseus replied.

"He wrestled a lion?"

"Strangled it."

Alex shook his head. "I'll find some other way," he said. "I'm not wrestling a lion."

Odysseus raised an eyebrow.

"I'm not wrestling a lion," Alex said once more. "You'll see."

"We'll see," Odysseus said with an unsettling smile.

"There has to be another way," Alex insisted.

Odysseus motioned to the net on the ground. "You could use that to slow him when he charges."

Alex crossed his arms over his chest. "At which point I'm supposed to jump on his back?"

"That's the general idea." The hero paused and then pointed further up the beach. "I've got another net for you as well. Take them both. If you miss with the first, you might be able to toss the second."

"I won't miss," Alex declared. "Anyway, that's not what I'm worried about."

"You know how to use them?"

"I used to fish with casting nets when I was little," Alex explained. "But that's not the point. The point is, when we did we didn't pull up five-hundred-pound killing machines. Even if we did get one, we would've tossed it back, not given it a belly rub."

"What strategy you use is up to you," Odysseus replied, "but you'll need that lion if you want your wife back, and if I were you, I'd want as many options as possible in regards to accomplishing that task."

"Fine. I'll take the nets," Alex said. "I'll be back before you know it."

"Good. There's one other thing I must mention."

"What's that?"

"Your friend will need to wait here. If she helps in defeating the lion, it could taint the spell. Not to mention, I don't think you want to chance her being eaten."

Jessica grimaced. "I'd rather not be a snack, so if it's all the same, I'll sit this one out."

"No worries. I understand."

Alex said his goodbyes and left. Once he was back on his chariot, he wondered how he could use the nets Odysseus had given him. Perhaps he could poison the animal once he had it snared. Surely its hide couldn't protect it against a good dose of cyanide, which he'd need to get. Or maybe he could crush its head with a boulder. Or maybe he could shoot the damn thing in the mouth. That had to be viable. Get it mad, let it roar, and jam a gun down its throat before pulling the trigger. Of course, that meant he'd need a pit stop back at Termessos, but that wouldn't take long.

Yes, that's what he'd do, he decided. Blast the lion right in its mouth. Quick. Simple. Easy. And best of all, it didn't involve wrestling a five-hundred-pound killing machine with his bare hands.

On a small hill, Alex stood on a broken wall and used his binoculars to scour the area. To his left grew a clump of trees that freely offered an oasis of shade to an otherwise flat and sun-beaten landscape. To his right, a small, rocky stream darted and bubbled through the field. About three hundred yards ahead of Alex, a family of deer meandered about, oblivious to the world, and as far as Alex was concerned, begging to be eaten by a lion. Despite these things that Alex was certain should attract any ferocious feline, there was no big cat anywhere to be seen.

"Why can't you be like all the other lions, Mister Lion?" Alex asked, taking a moment to clean his binoculars with the bottom of his jacket. "The ones on TV never hide. They aren't camera shy. They lounge and yawn, stretch, and yawn some more."

Alex pulled his nearly empty canteen off his web belt and took a swig of water. The drink did wonders for his parched mouth and throat, and if he was going to be out here much longer, he'd need a refill. "I know where you are, Mister Lion," said Alex, wiping his mouth and noting the sweaty feel of his back and chest. "You're avoiding this god-awful heat."

As if hearing his complaint, the world changed. The wind picked up, rustled the grass below, and whipped across his back. Clouds drifted across the sky, soon parking themselves between Alex and the setting sun. Subsequently the light dimmed, and the orange tint that covered the fields disappeared, leaving the land in a perpetual state of grey. Soon that light faded, and only the faintest orange glow peeked out from the horizon.

"I guess that's that," Alex said, rubbing his bleary eyes and deciding to pack it in. He could barely see the trees anymore, and where the deer were in that near-black landscape was anyone's guess. "Good night, Mister Lion," he said, easing himself off the wall. "Good work on wasting a day. Hope you sleep well. I'll most likely kill you in the morning."

Alex picked up the fishing net at his feet and began walking the three-mile trek back to where he had left his ponies. Out of habit, he checked his Garand for the umpteenth time. The magazine was full, and there was still a .30-06 round in the chamber. Not that he'd need any of that soon. No, what he needed now was something to eat and a nice bed to sleep in.

Alex smashed into the ground, face first. Something heavy landed on his back and trapped his hands and rifle under his chest. Pain exploded in both shoulders. His neck burned in agony. Alex struggled to get upright, but he quickly realized he was fighting a losing battle with something large, furry, and laden with teeth. Every few seconds, he felt the creature's jaw adjust, sending new waves of pain through his neck. It was only a matter of time before an artery or jugular was opened.

"Get off!" Alex screamed, but it did no good. Desperate and running out of options, he pulled the trigger to his Garand.

The rifle kicked like a rabid mule. The pressure on his neck and back was gone, and so was his attacker.

Alex, with ringing ears, planted the butt of the rifle in the ground and pushed himself up. Blood poured from open wounds. It stained his clothes and the ground below. His fingers went numb. Goosebumps covered his arms, and a chill ran through his body. Worst of all, a lion, five feet at the shoulder, boldly stepped into view. Even in the waning twilight, Alex could see the blood caked around its mouth and nose.

Alex tried to raise his rifle, but the strength in his arms had left him, indeed in his legs as well. He stumbled forward, dizzy and disoriented. Try as he might, he couldn't stay upright. Alex fell back, striking his head on the ground below. The lion pounced him, and clamping down on his neck, Mister Lion crushed the cartilage in Alex's neck.

Alex tried to scream, but the only thing that escaped his lips was a sputtering wheeze. His vision left him, and then so did the pain.

Alex opened an eye, groggy, confused, and unsure of everything. With a little concentration, he realized he was lying on a damp, limestone floor, unable to move or even feel his limbs. He couldn't see much of anything else, save the mouth of a cave a dozen yards away that led to a starry night.

Though his vision was lacking, he could still hear. Something snored loudly behind his back, and it didn't take long for Alex to realize what that something was; it was Mister Lion. Why Alex hadn't become a late-night snack, he had no idea. But he wasn't about to wake the feline to find out. All that mattered right now was to get up and get out. Once that was taken care of, he could figure out what next to do.

Alex summoned all his strength and tried to get to his feet. His arms, however, failed to respond in any controlled manner, and the moment he moved his legs, pain wracked his body. Alex gritted his teeth, and tears clouded his vision, but still he pushed on. Gods knew how many agonizing minutes it took for Alex to get on all fours, but eventually he did. True, he was a little lopsided, a little off balance, and near his mental breaking point, but he was up off the ground. And that, as far as Alex was concerned, was half the battle. Now all he needed to do was get out without making a sound.

When the stabbing pain in his body traded itself for a dull throb, Alex made another attempt to get to his feet. He didn't get far. Instead of going upright, his muscles contracted and he quickly found himself back on all fours.

Refusing to be defeated or stay in the cave a moment longer, Alex slowly crawled toward the mouth of the cave. With each push of a leg, every extension of an arm, it felt like nails were being driven into his limbs and twisted for good measure. By the time he had gone only a few paces, his body shook violently. By the time he neared the mouth of the cave, he'd nearly chewed through his lower lip to keep from whimpering.

Alex stopped, unable to go any farther. He thought about easing back to the ground to regain his strength, but he worried he might not be able to get up again.

I can make the light, he told himself, picking a more attainable goal. Whereas the mouth of the cave seemed like a mile away, the moonlight that poured into the cave was only a step or two in front of him. *Baby steps*, he thought. *Baby stepping to the light.*

Alex willed himself forward. The nails drove through his arms in an even greater number than before, but they did not stop him from reaching his goal. As Alex pushed himself into the moonlight, relief washed over him. That relief, however, was quickly drowned by terror.

Alex looked down to see that his left arm was gone at the elbow, a bloody, ragged stump in its place. His right arm fared only slightly better, its hand missing half its digits and a thumb. Alex almost caught the scream in his throat, but when he looked into a puddle of water and saw the reflection of a half-eaten, one-eyed face staring back, that scream shot out of his mouth like a runaway train.

The lion roared, and Alex scampered forward, but he didn't get far. His torn limbs could not begin to match the demands he set for them. Instead of bounding away like a nimble gazelle, he fell to the ground like a mutilated fawn.

A familiar weight of crushing, feline death landed on his back. Claws batted his head and sides. Teeth, *again,* locked around his neck. The lion jerked its head, and the last thing Alex heard was the sound of his vertebrae snapping.

Alex jerked awake.

Late morning sunlight poured into the empty cave, and with Mister Lion nowhere to be seen or heard, Alex looked himself over. He found his arms whole, thankfully. They were a little stiff, but not the chewed-up hunks of meat they once were. He had two hands and ten fingers, all intact. His torso was free of blemish and scar, but his clothes hung off him in bloody tatters.

Alex reached up and touched his face, trying to find any damage. His probe was ginger at first, but soon Alex was slapping his cheeks, relishing the wholeness of his head. As far as he could tell, he was tip top. No pain. No chunks of flesh missing. Hell, he even had two eyes. There was no time to argue or ponder why things were. He needed to get the hell out of there. Fortunately, he could hear birds chirping nearby, and if the birds were singing, surely Mister Lion was far away.

Alex jumped to his feet and rocketed out the mouth of the cave. The wind kissed his face and welcomed him to his newfound freedom. The sun cast its warm rays upon his skin, clearly wanting to bless his escape. Down the mountainside Alex ran, hurdling over shrubs and rocks, unsure of where he was going or where he wanted to be. All he knew was that any place had to be better than that cave.

Alex stopped next to a tree to get his bearings. The cave was about three hundred yards behind him at this point. If he squinted, to his right he thought he could make out the rock wall he'd been on the other day. It was far, maybe a mile away, but Alex felt certain he could cover the distance easily. The thought of being another feline snack only reinforced his determination.

"Wait till I see you again, Mister Lion," Alex said, taking off again. "We'll see who goes down then."

Mister Lion suddenly appeared in front of Alex's path, lazily walking out of some waist-high grass. Alex skidded to a halt, and the lion cocked his head and looked toward him as if perplexed as to why this man kept returning to life. Apparently, however, such mental musings weren't all that important to the lion, for he charged a moment later, teeth bared.

Alex swung at the creature, more out of reflex than anything else. His fist hit it directly in the nose with a satisfying thunk. Mister Lion, however, had far too much momentum to be stopped by such a silly attack and crashed into Alex with full force. The two rolled on the ground, claws and fists flying. Somehow, by fate or by luck, Alex ended up on top of his feline foe and rained blow after blow on its head.

"Oh, you want some of this, Mister Lion?" Alex screamed, completely enraged. His fists continued to pummel the creature's head, never slowing in the least. "Guess you picked the wrong goddamn supper! Guess you didn't know I just keep coming back!"

Alex's punches, while fast and furious, ultimately proved ineffective. This became clear when the lion, still on its back, raised its hind legs and hooked them under Alex's arms. Then with one powerful kick the lion sent Alex tumbling off.

"Run, Mister Lion! Run! I've been eaten by birds more ferocious than you!" Alex called out as the lion disappeared into the grass. "Next time I see you, you're going to be a pelt!"

Alex panted and smiled. Round three was his. True, his body was soaked in his own blood, but he was used to it by now, and he was clearly the victor. With that thought, Alex began the trek back to wherever his gear was. Now that he'd thoroughly spanked Mister Lion and sent him running home, he felt confident, bad ass, utterly unstoppable. He felt...knocked to the ground and torn to shreds.

When Alex opened his eyes, he was greeted with another morning. Once more he was back in the lion's den, and once again, his body had been made anew. This time, however, Mister Lion sat near the mouth of the cave and stared at Alex.

"Oh for fuck's sake," said Alex, shaking his head as the lion approached. "Now you're just being ridiculous."

One giant pounce later, Alex was back in the feline's jaws.

"I hope you choke on me," Alex spat.

CHAPTER TWENTY-EIGHT

Morning. The twelfth day. Alex had marked the cavern wall accordingly with a nearby rock.

Today will be different, he thought to himself. *Today, Mister Lion, you will not crush my throat, nor spill my guts, nor snap my neck. Nor will you have any other form of pre-meal entertainment. For I, Mister Lion, refuse to move.*

As such, Alex remained still, eyes closed tight, not once even daring to peek to see if the lion was near. He knew where he was. Mister Lion was lying down near the front of the cave, watching and waiting, as it had for the past two weeks. Alex could hear his occasional yawn or grunt from time to time. And why would Mister Lion move? He had a free meal delivered in home every morning. Alex's only real question at this point was why Mister Lion hadn't grown fat and lazy by now.

An hour passed, and then another. All the while Alex plotted against his feline foe. Victory would be his, oh yes. True, the past twelve days had seen Alex run down time and again, torn limb from limb, but during each of those days, Alex had been studying Mister

Lion's moves, learning his weaknesses. Today would see the end of Mister Lion, if only the damned thing would wander off.

At some point in the day, Alex realized he hadn't heard anything aside from the occasional bird or breeze for some time. When he opened his eyes and didn't see his archenemy lying or prowling about, he dared look around. The cave, for the moment, was empty.

Swiftly, silently, Alex slinked to the mouth of the cave, back pressed against the wall. He peered outside, checking nearby grass and scrub as much as he could. Mister Lion was nowhere to be seen, but Alex was wise to the ways of this feline. Mister Lion was out there, somewhere, but Alex wasn't afraid. Death had become more of an annoying setback than anything else at this point. That aside, he only had to make two short sprints before his masterful plan could be executed.

Alex glanced at his flanks one last time before he bolted. He bounded over the familiar rocks and crags of the mountainside, deftly avoided a few pitfalls he'd inadvertently hit before, and catapulted himself up a lone oak tree. Perched on a low branch, Alex paused long enough to ensure that Mister Lion wasn't right on his heels.

With no sign of the beast, Alex gripped a three-inch thick branch that grew above his head and pulled. For a second, the branch resisted, but soon it bent, splintered, and subsequently snapped under Alex's unyielding strength. He fell out of the tree and rolled when he hit the ground. He had no illusions of snapping off a branch gracefully, nor did he care. All he wanted was a weapon, and now he had it.

Alex was on his feet and running a second later. If Mister Lion wasn't tracking him before, the sound of an oak limb snapping would undoubtedly send him coming. And that meant Alex would soon have to make his stand. Fortunately, the stream wasn't far off, and that was exactly where he wanted to be.

Alex's feet pounded the ground, and his legs pumped without relent. The stream bubbled merrily, beckoning him closer. It promised him safety. Victory. The grass, on the other hand, tormented him. With each rustle made by the wind, every tall clump he passed, it promised him death by a whirlwind of fang and claw.

Alex ran on, never slowing. His eyes glanced left and right. His hands tightened on his club. His feet splashed in the shallow stream, and his mind commanded his body to halt, though it was tempting to run on.

With his club raised, Alex spun around. He grinned and laughed like the Mad Hatter. "Oh, Mister Lion," Alex cried out. "Your opportunity has passed!"

The lion didn't appear, and Alex kept his back to the stream, not because he expected the attack to come from the grass, but because he counted on Mister Lion to slink around for an attack on his rear. A few minutes passed, and Alex resisted the urge to run. Occasionally, he threw a glance over his shoulder, and after the fifth one, he kept his eyes forward and silently counted.

One...two...thee...four...five...six.

Alex whirled around at the sound of grass parting in time to see Mister Lion clearing the stream in a single bound. As the lion sailed through the air, Alex deftly stepped to the side and swung his club like he had been served a soft pitch at the bottom of the ninth with bases loaded.

The club connected with the side of Mister Lion's head with a loud crack. Mister Lion roared in defiance, and as he landed, Alex was on him again, swinging harder and faster than ever before. With every strike, Alex drove the lion into the ground and kept it stunned.

"That's for eating me yesterday," Alex yelled, landing a wicked uppercut with his club. Mister lion's head snapped back, and the feline rolled over, clearly punch drunk. Without losing any momentum in the attack, Alex brought the club high overhead and hit the creature again as it tried to come to its feet. "And that's for trying to eat me again today!"

The club struck Mister Lion directly on the forehead and snapped in two. Alex chucked his half of the club away and leapt on the back of Mister Lion before the feline had a chance to recover. Alex then wrapped his lower legs around the lion's waist and his arms around the lion's neck.

Mister Lion, with his strength returning, roared and tried to bite and claw his way to freedom. He thrashed about and slammed the back of his head into Alex's shoulder. When that didn't work, he rolled several times over, but that played directly into Alex's plan.

On Mister Lion's final roll, the two ended up in the stream. There, Alex wrestled with the great beast, dragging it deeper and deeper into the water. Alex had only one goal in mind the entire time, to keep his head above the water while keeping Mister Lion's beneath. If he couldn't stab, bludgeon, or shoot the animal to death, Alex was determined to drown the damn thing if that was the last thing he did.

Mister Lion bucked, and Alex fought hard to keep the animal down. More than once Alex almost lost his grip and paid for it each time with his blood. The stream turned red where they fought, and Alex knew his arms and legs wouldn't last forever. He could only hope the damage wasn't yet severe enough to allow Mister Lion to escape.

Sensing things were at a turning point, Alex kept the lion's head submerged with one hand and rained blows down with the other. The lion's fight weakened. Its body gave several violent spasms, then quit moving.

Exhausted, elated, bloodied and bruised, Alex dragged the waterlogged feline body from the stream. As he sat on the bank, he looked at his fallen foe. Part of him was sad that he had had to kill such a magnificent beast, but a greater part was glad it was over.

A small part of him, however, found humor in it all. "We're a lot alike, Mister Lion. We both fight to the death," he said, patting the creatures head. "So if you come back tomorrow morning, we'll call it a draw."

Jessica and Odysseus were not on the beach where Alex had left them. Alex spent the better part of a few hours scouring the island before he spied them inland and at the edge of a dense forest. When he reached them both, Alex hopped off his chariot with the lion carcass across his back and tossed it in front of them.

"You did it!" Jessica said, dropping the seven-foot spear she had in hand, running over and squeezing him tight. "I was getting worried, but Odysseus said we should give you at least a month before sending out a search party."

Alex raised an eyebrow at the fallen weapon. "What's that about?"

"Hunting lessons," Jessica said, beaming.

"Hunting what, exactly?"

"Anything. Everything. Oh my god, Alex, when this is all done, you've got to take me back here. Do you know how amazingly awesome it is to take down a chimera? I mean, I had help—lots of help—but still..."

"You did a fine job, Jessica," Odysseus said, casually leaning on his own spear. "I'm glad you made it back in one piece, Alex. Part of me wondered if the lion would eat you."

"He did eat me," Alex replied. "But that—"

"Wait," Jessica cut in. "What do you mean, he ate you? Like, ate ate you? Complete with chewing and swallowing and...stuff?"

"Yes, and more than once at that."

"Jesus. How's that possible?"

"Apparently, this ever-healing body of mine covers being lion food, too," said Alex. "At this point, I don't know if Hades blessed me or cursed me. Waking up in a cave, day after day, and being chewed up is unsettling."

Jessica cringed, and her eyes misted. "I don't even want to know."

"I imagine it must have been horrifying," said Odysseus. "Did you find what you need?"

Alex pointed down at the lion. "That's a dead cat, isn't it? One I killed without your stupid nets."

Odysseus glanced at the lion carcass and grinned. "Tell me, Alex," he said. "What kept you going? Being eaten time and again is not something most people would willingly face."

"Willpower," said Alex, thinking and rubbing his chin. His gaze drifted to the treetops, to where the wind gently swayed the leaves, and his mind drifted back to those gods-forsaken days of being trapped in a cave with only the breeze and birds to keep him company. "Determination to see this potion made and a healthy dose of insanity."

Odysseus raised an eyebrow. "Insanity?"

"Yeah, insanity," Alex said with a chuckle. "After about the third or fourth time I became a meal, the situation became too absurd to take seriously anymore."

A dog, tall and lean, bounded from the forest, interrupting the conversation. It ran up to Jessica, licked her hands, and then bounded over to Odysseus, its long, curled tail wagging the entire time with boundless enthusiasm. Once at Odysseus's side, it promptly sat with its chin up, ears pointed high, and never once barked or looked away.

"Alex, meet Argos," Odysseus said, scratching the dog behind its ears. "He's finer than any hound you'll ever meet, and he served me faithfully when I walked among the living. I can't begin to tell you about my elation when I learned he waited for me here in Elysium."

"I didn't realize pets went to heaven," said Alex.

Odysseus gave a surprised look. "And why not?" he asked. "Are they too not made by the gods? Do they not faithfully serve their masters?"

"I suppose some do."

Odysseus knelt, grabbed his dog with both hands, and playfully shook it around. "And those that do get to come here and play," he said to the hound. He then turned to Alex and said, "You should come with us for the afternoon. The boars we're about to hunt are things of legends. Three times as big and ten times as ferocious as any anywhere else. I'd wager that a relaxing afternoon spent hunting one down might do you some good, especially considering the ordeal you've just gone through."

"Thank you, but no," Alex said, holding up a hand. "I want to finish this potion so I can see where I'm at. Besides, I don't know the first thing about hunting pigs."

Odysseus stood and offered Alex his spear. "There's nothing to it," he said. "We can either corner the boar, at which point you'll need to stick it with a well-placed thrust. Or we can let Argos antagonize it enough so it charges."

"You let a boar charge you?" asked Alex incredulously. "Seems like that would be hard to dodge."

"You don't dodge it, my good man," said Odysseus, serious as ever before. "A stupid creature like that is blind to its rage. All you have to do is plant the spear in the ground and it will impale itself without a second thought. It's very exhilarating when it happens. You only need to be sure that the butt is seated and the point is aimed at his chest."

"Given my time with Mister Lion, I have no intentions of letting anything else charge me," said Alex. "But if I do end up doing something that stupid, I'll keep your pointers in mind."

"Perhaps next time you happen this way I can convince you to join us," said Odysseus. "But be warned, if Heracles is here when we do, he'll insist we tackle the beasts and strangle them."

Alex shook his head at the insanity of it all. "I'll keep that in mind as well. Can we get back to my potion now?"

"If you wish," he answered. "You'll need to see Hades this time and be sure to bring this necklace with you," Odysseus said, removing a small silver chain from his neck and handing it over. "The amulet attached, though plain to sight and touch, can capture what we seek."

"And what is it we seek?" asked Alex.

"Perseverance," he answered. "To get it, Hades must take you to Tartarus, for no mortal is allowed in on his own accord—so again, Jessica will need to stay here."

"Doing things on my own is becoming the norm, it seems," said Alex.

Odysseus nodded. "You will be more on your own in Tartarus than you've ever been. It is a place of righteous fire, where punishment for the most heinous is doled out. There you will be strapped to a wheel of fire on which you must remain for five days without rest or aid of any kind."

"You're chaining me to a wheel so I can be tortured?" Alex said, fear and anger in his voice. "Have you gone mad?"

"I am neither mad nor chaining you to anything," Odysseus replied. "You're free to keep my nets, but you won't be able to use them. They'll burn up the moment they touch that wheel."

"Which means?" Alex asked, knowing he didn't want to hear the answer.

"Which means you must hold on to the wheel of your own accord if you want to succeed," Odysseus answered. "I won't lie. It will be nothing short of excruciating. But it is the only way we can draw out and capture the purest form of perseverance, Alex. And love, true love, takes much of it."

Jessica put a soft hand on Alex's shoulders. "Alex, think about this for a second."

"I'm trying not to."

She turned him toward her. He could see in her eyes that there was much she wanted to say, but she only managed a few words. "This is insane. There's got to be some other way."

Odysseus shook his head, looking sympathetic to Alex's plight. "Suffering, I'm afraid, is sometimes necessary."

"Then say no," she said, her voice wavering. "You can't do this to yourself. Look at all you've done so far. No one is going to say you haven't tried."

Alex looked at Odysseus who nodded. "She's right on all counts. You've done a lot, and I'd say thus far you've tried as hard as any other man. What do you say to that?"

"I say I'm still without answers, so I've got no choice." Alex sighed heavily. "What happens if I fall off the wheel?"

"You'll have to start over," he said. "You must stay on that wheel for five days without break."

Alex shook his head. "She's right. This is insane."

"I agree, but you are the one choosing not to love your wife," Odysseus said. "If this path doesn't appeal to you, you can always walk away."

"And be back in love limbo where I started? No thank you. I need answers," Alex replied. "Let's get this flaming wheel of death over with."

CHAPTER TWENTY-NINE

Alex, trembling and speechless, stood next to Hades at the shores of Tartarus. A river of lava flowed a few feet away, roaring and churning as it completely encircled an island a quarter mile away. Jets of flame shot out from the molten rock, seemingly even more so whenever Alex was brave or stupid enough to draw near the shore's edge. The air was dense and smelled of sulfur. Volcanic ash covered the ground in a thick, deep carpet and made walking difficult. Well, it made walking difficult for Alex. Hades, on the other hand, appeared to have no difficulty whatsoever.

"When Zeus strapped Ixion to the wheel of fire, I thought the punishment a good one," Hades said, leading Alex to a narrow bridge. Since Alex's mention of voluntary torture, the god's attitude had shifted from depressive to unsettlingly eager. "I liked it so much I built a wheel of my own, but never got around to making locks that wouldn't melt," Hades went on. "I'm glad to see it will finally be put to use."

"Me too," said Alex, though he thoroughly was not.

"When this is over, remind your friend that she owes me pictures of my wife."

"I will," Alex said, feeling uneasy about Jessica suddenly being brought into the conversation.

"Good, and be sure to tell her all that you witnessed down here, for I promise she'll suffer the lot of it should she not come through on her promise."

"Over my dead body," almost came out of Alex's mouth, but he kept those words from passing his tongue when his mind realized such a threat was hollow when thrown at the God of the Underworld. So instead, he chose to alleviate Hades' concerns as best he could. "She'll come through. I promise."

Hades nodded in response, and with quick, purposeful steps, he led Alex across the bridge. It was a bridge, Alex noted, that was cool to the touch despite the scalding air. As they approached the other side, Alex saw that the island was circumscribed by a large wall, and in that large wall was only one gate. Atop that one gate was a *thing*—for what else could it be called—that made Alex stop in his tracks.

The creature had a dragon-like body of at least fifty yards in length, tail not included. It gripped its perch with claws that looked like they could easily peel a tank, and it watched Alex with fifty sets of eyes, each pair being set in one of fifty serpentine heads. Each head bared fangs like spears and screeched nonstop until Hades silenced them with a wave of his hand.

"Don't mind him," said Hades. "Those in the presence of an Olympian have nothing to fear."

"That's...comforting," Alex said, being sure he stayed near the god as he opened the gates. "Though I'm not sure how much I'll like that little tidbit when you leave."

"I will return in five days," Hades said as they passed through. "If for nothing else so that you can fetch my scepter. I'm not pleased that you forgot it, but I think this self-inflicted punishment of yours is good enough to stay my hand."

"Sorry about that, again," Alex said, hoping Hades didn't press the lie. "I promise it's perfectly safe." He then opted to try and change the subject so the matter would be forgotten. "How much farther is this wheel of yours?"

"Not far," Hades said. "Not far at all."

Inside the wall, Alex followed Hades over the barren terrain and down a long, gradual decline until they reached the island center. There, Alex stared at a pit the likes of which he'd never seen. It was at least four hundred yards across and gods knew how deep. A single staircase, narrow and broken, wound its way down the inside edge, flickering torches being the only things that illuminated the way.

"How deep?" asked Alex, fiddling with the necklace Odysseus had given him.

"Deep," Hades replied.

Alex picked up a small rock and tossed it over the edge. His eyes strained trying to follow it into the inky black. "Damn," he finally said after several moments. "I couldn't even hear it hit bottom."

"It will not hit bottom for seven days," said Hades, starting down the stairs. "If I were you, I'd mind my step."

"No kidding," said Alex, shying away from the edge and feeling dizzy. He fell in line behind Hades as the god descended into the pit, all the while wishing he could will a handrail into existence. Down they went, passing a myriad of dark tunnel entrances. Some were silent, others were not. From those that weren't came mournful wails, shrieks of terror, and cries of insanity.

Eventually, Hades entered one of the silent tunnels. The air felt stale, and though no echoes of madness bounced off the walls, Alex had the overwhelming urge to run.

The passage made a dozen turns before opening into a small cavern. Oblong and with a high, mossy ceiling, the cave offered ample space. In the middle floated a large wheel that slowly spun on an invisible axel.

Hades walked over to it, and with one hand he gripped the wheel's edge and brought it to a stop. "Climb on, Alex."

"On to what?" Alex replied. As far as he could tell, there was no chair to sit, grips to grip, or handles to clutch. It was merely a large wheel with eight spokes.

"As I said earlier, I have no chains that can withstand the heat," said Hades. "You will need to wrap your arms and legs around the wheel's edge if you are to remain affixed."

Alex walked over and after using a quick touch with a wet finger to see if the wheel was hot or not, he attached himself to the wheel's outer edge. There he hung upside down with arms and legs wrapped and locked together. "Now what?"

"Now you hold on for five days," Hades said. The corners of his mouth drew back. With one hand he set the wheel in motion and with the other, he conjured a ball of flame that hovered an inch above his open palm. "Any last requests?"

"Pint of morphine?" Alex said, eyes wide. He could feel the color drain from his face, and as much as he wanted to look away, he couldn't keep from staring at the flame.

"I don't know what this morphine of yours is, but I'm guessing it has to do with pain. So no, you can't have any."

The god flicked his wrist and the ball of fire hopped off his palm and onto the wheel. The flame raced in both directions along the wheel's edge. Alex clenched his teeth as the fire ran over his body with a roar. His skin peeled, and his hair vanished. Alex's screams were only answered by the sizzle of flesh.

The wheel glowed red, and Alex tried to shift his grip in his pain-deluded state, hoping that it might offer some relief. But to his horror, his arms stuck to the metal and pulling on them only exacerbated the pain.

Time crawled. Seconds turned into years and then into lifetimes in the single flick of a flame.

"Five days," he heard Hades say. "That's when I'll be back. Try not to let go, for your sake. I'd hate to see you start over."

Alex tried to force out a question, but it sounded so unintelligible, he wasn't sure if the god heard it, let alone understood it.

"How long has it been?" Hades said.

Alex whimpered while searching for some sort of mental hole to crawl into and shield himself from what he was suffering through.

"Almost thirty seconds," Hades said cheerfully. "Less than four hundred and thirty-two thousand to go."

Moments later, Alex was alone.

Tartarus. Oh, how Aphrodite hated coming to this place. How could anyone enjoy the intoxicating aroma of her perfume when the smell of sweat and blood permeated every nook and cranny? How could the wretched gaze upon her beauty when their eyes were plucked from their sockets? And who could listen to the melodious sound of her voice with that gods-awful howling strangling the air? It's not like anyone wanted to hear their cries of agony. After all, would it really kill the damned to shut up long enough for her to conclude her business in peace? Was it really asking too much to ask them to suffer in silence? It's not like they were lying in beds *they* hadn't made. It's not like they didn't *deserve* every last bit of punishment they had to endure. It's not like they had done what was right or paid homage to the gods when due. Had they done any of that, maybe they wouldn't be in the mess they were in.

The last thought further infuriated the goddess. Insolent, selfish, sufferers. Even in death they could only think of themselves. Even in death, they refused to learn their place. She had half a mind to waltz right into whatever tunnel the loudest group was in and show them what real agony was. Anything could be made worse with a broken heart.

Ultimately, Aphrodite decided against it. Lashing a poor soul with a few more stripes would increase the time she had to spend in such a miserable place, and since all she was here for was Alex, the sooner she saw him, the sooner she could leave and go back to being adored by all.

She entered his tunnel and paused. The screams—the ones she'd been loathing the most—were coming from this place, which meant Alex was the source of her irritation.

Aphrodite pressed her lips together and promised herself she'd rein in her displeasure long enough to get what she wanted.

Maybe.

With his arms around his knees, Alex sat in the far corner of the cave and slowly rocked. At the sound of approaching footsteps, he choked off his sobs and buried his emotional agony as best he could. A few seconds later, Aphrodite stepped into the cavern and stopped a few paces away from the wheel.

"Alex?" she said, looking around. Though the wheel burned steadily, the flames were not enough to illuminate the nook Alex was in. "Where are you, my dear?"

Alex didn't answer, and he prayed she'd leave soon. When she didn't and it was clear she was staying, he finally spoke. "Over here."

"Come out of the dark, silly," she said, beckoning him over with a wave of her hand.

"I'd rather stay."

"You want me to be all alone?" she said with a pouting lip. "I'm hurt that you'd leave me so."

Alex shook his head and decided nothing mattered one way or the other anymore. Stiffly, painfully, he took to his feet and limped toward her. When he stepped into the fire's light, he watched for her reaction.

Aphrodite gasped and covered her mouth with one hand.

"Am I that hideous?" he asked with a laugh. Of course he was. Though he couldn't see his face, he had felt it enough to know his nose, ears, and much of his mouth were gone. And he could certainly see the charred black stubs his hands and feet had become. Not to mention the places on his chest and midsection that looked like hamburger that had spent a good three hours on the grill.

"Alex, what did you do?" she said, recomposing herself. She closed the distance between them and took his hands in hers. "Talk to me."

Alex pulled away. "I've done nothing."

"No, no, no," she said, horror splashed over her face. "This is not nothing. This is serious."

"Stop—"

Aphrodite put a soothing hand on his shoulder. "This is needless, Alex."

"This is failure!" he yelled. Alex dropped to his knees and buried his face in his hands. "I tried to get what was needed, but I couldn't. I'm not strong enough."

"Get what?" she asked, kneeling beside him.

Alex looked around, but what he sought was nowhere to be seen. "The chain," he replied. "I was trying to capture perseverance like I was supposed to."

Aphrodite put her arm around his shoulders and pulled him close. "What are you talking about, Alex?"

Alex shut his eyes and allowed himself to be drawn into the goddess's embrace. Even with the smell of burnt flesh saturating Alex's nasal cavity, the aroma that came from her was strong enough and heavenly enough that for a moment, Alex forgot his worries, his pain, and his failure. A small squeeze from Aphrodite's arm prompted him to answer her question. "Odysseus said he could make me a love potion," he said. "I've been getting the ingredients he needs together."

"A love potion?" she said, sounding strangely amused.

Alex shook his head as he attempted to clarify. "Not a love potion," he replied. "Potion of Agape, I think he called it."

"And what, pray tell, does this potion do?"

Alex shrugged, knowing he wasn't entirely clear on its use. "Helps search the soul. Nothing fancy."

"Maybe I can help," she said. "What answers are you looking for?"

The question pierced his heart like a well-thrown spear. "Euryale," he managed to spit out. "I have to know whether or not this marriage was a mistake. I have to know if my heart is with her."

Aphrodite gently lifted his chin. She kept his eyes locked on hers, and if she found his appearance repulsive in any way, she didn't show it. "Alex," she whispered. "There is no such potion. Only you will ever know who you love."

"I know that," he snapped.

The Goddess of Love sighed. "You're not hearing me," she said. "This agape potion doesn't exist."

Alex looked at her dumbfounded. "What do you mean?"

"Odysseus lied," she said. "Or perhaps he's simply mistaken."

"No."

"Yes."

Tears welled in his eyes, but they never fell. Alex grew numb, but anger quickly surfaced as he refused to believe any such thing. "No," he said, pushing away her words. "You're trying to trick me."

Aphrodite took his hand, placed it on her chest, and covered it with one of hers. "I'm not lying, Alex," she said. "I swear by the River Styx that this Potion of Agape you speak of is not real."

Alex couldn't argue, though he wanted to. The seriousness of her oath made him confront reality. "Why would Odysseus do such a thing?"

"I don't know, Alex," she whispered. "I don't know."

Alex's head spun, a whirlwind of thought and emotion. "What will I do?"

"Alex, if I may," Aphrodite said after a few moments. "If you're still struggling with your feelings for you wife, maybe that means you two truly aren't meant for each other."

"Maybe," Alex said, hating himself for speaking those words, but he couldn't argue against the possibility anymore.

"It's okay, Alex," she went on. "Not every couple is the right match." She then laughed at her next thought. "If they were, I'd be out of a job."

"I had hoped otherwise," Alex said as he sank into her again.

"We all do," she said. "But it's not too late."

Alex looked up. "Not too late for what?"

"To make things right."

Alex sighed heavily. "I don't even know what that means anymore."

"I do," she said. "Euryale has a specialness to her. I can see why you liked her, but honestly, Alex, the last week aside, who has always consumed your thoughts?"

"Jessica."

"And who's been at your side through all of this?"

"Jessica, but only because Euryale's been locked up."

Aphrodite nodded. "Fair enough, but Jessica's risked life and limb to help you. Could Euryale, an immortal, ever do the same? Jessica still loves you, even if she won't say it."

"Like you made her?" Alex said with a snort.

Aphrodite let a short growl slip. "I erred forcing it, I admit," she said, recomposing herself. "But what I did wasn't a lie. I can't make anyone say anything that they don't already believe is true. I freed her heart and yours. I didn't enslave it."

Alex looked away as he wrestled with her words. He couldn't deny that he had loved hearing Jessica's confession for him, but he hated himself for it at the same time. A man cannot serve two masters. Or dedicate himself fully to two lovers. To that end, all he could do was shrug in reply.

"Come, Alex, think this over," she said. "Despite what I may have said or done, who's the one really enslaving you? I'm offering you a choice. Can you really say that about what others have offered?"

"Things are such a mess," he said. "All I want is for both of them to be happy and for this to be over."

"Then divorce yourself from this relationship and let me work," she said. "I can see to it that you and Jessica have a relationship that lasts beyond the ages, the envy of all, and at the same time, you have my word I'll see to it that Euryale finds the love she's searching for. Everyone can have their happy ending."

Alex buried his face in his hands. "This feels too easy. Too easy and too wrong."

"Torturing yourself in a vain search for some non-existent feeling is wrong, Alex," she said. "Athena falsely promising you hope and bliss is wrong. All your needless suffering is wrong. Even if she did set the two of you up, Love is my domain. I'm still obligated to fix her mistakes."

Her words trailed off and Alex mulled them over in silence. Maybe she was right. Maybe he couldn't find this elusive feeling of love because it didn't exist in him for Euryale in the first place. Maybe all he felt was a momentary infatuation. A crush. A lust. A substitute for Jessica. God, if that were true, his marriage to the gorgon would never stand eternity.

"What about Ares?" Alex asked. "He still wants to crush me."

"I'll make him release Euryale and bother you no more," she replied. "He does what I tell him, like a good boy."

"And the scepter? I need it back. I can't trade a war with Ares for a war with Hades."

Aphrodite smiled, and Alex felt his worries vanish. "You'll have the scepter back. I wouldn't want anyone turning you to a mortal again, now would I? That would completely muck up my plans for your eternal bliss."

Alex knew he had to decide. On the one hand, the path he was on now promised nothing and was filled with pain, uncertainty, and lies. The other would see Hades' scepter returned, the war put to an end, Euryale freed, and love found for both him and her. Maybe the goddess was right. Maybe a happy ending could be had by all. Not that he wanted to give Euryale up, or that he liked the idea of her being distraught—no crushed—by his surrender, but in the end, wouldn't she be better off?

"Okay, we'll do it your way" he said, taking a deep breath and gathering his resolve. "What do I have to do?"

Aphrodite smiled. "I need you to divorce your wife and pray for my aid and favor. I will take care of the rest."

"Do I need a lawyer?" Alex said with a brief smile.

Aphrodite shook her head. "No. Being in the presence of Zeus will be enough. I will fetch him, and he will annul your vows with myself, Ares, and Athena present as witnesses tomorrow morning."

Alex popped his knuckles as he tried to convince himself this was the right thing to do. "Will this be at Termessos? I want to make sure Ares releases Euryale right after."

"Of course," she said, grabbing his hand and laughing. "You worry too much. It's all under control."

"Promise?"

"Most definitely," she said. "You've made the right choice, my dear. This will be over before you know it."

CHAPTER THIRTY

Alex, with a mostly rejuvenated body, raced back to the Elysium fields. He figured since he had some time before his marriage was dissolved, he should pick up Jessica and rip Odysseus a new one.

Alex found the ancient hero at the tip of a long, wooden jetty. There Odysseus sat with his bare feet dangling in the water and his eyes looking out to the western horizon. The sun had begun to set and cast a warm glow over the ocean. Aside from the brief neighing of Alex's ponies, which Odysseus apparently either ignored or did not hear, the only sounds about were the lapping of the tide and the occasional cry of a seagull overhead. The air smelled of its usual salt, but had a crispness to it as well. Altogether, Alex knew he would have found it a relaxing scene, had he not been so utterly pissed off.

"Get up," Alex said, stepping off his chariot and marching up behind the man. "You've got some explaining to do."

"In a minute," he said, still sitting and looking out over the waters. "Why don't you join me for one last sunset?" he asked. "A lasting image might help you endure your journey in Tartarus."

"I've been to Tartarus already," Alex replied. He nudged the man with his foot. Sure, it was probably rude, but it wasn't as bad as a kick to the head, and that was about to follow if Alex didn't get what he wanted.

Odysseus glanced over his shoulder, looking ready for a fight, but the man's anger dissolved in a flash. His eyes softened, and he jumped to his feet. "The wheel was not kind to you, I see."

Alex looked himself over. His fingers had regrown, as had his ears and nose. Patches of charred skin remained, but most of it was a bright, rosy pink. "I've looked worse," he stated, still in pain.

"I suspect you have," Odysseus replied. "Did you find what you need?"

"Find what I need?" Alex said, twirling the chain Odysseus had given him. "Tell me, good sir, what exactly do I need?"

"Seems you need a lot more than I had originally thought," Odysseus said. "I know I had said five days on the wheel, but I suppose what you've done must do. On to your next task."

"There's no next task!" Alex said, swinging at the man's chin with a right hook.

Odysseus stepped into the attack. He caught Alex's forearm with his left hand, and at the same time, he smashed his right elbow across Alex's chin. "For twenty years I fought," he said as Alex stumbled away. "Ten on the shores of Troy and ten more trying to come home to my dearest Penelope. You think you can beat me with such a pathetic attack? Have you gone mad?"

Alex grunted as he crouched. Odysseus's words barely registered in his mind, and all Alex could think about was how best to take down this new enemy of his that stood tall, proud, and mocking.

Alex drove forward and caught Odysseus about the midsection. Blows rained on his head and sides, but he didn't care. The two struggled, trading punches and kicks. Alex tried several times to take the man to the ground and finish him there, but Odysseus was too skilled to be brought off his feet.

"An angry warrior is a dead warrior," Odysseus said, locking his arms with Alex's and laughing. "You're like the boars we hunt. Angry and blind to everything that matters."

Alex broke apart from the entanglement, and when Odysseus did not follow up with an attack, he took the moment to regain his breath. "You sent me on a wild goose chase!"

"I sent you for ingredients, not a goose," Odysseus replied.

"For something that doesn't exist!" Alex said. "This agape potion of yours is a farce!"

"My help is no farce."

"You promised me a potion!" Alex said, muscles tightening and ready to spring him back into the fight.

"I promised you answers!" Odysseus retorted. "Are you so dense you can't see them?"

Alex, thrown by the man's response, straightened. "What the hell are you talking about? I've gotten no answers. I've got nothing to show. I'm exactly where I was when I first came here."

"Not true," Odysseus said. "You've done and gone through much."

"Yeah," Alex said, smirking. "You're right. I've been beaten, broken, eaten, and burned. All for what?"

"You tell me, Alex," the hero replied, dropping his guard. "Why did you do that?"

Alex laughed at the stupidity of such a question. "What do you mean why? You told me to. You told me to fetch you supplies for your moronic, non-existent potion."

"Why did you want the potion, Alex?"

"Is this twenty questions now?" Alex said, shaking his head. "See? I can do it too."

"It's only as many questions as it takes to get through that thick skull of yours," he said. "Humor me. Why did you want the potion?"

"To find out where my heart was!" Alex said, throwing up his hands.

"Oh," Odysseus replied. "I was under the impression you wanted to have an adventure."

"Adventure?" Alex yelled. He brought his face only a few inches away from the Odysseus's. "You think I did this for fun? Because I was bored?"

"Well, you are a hero," Odysseus replied calmly.

The man's lackadaisical attitude boiled Alex's blood. He couldn't think. He couldn't stand still. He wanted to drive his fist through the man's teeth but didn't, only because he knew he wanted to inflict more pain than that.

"You are on Elysium," Odysseus went on. "Being a hero is the national pastime around here."

"This is not a damn game!" Alex yelled. "You think I'd suffer through all this needless garbage for fun?"

"You wouldn't?"

"No, I wouldn't! I'm doing this to hopefully save my wife, my marriage. I suffered for her, damn it—" Alex cut short his frenzy-filled monologue as his last words drilled home. "I suffered for her," he softly repeated.

Odysseus smiled knowingly. "Do you have what you need now?"

"Yeah, I think I do," Alex said, his inner fire now extinguished. Could he not be loving someone in the face of so much self-sacrifice? Surely he must be. The only thing he wondered now is how such an obvious answer had eluded him for so long. Alex extended his hand, sheepishly. "I'm sorry," he said. "I feel like an ass. I hope you accept my apology."

"I do," Odysseus said, shaking his hand.

Alex avoided the man's gaze for the moment, still feeling a little off. "Now what?"

"You tell me," Odysseus replied. "Love is a choice. What are you going to choose to do, Alex?"

"I'm meeting Aphrodite in the morning," Alex said, fearful at what it would entail but elated now that his heart soared above the clouds. "Once I decline her help, Ares is going to come at me again and again and again. So I've got until then to figure something out."

"I'd help in that regard if I could," said Odysseus, rubbing his chin and looking out over the water. "But as I said when we first met, Ares is one of the most powerful Olympians. No mortal has truly defeated him in battle, only sent him running to lick his wounds."

"Yeah," Alex said with a smile. "I managed to do that once."

"You did?" Odysseus said, turning toward Alex and sounding impressed. "Do tell. I was under the impression that you beat him in the Olympics, not in mortal combat. The only other man that hurt Ares was Diomedes."

"I did beat Ares in the Olympics," Alex said, feeling his head swell. "Granted, I had a javelin from Artemis, but I won just the same. After that, I beat him in an arena."

"Diomedes used a spear from Athena," Odysseus said. "Did you use the same to beat Ares?"

"No. I had a pineapple from Hephaestus," Alex replied with a smile. "It's not a fruit," he quickly added, realizing that Odysseus would be at a loss as to what he was talking about. "It's a weapon we invented not too long ago. I knew Ares wouldn't know what it was, at least, not until it blew up in his face. Literally."

"Clever," said Odysseus. "Perhaps you can use that same ingenuity again."

Alex shook his head. "Ares will never fall for the same trick twice."

"He might not fall for the same trick twice, but I suspect you could lure him into another ruse," Odysseus said. "A man as creative as you should be able to come up with any number of things."

"I'm open to suggestions," Alex admitted. At this point, he was open to a complete game plan since the number of viable ideas he'd come up with could be counted on no hands.

"What do you have to work with?"

Alex shrugged. "Wedding presents. Plenty of those. Winged sandals. Ponies with chariot. And some yarn."

"Going to battle is as much preparation as it is determination," Odysseus said. "If I were you, I'd do three things. First, take an exact inventory of what you have and what you may need. Second, study your opponent and study him well. Learn his habits and his weaknesses so you can exploit them. You'll not conquer Ares otherwise. Last, I would go to Hephaestus again. If any Olympian will aid your cause one more time, it will be him."

Alex committed Odysseus's list to memory. Though the instructions were simple and made a lot of sense, he had reservations about the hero's last point.

"Hephaestus might help, but even if he makes me another weapon, so what?" Alex said. "I can't kill Ares no matter what Hephaestus gives me, and he'll keep coming at me over and over."

"You don't have to kill him, just beat him."

"Easier said than done."

"You don't even have to beat him," Jessica said from behind.

"How's that?" Alex said, turning to face her.

"All you have to do is to remove Ares's desire to fight you," she said.

Alex chuckled. "You think I can turn Ares into a pacifist? I'm not sure I can really picture him with flowers on his head singing *Let There Be Peace on Earth*."

"I don't think that's what she meant," Odysseus said, his face beaming with approval. "Whatever you do, if you can get Ares to not want to fight you specifically, that will be good enough. Perhaps you can convince him that a better battle elsewhere will satiate his lust for war."

"Or get him to realize any victory over you is a Pyrrhic one at best," Jessica added.

"I like it," Alex said, thoughtfully. "I like it a lot. How did you come up with that?"

"Bumped into a harpy earlier after Heracles ran after a manticore," she said. She then nodded to the spear she was carrying. "Not sure if I'd have won, damn thing was scary and fast, but I put up enough of a show that she knew I wasn't worth the risk."

Alex whistled, thoroughly impressed. "Jessica the Monster Slayer. Has a nice ring to it, don't you think?"

"I do," she replied. "When I get home, I'm going to make that into a book and then a movie and then a huge line of toys."

"Getting a little ahead of yourself, aren't you?"

Jessica shrugged. "Never too early to think about merchandising."

"I'll leave that up to you," Alex said. "I've got to get going." Jessica planted the spear in the ground. "Why am I not surprised you're leaving me again. I came to help, remember?"

"I know," Alex said. "And you have been, immensely." He hugged her tight. "But this last fight is mine alone."

Jessica settled into the embrace. "Fine, be that way. It was good seeing you again, though."

"Hey, don't act like I'm not coming back."

"You will. I know," she said. "But when you do, you'll have your bride back and this will be over, and I'll have to go back to the mundane life."

Alex straightened his arms so he could look her in the eyes. "I'll pull some strings," he said, smiling. "Your adventures don't have to end here."

"Promise?"

"Absolutely."

As Alex turned and went for his ponies, Jessica called out one last time. "Hey, one other thing, if you could?"

"What's that?"

"If you meet any single, hottie Greek heroes, send them my way?"

Alex laughed. "As you wish."

* * *

Alex bolted down the dark tunnel the moment he saw the warm glow of Hephaestus's forge. He stubbed his toes and bruised his shins a half dozen times along the way, but he cared not. Eagerness drove Alex forward, eagerness to see his plan come to fruition. All he lacked was one little item from the god's armory.

"Alex, good friend," Hephaestus said as Alex exited the tunnel. "Back sooner than I thought, yes, but back the victor."

Alex skidded to a stop a few feet behind the still-working god. "I haven't won yet," he said, raising his voice so he could be heard over the sounds of hammer and anvil. "But I will soon."

Hephaestus's arm froze, mid stroke, and he turned around, confusion on his face. "We beat him in the arena, did we not? We used our weapon, our pineapple, and sent him running."

"We did," Alex replied, fidgeting with the bag that was slung over his shoulder. "Sadly that wasn't enough. He cheated me out of my victory."

Hephaestus narrowed his eyes and let slip a low growl. "Cheat, yes. Ares cheats often, as do others," he said, returning to his work. "They're all cheats. We should've known better."

"I fight him again tomorrow morning," Alex declared.

"We wish you the best," the god flatly replied.

Alex stepped forward. "But I need your help."

"We helped you once already," Hephaestus replied. His face hardened and the blows from his hammer fell faster and heavier.

"I appreciate it to no end," Alex said. "As you said before, we beat him in the arena. We can beat him again."

Hephaestus grunted and smirked. "To what end? We waste our time fighting. We try, and he always escapes, always laughs at us."

"I know," said Alex, gritting his teeth and sharing the god's frustration. "This stupid war should've never happened, but it did. It should've ended, but it didn't. I know I can't beat Ares—"

"This is supposed to give us confidence?" Hephaestus interrupted with a smirk.

"No," Alex replied, shaking his head. "But I know how to get him to stop. All I need is your net."

Hephaestus laughed heartily. "You think we'd give our prized possession so easily so that Ares can take it from you?"

Alex backed, hands up. "No, you've got it all wrong," he said. "I'm not going to give him your net. I'm going to take him down with it."

Hephaestus shook his head. "No, good friend, he'll take it from you as he took Hades' scepter."

"I swear by the River Styx he'll do no such thing," Alex said, hopeful that the oath would sway the god's mind.

Hephaestus motioned to the countless weapons and shields that hung on the walls. "You may use anything else," he said, returning to his work. "We must have our net. We must have it to catch them again when the time is right. We cannot make another."

Alex pulled the bag off his shoulder and took out the recently purchased laptop from inside. "Hephaestus," he said, waiting until he had the god's attention before going on. "Hear me out before you say no."

Hephaestus put down his hammer. "What is that?"

"A laptop," Alex said, flipping it open and booting it up. "I downloaded some movies off the Internet. Movies of Ares fighting Athena."

The look on Hephaestus's face changed from skeptical to inquisitive. He walked over and inspected the laptop like any master craftsman would marveling at something new. "Tell us plainly what you mean."

"People can make movies with things called cameras," Alex explained. With a few taps of the touchpad, he opened one of the movies he had downloaded for Hephaestus to see. It was a video Alex had found that one of his old neighbors had made when Athena and Ares decided to duke it out in front of his former home.

The audio was crap and filled with expletives, and some of the shots were ruined by someone swinging the camera wildly, but it still managed to faithfully capture most of the fight.

"Cameras record events as they happen," Alex explained. "That way people can come back later and see what happened."

Hephaestus smiled like a father proud of his children. "What fine smiths you mortals have become to produce such a thing,"

Alex hit the replay button once the video finished. "I've studied this countless times and learned a few things about Ares," Alex said. He watched the timer at the bottom of the screen, and when it reached 0:42, he paused the video. "This is the second time Ares throws a car at Athena. At first glance, it looks like a good throw, but he always throws a little right of center. Always. The first throw was the same, but it's harder to see thanks to the terrible camera angle."

Hephaestus didn't immediately reply, and Alex resumed the movie until another thirty seconds had passed at which point he stopped it again. This time, instead of a frame displaying an airborne auto, the screen showed Athena deftly spinning out of one of Ares' holds. "This is Athena getting away, obviously," Alex said. "Ares likes to grab the forearms and pull in close. I imagine he likes to be up close as he pummels his victim."

"Athena fights better than we do," Hephaestus said.

"She does," Alex acknowledged. He then moved the play bar up a few minutes to where Ares and Athena wrestled on the ground, covered in the remains of Alex's house. "But I'm not about to fight Ares hand to hand," he said. "This is after they nuked my house, my fish...my piano. You can see Athena is trying to get out of her brother's hold on the ground, but she's struggling a lot at this point."

"Which means what?"

"It means Ares knows he excels when the fight hits the ground," Alex explained. "If the fight lasts long enough, he'll want to play to that strength and get things on the ground as quickly as possible."

"Knowing he'll probably charge is one thing, knowing when he will is something else."

"True," said Alex. He backed the movie up about twenty seconds. "But look what happens when Athena turns her back on him right before they obliterate my house," he said as the video played. "It takes a few seconds, but what she does really pisses him off. I know you can't see it well, but I was there. He turned crimson right before he charged. I don't think he could control himself if his life depended on it at that point."

Alex checked his watch. "I'm out of time," he said. "I've got to get back soon, and I've still got to get to the River Acheron. Please, we could easily be here another hour discussing everything. Lend me your net. I can get him to run right into it, thus defeating him, ending this war, and regaining my bride."

When Hephaestus hesitated, Alex quickly added, "I'll even have him promise to leave your wife alone."

The god cracked a brief grin. "We appreciate your friendship," he said. "But even if you could end his lies, what would it matter? She still sneaks about. She still takes advantage of us when our back is turned. No, good friend, ridding us of Ares does not solve our problem. It does not save the marriage."

"Then what would?" asked Alex.

Hephaestus grunted. "Don't pretend you can fix such things. We've tried for eons, but they are so elusive now. How can we confront her lies without proof? And if we cannot confront those lies, how will we ever fix that which is broken? How can we convince the others that they are still sneaking off behind our back?"

Alex chuckled, then immediately straightened, looking mortified at his behavior. "Sorry," he said, hoping he didn't have to dodge a hammer. "But if all you need is a way to keep an eye on her, take my laptop. We can put some webcams around and voila! You'll not only see what's going on, but have proof of it, too."

"Won't she see these cameras?"

"No," he said. "They're super tiny now. And you can always disguise them as anything you want and place them anywhere you need. Play to her vanity if you must and give her one as a gift."

The god sucked in a long, slow breath, and smiled. "This could work."

"It will work!"

"Then in exchange for your laptop and help getting cameras, and most of all for being a good friend and keeping your word and your desire to help, we will loan you our net."

"Thank you!" Alex said, grabbing the god's hand and shaking it. "You've no idea how appreciative I am."

"And you have no idea what we will do to you if it's lost," said Hephaestus. "Hades might not be able to make chains for his wheel, but we can. We can make a great number of things that can tear flesh and sanity with ease."

The God of Smiths limped away and plucked the net from the wall. A brief twist of its links turned it invisible. "Do like this and it fades from sight," he said. "Twist back or catch your prey and all can see its golden links. My net will close on whatever you cast it upon, and it will only release when you desire it to."

Alex took the net from Hephaestus, noting it was far lighter than he had expected. "Thank you again, Hephaestus. The next time you see me, I'll return your net and give my eternal thanks once more."

CHAPTER THIRTY-ONE

Alex flew to Termessos as fast as his little ponies would go. They breathed heavily and grunted often, and Alex wondered if he might run them to death. That was a chance he was willing to take, however, since he'd spent too long in the Underworld, and he feared Aphrodite might get frustrated at having to wait and do something to ruin his plan. More than once Alex told himself that these little ponies came from the same farm that bred horses to pull the sun. Thus having them blaze a trail from the Underworld to Termessos ought to be nothing more than a fun run. Thankfully, his worries never materialized, and with two live, happy ponies, Alex reached Ares' fortress.

"Sorry I'm late," Alex said to all once he arrived. He checked the ponies' bridles one last time before approaching Ares, Athena, Aphrodite and Zeus, all of whom stood outside the fortress gates. "Lost track of time."

Athena took a quick step forward. "Wasting time fishing, Alex?" she asked with annoyance. "Or are those for decoration?"

Alex glanced over his shoulder to where two rope nets hung from his chariot's side. "No," he replied. "Odysseus gave me the nets a while ago when I was hunting lions. I guess I haven't figured out what else to do with them."

"Perhaps when we're done here you can use them on another hunt," Zeus said. "There's many a ferocious creature you can tackle with them, but they will take time and cunning to persevere over."

"All the more reason for us to wrap this up quickly," said Aphrodite.

"Yes. Let's get this done," said Alex, adjusting the rifle sling to the Garand he had over his shoulder.

Athena pressed her lips together and folded her arms over her chest. "I can't believe you're doing this to your wife."

"I only want everyone to be happy," he replied. He then turned to Ares. "You have Hades' scepter?"

Said scepter appeared in Ares' hands, and the god answered. "I do."

"Good." Alex sucked in a breath and steeled himself for the performance of a lifetime. He turned and faced the God of Thunder. "Mighty Zeus, ruler of the Olympians, I humbly beseech you to grant me one favor."

Zeus chuckled. "If it will settle a squabble between my children, I'm listening. The three of them won't leave me alone! It makes disappearing...difficult, as of late."

"Yes, this will end the squabble," Alex said. He paused as he caught Aphrodite nudge Ares with an elbow and Athena sigh in disgust. "For far too long I questioned my love for Euryale, and it took our separation and untold amounts of suffering to realize my love for her is always a choice, never a feeling. Thus, I'm here to say to all of you, my vows I made in front of you, Zeus, and her father, The Old Man, are stronger than ever before."

Aphrodite's mouth hung open. She stammered over a half dozen words as her face burned bright. The fact that Athena's face had the smuggest grin Alex had ever seen probably didn't help either. "You think this will end things?" she finally got out.

Alex shook his head, and kept his attention on the God of the Sky. "Zeus, make me your champion, and let me put an end to how Ares mocks your ruling. Every time he challenges me, intent on breaking the bonds between myself and Euryale, he is intent on destroying what you have sanctified."

Zeus held up a hand, keeping both Ares and Aphrodite in check. "You make a fine argument, Alex, but I have spoken with Ares in private. He has a right to challenge you."

Alex nodded. "Then let this be the final challenge. Let everything be decided between us with this last battle. We shall go, nonstop, till the other tires of combat and yields to the other."

"What say you?" Zeus said to the God of War.

"I always knew you were a true warrior," Ares said, beaming with pride. "I accept your challenge. We shall take to the field of battle one last time and engage in glorious combat! Let us shake hands as friends before we fight as enemies!"

"I don't think so," Alex said as apathetically as he could. He pulled a piece of *Hot-N-Tuff* from his pocket and began to chew, hoping such an act would add further insult to the god. "I don't want to lower myself by touching the hand of someone about to be defeated."

Alex turned around and strutted to his chariot, all the while counting silently in his head. He resisted the urge to look over his shoulder. At the count of five, being the same time it took Ares to attack Athena on the video, Alex jumped to his left, spun, and brought his rifle to bear.

Ares' spear zipped by the left side of his head. A split-second later, Alex pulled the trigger. The Garand kicked, and though it hadn't been properly seated in his shoulder, his aim was good enough. The round struck Ares on his right thigh, and the god dropped to one knee screaming in pain.

Alex jumped on to his chariot and cracked the reins. His ponies bolted into the air, but Alex didn't let them go too far. He brought the chariot around in a large, slow circle as Ares took his feet. "You like that?" Alex yelled. "I dipped them in the River Acheron. They've got a nice sting to them now, don't they?"

Ares, face contorted and red with rage, cried out with the voice of a thousand charging men. He drove across the battlefield, leaving a stunned Aphrodite and Zeus (but an amused Athena) behind as he scooped up his spear.

Alex aimed and fired again, and then a third and fourth time. But not a single shot found its mark, for wherever Ares was when Alex pulled the trigger, by the time the bullet flew from the weapon, the god had already moved. Shaken at Ares' blinding speed, Alex cracked the reins again and tore across the sky. The sudden acceleration nearly threw Alex from the body of the chariot, but he managed to catch himself on the edge.

"Will you run forever, Alex?" Ares shouted. "How long do you think your ponies can keep you safe?"

Alex didn't bother to reply or even look at the god. No doubt Ares was lining up another throw. With that thought forefront in Alex's mind, he yanked his reins down and to the right, sending his ponies into an earth-bound spiral.

Something whooshed past his head, and Ares bellowed a curse from below.

The ground rushed up to meet Alex, and he quickly righted his ponies' path. Skimming across the rocky terrain, he glanced to his left, back to where he guessed Ares would be, and saw the god as he brought his spear up and over his shoulder.

Alex dropped in the chariot's body and pulled left on the reins with all his might. The ponies swerved, and physics weighed in on the situation. The chariot's body, heavy and full of momentum, tipped to the side as the ponies made their sharp turn. The chariot almost righted itself, tugging on the bridles, but then some of the buckles failed and the straps slipped free. The ponies sped off in one direction, and the chariot, with Alex still inside, tumbled in another.

The tumbling chariot threw Alex clear. He rolled across the ground, head tucked and covered, and he bounced off a few rocks before coming to a halt. Once he did, Alex jumped to his feet. About three hundred yards away, he saw Ares running toward him. His rifle was nowhere to be seen, but his javelin was embedded in the ground, some fifty yards away and on the far side of his overturned chariot.

Alex ran faster than he had ever thought possible, perhaps even faster than Hermes himself. He used his hands and vaulted over the chariot. Once he landed, in one swift motion, he spun around, pulled one of the rope nets from the chariot's side, and let it fly back the way he came.

It wasn't the best of throws, but it was good enough. The net opened and sailed directly at Ares. The god, no more than ten yards away, sprang to the side.

"Is that all you've got?" Ares said as the net passed by. "You think you can trap me with such toys?"

"It scared you, didn't it?" Alex taunted, fumbling as he pulled the other net out from under the chariot's body.

Ares narrowed his eyes. He walked over a few paces, picked up the net, and held it up for Alex to see. "This is what I think of your toys," he said, tearing it apart like a sheet of papyrus. "Now what do you have to say?"

Alex's mouth went dry. He adjusted his grip on the second net as Ares circled around the chariot, no doubt to get a clear run at him. The thought that maybe he should have planned more for this final showdown crossed Alex's mind more than once in the span of three nanoseconds. "Well," Alex finally said. "I think no matter what you say, it's pretty obvious why Athena beats you all the time. You're scared of a fishing net."

Ares growled and balled his fists. "You're big in talk but small in deed."

"Maybe," Alex said, inching back. "But at least I'm not a coward. You don't see me being a god and running from mortals."

Ares gave a guttural yell and charged. Alex threw the net and rolled to his left. Like the first, the net opened fully, but this time, Ares didn't dodge. Instead, the god caught the net with both hands, no doubt intending to tear through it on the first stride and then tear through Alex on the second.

Ares' muscles bulged as he tried to pull it apart. It held fast, fully enveloping him. Ares tumbled to the ground, both arms and one knee pinned against his chest. The more he struggled, the tighter the net grew. A few seconds later, Ares, a scarlet faced, seething mass of muscle, lay trapped, unable to move.

"Impossible!" he yelled, wiggling as best he could. "Rope is not stronger!"

Alex exhaled, remembering to breathe. Once he was convinced the god wasn't going anywhere, he calmly pulled his javelin from the ground and walked over to Ares' feet. "Well, it's not all rope," he said. "I might have reinforced it with a little something special." He then reached down and twisted something in the air, and Hephaestus' golden net shimmered into view, affixed to the fishing net with countless pieces of brown yarn.

"If you don't let me go, mortal, I'll see you cursed unlike any other," Ares said.

Alex crossed his arms. "I'm not letting you go until you surrender."

"You dare make demands of me?" he bellowed. "How long do you think it will be before Zeus orders my release? Before Aphrodite frees me herself? I can wait and plot your destruction, mortal. You've only sealed your fate."

"I figured you'd be like this," Alex said. "But I think I can change your mind."

Ares rolled around again, but like the previous escape attempts, his efforts proved futile. "Let me out this moment!"

Alex ignored him and righted his chariot. Then he whistled and called his miniature equines back over before reattaching their bridles to the chariot. A brief inspection of the straps and buckles thankfully showed them to be in good working order.

"I saw those bridles break," Ares said with confusion.

"You saw what I wanted you to see," Alex boasted. The corners of his mouth drew back as he relished the moment. "I loosened the straps before I arrived."

Ares glared. "No matter," he said. "Your feints will not save you. I will never cave to your demands."

"I know," Alex said nonchalantly. "You said that already."

With a great deal of caution, Alex loaded the god onto the chariot and climbed on to the back of one of the ponies. He'd never actually ridden a pony before, save for once when he was nine, but it didn't look too hard. It was awkward, but manageable, and he figured he'd be fine if he took it slow. Whatever the difficulty of riding a flying pony bareback was, one thing was certain: Alex wasn't about to ride in the chariot with Ares.

"Where are you taking me?" Ares demanded.

"To the Underworld," Alex said, patting his pony and nudging it forward. "Try not to fall out along the way."

Alex stopped his ponies atop a tall bank alongside the River Acheron. Down below, beyond the bank's steep slope and its sudden drop, the dark waters flowed, shrouded by fog. As Alex dismounted, the only things that carried in the heavy air were his ponies' occasional snorts and Ares' continued rants.

"I'm going to use your eyes for pincushions," Ares said, still lying trapped in the chariot. "The needles I'll use will be dull and rusty."

Alex ignored the threats, and using the net, he pulled the god down onto the ground.

Ares hit the dirt with a thump and a grunt. "Are you listening to me, mortal?" he growled. "Your eyes will be my pincushions.

And when I tire of that, I'll suspend you from hooks by your groin and pour molten bronze down your throat."

"I want you to listen to me now," Alex calmly said. "The Acheron runs deep here. Even with the longest branch I could find, I could not touch bottom when I stuck it in."

"Your drivel only adds untold miseries, mortal! You cannot bind me forever!"

"You'll be bound as long as this takes," Alex replied.

"Release me this instant and pray for my mercy!"

Alex sighed heavily and made his way down the footpath, wishing it didn't have to come to this. When he reached the water's edge, he dipped his javelin into the river and returned.

"What are you doing?" Ares said warily.

"Only what you make me do," Alex said. "If you swear by the River Styx to free Euryale and harm neither of us, I'll release you this instant."

"And when I don't?"

Alex brought the tip of the javelin near Ares' leg and raised an eyebrow. A small bead of water ran from the shaft and dripped off the tip. Ares flinched as it hit the ground. "Do you need to ask?" Alex said, hovering the weapon over the god.

Despite the threat, Ares did not capitulate. "A warrior never surrenders," he said.

Alex shrugged. "Have it your way," he said and pressed the javelin against Ares' leg.

Ares roared like a pride of wounded lions and thrashed madly, but Hephaestus' net held.

"There's a lot of water down there," Alex said once the god ceased his struggles. "Do I need to get more?"

"I've had worse," Ares said with a glare.

"You lie!"

Ares grit his teeth. "Do I?"

Alex shook his head in disbelief. He went down to the banks once more, dipped his javelin into the water, and returned. "Do you surrender to my terms?"

"Whatever you do to me I will return back to you a hundred fold!" Ares yelled.

Alex pressed his weapon into the god's leg a second time. "Surrender, damn you!"

"Never!" Ares shouted. The god clenched his jaw as visible waves of pain rippled through his body.

Alex kicked him in the back out of pure frustration. "I swear I'll roll you in. How much pain can you stand?"

Ares laughed like a madman. "Enjoy yourself now, mortal. Eternity is a long time."

"God, how stupid are you?" Alex shouted. "You think I like doing this? That I'm getting some sort of sick payback? I just want my wife and for you to leave us alone!"

"I don't care what you want," Ares evenly replied. "When I get out, your suffering will never end, and I will ravage your bride until her body is worn and broken."

Alex boiled with rage. He drove his javelin into the ground at an angle under Ares' back. "Fine," he said. "Let's see what you can do when you're at the bottom of the river."

Ares' eyes went wide. "What—"

But that was all the god got out. Alex grabbed the top of the javelin and heaved forward. Ares' body lifted in under the makeshift lever and then rolled down the bank.

"Stop, mortal!" Ares screamed in abject terror. He kicked and pushed as best he could inside the net, trying to stop himself from falling in the waters. His body skid to a stop a few feet from the drop. However, the soil underneath began to shift under his weight, and it was clear his stay of execution was only temporary.

Alex looked down from the top of the riverbank with neither action nor remorse. "You had your chance," he spat.

Ares ceased his struggle, though his face was filled with fear. "Please, mortal," he begged. "Don't let me fall in. I'll swear to all you've demanded of me. By the River Styx, my involvement with you and your wife is over this very moment if you save me!"

Alex hesitated. How he longed to see Ares slip into the dark waters! How he longed to know the god would writhe in limitless pain!

"Euryale is still in danger," Ares said. "Think of her if nothing else!"

Alex stared blankly at the god, unsure what he meant. "What are you on about?"

"Aphrodite is driving all of this," he replied. "Taking your anger out on me will not free your bride. Aphrodite will never let her go."

Alex shook his head. "No. You're the one who took Euryale."

"At Aphrodite's request!" said Ares. "She's infuriated that Athena brought you two together. Athena can claim victory if your marriage survives Aphrodite's trials, and then she can take Aphrodite's station as Goddess of Love. Aphrodite will never stop fighting you!"

"Son of a bitch," Alex muttered as he connected the dots. "That's why I've suffered? Why Aphrodite offered her help, and Athena refused hers? To see who's the best matchmaker?"

"Mortal!" Ares cried out. The ground below the god shifted again and he slid a few more inches toward the edge. "Set me free and I'll answer your questions!"

Not thinking, Alex ran down the bank. The soil was thinner and looser than he had realized. Alex lost his footing and tumbled down the slope. His hands and fingers tore at the slope and cut themselves on jagged rock. Finally, he came to a halt a foot from Ares and no more than two from the bank's sudden drop.

Ares laughed heartily. "For all your planning, this is how you save me?"

"Yeah, well, I didn't plan this part," Alex said, forcing a nervous smile. "I'm open to suggestions."

The ground shifted, and the two slid some more.

"Free me, mortal," Ares said. "I've given my oaths. You have nothing to fear."

Alex nodded and flat on his belly, carefully reached for the net. True to the god-smith's words, the moment Alex touched it and wanted Ares to be free, the net relaxed.

Ares slipped out of his prison. Now lying on his stomach, he took Hephaestus's net and threw it to the top of the bank. He then drove his left hand deep into the ground.

Though the god was now anchored, the shockwave sent Alex sliding. But as he went, Ares snatched him up with his right hand and held him close.

"I swore by the River Styx I would leave you alone," Ares said, grinning wide. "We both know how important it is to abide by those oaths."

Alex felt his heart stop and his mouth hang open. "You swore not to harm either of us as well."

"I know," Ares said with a wink. "But I had to see the look on your face. Consider it harmless payback for what you've done today."

"Not funny," Alex replied. "Let's get out of here."

Ares held his smile. "Yes, let's," he said before sending Alex flying.

With ponies waiting outside and Ares gone for good, Alex bounded up the tower stairs with an iron key in hand. By the time he reached the top and burst through the oak door, he was out of breath and dripping in sweat. The jail, however, was empty.

The cell bars that once held Euryale were bent outward a few inches, but not enough for anyone to squeeze through. The door hung open, and a water-filled basin sat nearby. In its reflection was a shadowy image of someone bound, blindfolded, and huddled in a dark corner.

"Jessica?" Alex said, leaning in for a better look. The waters swirled, and the image faded. "What the hell is going on?"

"Message for you."

Alex spun. Hermes was bouncing on the balls of his feet, scroll in hand and arm outstretched. Alex snorted. "Do I need to sign?"

"Not this time," the messenger god replied, handing the scroll over. "Given the contents of what's inside, I wouldn't waste your time like that."

Alex snatched the scroll and undid the ribbon that kept it tied. Creases formed in his brow as he read.

> *Aphrodite, patron of Cyprus and Goddess of Love, to the stubborn and deceiving Alex, husband of Euryale and lover of Jessica. I have written to inform you that both your wife and former girlfriend are in the labyrinth of Crete. One of them will die—which one is up to you.*

"You've got to be kidding me!" he said, slamming a fist into the stone wall. "I don't even know how to get there!"

"I do," Hermes replied. "Think your ponies can keep up?"

CHAPTER THIRTY-TWO

Alex left a wake taller than a titan as his ponies shot across the Mediterranean and followed Hermes. Ships flashed by on the horizon, and jets above couldn't dream of keeping up with the speed he had. In less than fifteen minutes, Alex covered the distance between Termessos and Crete, and when he landed he saw his ponies pant for breath for the first time ever.

Alex jumped off his chariot and ran toward a stone archway that was flanked by a pair of lit torches and that appeared to lead into the depths of a mountain. Nearby stood Athena, who looked genuinely concerned for him, and Aphrodite, who twirled Hades' scepter and sported a cruel grin.

"Where are they?" Alex asked, barely able to get the words out without choking on tears.

"Jessica is bound in one of the labyrinth's alcoves," Aphrodite said, motioning with her head to the tunnel entrance. "And Euryale is in a cage in the center that will open when the sun sets, which is in about a minute. So unless you want her to rip Jessica apart or turn her to stone, I'd get moving if I were you."

"Let me guess, you're still not going to help," Alex said to Athena.

"No," she replied. "But I am here to tell you that however this ends, that will be it."

"You're damn right it will be."

Alex started for the dark tunnel, but stopped when Aphrodite called his name.

"You'll need this," Aphrodite said, tossing him Hades' scepter.

"Why? Am I to raise an army to rescue her?"

Aphrodite shook her head. "No, silly. It's to give you a choice. It's the only thing that can turn your wife mortal and stop her from slaughtering your childhood sweetheart."

Alex's stomach churned. Thankfully, he managed to catch the bile rising in his throat before it turned into a projectile. "You're sick," he spat. "I'll never make that choice."

A mournful howl echoed from deep inside the labyrinth's halls. Aphrodite smiled. "Then the choice will be made for you."

Alex cursed them both under his breath and bolted through the stone archway, snagging one of the torches as he did. The halls he ran through were tight, and his feet pounded against the chipped, rocky floors. He didn't know where to go, but at least the torch he held cast its light a good twenty yards in every direction, and he wondered if a god—Athena even—had blessed it in secret. Regardless, he was thankful for the extra light it provided.

"Euryale? Jessica?" he yelled, not sure who he ought to try and find first. Should he try and free Jessica and get her out of the maze before Euryale could catch her? Or should he try to find his wife and calm her down? He didn't know if that was possible, let alone what Euryale had become, but if the brief preview he had seen of her monstrous form right after the wedding was any indication, both he and Jessica were in dire straits.

Alex rounded a corner and stumbled as the floor dropped an inch into shallow standing water. After catching himself on the wall, he continued until he reached a four-way intersection.

Shadows danced on the walls, and nothing gave any indication which way to go.

"Someone. Anyone. Answer me!" he called.

A guttural cry echoed in the air. He thought it came from one of the tunnels on his right, but he wasn't sure which. Feeling as if time was against him, he arbitrarily picked a tunnel and sprinted down it. The passage twisted constantly and branched time and again, sometimes leading up or down stairwells.

Alcoves and large rooms populated the labyrinth as well. Some were empty. Others had junk well past their prime, and a few had the remains of less fortunate souls. None, however, held Jessica nor his wife, and given how all the halls looked the same, Alex feared he'd go mad long before he found either of them.

He came to an abrupt halt when he entered an oblong cave that held four other exits spaced evenly about. A pit was in the center, one that was deep enough that the torchlight could not reach its bottom. Alex was about to kick a rock to test its depth when something entered the room from one of the other halls.

The monster that greeted him was covered in scales and had claws like daggers and fangs that could puncture dragon scale. It slithered farther into the torch light on a serpentine tale, and its head full of vipers hissed at him. When he spied the pair of red ones in the back, there was no question as to who this creature could be. All Alex could do was pray some shred of his wife was still inside the nightmare she'd become.

"Euryale," Alex said, trying to stay strong for his sake as much as hers. "It's me. We can go home now."

"Liar!" she roared, driving toward him with her razor-sharp talons outstretched.

Alex backpedaled, unsure what to do. He managed to bat her claws away, but Euryale rammed her shoulder into his chest, knocking the wind from his lungs and tossing him onto his back. His head struck the unyielding floor with a wet thump as both the torch and scepter flew from his grasp.

Euryale jumped on top of him. Her talons tore into his flesh with a ferocity that put Mister Lion to shame. "I gave you my heart and swore to the Fates you'd never leave me, and what do you do?" she screeched as the blows came down. "You leave me for a harlot the second you could!"

"I swear, I haven't!" Alex said.

"Alex? Where are you?"

The cry was soft and distant, but it was enough to pause Euryale's attack. The gorgon straightened and turned her head. When Alex's name was called out a second time, she darted away.

"Euryale, stop!" Alex said, pushing past the pain in his arms so he could get to his feet. "Come back!"

The gorgon disappeared into the dark, and Alex raced after her, barely remembering to scoop up both the torch and the scepter as he went. He raced through the tunnels, using the sounds of Euryale's own chase to guide him. The labyrinth was not kind to those using such methods of navigation. Sounds bounced from all over, and more than once Alex wondered if he was chasing the echoes of his own footsteps as much as he was chasing the noise of Euryale's pursuit.

Alex rounded a corner and found himself back at the circular room with the pit where he had first run into his wife, only this time, he entered from a different passage. How he'd managed to return to this spot, he didn't know, but apparently neither did Euryale, for she was a dozen yards away and switching her gaze between three separate exits.

"Euryale, please," he said.

The gorgon turned and snarled at him, and then when Jessica's soft cries drifted in to the room from one of the halls, she roared and charged.

Alex intercepted his wife an instant before she escaped down a passage. He had to drop both torch and scepter again to make the tackle, but he managed to wrap his arms and legs around her body and drag her to the ground. "I know you're in there," he said as they wrestled. "I'm not going anywhere."

"Good because then you can witness every drop of her blood spill from her precious little body," Euryale replied.

"I love you, but I'm not going to let you hurt her."

"Save your hollow words for someone else," she said before sinking her fangs deep into his arms. Her vipers followed suit, striking his face, neck and shoulders.

Alex screamed, and the pain that radiated from each new wound was tenfold stronger than what he'd suffered while on Hades' wheel, but still he held onto his wife. He held on, that is, until his arms began to numb and his grip on Euryale began to falter.

"You'll never stop me, *dear*," she said with as much venom in her words as her vipers had in their mouths. "If anything, you should give your whore a quick, merciful death before I reach her."

Water formed in Alex's eyes. He knew she was right. He wouldn't be able to stop her forever, but he might be able to delay her long enough to come up with a plan that was better than wrestling her for eternity. He tucked his knees beneath him and summoned what strength he had left in his hands to keep his arms locked around Euryale and dragged her back to the pit.

"Get off me!" Euryale screamed, striking at him with fang and claw yet again.

"Forgive me," Alex said. He jerked back, spun, and let his wife go.

She fell into the pit and was swallowed by darkness, cursing his name the entire time.

CHAPTER THIRTY-THREE

Alex stumbled.

His vision had blurred long ago, making navigating the treacherous labyrinth difficult at best. Furthermore, the walls had grown three times their size over the past few hours—assuming his sense of time was right, which he was mostly sure wasn't—so he'd been spending more time looking up than down, and thus his feet often found debris and divots in the ground he'd normally sidestep with ease.

"Oh, Alex," Aphrodite said as he rounded a corner and came to an intersection. "How long are you going to delay the inevitable?"

"Get away from me," he said, swinging both scepter and torch like a drunk playing with the equipment in a batting cage. This in turn exacerbated the headache he had, like a migraine worsened by a jackhammer.

Aphrodite laughed and didn't bother to move as his clumsy attack missed by three feet. "I'm not the one you should be swinging at."

A deep grumble came from Alex's stomach. He dropped with his hands on his knees before puking. He wiped his mouth with the back of his hand before spitting in a vain effort to rid himself of the acrid taste in his mouth. "What's going on?"

"Euryale's venom is ravaging your body. I could help if you want."

"Take your help and shove it up your ass," was what Alex tried to say. His tongue, however, was puffed like a marshmallow in a microwave, and all that came out was an unintelligible mash of noise. As such, he willed himself past the goddess, intent on finding Jessica and seeing her out of the maze before Euryale caught up with them both.

"She'll be out of that pit soon," Aphrodite said, waiting for him at the next intersection. "Won't be very long after that."

Alex grunted and went right. The hall that way had a cooler air to it, and somewhere in his delirious mind he reasoned that this meant Jessica had to be wherever it led because she'd always been the cool one growing up.

He rounded a corner and successfully navigated a half dozen steps down before bumping into the goddess again. This time, she leaned against an open doorway.

"You should rest. Think this through."

Alex wiped the sweat off his brow and out of his eyes before shaking his head. Even if Aphrodite was telling the truth and Euryale was still in the pit, he couldn't spare even a moment.

A gentle hand took his shoulder from behind and rooted him in place. "Here, let me help," she whispered in his ear. "Her venom is too much for you, despite your body from Hades."

Alex inhaled deeply and fell against the wall. The unseen vise around his head loosened its grip, and the fever that accompanied it faded. In the first moment of blissful relief, he praised the goddess before he remembered how much he hated all she'd done. "Thank you. You have no idea how good that feels."

"Anytime, love," she said.

"This doesn't change anything," he said, pushing off the wall and setting his jaw in determination. "I'm not giving up either one of them."

Aphrodite giggled, and she followed Alex. Though he charged through halls faster than a fool charges headlong into love, Aphrodite followed effortlessly behind, gliding along on a cushion of air. "What do you think you'll accomplish, racing around like this?"

Alex paused at a T in the maze to catch his breath. "How are you keeping up so easily?"

"You can never escape things that whisper to your heart," she said. "But back to my point: you know you can't save them both. What will you do other than watch Euryale kill Jessica while you pant for air?"

"I'll wrestle her for the next hundred years if that's what it takes before she comes to her senses," Alex said. "She's only like this because you enraged her."

Aphrodite touched his forearm as she placed a hand over her chest. "Oh, Alex," she said. "You give me too much credit. I didn't wound her heart. You did when you indulged in your feelings for Jessica. You made that choice. Not me."

"Under your spell," Alex added.

Aphrodite shrugged. "If you say. That still doesn't change the fact Euryale's so worked up that she won't be herself until she's taken a life, be it by blood or stone. Trust me on that one."

"You're lying."

"You know I'm not."

Tightness gripped his chest, and a lump formed in Alex's throat. Whatever tricks the goddess might be playing, in the deepest parts of his soul, he knew she was telling the truth. Euryale would never tire or revert to herself until someone was dead, and the only mortal in the labyrinth happened to be the only person she wanted to kill.

"There's the face I was looking for," Aphrodite said. "Tell me, Alex, will you still love your wife when the image of what she's about to do haunts you through eternity?"

"Stop it."

"Or will you use that scepter of yours to protect your fair maiden in distress? All you have to do is stab Euryale with the pointy end and wish away her immortality. The scepter will do the rest. It's quite easy."

"I said stop!"

A growl, ancient and powerful, thundered down the halls, seemingly coming from everywhere at once.

Aphrodite smiled. "Time is almost up. Best say your goodbyes now."

"I'm not saying goodbye to anyone," Alex replied, eyes narrowing and heart hardening. "By the River Styx, I swear I won't let either of them die."

Aphrodite cringed, but it was plainly all for show. "Such oaths won't protect her from the gruesome fate that awaits, I'm afraid. You can try all you like. The outcome will be the same."

"We'll see."

Aphrodite pointed down the passage to his right. "She's that way," she said. "Take your second left and then your fourth right. You'll find her huddled in a corner. I'd hurry though. Euryale will be there sooner than you think."

Most of Alex was wary about trusting Aphrodite's directions, but not enough of him to keep him in place. Time was not his friend, and he was desperate to find Jessica, so he followed the goddess's directions. To his elation, she'd been telling the truth, and he found Jessica pressed into the corner of a triangular room.

Thick ropes held her wrists tightly behind her back while also keeping her ankles firmly together. Though her blindfold had fallen off, it was clear she hadn't seen anything in a long time. She shut her eyes and turned away when the torch light struck her face.

"Please god tell me that's you, Alex," she said, hopeful and terrified.

Alex bolted to her side and made short work of her bindings. "It's me."

Jessica threw her arms around him. At first, Alex thought it the simple embrace of a friend who hadn't seen another in a long time, but when she fell into him, sobbing, he understood the primal fear she'd been wrestling with.

"I'm sorry," he said, stroking the back of her head. "I should've sent you home right after the wedding. You should never have been caught up in this."

"I'm going to die, aren't I?"

"No."

"Promise?"

"Promise." Alex kissed the top of her forehead before standing and helping her to her feet. "But unless you want to make me a liar, we've got to get moving. Now."

"Then why are we still standing here?"

They'd barely gone two paces before Euryale appeared in the doorway, her serpentine body easily blocking the exit. Before her eyes could meet Jessica's, Alex spun Jessica around and quickly put himself between her and Euryale.

Euryale snarled and barreled toward them, claws and vipers ready to strike. Alex caught the brunt of the attack with his hands. Muscles bulged in his legs and arms as he pulled the gorgon off balance and they both fell to the ground.

The fight between himself and his wife felt ten times more frantic than it had ever before. Euryale twisted in his grasp and assaulted his body with talon and fang. Alex, operating out of instinct to protect himself and one he held dear, swung with the scepter. Its head connected with the side of Euryale's and she fell to the side, stunned.

In the lull, Alex turned to Jessica and yelled, "What are you waiting for? Get out of here!"

Jessica, torch in hand and eyes averted, hesitated. "Aren't you coming?"

Alex went to follow, but didn't get a stride before he bent over and emptied his stomach. Euryale's venom coursed through his veins. Alex heaved again before barking an order. "Go! I'll catch up!"

Jessica ran, one hand guiding the way as she made sure not to look anywhere near Alex or the gorgon. She'd scarcely left the room when Euryale came out of her daze and gave chase. Alex managed to intercept her one last time, locking his arms with her and keeping her from escaping.

Euryale bellowed, but with Alex's arms squeezed around her chest, it was not nearly as loud or mournful as it could have been. Its effects, however, were far from benign. A spider web of agony spread from Alex's heart to his arms, neck, and head. His strength vanished, and he crumpled.

He hit the ground, face first, and Euryale pulled free from his grasp. At the far end of the corridor, he could see Jessica, curled in a fetal position, hands covering her ears. The torch lay burning nearby while blood streamed from her nose, pooling on the stone floor. She rocked, eyes shut tight while Euryale methodically approached.

"Euryale, you don't have to do this," Alex said, pushing himself up. It hurt to stand, to move, to think.

"Have to and want to are separate things."

Alex staggered after her. A few of her vipers turned and hissed at his approach, but she kept her back to him. She didn't need to pay him any heed. Her prey lay helpless before her, and he could barely walk. They both knew he couldn't stop her, not without...

"Are you ready to use that on me?" she taunted. "Or do you still want to pretend I mean more to you than she does."

Alex glanced at the scepter and only then did he realize he'd been thumping it in his other hand. The spike at the bottom looked as if it could shatter a diamond, and a hungering feeling seemed to emanate from it. "I'm not pretending," he said. "I love you, will love you, always."

"I've heard those words before," she said. Euryale bent down and effortlessly lifted Jessica off the ground. She traced the edge of Jessica's face with a single claw. "Come, sweet thing. Open your eyes."

Alex limped on. Ten paces to go. Five. He shifted his grip on the scepter, sensing Euryale's playtime was ending. "Don't make me do this. It doesn't have to end like this."

"This ends in stone or blood," she hissed.

Euryale raised her free hand, claws spread, and swung at Jessica's neck. Alex lunged, hooking an arm around hers to stop the strike. The gorgon spun, her face contorting not in rage, but shock, as the scepter's point pierced flesh and heart.

CHAPTER THIRTY-FOUR

What have I done?" Euryale said, voice weak and body weaker. She stared at her Alex with eyes of sorrow, and her hands, free of talon and vengeance, caressed the sides of his face. Tears welled in her eyes as one hand slipped down his neck to where the scepter stuck from his chest. Her throat closed as she yanked it free, letting it hit the ground with a thud. She then wrapped her arms around his neck and leaned into him, desperate for his touch, but all she received was the cold press of stone against her skin.

"You killed him," Jessica whispered from behind.

Euryale heard the woman take the scepter from the ground and push herself to her feet, but she refused to part even an inch from what was left of her husband. "Take my life if you wish," she said. "A monster like me deserves no less."

Jessica thumped the scepter in her hands a dozen times before answering. "No," she said. "He suffered more than anyone should have just to learn how much he was willing to dedicate himself to you, and even when you came at him—at me—he never gave up. I won't dishonor his life."

An uneasy silence smothered the two of them. It lingered for what felt like eons to Euryale, and in that span of time, Euryale could do nothing but sob as the weight of her actions crushed her heart and her dreams.

"What in the name of Cronus is this?"

Euryale peeked over Alex's stone shoulders to find Aphrodite a few paces away, crass, with Athena next to her looking impressed. "He's gone," the gorgon spat. "I hope the two of you are happy."

"Do I look happy, you beast of a thing?" Aphrodite said, stepping forward.

"You look like a vile, pitiful creature that could never be happy," Euryale shot back.

"You stupid, insolent—"

Athena yanked her sister back by the shoulder and put herself between her and the gorgon. "It's over."

"It's not over! He cheated! He was supposed to pick!"

"He did," Athena said. "Now leave."

Aphrodite narrowed her eyes. "And if I don't?"

"Then I won't let you call this a draw," Athena said. "And before you reject my offer, I'd suggest you consult with Ares on what happens to those who continue to fight me."

Aphrodite pressed her lips together. Her nostrils flared, and she breathed deep before pointing an accusing finger at Athena. "Fine. This is a draw, but between us, it's far from settled. I'll see you in my temple and on your knees, begging my favor, soon enough."

Euryale waited in stunned silence for the Goddess of Love to leave before speaking. "Why?"

"Because I defend my champions," Athena said. "She can call it a draw all she likes. The winner is clear."

"Then why not press the victory?" Euryale said, this time with spite. "Isn't that what you wanted out of this, bragging rights?"

"No, I wanted to know if the man I picked could be the champion I wanted," Athena said. She reached behind the gorgon and took the scepter from Jessica before putting a gentle hand on Euryale's shoulder. "I'll take you home and get this to Hades. I suppose that's the least I can do, seeing how I promised Alex something special should he persevere."

"Wait!" Jessica said, nearly lunging at Athena. "He's not dead though, right? I mean, he's in the underworld somewhere. We can see him again? Take him out?"

Athena shook her head. "He gave up his immortality," she said. "He'll go to the asphodel fields where every other mortal goes..."

The goddess's voice trailed, remorse lingering in the words. Though she didn't finish the rest, Jessica didn't need her to. "And forget everything he's ever done, and everyone he's ever met, and become a witless shade."

"Unless you make him a hero," Euryale said as she kept her gaze away from Jessica. "Then he goes to Elysium."

"That's up to Minos," she said after a moment's thought. "Zeus gave him the sole honor of bestowing the title of hero some time ago, but he hasn't granted that title in a long, long time."

"Surely there's something you can do," Jessica said. "Alex deserves more than to end up a shadow."

"I can give him a chance," she said. "But the final decision will not be mine."

CHAPTER THIRTY-FIVE

I see you got a new skiff," Alex said with a sheepish grin. "Looks roomier than the one you had before."

Kharon, still sporting his red tunic and conical hat, continued to lean on his staff as he narrowed his eyes. Slowly, he outstretched an open palm. "One—nay two—obols, if you wish to cross."

Alex playfully patted himself down. "Left my wallet above ground. Let me through and I'll get you twenty."

"Step aside."

Alex didn't.

Kharon whipped his staff around and brought it to a halt at Alex's neck. "Everyone pays. No exceptions. Since you can't pay, from here on out you can spend the rest of eternity wandering the banks."

"Apparently, you haven't heard about what I've done since we met," Alex said, pushing the staff away. "I'm married to Euryale, daughter of Phorcys. I've beaten the descendant of the Nemian lion, wrestled a wheel of fire, and brought Ares to his knees."

Kharon jabbed his staff into Alex's chest, and he went flying back as if Zeus himself had driven a lightning-charged fist into his sternum. "Every mortal pays. No exceptions."

Alex grimaced as he took to his feet, several yards away from where he had been standing. His chest ached, and he cursed again as Kharon tended to the line of deceased that was still waiting. After a few minutes of watching several more unfortunate souls get turned away, Alex felt a tap on his shoulder.

"Time to leave," Hermes said, handing Alex a pair of winged slippers. "Your presence is requested in Olympus."

"No!" Kharon protested. "The dead stay here."

"He's not quite dead, yet," Hermes said.

Kharon went to object again, but before he'd spit out his first word, Hermes led Alex away. Off the two flew, cutting through the fog that enshrouded the bank before eventually breaking into fresh air and daylight. Alex relished the smell of freedom the outside brought, but he couldn't enjoy it. Hermes kept running up, up, up, high into the clouds, and Alex had to give it his all to keep up.

They shot through the Gates of Olympus and down the city's many streets and stopped only when they reached the steps that led to the Great Hall. There Alex found Athena and Euryale waiting for him.

Before he could get a word out, Euryale pounced on him and nearly bowled him over. She assaulted his face with kisses, and her vipers did the same. Somewhere in the midst of that flurry, she managed three little words. "I hate you."

Alex pulled back. His brow furrowed as his hands gently framed her face. "Come again? Did you say you hate me?"

She laughed, tears in her eyes. "Yes, for what you made me do to you."

"I only did it because of what you were about to do."

"For what it's worth, I didn't kill her, and Athena had Hermes take her home." Euryale's head dropped, and she looked away in shame. "I told you I was a monster."

"You're my monster," he replied, turning her face toward him. "Even after what I did? What I can still do?"

Alex nodded. "We can work through it, if you're willing."

"How are you so sure?"

"Love is a choice."

Athena cleared her throat, and Alex looked over his wife's shoulder to see what the goddess wanted. "If you two love birds are done," Athena said, "you've got one last fight."

Alex groaned and muttered a slew of curses. Being killed twice, it seems, wasn't enough for The Fates. "I should've guessed. What sort of fight?"

"Nothing too terrible," she said. "You only need to make a convincing case that you're worthy of the title hero. Do that and you can live on Elysium. Otherwise, it's off to the asphodel fields for you, where you'll continue on as a witless shade."

"Wonderful," Alex said. "Any pointers?"

"I can't tell you anything you don't already know," she said. "But I'd start by giving these back to Hades and Hephaestus. Neither will side with you if you don't."

Alex took the scepter and net that she gave him and steeled himself for what was about to come. "Alright, let's go."

In the group went, through the gargantuan doors and into the Great Hall. Inside was a whirlwind of divine activity. All the gods stood in the hall, arguing between themselves. All, that is, except for Zeus and Hera, who sat upon their respective thrones (but still argued).

"This is obscene. The only reason he's here is because Athena knows Minos will never make him a hero," Aphrodite said, looking at Zeus but pointing an accusing finger at Alex. "Our time is better spent elsewhere."

"Minos judges mortals," Athena countered. Her tone was even, as if she were a teacher working with a troublesome student, something Alex was certain she'd done intentionally to dig under Aphrodite's skin.

"Alex gave up his immortality!"

"Technicality at best."

"Enough! Both of you!" Zeus bellowed as he came out of his seat. "The matter is before us now." The two goddesses exchanged glares but said no more. Once they went to their respective thrones, Zeus addressed Alex directly. "Alex, there are some here who think you should be declared a hero and given full honors due to one. Do you think you're worthy of such a title?"

Alex felt his throat tighten. He placed his hands behind his back and sucked in a breath to steady himself, knowing this first impression was more paramount than any other he'd ever made. "All of you here have seen what great men and women are capable of," he said. "I don't know how I measure up with them, but I believe I did all that was expected of me and proved I would always love my wife. I hope everyone here agrees, especially her father."

"Her father does," Phorcys replied. "He is not the son-in-law I expected, but he has shown he navigates treacherous seas with the skill of a seasoned admiral. I am proud to have him wed to my daughter."

"Then we shall make this quick." Zeus paused long enough to hold up a staying hand when both Aphrodite and Athena looked to jump in on the matter. When they settled, he continued. "If more of us declare you fit than not, you'll have your place on Elysium."

Alex counted the number of deities in the hall. Twelve. To his dismay, he thought he only had three at best in his corner, maybe four. Could he swing three more? What if he could only swing two? Thus, he asked the obvious question. "What if it's a tie?"

"Then you'll join the rest of the mortals in the fields of asphodel," Zeus said. "I believe you have items to return first, however."

Alex nodded. With purpose, he stepped up to Hades and handed him back his scepter. "Your help was nothing short of immensely gracious, and I pray you look well upon how I wielded your army of the dead. Moreover, I pray the extra time you had with your wife, Persephone, went well and will always be well."

The God of the Underworld dipped his head slightly, but the hardness to his face foreshadowed the god's vote. "A hero would not have lost my scepter, even if the loss was temporary. I vote nay."

Alex felt his gut drop. He bowed and moved on, knowing there was nothing he could do. Next he came to Hephaestus. Alex handed back the net to the God of Smiths. "You will always have my eternal gratitude, and I hope I've wielded the tools you've given me in a manner worthy of your name so that we can enjoy each other's company as frequently as The Fates will allow."

Hephaestus smiled. "You have my vote and my confidence. A true hero, both in action and in word."

Emboldened that he had a vote, Alex managed to relax. That momentary relief disappeared when Zeus decided to drive everything to a finish.

"Hermes, what say you?"

"Abstaining," Hermes replied. "Just a messenger."

Zeus nodded. "Dionysus?"

"Abstaining."

Zeus raised an eyebrow. "Demeter?"

Alex perked. The goddess looked calm in her teal chiton, which Alex thought was a good sign. Furthermore, although he'd only spoken to her briefly at the wedding, he felt their encounter was pleasant and he'd left a good impression on her. Last, and certainly not least, her daughter Persephone would have undoubtedly had a few good words to say about him as well.

"Against," the goddess replied with an unsettling tone. She turned her icy-blue eyes to Alex and elaborated. "A hero does not prolong the separation of a mother and her daughter."

"But she—" Alex caught himself before he finished his objection. Arguing, he realized, would only make things worse.

Zeus, thankfully, kept things moving. "Phorcys?"

"Do you even need to ask?" the Old Man replied. "Yes."

"Poseidon?"

The Lord of the Sea grumbled to himself as he eyed both Athena and Aphrodite. "There's a strong case either way," he finally said. "Since I don't know his exploits enough, I'll leave it to others to decide. I abstain."

"So be it," Zeus said. "Apollo?"

Apollo smiled brightly at Alex which helped bolster his hope. "I've seen everything that man has done under the sun. No mere mortal could have accomplished a tenth of what he has, and certainly The Fates would not have entertained someone who is not a champion's champion. I vote yes."

Zeus turned to his left and spoke to his wife. "Hera?"

The goddess didn't hesitate in sinking Alex's heart. "I'd vote no twice if I could. A husband shouldn't have even the hint of infidelity."

Again, Alex went to argue since Aphrodite had put a spell on Jessica, but Zeus moved on. At least Phorcys seemed unfazed by the accusation, and Alex guessed he understood the circumstances.

"Marriages are not so black and white," Zeus said. "Alex has performed dutifully and then some. A yes from me."

"Thank goodness," Alex whispered. Alex double checked the math. That left him with four votes saying yes, and only three saying no. His heart leapt for joy, but plummeted into a bottomless pit of despair when he saw that the only ones who had yet to vote were Athena, Aphrodite and Ares. Even with Athena's vote, the best he could hope for was a tie.

His wife's hand found his, and she gave it a squeeze. "It'll be okay."

"Yeah," he said as Aphrodite gave him a wicked grin. "Though I can't possibly see how."

CHAPTER THIRTY-SIX

Athena?" Zeus said, grabbing his daughter's attention.

"Alex is a hero as much as any other," she said, nodding toward him. "Granted, a stubborn man in the beginning, and one that had to learn his place before he could fulfil his potential, but he's persisted. Even the famed Odysseus and Heracles see him as one of them, and I hear both are eager to tackle the monsters of Elysium with Alex once he returns."

"Too bad he'll never get the chance," Aphrodite said. "I vote no. And with Ares doing the same, it's a tie."

Zeus looked around the Great Hall and made a quick, soft count to himself. "That it does."

"Wait!" Alex jumped forward with the desperation of a dead man walking. "He still has to cast his vote. She can't speak for him."

Zeus shrugged and let out a sigh filled with sympathy. "He's right, Ares," he said. "Let's make it official."

"And do you want to be known as the god who was beaten by a man?" Alex tossed in before Ares had a chance to answer.

Every deity, save Athena and Aphrodite, sucked in a collective breath. Athena chuckled softly, and Alex was sure he caught a subtle, acknowledging nod directed his way. Aphrodite, on the other hand, turned statuesque as her fair skin turned red.

Ares set his jaw and spent the next few seconds looking back and forth from Alex to Aphrodite. With a growl and a reluctant voice, he finally cast his vote. "I will not bestow such an honor on a recent enemy," he said. He paused and grumbled to himself while Aphrodite straightened and smiled. "But nor will I admit I am so weak that a mere man can compete with me. I abstain."

"You can't abstain!" Aphrodite shouted. "If you do, I'll—" The goddess stopped as the rest of the Olympians watched with interest how the triangle between her, Ares, and Hephaestus would play out. She backed away from her threat, adjusted her chiton, and stormed out.

"By my count, that's five in favor and four against," Zeus said. He clapped a hand on Alex's shoulder that sent tiny bolts of lightning into the air. "It is my pleasure and honor to be the first to call you, Alexander Weiss, the first hero of the new age. May Elysium forever provide you with the challenge and life you deserve."

EPILOGUE

Alex sat at the end of a wooden pier, feet dangling in the water and Euryale's head resting on his shoulder. For the past year they'd spent the end of each day this way, and as far as he was concerned, they could spend the end of the next thousand the same.

"What do you want to do tomorrow?" she asked.

"Odysseus wants to try and get that new hydra," he replied. "I think I'll pass, though. Thought we could slip out and see your dad. It's been a bit."

"He'd like that." Euryale snuggled into him further. "I would, too."

"Still have some jerky for Cerberus? We'll need to bribe him as usual."

Euryale laughed. She put a hand over her mouth and tried to stop, but was unsuccessful.

"What?"

"Nothing."

Alex turned to his wife. "What? C'mon, tell me."

"Heroes can leave whenever they want," she said. "It's just sort of a joke played on the newcomers, see how long it takes them to figure it out."

"No..."

"Yes."

"But Heracles, Achilles, Perseus—"

"Are never always around when you go looking for them, are they?" Euryale interjected with a smile.

"Well, it's a big island..." Alex shook his head before he laughed and hit the pier with the bottom of his fist. "Son of a bitch. We can really go whenever we like?"

"Pretty much, as long as we keep things lowkey."

"Well, I'm really, really glad to hear that," said a familiar voice from behind.

Alex twisted in place to see Jessica standing a few paces away. Her hair, pulled back in a ponytail, looked like it hadn't been washed in a week. Dirt clung to portions of her skin, and a few bruises showed as well. Her tank top, khaki shorts and hiking boots had all seen better days, too. Despite all this, Alex leapt to his feet and ran over to her. "Jessica! It's so great to see you! How have you been?"

"Never better," she said. "Got home last year and became rich and famous with all those pictures I'd taken. People are still trying to wrap their heads around the gods showing up, but getting in on the action from the start has been lucrative, to say the least. A wee bit dangerous, too, I might add."

Alex's shoulders fell, and he cursed. "Oh damn. You're dead, aren't you?"

"No," she said, laughing. "I'm not quite dead, yet. Got a little spell of protection from all things gorgon cast on me courtesy of The Old Man. That said, I need help from the both of you—if you're up to it."

Alex glanced back at his smiling wife who gave an encouraging nod. "I hope this doesn't involve us going to war with Ares."

"Nope. But by the time this is over, you might wish we were."

The End

ACKNOWLEDGEMENTS

Strange as it may sound, I'd like to first thank those who read a very early draft of The Gorgon Bride and destroyed it completely, for without getting multiple proverbial kicks in the teeth, the story would never have been changed from something I liked into something I love.

I can't thank enough all the other readers down the line as well that helped shape the text and read constant revisions so that what started out as merely an opening idea for a scene—a poor guy stuck on the banks of Acheron—into this fun epic tale.

My wonderful editor, Crystal Watanabe, once again helped put the much-needed finishing touches...

And most of all, I must thank my wife, Mary Beth, who is dying for the sequel to come out now.

ABOUT THE AUTHOR

When not writing, Galen Surlak-Ramsey has been known to throw himself out of an airplane, teach others how to throw themselves out of an airplane, take pictures of the deep space, and wrangle his four children somewhere in Southwest Florida.

He also manages to pay the bills as a chaplain for a local hospice.

Drop by his website www.galensurlak.com to see what other books he has out, what's coming soon, and check out the newsletter (well, sign up for the newsletter and get access to awesome goodies, contests, exclusive content, etc.).

About the Publisher

Tiny Fox Press LLC
5020 Kingsley Road
North Port, FL 34287

www.tinyfoxpress.com